WHITE BONES

GRAHAM MASTERTON was an internationally bestselling writer for many years before he turned his talents to crime writing. He lived in Cork for five years, an experience that inspired the Katie Maguire series.

WHITE BONES

GRAHAM MASTERTON

HEAD
ZEUS

First published in the UK in 2013 by Head of Zeus Ltd.
This paperback edition published in the UK in 2013
by Head of Zeus Ltd.

9 7 5 3 1 2 4 6 8

A CIP catalogue record for this book is available from
the British Library.

ISBN (MMP) 978178182163
ISBN (E) 9781781852170

Printed and bound by CPI Group (UK) Ltd.,
Croydon CR0 4YY.

Head of Zeus Ltd
Clerkenwell House
45-47 Clerkenwell Green
London EC1R 0HT

www.headofzeus.com

"Ar scáth a chéile a mhaireas na daoine."
"People live in one another's shadow."

Irish proverb

One

John had never seen so many hooded crows circling around the farm as he did that wet November morning. His father always used to say that whenever you saw more than seven hooded crows gathered together, they had come to gloat over a human tragedy.

It was tragedy weather, too. Curtains of rain had been trailing across the Nagle Mountains since well before dawn, and the north-west field was so heavy that it had taken him more than three hours to plow it. He was turning the tractor around by the top corner, close to the copse called Iollan's Wood, when he saw Gabriel frantically waving from the gate.

John waved back. Jesus, what did the idiot want now? If you gave Gabriel a job to do, you might just as well do it yourself, because he was always asking what to do next, and was it screws or nails you wanted, and what sort of wood were you after having this made from? John kept on steadily plowing, with big lumps of sticky mud pattering off the wheels, but Gabriel came struggling up the field toward him, still waving, with crows irritably flapping all around him. He was obviously shouting, too, although John couldn't hear him.

As Gabriel came puffing up to him in his raggedy old brown tweeds and gumboots, John switched off the tractor's engine and took off his ear-protectors.

"What's wrong now, Gabe? Did you forget which end of

the shovel you're supposed to be digging with?"

"There's bones, John! *Bones!* So many fecking bones you can't even count them!"

John wiped the rain off his face with the back of his hand. "Bones? Where? What kind of bones?"

"Under the floor, John! *People's* bones! Come and see for yourself! The whole place looks like a fecking graveyard!"

John climbed down from the tractor and ankle-deep into the mud. Close up, Gabriel smelled strongly of stale beer, but John was quite aware that he drank while he worked, even though he went to considerable pains to conceal his cans of Murphy's under a heap of sacking at the back of the barn.

"We was digging the foundations close to the house when the boy says there's something in the ground here, and he digs away with his fingers and out comes this human skull with its eyes full of dirt. Then we were after digging some more and there was four more skulls and bones like you never seen the like of, leg-bones and arm-bones and finger-bones and rib-bones."

John strode long-legged down toward the gate. He was tall and dark, with thick black hair and almost Spanish good looks. He had only been back in Ireland for just over a year, and he was still finding it difficult to cope with running a farm. One sunny May morning he had been just about to close the door of his apartment on Jones Street in San Francisco when the telephone had rung, and it had been his mother, telling him that his father had suffered a massive stroke. And then, two days later, that his father was dead.

He hadn't intended to come back to Ireland, let alone take over the farm. But his mother had simply assumed that he would, him being the eldest boy, and all his uncles and aunts and cousins had greeted him as if he were head of the Meagher family now. He had flown back to San Francisco to sell his dot.com alternative medicine business and say goodbye to his friends, and here he was, walking through the gate of Meagher's Farm in a steady drizzle, with a beery-breathed Gabriel following close behind him.

"I'd say it was a mass murder," Gabriel panted.

"Well, we'll see."

The farmhouse was a wide green-painted building with a gray slate roof, with six or seven leafless elms standing at its south-eastern side like an embarrassed crowd of naked bathers. A sharply-sloping driveway led down to the road to Ballyhooly, to the north, and Cork City, eleven miles to the south. John crossed the muddy tarmac courtyard and went around to the north side of the house, where Gabriel and a boy called Finbar had already knocked down a rotten old feed store and were now excavating the foundations for a modernized boiler-house.

They had cleared an area twelve feet by twenty. The earth was black and raw and had the sour, distinctive smell of peat. Finbar was standing on the far side of the excavation, mournfully holding a shovel. He was a thin, pasty-faced lad with a closely-cropped head, protruding ears, and a soggy gray jumper.

On the ground in front of him, like a scene from Pol Pot's Cambodia, lay four human skulls. Nearer to the damp, cement-rendered wall of the farmhouse, there was a hole which was crowded with muddy human bones.

John hunkered down and stared at the skulls as if he were expecting them to explain themselves.

"God Almighty. These must have been here for a pretty long time. There isn't a scrap of flesh left on any of them."

"An unmarked grave, I'd say," put in Gabriel. "A bunch of fellows who got on the wrong side of the IRA."

"Scared the shite out of me," said Finbar, wiping his nose on his sleeve. "I was digging away and all of a sudden there was

3

this skull grinning up at me like my old uncle Billy."

John picked up a long iron spike and prodded amongst the bones. He saw a jawbone, and part of a ribcage, and another skull. That made at least five bodies. There was only one thing to do, and that was to call the Garda.

"You don't think your dad knew about this?" asked Gabriel, as John walked back to the house.

"What do you mean? Of course he didn't know."

"Well, he was a great republican, your dad."

John stopped and stared at him. "What are you trying to say?"

"I'm not trying to say nothing, but if certain people wanted a place to hide certain remains that they didn't want nobody to find, your dad might have possibly obliged them, if you see what I mean."

"Oh, come on, Gabriel. My dad wouldn't have allowed bodies to be buried on his property."

"I wouldn't be too sure, John. There was certain stuff buried here once, under the cowshed, for a while."

"You mean guns?"

"I'm just saying that it might be better for all concerned if we forgot what we found here. They're dead and buried already, these fellows, why disturb them? Your dad's dead and buried, too, you don't want people raking over his reputation now, do you?"

John said, "Gabe, these are human beings, for Christ's sake. If we just cover them up, there are going to be five families who will never know where their sons or their husbands went. Can you imagine anything worse than that?"

"Well, I suppose you're right. But it still strikes me as stirring up trouble when there's no particular call to."

John went into the house. It was gloomy inside, and it always smelled of damp at this time of year. He took off his boots and washed his hands in the small cloakroom at the side of the hall. Then he went into the large quarry-tiled kitchen where his mother was baking. She seemed so small these days, with her white hair and her stooped back and her eyes as pale as milk. She was sieving out flour for tea brack.

"Did you finish the plowing, John?" she asked him.

"Not quite. I have to use the telephone."

He hesitated. She looked up and frowned at him. "Is everything all right?"

"Of course, mam. I have to make a phone call, that's all."

"You were going to ask me something." Oh, she was cute, his mother.

"Ask you something? No. Don't worry about it." If his father really had allowed the IRA to bury bodies on his land, he very much doubted that he would have confided in his mother. What you don't know can't knock on your door in the middle of the night.

He went into the living-room with its tapestry-covered furniture and its big red-brick fireplace, where three huge logs were crackling and Lucifer the black Labrador was stretched out on the rug with his legs indecently wide apart. He picked up the old-fashioned black telephone and dialed 112.

"Hallo? I want the Garda. I need to speak to somebody in charge. Yes. Well, this is John Meagher up at Meagher's Farm in Knocknadeenly. We've dug up some bodies."

Two

It was raining even harder by the time Katie Maguire arrived at Meagher's Farm in her muddy silver Mondeo. She could see that Detective Inspector Liam Fennessy was already there, as well as two other detectives and three or four uniformed gardaí who were struggling against the gusty wind to erect bright blue plastic screens.

She climbed out of the car and walked across the farmyard with her raincoat collar turned up. Liam was standing by the open grave with his hands in the pockets of his long brown herring-bone overcoat, undeterred by the rain, smoking a cigarette. Detective Garda Patrick O'Sullivan was hunkered down in his windcheater, frowning at the bones with a studious expression on his face, while Detective Sergeant Jimmy O'Rourke was standing under the shelter of the farmhouse roof, talking to John Meagher.

"Afternoon, superintendent," said Liam. He was thin and hollow-cheeked, with fair, greased-back hair and circular wire-rimmed spectacles, which were spotted with rain. He looked more like a young James Joyce than a Garda inspector. "Seems as if we've got a few bones to pick, doesn't it?"

"God almighty." She had never seen anything like this in her entire career. "How long before the team from the technical bureau get here?"

"Half-an-hour I'd say. And the venerable Dr Owen Reidy is

coming down first thing tomorrow morning. Reidy the Ripper. He'd have your duodenum for a fancy necktie before you even breathed your last gasp."

Katie gave him the faintest of smiles. "Did you talk to Superintendent O'Connell in Naas?"

Jerry O'Connell was in charge of Operation Trace, which had spent the last nine years looking for eight young women who had disappeared without trace in the eastern counties of Ireland.

Liam said, "I put a message in, yes."

Katie walked slowly around the excavation, trying to make sense of all the bones that were lying there, jumbled up like pick-a-sticks as if somebody had tossed them up into the air and let them scatter at random. She could make out at least three pelvises, and two breastbones, and innumerable vertebrae.

She was used to dead bodies – three or four bluey-green floaters were fished out of the River Lee every week, and then there were the blackened and bloated druggies they regularly found in Lower Shandon Street, and the maroon-faced winos crouched in shop doorways in Maylor Street, their hearts stopped by Paddy's whiskey and hypothermia.

But this was different. This was wholesale butchery. She could almost smell the dread of what had happened here, along with the peaty reek of the rain-soaked soil.

Sergeant O'Rourke came up to her. He was a short, sandy-haired man with a rough-hewn block of a head, like an unfinished sculpture. "What do you think, Jimmy?" she asked him.

"I never saw nothing like it, ma'am, except in a picture on Father Francis' wall, at St Michael's, which had heaven at the top and hell at the bottom, you know, and this is what hell looked like. All skeletons, all in a heap."

Katie said, "This is John Meagher, is it?"

"That's right. John – this is Detective Superintendent Kathleen Maguire. She's in charge of this investigation."

John held out his hand. "Oh, I see. I'm sorry, I didn't realize that – "

"That's all right, John," said Katie. "An Garda Síochána is an equal-opportunity employer, and occasionally they bend over backwards to be *very* equal."

"It looks so far like there could be six skeletons, or even seven," said Sergeant O'Rourke. "Kevin's counted thirteen ankle-bones so far."

"Do you have any idea at all how these remains might have come to be buried here?" Katie asked John.

John shook his head. "None at all. Absolutely none. I've been running the farm for fourteen months now so nobody could have buried them here after I took over."

"What about *before* you took over?"

"Meagher's Farm has been in my family since 1935. I can't see my father burying any bodies here. Why would he? Nor my grandfather, either."

Katie nodded. "Does anybody else have access to your property here? Like tenant farmers, anybody like that? Or holidaymakers? Or Travelers?"

"There's nobody here but me and Gabriel and the Ryan brothers, Denis and Bryan. They do the general laboring, and Maureen O'Donovan helps me to run the creamery."

"I'll be wanting to talk to them, too."

"Sure, absolutely. But this is a total mystery, so far as I'm concerned. I'm no expert, but it looks me as if these people have been dead for a heck of a long time."

Katie said nothing, but stood looking at the bones with her hand pressed over her mouth.

John waited until Katie had walked around to the other side

of the excavation before he said to Sergeant O'Rourke, "Kind of *intense*, isn't she?"

"Oh, not usually. But she's very humorless when it comes to homicide, Superintendent Maguire. Doesn't see the funny side of it, if you know what I mean."

John watched her as she circled around the bones. A very striking woman, he thought, not more than 5ft 5ins, just turned 40 maybe, with cropped coppery hair and sage-green eyes and sharply-chiseled cheekbones. She had that Irish-elfin look of being related to the fairy folk, ten generations removed. The sort of woman you find yourself looking at a second time, and then again. But then she glanced up and caught him looking at her and he found himself immediately turning away, as if he had something to be guilty about. God knows how she would make him feel if he actually knew how these skeletons had come to be buried here.

Eventually she came back over. The raindrops were sparkling in her hair. "You haven't heard any local stories about anybody going missing? Not necessarily recent stories. Something that might give us a rough idea when these people died."

"I don't have too much time for local gossip, I'm afraid. I go down to Ballyvolane once in a while and have a couple of drinks at the Fox and Hounds. But I'm still a foreigner, as far as the locals are concerned. Not surprising, really. I still can't understand the Cork accent and up until I came here I thought that hurling was something you did after drinking too much Guinness."

"All right, John," said Katie. "You won't be going anywhere, will you? Once we've had the chance to clear this site properly; and the State Pathologist has examined the remains, there'll be quite a few more questions that are going to need answering."

"Listen, whatever I can do."

Katie went over to her car and picked up her mobile phone. "Paul? It's me. I'm up at Knocknadeenly. Yes, somebody's found some remains. Yes, I know. Listen, it doesn't look as if I'm going to be home until late. There's a Marks & Spencer chicken pie in the freezer. You put it in a pre-heated oven at gas mark 8. Yes. Well, you know how to peel a potato, don't you? All right, go to the pub if you like, it's up to you, but eat something decent. I'll call you later."

A white Garda van was coming up the driveway. The technical bureau. Katie walked back to the excavation and waited for them to kit up in their Tyvek suits and their rubber boots. She looked down at the heap of bones and wondered who on earth they had belonged to. Normally, when she attended a death scene, it was immediately obvious who had done what to whom, and why. Bloody carving-knives in the kitchen sink. Babies, gray-faced from suffocation. Girls lying face-down and muddy-thighed in a ditch somewhere, strangled with their own scarves.

But this was something very different, and until she knew how long these people had been lying here it was futile for her to try and guess who might have killed them, or why. All that was immediately apparent was that none of the skulls had a bullet-hole in the back. That would have been very strong evidence that they were the victims of a political execution, or maybe a revenge killing by one of the local gangs.

Although she was going to inform Operation Trace about these skeletons as a matter of protocol, she didn't think that they were connected with Superintendent O'Connell's investigation. The girls he was looking for had disappeared one by one over nearly a decade – the last one in July, 1998 – and Katie's immediate impression was that these bodies had been buried all at once.

Liam came up to her and offered her an extra-strong mint. "What do you think? Could have been Meagher's father who did it, possibly?"

"We won't know that until we find out who all these people were, and when they were killed, and why."

"You're not looking for a motive? Look around you – a Godforsaken place like this. Struggling from dawn to dusk to scrape a half-decent living and nobody to take out your economic and sexual frustrations on, except the livestock, or the occasional passing cyclist, looking for somewhere to spend the night. Remember that bed-and-breakfast business, down in Crosshaven? Three of them, stuffed in an airing-cupboard?"

Katie lifted her hand to shield her eyes against the rain. "I don't know. I don't get that kind of a feeling. I wouldn't totally rule it out, but there's something very dark about this. The way the different skeletons are all tangled up... it's like they were all taken apart before they were buried."

A series of lightning-bright flashes illuminated the blue plastic screens. The photographer was getting to work, and now the forensic retrieval team were waddling around in their protective suits, marking out the positions of skulls and ribcages.

One of them picked up a thighbone which appeared to have something dangling from the end of it. Then he bent over and picked up another, and another. He examined them for a while and then he came over to Katie and said, "Superintendent? Have a sconce at these."

Katie tugged on a tight plastic glove and accepted one of the bones. It had been pierced at the upper end, where it would have fitted into the hip socket, and a short length of greasy twine had been tied through the hole. On the end of the twine dangled a small doll-like figure, apparently fashioned out of twisted gray rags, with six or seven rusted nails and hooks pushed into it.

Every thighbone had been pierced in the same way; and every one had a tiny rag doll tied onto it.

"What do you make of this, Liam?" Katie asked him. "Ever see anything like this before?"

Liam peered at the little figure closely, and shook his head. "Never. It looks like one of your voodoo effigies, doesn't it, the ones you stick pins in to get your revenge on people."

"Voodoo? In Knocknadeenly?"

The scene-of-crimes officer took the thighbone and went back to work. Katie said, "I don't know what happened here, Liam, but it was seriously strange."

At that moment, John came over and said, "What about a drink, superintendent?"

She would have done anything for a double vodka, but she said, "Tea, thank you. No milk, no sugar."

"And you, inspector?"

"Three sugars, please. And unstirred, if you don't mind. I'm very partial to the sludge at the bottom."

Gradually, the weather began to clear from the west, and the farm was illuminated by a watery gray sunlight. Katie went into the house to talk to John's mother. She was sitting in the living-room with a pond-green cardigan draped around her shoulders, watching *Fair City* and stroking the dog. A large photograph of a white-haired man who looked almost exactly like an older John was standing on the table next to her, along with an empty tea-cup and a crowded ashtray.

"I'm going to have to ask you some questions, Mrs Meagher."

"Oh, yes?" said John's mother, without taking her eyes off the television.

"Do you mind if I sit down?"

"You'll be after taking off your raincoat."

12

"I will, of course." Katie took off her coat and folded it over the back of a wooden chair that was standing behind the door. Underneath she wore a smart gray suit and a coppery-colored blouse that almost matched her hair. She sat down opposite Mrs Meagher but Mrs Meagher still kept her attention focused on her soap opera. The living-room smelled of damp and food and lavender furniture-polish.

"So far we've discovered the remains of eight people, and it looks as though there may be more."

"God rest their souls."

"You wouldn't have any idea who might have buried them there?"

"Well, it must have been somebody, mustn't it? They weren't after burying themselves."

"No, Mrs Meagher, I'd be very surprised if they did. But I'd be interested to know if you were ever aware that your late husband was doing any work in the old feedstore."

"He was always in and out of there. The cattle needed feeding, didn't they?"

"Of course. But what I meant was – were you ever aware that he was doing anything unusual in there? Like construction work, or digging?"

"Sacred heart of Jesus, you're not suggesting for a moment that my Michael buried these poor folk, are you?"

"I'm just trying to get some idea of how they got there, and when."

"I'm sure I don't have a clue. It would have taken a lot of work, wouldn't it, to bury so many people, and Michael would never have had the time for anything like that. He always said that he worked harder than two horses and a brown donkey."

"Did he take any interest in politics?"

"I know what you're saying. He read *An Phoblacht* but

he never had the time for anything like that, either. Not the meetings. It was all I could do to get him to Mass on Sunday."

"Did he have any special friends that you know of?"

"One or two fellows he met in The Roundy House in Ballyhooly. He used to play the accordion with them sometimes, on a Thursday night. That was the only time he was ever away from the farm, on a Thursday night. But it was feeble old fellows they were, couldn't have killed a fly, let alone find the strength to bury the poor creature afterwards."

"Did anybody strange ever come to visit him? Anybody you didn't know yourself?"

Mrs Meagher shook her head. "Michael liked his family around him but he wasn't one for entertaining. Whenever that fat good-for-nothing priest Father Morrissey came visiting and I gave him a piece of cake or a ham sandwich, Michael used to say that he felt like cutting his belly open to get it back, to think of all the hard work that every mouthful had cost him."

"I see. Was he a difficult man, Michael, would you say? I don't mean to speak ill of him."

Mrs Meagher sniffed sharply. "He had his opinions and he didn't care for eejits. But, no – *tut* – he wasn't any more difficult than any other man." As if all men were quite impossible.

"Did he ever have any long-running arguments with anybody?"

"What? He hardly spoke a single word to anyone from one day's end to the next, leave alone argue."

"One more thing. Did you ever hear any stories about people going missing anywhere in the area? Not necessarily recently, but at any time?"

"People going missing?" Mrs Meagher took her attention away from the television for the first time. "No, I never heard of anybody going missing. Of course, when I was a girl my

14

mother was always telling us tales about folk who had been taken by the fairies, off to the Invisible Kingdom, but that was just to frighten us into eating our potatoes."

Katie smiled and nodded. Then she said, "One more thing. Have you ever seen anything like this before?" She reached into her pocket and took out a sealed plastic evidence bag, with one of the little gray rag dolls in it.

"What's that, then?"

"You've never seen anything like it before?"

"That's not a very good toy for a child, now, is it? Full of hooks and all."

"I don't think it's a toy, Mrs Meagher. To be quite honest with you, I don't know what it is. But I'd prefer it if you didn't mention it to anyone."

"Why should I?"

"Well, just in case anybody asks. Anybody from the newspapers or the TV."

Mrs Meagher picked up a half-empty pack of Carroll's cigarettes, and offered one to Katie. "No? Well, I shouldn't either, with my chest. The doctor says I've got a shadow on my lung."

"Why don't you give them up?"

She lit her cigarette and blew out a long stream of smoke. "Give them up? Why in God's name would I try to do something when I know for sure that I'd never be able to do it?"

Three

By the time it grew dark, the technical team had uncovered eleven human skulls and most of the skeletons that went with them – as well as nineteen thighbones pierced and hung with little gray dolls. The excavation had been photographed at every stage, and the position of every bone precisely marked with little white flags and logged on computer. At first light tomorrow, they would begin the careful process of bagging and removing the remains and taking them to the pathology department at Cork University Hospital. There they would be examined by Dr Owen Reidy, the State Pathologist, who was flying down from Dublin bringing his black bag and his famous bad temper.

Liam came over as Katie left the house. "Well?" he asked her, chafing his hands together.

"Nothing. It's hard to believe that John Meagher's father had anything to do with this. But someone managed to excavate a hole in the floor of his feedstore and bury eleven skeletons in it, not to mention drilling their thighbones and decorating them with little dollies, and how they did that without Michael Meagher being aware of it, I can't imagine. As Mrs Meagher says, he was in and out of there every single day, fetching and carrying feed."

"So, it stands to reason. He *must* have known what was going on."

"And what do we deduce from that? That he conspired with an execution squad?"

"I don't think these *were* executions," said Liam. "With executions it's almost always *phutt!* in the back of the head, after all. And what about all these dollies? What execution squad would bother to dismember their victims and drill holes in their thighbones? They'd have the graves dug and the bodies thrown in and they'd be off. But even if this *was* an execution, and John's father *did* bury the bodies, we can't necessarily assume that he did it willingly. He might have been warned to keep his mouth shut or else the same thing would happen to him."

Katie took out a handkerchief and wiped her nose. "I don't know. I think we're going to have to look somewhere else for the answer to this."

"Well, let's keep an open mind about our Michael Meagher. Like I said, there's something about these out-of-the-way farms that puts me in mind of *The Texas Chain Saw Massacre*. The rain, the mud, and nobody to tell your woes to but the pigs and the cows. It's not good for a man's sanity to be speaking nothing but Piggish and Cattle-onian all day."

Katie checked her watch. "We've done all we can for tonight. General briefing at ten o'clock tomorrow morning, sharp. Meanwhile, can you get Patrick started on a comprehensive check of missing persons in the North Cork district for the past ten years? Tell him to pay special attention to people who went missing in groups, and anybody who was cycling or hitch-hiking or backpacking. They're always the most vulnerable.

"Have Jimmy talk to his Traveler friends... they might know something."

"And me?"

"You know what I'm going to ask you to do. Go and have a drink with Eugene Ó Béara."

"You don't think he's really going to tell me anything, do you?"

"If the Provos had a hand in this, no. But you might persuade him to confirm that they didn't, which would save me a whole lot of time and aggravation and a few hundred euros of wasted budget."

Four

It was nearly 10 o'clock when she finally got home, turning into the gates of their bungalow in Cobh, and parking her Mondeo next to Paul's Pajero 4x4. The rain was falling from the west as soft as thistledown. Paul still hadn't drawn the curtains, and as she walked up the drive she could see him in the living-room, pacing up and down and talking on the phone. She tapped on the window with her doorkey, and he lifted his whiskey tumbler in salute.

She let herself in and was immediately pounced on by Sergeant, her black Labrador, his tail pattering furiously against the radiator like a bodhrán drum.

"Hallo, boy, how are you? Did your daddy take you for a walk yet?"

"Haven't had the time, pet," called Paul. "I've been talking to Dave MacSweeny all evening, trying to sort out this Youghal contract. I'll take him out in a minute."

"Poor creature. He'll be ready to burst."

Katie pried off her shoes and hung up her coat and went through to the living-room. It was brightly-lit by a crystal chandelier, with mock-Regency furniture, all pink cushions and white and gilt. The walls were hung with gilt-framed reproductions, seascapes mostly, with yachts tilting against the wind. One corner of the room was dominated by an enormous Sony widescreen television, with a barometer on top of it in the shape of a ship's wheel. In the opposite corner stood a large copper vase, filled with pink-dyed pampas grass.

Paul said, "Okay, Dave. Grand. I'll talk to you first thing tomorrow. That's right. You have my word on that."

Katie opened up the white Regency-style sideboard and took out a bottle of Smirnoff Black Label. She poured herself a large drink in a cut-crystal glass and then went over to draw the curtains. Sergeant followed her, sniffing intently at her feet.

Paul wrapped his arms around her waist and gave her a kiss on the back of the neck. "Well, now. How's everything? I saw you on the TV news at eight o'clock. You looked gorgeous. If I wasn't married to you already I would have called the TV station and asked for your phone number."

She turned and kissed him back. "I'd have had you arrested for harassment."

Paul Maguire was a short, pillowy man, only two or three inches taller than she was, with a chubby face and dark-brown curly hair that came down over the collar of his bright green shirt in the 1980s style that used to be called a "mullet." His eyes were bright blue and slightly-bulging and he always looked eager to please. He hadn't always been overweight. When she had married him seven-and-a-half years ago he had taken a 15-inch collar and a 30-inch waist and had regularly played football for the Glanmire Gaelic Athletic Association.

But five years ago his construction business had suffered one serious loss after another; and his confidence had taken a beating from which he hadn't yet recovered. These days he spent most of his time trying to make quick, profitable fixes – wheeling and dealing in anything from used Toyotas to cut-price building supplies. There were too many late nights, too many pub lunches with men in wide-shouldered Gentleman's Quarters suits who said they could get him something for next-to-nothing.

"Did you eat, in the end?" Katie asked him.

"I had a ham-and-cheese toastie at O'Leary's. And a packet of dry-roasted."

"That's not eating, for God's sake."

"Oh, don't worry about it. I don't have much of an appetite, if you must know."

"The whiskey's killed it, that's why."

"Come on, now, Katie, you know what pressure I've been under, working this deal out with Dave MacSweeny."

"I wouldn't mention Dave MacSweeny and a decent man on the same day. I don't know why you have anything to do with him."

"He went inside just the once, and what was that for? Receiving a stolen church piano. Not exactly Al Capone, is he?"

"He's still a chancer."

She went through to the kitchen, with Sergeant still pursuing her feet. Paul followed her as she opened the breadbin and took out a cut bran loaf. "This is always the way, isn't it? I'm married to the only female detective superintendent in the whole of Ireland, so no matter what I do I have to conduct myself like a saint."

"Not a saint, Paul. Just a law-abiding citizen who doesn't have any dealings with people who hijack JCBs from public roadworks and smuggle cigarettes through the quays and steal lorryloads of car tires from Hi-Q Motors."

Paul watched her in frustration as she cut herself a thick slice of red cheddar and started to slice up some tomatoes. "I'm doing my best, Katie. You know that. But I can't check the credentials of everybody I do business with, can I? They wouldn't give me the time of day if I did. It's bad enough you being a cop."

Katie sprinkled salt on her sandwich and cut it into quarters. "Hasn't it ever occurred to you that my being a cop is precisely *why* they do business with you? Who's going to touch you, garda or villain, when you're Mr Detective Superintendent Kathleen Maguire?"

Paul was about to say something else, but he stopped himself. He followed Katie back into the living-room, stumbling over Sergeant as he did so. "Would you ever hump off, you maniac?"

Katie sat down and took a large bite of sandwich, using the remote to switch on the television. Paul sat beside her and said, "Anyway, forget about Dave MacSweeny. How was your day? What's all these skeletons about? They said on the news there was nearly a dozen."

Katie's mouth was full of sandwich, but with eerie timing her own face suddenly appeared on the screen, standing in the afternoon gloom up at Meagher's Farm, and she turned the volume up. "*We can't tell yet how long these people have been buried here, or how they died. We're not excluding any possibility at all. We could be looking at a mass execution or a series of individual murders or even death by natural causes. First of all the remains have to be examined by the State Pathologist, and as soon as he's given us some indication of the time and cause of death, you can be sure that we'll be pursuing our enquiries with the utmost rigor.*"

"There," said Katie. "Now you know as much as I do."

"That's it? You don't have any clues at all?"

"Nothing. It could have been an innocent family who died of typhus, and who were buried on the farm because they couldn't afford the funerals. Or it could have been eleven fellows who upset somebody nasty in the Cork criminal fraternity."

"I hope you're not making a point."

"No, Paul. I'm very tired, that's all. Now how about you taking Sergeant out to do his business, so that we can go to bed and get some sleep?"

While Paul put on his raincoat and took Sergeant for his run, Katie went through to the small room at the back of the house where she kept her desk and her PC. They still called it The Nursery, although they had stripped off the pale blue wallpaper, and the sole reminder of little Seamus was a small color photograph taken on his first and only birthday.

She took her nickel-plated Smith & Wesson .38 revolver out of the flat TJS holster on her hip and locked it in the top drawer of her desk. Then she sat for a long time staring at her reflection in the gray screen of her computer. When she was young she used to sit on the window-seat at night, looking out of the window, and imagine that there was a ghostly girl looking back at her out of the darkness. She even used to talk to her reflection, sometimes. *Who are you, and what are you doing, floating in the night, and why do you look so sad?*

She didn't fully understand why, but today's discovery up at Meagher's Farm had given her a feeling of deep disquiet… as if something terrible was about to happen. The last time she had felt anything like this was late last spring, when the coastguard had discovered the body of a Romanian woman, washed up on the beach at Carrigadda Bay, in her multi-colored dress. During the course of the next few weeks, all along the coastline as far as Kinsale, they had discovered thirty-seven more. Each woman had paid £2,000 to be smuggled illegally into Ireland, but they had been thrown into the sea a hundred yards offshore, with all of their belongings, and none of them could swim.

During the night, Paul rolled over onto his back and started to snore. Katie elbowed him and hissed, "*Shut up, will you?*" and he stopped for a while, but then he started up again, even louder. She buried her head under the duvet and tried to get back to sleep, but all the time she could hear that high, repetitive rasping.

She found herself walking through a dark, dripping abattoir. She wasn't aware that she was asleep. Somewhere close by she could hear a shrill chorus of bandsaws, and the sound of men whistling as they worked.

She turned a corner and found herself on the killing floor. Five or six slaughtermen were standing around steel-topped tables, wearing long leather aprons and strangely-folded linen hats. They were nonchalantly cutting up carcasses, and tossing them into heaps. Arms on one heap, legs on another, heads in the opposite corner.

Katie walked toward them, even though the floor was slimy with connective tissue and she could feel the blood sticking to her bare feet. As she came closer, she suddenly saw that the carcasses were human – men, women and children.

She came up behind one of the slaughtermen and lifted her hand to touch him on the shoulder. "*Stop*," she mouthed, but no sound came out. He was lining up a decapitated human head, ready to saw it in half.

"*Stop*," she repeated, still silently. At that moment, the decapitated head opened its eyes and stared at her. It started to jabber and babble, and with a thrill of horror she realized that it was trying to explain to her what had happened up at Meagher's Farm.

"*The Gray-Dolly Man! You have to look for the Gray-Dolly Man!*"

"Stop! I'm a police officer!" Katie screamed at the slaughterman. But without hesitation he pushed the head into his bandsaw. There was a screech of steel against bone, and Katie's face was sprayed with blood.

Katie woke up with a jolt. Paul was still snoring, and rain was spattering against the window. She waited for a few minutes, then she climbed out of bed and went through to the kitchen for a drink of sparkling Ballygowan water. She could see herself reflected in the blackness of the window as she drank directly out of the neck of the bottle. The ghost again, looking back at her.

You need a break, she told herself. She and Paul hadn't had a holiday since February, when they had taken a cheap package to Lanzarote for ten days and it had rained for nine of them. Or maybe she needed a different kind of break. A break from her entire life. A break from pain and violence and kicking down doors to damp-smelling apartments. A break from her guilt about little Seamus.

But she couldn't forget those eleven skulls, lined up higgledy-piggledy beside the excavation where the rest of their bodies were strewn. And she couldn't forget those little rag dolls, dangling from their thighbones. Eleven people, deserving of justice. She just prayed to God that they hadn't suffered too much.

Five

Wednesday was colder but very much brighter, and Katie had to wear sunglasses when she drove into the city. The roads were shining silvery-wet from the early-morning rain, and the Lee was glittering like a river of broken glass.

She took the road that ran alongside the quays, where red-and-white tankers and cattle-ships were moored, as well as a three-masted German training clipper. The river divided into two branches as it reached the large Victorian custom-house, so the center of the city was built on an island less than a mile wide and two miles long, connected by more than a dozen bridges and criss-crossed with narrow, devious streets and hidden lanes.

The buildings along the river were painted in greens and oranges and blues, which gave Cork the appearance of somewhere in Denmark, rather than the late-Victorian English-built city it actually was.

Katie drove past City Hall and turned south on Anglesea Street to the modern concrete block of the Garda headquarters. As she climbed out of her car in the car-park, she saw seven hooded crows sitting on the barbed-wire fence at the back. They stayed there even when she walked close by, their feathers ruffled by the sharp early-morning breeze, their eyes as black as buttons.

She remembered that one of the nuns at Our Lady of Lourdes had told her that crows had once been white, but when Noah sent a crow from the Ark to look for land, it had never returned, so God had tarred its feathers so that it looked as black as Satan.

She collected a plastic cup of cappuccino from the machine at the end of the corridor, and then walked along to her office. Sergeant Jimmy O'Rourke was standing outside her door waiting for her in a cloud of cigarette-smoke.

"Dr Reidy's office sent us an e-mail this morning. I'll go up to the airport to meet him at half-past eleven."

She hung up her raincoat. Today she was wearing a green jacket in herringbone tweed and a black sweater. "That's okay," she said. "I'd like to pick him up myself."

"Patrick's left a printout of missing persons on your desk. I've sent Dockery and O'Donovan out to call on all of the farms around the Meagher place. But for what it's worth, I heard something that could be interesting. I called up to the halting site at Hollyhill last night, and one of the Travelers happened to mention that Tómas Ó Conaill had been seen around Cork, him and some of his family."

"Ó Conaill? That devil? I thought he was in Donegal."

"He was, but he and his family haven't been seen since the middle of August at least. Never mind, wherever he is, I'll find him."

"Thanks, Jimmy."

Katie sat down at her desk and wrote "Tómas Ó Conaill" on her jotter, and underlined it three times. Two years ago, she had arrested Tómas Ó Conaill for a vicious attack on a pregnant girl in Mallow, almost disemboweling her with a chisel, but nobody had been prepared to testify against him, not even the girl herself. He was intelligent and charismatic, but he was an out-and-out sociopath who gave the Traveling people a bad name that they didn't deserve – using their cant language and their intense secrecy to conceal his activities from the law.

Tómas Ó Conaill. If anybody was capable of killing and dismembering eleven people, it was him.

As she sipped her cappuccino, she glanced out of the window toward the new multi-story car-park at the back of the Garda station, and saw over a dozen crows clustered along the top of it.

She stood up and went to the window and stared at them. She had never been seriously superstitious, although she never walked under ladders. But the all these crows on the car-park roof strengthened her conviction that something bad was about to happen.

She sat down again. Next to her computer terminal stood a framed photograph of herself and Paul, on their wedding-day, four years ago. She had never noticed before that Paul's right eye seemed to be looking one way, while the left eye was looking another. She reached out and touched the photograph with her fingertips and whispered, "Sorry."

At 7:35 am there was a rap at her open door and Chief Superintendent Dermot O'Driscoll came in, eating a piece of toast. He was a huge, sprawling man with a high white quiff and a pinkish-gray face like a joint of corned beef. His hairy white belly bulged out between his shirt-buttons. He heaved himself into one of Katie's chairs and said, "Well, Kathleen? How's tricks? I hope you realize that the eyes of the world are on us."

"I saw Sky News this morning, yes. But until I get Dr Reidy's analysis – "

"All right. It's just that the media are getting very impatient for fresh developments. And I've already had two calls from Dublin this morning, asking for progress reports."

Katie liked Dermot, and trusted him. After she was unexpectedly promoted to detective superintendent, he had protected her from some very rancid criticism, especially from some of the male detectives who had been passed over. But she didn't care much what the press thought about her, unless they got their facts arse-about-face, and she was too impatient to get results to share his constant concern about "presentation."

"I'm sure we can handle it here, sir," she told him. "We have all the manpower and all the facilities we need. But I think there's more to this case than meets the eye and the last thing I want to do is jump to any lurid conclusions for the sake of amusing the media."

"So where are we so far?"

Katie held up the file that Detective Garda O'Sullivan had left for her. "In the past ten years, over four hundred and fifty people have gone missing without trace in the North Cork area, although never more than three together at any one time, and that was in 1997 near Fermoy. Even when eleven people or more have gone missing in a short space of time, there hasn't been any kind of connection or consistency between them. Summer, 1995: A 45-year-old Waterford man disappeared from the bridge over the River Bride near Bridebridge. The next day a 13-year-old English girl vanished from her parents' caravan at Shanballymore. The same evening, a 33-year-old electrician failed to return home to his family in Castletownroche. Eight other people went missing in the next two days. That's eleven in total. But they didn't have anything in common – not sex, or appearance, or age, or financial background, or even where they were last sighted, and none of them gave any evidence of being distressed or upset before they left."

"What about revenge killings, or executions?"

"Far too soon to tell. It could have been political, it could have been criminal. We really don't know. Liam's talking to Eugene Ó Béara but I'm not especially hopeful."

"How about Eamonn Collins?"

"I'll talk to him myself, later today."

"You said yourself it could have been a natural disaster – an epidemic?"

"Patrick O'Sullivan's looking into that... going back over hospital and doctors' records for the Mallow and Fermoy and Mitchelstown area. But eleven people... that's a lot of people to die at once and nobody to notice it. And of course we've got these mysterious little dolls."

"Do you have any ideas what *they're* all about?"

"None at all. They suggest some kind of folk ritual, don't they? But none of us have ever come across any ritual like this before."

"Any other leads?"

"Jimmy's been talking to some of his contacts in the Traveling community. Apparently Tómas Ó Conaill's been seen in the area."

"Ó Conaill? That piece of work. I thought he was up north these days. Ireland's answer to Charles Manson."

"Well, he may be nothing to do with any of this, but I want to be sure. Apart from that, I'd like at least twenty guards so that we can make house-to-house inquiries around the Knocknadeenly area, and make a thorough search of the whole of the Meagher Farm."

"And what should I be after telling the media?"

"You can tell them we're on top of it."

"Well, Katie, they may want something a little more exciting than that."

"This isn't entertainment, sir, with all due respect."

"Katie – come on, now. Diplomacy. You know as well as I do that if you want their assistance, you'll have to give the media fellows something to keep their salivatory juices flowing. You're a story in yourself, don't forget."

"I don't want to release anything about the dolls, not yet. Not till we know what their significance is."

"Fair enough. But what *can* you release?"

"I'll tell them we're trying some secret new techniques to establish the victims' identities."

"That's good. I like that. And what secret new techniques might these be?"

"I don't know. That's why they're secret."

Chief Superintendent O'Driscoll shook his head. "You're a great detective, Katie. One of the best I've ever had. But you have to understand that the job requires some *tact,* my love, as well as skill."

"When I find out who dismembered eleven people and buried them on Meagher's Farm, sir, then I'll be sweetness itself."

The briefing was short and inconclusive and full of smoke. The technical team showed pictures of the scattered skeletons, but there didn't appear to be any pattern to their disposal. All that they could usefully deduce was that the bodies must have been dismembered before they were buried, because nine femurs were located at the bottom level of the excavation, with three ribcages on top, and then dozens of assorted tibias and fibulas and scapulas, with finger-bones and toe-bones and skulls.

And, of course, the legs must have been cut off so that holes could be drilled, and little rag dolls tied onto them.

Detective Sergeant Edmond O'Leary pointed mournfully to the blown-up photographs. "There was no way of telling for certain which thighbone belonged to which pelvis; or which patella belonged to which thighbone; or which anything belonged to anything else."

At the back of the room, Liam sang, under his breath, "*The hipbone was disconnected from the... thighbone! The*

31

thighbone was disconnected from the... kneebone!"

Katie turned around and gave him an exasperated frown, but he gave her a grin of apology and a wave of his hand.

"Until we have a full pathological report, all we can say for sure is that these skeletons were probably all buried under the feedstore in Meagher's Farm at the same time... even though they may not have actually died or been killed at Meagher's Farm. Their remains may have been transported from another location, and we don't yet have any evidence that they died or were killed on the very same day."

"Any footprints found?" asked Liam.

"Only John Meagher's, and his mother's, and those of his various laborers."

"Tire-tracks?"

"John Meagher's Land Rover Discovery, that's all. And the milk lorry from Dawn Dairies. And the young boy's bicycle."

"Any clothing found, or shoes?" asked Katie.

"No, nothing."

"Any buttons, or hooks-and-eyes, or zippers, or fastenings of any kind?"

"No, and that was unusual, peaty soil being such a preservative."

"So we could be looking for clothes, as a possible clue?"

"We could, yes. And jewelry, of course. They were all adults, by the size of them, and it would be rare to find eleven adults without a single crucifix, or wristwatch, or wedding-ring between them."

"Get onto that," Katie told Edmond O'Leary. "Ask around the jeweler's shops in Cork, in particular... see if they've been offered a quantity of wedding-rings and other personal knick-knacks. Lenihan's would be a good bet, in French Church Street. We pulled in Gerry Lenihan twice last year for fencing stolen rings."

"The only other thing I can tell you so far is that the bones were probably those of young adult females, although I will obviously bow to Dr Reidy's greater expertise in this matter if he says different."

At that moment, Garda Maureen Dennehy came into the briefing-room and handed Katie a note. *Eamonn Collins: Dan Lowery's, 2:30 pm.*

"Thanks, Maureen."

"By the way, your husband called you, too. He said he may have to go to Limerick tonight, so don't wait up for him."

"All right," Katie nodded, thinking to herself, *what the hell is Paul up to now?*

Six

She was talking to one of the airport security police when Dr Owen Reidy came through the automatic sliding doors, impatiently pushing two young children aside. He was wearing a billowing tan trenchcoat that was belted too tight in the middle and a wide-brimmed trilby hat.

"They kept us waiting on the runway at Dublin for over twenty minutes," he grumbled, pushing his medical bag and his bulging overnight case at the young garda. "What do they think, we have time to waste waiting for these package holidaymakers to land from Florida? They should make them circle until they run out of fuel. And crash. And burn."

Dr Reidy had a big, mottled face and sumptuous ginger eyebrows, and he always sported a huge spotted bow-tie. He had been closely involved with Charlie Haughey, when he was Taoiseach, and the *Irish Examiner* had claimed that he was "the fifth man" in a middle-aged orgy at the Grafton Hotel in Dublin, which Dr Reidy had always firmly denied. Deny it or not, he was a grand stegosaurus from the mid-1980s, when the Irish economy had begun to boom, and certain people had made a great deal of money, thanks to nods and winks and tax-breaks and special favors, and he still expected to be treated like one of the great and the good.

"Glad to see you're well, Dr Reidy," said Katie, as they walked out into the sunshine,

"*Pphh*! I was hoping for two days of golf in Killarney. Not picking over skeletons in Cork."

"So far, we've exhumed eleven skulls; which presupposes eleven different individuals, and a corresponding collection of assorted bones."

"Well, your people can count then, can they? That's one mercy."

"We don't have any suspects yet. It depends very largely on the way they died, and when."

"So – as usual – you'll be depending on me to crack your case for you."

"You're a great pathologist, Dr Reidy."

"And you, detective superintendent, should be home minding your kids."

Katie looked out of the car window as they were driven down the long hill toward Kinsale Roundabout, and Cork. She could have said all kinds of things in answer to that. She could have been dismissive, or bitter, or told him how she had gone to feed Seamus on that chilly January morning and found him dead, not breathing.

Instead, she said, "We've booked you your usual room, up at the Arbutus Lodge. I'll have to warn you, though... it's changed hands since you were here last, and the food's not what it used to be."

"I'll take my chances with that, inspector."

They drove into the city, and dropped Katie off in Anglesea Street. Dr Reidy said, "I'll be letting you know my findings as soon as I can. I'm aiming to get at least two days' golf in, after all."

Katie said nothing, but closed the car door and watched him being driven off, his car bouncing and swaying over the potholes. She crossed the road and walked back into the Garda headquarters, her head bowed, and when Garda Maureen Dennehy said, "Chief Superintendent O'Driscoll has been looking for you, ma'am," she didn't look up, not once.

Eamonn "Foxy" Collins was already waiting for her when she walked into Dan Lowery's pub in MacCurtain Street. It was a small pub, its walls crowded with bottles and mirrors advertising Murphy's stout and souvenirs and vases of dried flowers. Eamonn Collins liked it partly because of its theatrical connections (it was right next door to the Everyman Palace theater) but mainly because of its gloomy stained-glass window, which had originally come from a church in Killarney, and which made it impossible for anybody to see into the pub from the pavement outside.

He was sitting in the small back room where he could watch both the front door and the stairs which led up to the toilets. Opposite him sat a big silent man with a blue-shaved head and protruding ears and python tattoos crawling out of the neck of his sweatshirt. Eamonn himself was lean and dapper, with russet brushed-back hair that was beginning to turn white in the front and which had earned him his nickname. He wore a beautifully-tailored two-piece suit in mottled gray tweed, a black waistcoat and very shiny black Oxfords.

Katie sat down opposite him, deliberately obscuring his view of the front door.

"Will I buy you a drink?" he asked her. They didn't need to exchange any pleasantries. His eyes were like two gray stones lying on a beach in winter.

"A glass of water will do."

"Jerry," said Eamonn, and the big silent man stood up and went to the bar.

"You've been taking it very easy lately," said Katie. "Five

36

days' fishing in Sligo... two weeks golf in South Carolina."

"It's good to know that I'm missed."

"I miss you like a dose of hepatitis A."

"You're the light of my life, detective superintendent. But a little more live-and-let-live would go a long way."

"I don't think that drugs have anything much to do with letting people live, do you?"

Eamonn gave a one-shouldered shrug. "What I always say is, you shouldn't let nefarious activities fall into the wrong hands; you have to keep crime clean."

"Is that what happened up at Meagher's Farm? Somebody was keeping crime clean?"

"I don't know what happened up at Meagher's Farm, I'm sorry to say. Things have been very peaceful here in Cork in the past few months, that's why I went off on two weeks' holliers. The only thing I can tell you for sure is that it wasn't anything to do with me; or with anybody else that I know of."

Eamonn was the only man she knew who actually pronounced his semi-colons, sticking out the tip of his tongue and making a soft little clicking sound. She had always found his fastidiousness to be the most alarming thing about him. He ran one of the most profitable drug rackets in the city, and he had been personally responsible for the brutal murders of at least five people. Yet all his clothes were handmade in Dublin and he was always quoting from Yeats and Moore.

There weren't many of Cork's criminals who actually gave her that bristling-down-the-back-of-the-neck feeling, but "Foxy" Collins did.

"Have you eaten at all?" he asked her. "I know that you detectives are often too busy to eat, and the beef sandwiches here are particularly good. Or the Kinsale fish chowder."

"I've had lunch already, thank you," Katie lied. "What I

need to know from you is who's gone missing in the past six months. Eleven people, that's a lot of bodies. If they're *your* bodies, I'm sure that you'll be anxious to have your revenge. If they're not, then I'm sure you'll be equally anxious to make sure that one of your competitors gets what's coming to him."

"But what if *I'm* responsible?" asked Eamonn. "I wouldn't tell you that, now would I?"

"I don't think you *are* responsible. You're more flamboyant than that. When you deal with somebody, you like the whole world to know about it. Like that time you set fire to Jacky O'Malley in the middle of Patrick Street."

Eamonn came close to smiling. He took a sip of his Power's whiskey and fixed her over the rim of his glass with those stones for eyes. "You know what it looks like to me, this massacre of yours? It looks like the work of knackers. There's been some bad blood feuds between some of the families, and if I were you I'd be looking to talk to some of the Traveling folk.

"Tómas Ó Conaill?"

"That wouldn't surprise me. He was always a vicious bastard, and his head was always full of fairy nonsense."

There was a long silence between them. In the front of the pub, a businessman was shouting on his mobile phone. "I will, yeah. I did, yeah. I am, yeah." Eventually Eamonn leaned forward and traced a pattern on top of the varnished table with his well-manicured fingertip.

"The way it was done, you see. The bones all mixed up like that. The knackers do that to stop a person from being admitted to heaven. If you can't find your feet, how can you walk through the Pearly Gates?"

Katie said, "I didn't know that you were such an expert on Irish superstitions."

"I take a very keen interest in anything that's a matter of luck."

38

"Well, you'll let me know, won't you, if you hear about anybody whose luck ran out up at Meagher's Farm?"

"I will, of course. It's always been my policy to co-operate with the Garda."

"One day, Eamonn, I promise, I will break you."

Eamonn gave her a smile. "'You may break, you may shatter the vase, if you will… but the scent of the roses will hang round it still.'"

She left the pub without touching her glass of water and without saying goodbye. The big silent man with the shaved head followed her to the door and opened it for her.

Seven

Dr Reidy called her from the University Hospital at 11:25 on Friday morning.

"I'll be finishing my written report over the weekend, detective superintendent. But I think you ought to come over to the path lab so that I can give you some preliminary findings. Which will surprise you."

"Surprise me? Why?" asked Katie, but he had already banged down the phone.

Liam drove her to the hospital. It was a gray day, dry, and not particularly chilly, but with low cloud pouring endlessly over the city from the west. One of those days when you could easily imagine that you would never see the sun again, for the rest of your life.

She didn't need an overcoat: just her prune-colored wool suit with the red speckles and a cream-colored rollneck sweater. Liam wore his new black leather jacket.

Liam said, "There's no doubt about it, so far as I'm concerned. Whichever way you look at it, Michael Meagher *had* to know that the bodies were buried under his feedstore. I know that Mrs Meagher plays down his republican connections, but it's totally possible that he never told her what he was doing, most of the time."

"Eugene Ó Béara denied any knowledge, though, didn't he?"

"He did, yes, but that was hardly the surprise of the century."

They parked at the front of the hospital and Katie led the way through the double swing doors and along the corridor to the pathology laboratory. An old man in a plaid dressing-gown sat in a wheelchair at the end of the corridor, and frowned at her through glasses that were so fingerprinted that they were almost opaque. He looked the spitting double of Samuel Beckett, but if you had said to him "nothing happens, nobody comes, nobody goes, it's awful!" he might very well have agreed with you but he wouldn't have known that it came from *Waiting for Godot*.

Dr Reidy was standing at the far end of the pathology laboratory wrapped in a green plastic apron. The pearly gray light from the clerestory windows lent him a halo. Eleven trestle tables were arranged in two lines, each table draped in a dark green sheet, and on each table lay a collection of bones, with paper labels attached to every one of them. When Katie saw them like this, she thought they looked even more vulnerable and pathetic than they had when she had first seen them up at Meagher's Farm, a family of fleshless orphans. She felt a sense of desperate sadness, not least because it was far too late to do anything to save them.

Three laboratory assistants were still carefully sorting through the bones, trying to reassemble the skeletons into their previous selves. They were using a wallchart with eleven skeletal diagrams on it to chart their progress.

Dr Reidy blew his nose into a large white handkerchief. "We have identified most of the component parts of these unfortunate individuals – and, yes, they were all female, of varying ages. I will be giving you a list of the bones that are still missing so that you can send your officers back up to Meagher's Farm to search with rather more diligence than they obviously did before. I will attach drawings of what each particular bone

41

looks like. I don't have any optimism that any of your officers can tell their coccyx from their humerus."

"You mean their arse from their elbow," said Katie, without smiling.

"Quite, detective superintendent. What an anatomist you are."

Katie walked around the nearest table and looked at the skull lying forlornly at one end, its bones arranged beneath it. "You said you had a surprise for me, doctor."

"That's right. Not an unpleasant surprise, you'll be happy to know. I've made some preliminary tests on these bones and I can tell you with absolute certainty that none of these ladies died in your lifetime... or even *my* lifetime, so we can forget about Operation Trace. All the marrow's decayed but I should be able to retrieve some identifiable DNA. I've also sent some bone-samples off to Dublin for full amino-acid racemization and when I get the results back I should be able to give you a much more accurate date. But you'll probably be relieved to know that you're not looking for a murderer who's likely to be still alive today."

"You're sure they were murdered?"

"I think it's ninety-nine percent likely but not totally certain. Apart from the holes drilled in the top of the femurs, and the doll-figures attached, each had a narrow chisel-like object pushed into both eye-sockets. Each was obviously dismembered, but it won't be possible for me to determine whether this process began before or after death. There's something else very interesting, too."

"Oh, yes?"

Dr Reidy lifted a tibia from the table in front of them and handed it over so that Katie could examine it more closely. "What do you make of that?"

"It's a leg-bone."

"Of course it's a leg-bone, detective superintendent. But do what detectives are supposed to do and detect what's noteworthy about it."

Katie turned it this way and that. "I don't know. What am I looking for?"

With one blunt, trembling, nicotine-stained forefinger, Dr Reidy pointed to a series of diagonal scratches all the way down the side of the bone. "These striations," he said. "They appear to have been made with a very sharp short-bladed knife of the kind that butchers use for trimming ribs."

"Meaning?"

"Meaning that their flesh didn't naturally decay. Before they were interred, every one of them was completely boned."

Katie said nothing, but looked around the laboratory at the ivory litter of human remains. There was something so tragic about them. Unknown, unburied and unmourned. And God alone knew what they must have suffered, before they were killed.

Liam lifted his spectacles so that he could take a closer look. "What are we talking about here, sir? Why would somebody want to scrape people's flesh off?"

Dr Reidy struggled under his plastic apron, found a handkerchief, and loudly blew his nose. "Cannibalism?" he suggested.

"Cannibalism? Jesus, this isn't Fiji."

"I'm just giving you the forensic findings, Inspector Fennessy. But the findings are that quite apart from the obvious attachment of small cloth figures to their femurs, all of these skeletons had the flesh scraped off them, with considerable care and effort, as if it was being done for a specific, ritualized purpose. Of which cannibalism may have been part."

43

Katie said, "Can you give me just a rough idea of how old these skeletons are?"

"From the tests I've done so far, which – as I say – are not at all conclusive, I'd say that their bones have been lying under Meagher's feedstore for about eighty years, and possibly more. Long before John Meagher's grandfather bought the property, and long before Michael Meagher owned it."

"What about the dolls?"

"They're all made out of linen, knotted and wound around like the funeral-windings of a mummy. The screws and nails and hooks are handmade, most of them, and we can probably date them very accurately indeed. Certainly their corrosion is consistent with them having been buried for at least three-quarters of a century, and possibly longer."

Katie said, "Have you ever come across any killings like this, ever before?"

Dr Reidy shook his head. "Never. As I say, there was obviously some ritualistic element in what happened to these women, but precisely what it was I can't tell you. I never saw bones so methodically stripped of their flesh before. And I've never seen anything like these dolls. And that's in twenty-nine years of medical jurisprudence."

"So what do we do now?"

"My dear, I really can't tell you. I'm going off to play golf in Killarney. You, presumably, will be trying to find what kind of people could have committed such an idiosyncratic crime, and why."

Katie stood close to Dr Reidy for a while, looking at all of the eleven skulls with their crooked, jawless grins. Then she simply said, "Thank you."

"You're quite welcome," Dr Reidy replied, laying an unchar-acteristically avuncular hand on her shoulder. "It always makes life more interesting to see something new, even if it is rather stomach-churning."

That afternoon, she held a media conference at Anglesea Street. The conference room was dazzled by television floods and the epileptic flickering of flashlights. She held her hand up in front of her face to shield her eyes.

"Early forensic examination indicates that these skeletons were interred over eighty years ago. Until we receive more information from Dublin, we won't have a precise date, but it looks as if they could have been victims of a some kind of ritual massacre."

"A Celtic ritual?" asked Dermot Murphy, from the *Irish Examiner*, lifting his ballpen.

"We don't know yet. But we'll be talking to several experts on Irish folklore, to see if there's any kind of religious or social precedent for killings like these."

"You said that the bones had been cleaned by a butcher's knife. Could this be cannibalism we're talking about here? Or a farmer feeding human beings off to his livestock? I read a horror story about that once."

"This is not a story, Dermot. This is reality."

"So what can we say? Without being too sensational?"

"You can simply say that we'll be calling in all of the qualified assistance that we can. We're also appealing for anybody who has any knowledge of similar killings to come forward and share their information with us, no matter how inconsequential they think it may be. This is a difficult and highly unusual case, but you can rest assured that we're making progress."

"Is there any point in continuing a full-scale investigation?" asked Gerry O'Ryan, from the *Irish Times*. "The murderer's more than likely dead by now, surely?"

"So far the investigation is still open," said Katie. "I'm going to be talking to Chief Superintendent O'Driscoll tomorrow morning, and we'll decide what action to take next. Obviously we don't want to waste taxpayers' money on pursuing a case that will give us no useful result."

The media conference broke up, and the television lights were switched off, leaving the room in sudden gloom. Katie talked for a while to Jim McReady from RTÉ News, and then she walked back to her office.

She was halfway there when she heard the jingling of loose change as somebody tried to catch up with her. "Superintendent!" called a voice. It was Hugh McGarvey, a freelance journalist from Limerick, a skinny little scarecrow of a man with a withered neck and a beaky nose. "You're right on top of this case, then, superintendent?"

"I'm doing everything I possibly can, yes."

"Would it be impertinent of me to ask you, then, who your husband is on top of?"

"*What*?" she said, baffled.

"Your husband, Paul. I was having a few drinks with some friends at the Sarsfield Hotel in Limerick on Thursday night and lo and behold I saw your husband stepping into the lift with some dark-haired girl in a short blue dress. A fine half she was, very vivacious. And very friendly they looked, too."

Katie suddenly felt short of breath, as if somebody had slapped her in the stomach.

Hugh McGarvey added, "There was no Paul Maguire in the hotel register that night, but then, well, you wouldn't have expected there to be, would you?"

"Mistaken identity," said Katie. "You should be careful of that, Hugh. A lot of people get themselves into serious trouble, pointing the finger at the wrong person."

"Oh, I'm pretty sure it was him."

"Couldn't have been. He wasn't even staying at the Sarsfield."

"I was only checking, superintendent. It would make a bit of a story, wouldn't it, if it was true?"

"Listen," said Katie. "You were invited here for a media conference about a serious crime – even though that crime was committed over eighty years ago. That's the story. Not me."

"You'll always be the story. At least you will be until another woman makes the rank of detective superintendent."

"Your breath smells," said Katie.

Paul said, "Nothing happened in Limerick, Katie. I was trying to buy some building supplies from Jerry O'Connell, that's all. We had a bite to eat together, and a couple of drinks, and then I went to bed. On my own."

"You were staying at the Sarsfield, though? You told me you were staying at Dwyer's."

"I was going to stay at Dwyer's but they didn't have a room."

"Dwyer's didn't have a room? *Dwyer's*? In the middle of the week?"

"For God's sake, Katie. Outside of this house you're a detective superintendent, but inside of this house you're my wife. I don't expect you to put me through the third degree just because some ratty reporter imagined he saw me with some fictitious woman."

Katie said, "All right. Sorry. You're right."

"It's always the same. You're always making me feel guilty even when I haven't done anything."

"I said I'm sorry."

"Jesus Christ," said Paul. "I love you and this is what I get in return."

Katie didn't know whether to believe his protestations

of innocence or not. If he had been one of her suspects, she wouldn't have accepted his story for a second. Of course she could call Dwyer's and check if he was telling the truth, and she could call the manager at Sarsfield's, too, but what good would that do? Paul was her husband and at some point she had to trust him, not just because she felt so responsible for him, not just out of loyalty, but also because she wasn't yet ready to face the alternative. She didn't want to choose which CDs were hers and which were his. She didn't want to sell the house, because The Nursery was here, and she couldn't leave The Nursery.

Not to be able to walk into that room again, and close her eyes, and imagine that she could still smell that baby-smell of talcum-powder, and still hear that clogged, high-pitched breathing – just now, that would be more than she could bear.

Paul swallowed whiskey and said, "Hugh McGarvey's stirring it, that's all. He's a scumbag. He's probably still sore because you complained about that rubbish he wrote about police overtime."

"Forget it, Paul. He made a mistake, that's all."

"Me and Jerry went through a whole bottle of whiskey between us. I couldn't have flahed anybody if I'd wanted to."

"I said forget it."

He sat down on the pink-upholstered sofa next to her, and stroked her cheek. "There's only one woman I love, Katie, and that's you."

"What's wrong with you, Paul? Why can't you tell me?"

"There's nothing at all wrong with me, Katie. I'm just trying to find my feet again, that's all. Can't you ever give me a chance, for Christ's sake?"

"I'm always giving you a chance. But what happened to the happiness, Paul?"

He was just about to say something when the phone rang. Katie picked it up and it was Liam, and he sounded as if he were standing next to a busy road-junction.

"I've had a call from Eugene Ó Béara. He says that there's somebody who wants to talk to us. Three o'clock on Sunday, in Blackpool."

"All right, then. He didn't give you any idea what it was about?"

"No, he was being all mysterious."

Katie put down the phone. She looked at Paul but Paul looked back at her with an expression that said nothing but: *what*? She wanted so much for him to give her some hope. She wanted him to say that he had got his self-confidence back, that everything was going to be different. But Paul took another swallow of whiskey, and tugged at Sergeant's ears, and said, "You like that, boy, don't you? You like that."

Eight

By the time the two builders had dropped her off at the bridge by the Angler's Rest, on the way to Blarney, the tarmac-gray sky grew even darker, and huge spots of rain had begun to fall across the road. The builders gave her a wave and a toot of their horn and turned off westward toward Dripsey. She crossed the road and stood with her thumb sticking out.

The breeze blew the long blonde hair that streamed out from underneath her knitted woolen cap. She was a tall, athletic-looking girl, with a honey-colored California suntan. She was wearing a navy blue windcheater and blue denim jeans and Timberland hiking-boots, and carrying a rucksack.

Hitch-hiking through Ireland had been magical for her. She had planned this trip for over eighteen months, sitting on the verandah of her parents' home in Santa Barbara, poring over photographs of misty green mountains and rugged beaches and picturesque pubs with raspberry-painted frontages and bicycles propped outside. Most of those pictures had come to life, and she had stood on the rocks on the Ring of Kerry overlooking the pale turquoise sea, and tapped her feet to Gaelic music in tiny one-room bars, and walked along the banks of the Shannon and the Lee, knee-deep in wet green grass.

Now she was on her way to Blarney Castle, a few miles north-west of Cork City, to do what all conscientious tourists were obliged to do, and kiss the Blarney Stone.

She had only been thumbing for a lift for five minutes before a black Mercedes pulled into the side of the road and waited for her with its engine running. Its hood was highly-polished but its sides and trunk were thickly coated with brown mud. She ran up to it and opened the door.

"Pardon me, are you going through Blarney?"

"Blarney?" he said. "I can take you anywhere your heart desires."

"I only need to get to Blarney."

"Then, of course."

She climbed into the front passenger seat. The interior of the car was immaculately clean and smelled of leather. "I'm not taking you out of your way?" she said, tossing her rucksack onto the back seat.

"Of course not. I *am* the way."

They drove smoothly off toward Blarney. Although it was only three o'clock in the afternoon, the day grew suddenly so dark that the driver had to switch on his lights. There were no other cars in sight, and both sides of the road were overhung with shadowy green woods.

"You're American," he said.

"Yes, but Irish heritage. Fiona Kelly, I'm from Santa Barbara, California. My great-great-grandfather came from Cork, and he emigrated to New York in 1886."

"So you're rediscovering your roots?"

"It's something I've always wanted to do. I don't really know why. My parents have never been back here, but I saw a Discovery program about Ireland two or three years ago, and do you know, the minute I saw those mountains, and those fabulous green meadows..."

"Ah, yes. They say that if you come from Ireland, you have to come back to Ireland to say your last words. *In articulo vel periculo mortis.* If you're dying, you know, your last plea for absolution can be heard by any priest at all, even if degraded or apostate, even if you've committed grievous sins which can normally be forgiven only by some ecclesiastical superior."

"Well, wow. You seem to be pretty well versed. Are you a priest?"

"No," he smiled. "I'm not a priest. But, yes, I'm pretty well versed, as you put it."

Suddenly, it began to rain thunderously hard. The driver slowed down, but his windshield wipers were still whacking from side to side at full speed, and Fiona found it almost impossible to see where they were going.

"Maybe we should pull over," Fiona suggested, nervously.

"Oh, no, we're going to be fine. We're almost there now."

She peered through the windshield but she still couldn't see any signs saying Blarney.

"I have to kiss the Blarney Stone. That was something my dad made me promise."

"Well, of course. Everybody who comes to Cork has to kiss the Blarney Stone. It gives you the gift of a silver tongue."

At last the rain began to die away, and the driver switched off the windshield wipers, and unexpectedly a pale golden sun came swimming out of the clouds. The driver remarked, "They say that we don't have a climate here, only weather."

He turned sharp left, and up a steep muddy road with a sign saying Sheehan's Nurseries. The road became narrower and narrower, and eventually Fiona said, "This isn't the way to Blarney, is it?"

"It's a detour, that's all. We'll be there in a trice."

"No, no. I really don't think so. I want you to stop, right now, and I want to get out."

"Don't be ridiculous. It's only a half-a-mile into Blarney from here."

"In that case, I can walk it, okay? I want to get out."

"You're not frightened, are you?"

"No, I'm not. But I want to get out. It's stopped raining and I can walk the rest of the way."

"Hm," said the driver, and suddenly put his foot down, so that the Mercedes surged forward, and its rear tires slithered on the muddy road.

"Stop, will you?" Fiona demanded. "I want to get out!"

"Sorry, Fiona Kelly. That's not really an option."

Fiona reached into her jeans pocket and tugged out her mobile phone. "Are you going to stop and let me out or am I going to call the police?"

Without warning, the driver wrenched the mobile phone out of her hand and then punched her on the cheek. He hit her so hard that her head banged against the window.

"Oh God!" she screamed. "Stop! Let me out! *Stop*!"

The driver slammed his foot on the brake. The car slewed sideways and stopped halfway up the verge. Fiona grappled with the door-handle but it was centrally-locked and she couldn't open it.

"*Let me out*! Are you crazy? *Let me out*!"

The driver punched her a second time, right in the side of the nose, snapping her cartilage. The front of the car was suddenly spattered with blood. Then he seized her shoulders and hit her head against the window again and again, while she struggled and pushed and flailed her arms.

"You could have – saved me from – doing this," he grunted, as he thumped her head against the glass, and then against the door-pillar. "You could have – sat there – and behaved yourself – like a good little – girl."

He seized a handful of long blonde hair, pulled her head toward him, and then knocked her head so hard against the window that she slumped unconscious, with blood pouring from her nose in a thin, continuous river.

He sat where he was for two or three minutes, breathing heavily. "Shit," he said, under his breath. Then he started up the car again, backed it off the verge, and continued to drive down the lane. Fiona sat next to him, joggling limply as he drove over lumps and potholes. Every now and then he glanced across at her and shook his head in annoyance. He wasn't used to girls who twigged so quickly that he was trying to take them away. Usually they were still smiling right up to the moment when he produced the ropes – and, sometimes, even after he'd tied them up.

He turned left up a steep, winding hill, where the nettles and the brown-seeded foxgloves crowded even closer. At the top of the hill there was a sagging five-bar gate, every bar still bejeweled with raindrops, and beyond that stood a damp-looking cottage, with one side thickly shrouded in creeper. He drove the Mercedes all the way around the cottage to the back garden, so that it couldn't be seen from the lane, and parked it beside the overgrown vegetable patch. As he climbed out of the car he saw dozens of hooded crows perched on the telephone-lines above his head. He clapped his hands and shouted, "*Hoi!*" but they stayed where they were, all facing south-west, into the wind.

Opening the passenger door, he dragged Fiona out of the car and across the yard, her heels bumping on the broken concrete. She was still unconscious, but her nose had stopped bleeding, and she had a congealed black moustache. He propped her up against the side of the porch as he searched in his pocket for his keys.

"Shit," he repeated, like a litany.

He managed to turn the key in the green-painted cottage door, and nudge it open with his shoulder. Winding Fiona's arm around his neck, he shuffled her inside, and across the hallway, and into the gloomy, damp-smelling living-room. He dropped her onto the worn-out couch, with its mustard-colored throw, and then he went back to close the front door, and lock it.

"Now," he said to himself. He crossed the living-room and drew the cheap yellow cotton drapes. Then he shrugged off his coat and tossed it across the back of one of the armchairs, and rolled up his shirtsleeves. "*Couldn't* be nice, could you? Couldn't be agreeable. Had to put up a fight."

The clock on the mantelpiece chimed four. Fiona, on the couch, started to stir, and groan. Immediately, and very quickly, he unlaced her boots, and pulled them off her feet, and let them tumble onto the floor. Then her thick red hiking-socks.

She groaned again, and tried to lift her arm. He leaned over her and said, "Shush, shush, everything's fine. You're going to be fine in a minute." He unbuckled her belt, opened up her jeans, and wrenched them halfway down her thighs. He was surprised and mildly aroused to find that she wasn't wearing any panties. Then he pulled off her denim jacket, and her red ribbed sweater. She mumbled, "Mom… what's happening, mom? Don't want to go to bed."

"Everything's fine. Don't worry about it."

"Mom, my head hurts."

"It's okay… I'll bring you some aspirin. Just lie still."

He took off her jeans and threw them into the corner of the room. He lifted her up, so that she was sitting, and then he knelt in front of her and tilted her over his shoulder. Panting with effort, he stood up, and carried her into the hallway, her arms dangling down his back, and into the bedroom next door. She

55

was a big girl, well-nourished, and by the time he managed to lower her onto the bed he was trembling with the strain.

"Shit," he said.

The bed had a green cast-iron frame and no mattress or blankets, but several thicknesses of newspaper had been spread on the floor underneath it. Its springs creaked and complained as he tied her wrists with cords, and then her ankles. She opened her eyes for a moment and said, "What… what's happening?" but then she closed them again and started to breathe thickly through her open mouth.

He stood up and looked at her. His expression was completely impassive, although he was gripping his genitals through his black corduroy pants, and systematically squeezing them. After a while he went through to the kitchen and came back with a pair of orange-handled scissors. He cut through the front of her bra, and then the straps, and took the pieces away.

"Mom?" she said.

He reached out and stroked her forehead, and the crusted blood on her upper lip. He didn't know why victimhood made girls so appealing, but it always did. It made them so much more feminine and vulnerable, no matter how strong and self-confident they had acted when he first met them. *Stop the car and let me out*! It was such a futile, arrogant demand that it made him smile to think about it.

Eventually he went back into the kitchen and came back with the coil of thin nylon cord. He looped it around the top of her left thigh, and knotted it, and pulled it as tight as he could, one foot braced against the bed-frame. It cut deep into her suntanned flesh, so deep that it almost disappeared. She suddenly blinked her eyes and started to struggle.

"Oh God, that hurts! What are you doing to me? What are you doing?"

He leaned over her and touched his finger against her lips. "Don't shout, nobody can hear you. You're miles and miles from anywhere."

"God, you're hurting my leg, you're hurting my leg!"

"That's necessary, I'm afraid. You wouldn't want to bleed to death, would you?"

Her eyes flicked wildly from side to side. "What do you mean? What are you talking about? Where am I?"

"You're alone with me, that's all you need to know. You're alone with me and Morgan."

"Listen, you creep, you'd better let me go. My father's president of CalForce Electronics."

"Oh, CalForce Electronics? Never heard of them, I'm sorry to say."

"You're really, really hurting my leg."

"I know, my sweet. I'm sorry. But, as I say, it's necessary for your survival."

"What do you want? What are you going to do to me? My father can pay you money."

"I expect he can. But I'm not interested in money. Not in the slightest."

"Then what? What do you want? Are you going to rape me, or what?"

"Rape you? Of course not. You don't think I look like a *rapist*, do you?"

"I don't know. But please take this cord off my leg. It's so tight."

"I know. It's supposed to be."

"For what *reason*? What are you going to do? Look at my leg, it's turning blue."

"That's a very good sign. Shows that I've restricted your circulation."

"Please," begged Fiona. "If anything happens to me, my parents are going to be devastated."

"Well, that's very selfless of you. But I'm afraid that you have a destiny which far supersedes any consideration for your parents."

"What do you mean? Please... if you let me go, I won't tell anybody what happened here. I'll go right back home and I won't mention any of this to anybody."

He nodded, almost ruefully. "Of course you won't, because you'll be dead."

"You're going to kill me?"

"It's a regrettable but inevitable part of the ritual."

"Please. I'm twenty-two years old."

"Yes?"

Tears suddenly started to drip down her cheeks. "I'm twenty-two years old and I haven't lived any kind of life yet. I've seen Ireland, and that's about all. I want to do so much more. I want to be a teacher, and teach little kids."

"Do you have a boyfriend?"

Fiona nodded, still snuffling. "His name's Richard. I've known him since I was fourteen."

"Um. He's going to miss you, then."

"Please don't kill me. Please don't kill me. I'll do anything."

"Now, then. Don't be too hasty in what you wish for. By the time tomorrow morning comes, you'll be pleading with me to have it done with, believe me."

"Please."

He looked at his watch and gave a little negative shake of his head. "I'm going to have to leave you for a while. Only about half-an-hour... but you took me by surprise, you see. I wasn't expecting to come across somebody so suitable so soon. I have to make a few purchases, to see us through the next few days."

"I'll do anything you want. I can call my father and ask him to send you money."

"*Money?*"

"I don't know... anything you want. Anything."

"I'll see you later," he said. "And, really, don't bother to scream."

Nine

The afternoon went past like a strange grainy dream. Fiona heard his car scrunching out of the driveway in front of the cottage, and then the only sounds were the cawing of the crows and the whispering of the ivy against the window.

For the first five or ten minutes she struggled furiously to get herself free, but he had tied her with such complicated knots that all she managed to do was tug them even tighter. In spite of what he had said, she tried shouting for help, but it was obvious that he had been telling her the truth. The cottage was far too isolated for anybody to be able to hear her.

She shivered with cold and wept with self-pity. Her right leg had turned a pale turquoise color and she couldn't feel it at all. She tried talking to her mother, in the hope that her mother would somehow sense that she was in danger, like people did in Stephen King stories.

But then there was nothing but the crows, and the surreptitious sniggering of the ivy, and the throb, throb, throb of her circulation in her ears.

He came back in less than an hour. He didn't go straight in to see her. Instead, he went directly to the kitchen and heaped his bags of groceries onto the Formica-topped table. "How are we feeling?" he called, but she didn't reply. He filled the kettle and put it onto the old-fashioned gas-stove, lighting the hob with a newspaper spill. Then he put away his cans of baked beans and his packets of biscuits, slamming the cupboard doors. He hadn't bought much in the way of frozen food: there was a refrigerator in the corner which rattled and coughed like a wardful of emphysema victims but only managed to keep food somewhere just below tepid.

He made himself a mug of instant coffee, and stirred it with an irritating tinkle. He could hear Fiona weeping quietly in the bedroom. On the wall beside the stove hung a yellowed calendar for 1991, with a picture of Jesus on it, entering Jerusalem in triumph. As he sipped his coffee, he leafed through the months. On June 11, somebody called Pat had died. On June 14, Pat had been buried. *Requiescat in pace*, Pat, he thought.

Eventually, he rinsed his mug and left it upside-down on the draining-board. Then he went back into the bedroom, and switched on a dazzling Anglepoise lamp beside the bed. Fiona flinched and turned her face away from it.

"Well, then! Sorry it's so bright, but I have to see what I'm doing."

"Please," she sobbed. "I can hardly feel my leg at all."

"Well, that's good. That's *very* good. From your point of view, anyhow."

"You're not going to hurt me, are you?"

He looked down at her with a thoughtful expression on his face. "Yes," he said. "I probably am."

"Can't you give me something to deaden the pain? Aspirins, anything."

"Of course. I'm not a sadist."

"Then *why*?" she said, her voice rising in hysteria. "Why are you doing this? If you're not a sadist, *why*?"

"There are things I need to know, that's all."

"What things? I don't understand."

61

"There are other worlds, apart from this. Other existences. Darker places, inhabited by dark monstrosities. I need to know if they can be summoned. I need to know if any of the rituals really work."

"Oh dear God, why do you have to do it to *me*?"

"No special reason, Fiona. You were there, that's all, standing by the side of the road. Fate. *Kismet*. Or just plain shitty luck."

"But you don't know me. You don't know anything about me. How can you kill me?"

"If it wasn't you, it would have to be somebody else."

"Then let it be somebody else. Please. Not me. I don't want to die."

This time he said nothing, but left the room again, and came back a minute later with a mug of water and a brown glass bottle of aspirin tablets. He held the tablets out in front of her in the palm of his hand, as if he were feeding an animal, and she bent her head forward and choked them down, three and four at a time, crunching some of them between her teeth and swallowing some of them whole. All the time she was mewling and sobbing and the tears were streaming down her cheeks.

"Imagine that you're going on a journey," he said, and his voice became curiously monotonous, as if he were trying to hypnotize her. "Imagine that you're going to be traveling not through some undiscovered country, but through the landscape of your own suffering. Instead of forests you will walk through the thorns and brambles of tearing nerves, and instead of snowy mountain-tops, you will see the white peaks of utter agony."

He held the mug against her lips and she drank as much water as she could, even though most of it ran down her chin.

"I'll do anything," she said. "Just let me go, please. I'll do anything at all."

"You don't understand, Fiona. I simply want you to lie back and experience what's coming to you."

Maybe it was the effect of the aspirins; or maybe it was shock, but Fiona suddenly stopped sobbing and lowered her head, and stared at the end of the bed with oddly unfocused eyes. Maybe it was despair – the realization that no matter how much she begged, he was going to kill her anyway.

There was a brown leather briefcase standing on the floor next to the cheap walnut-veneered wardrobe. He picked it up, and sat down on the side of the bed-frame, and opened it. Fiona didn't take her eyes away from the end of the bed, even when he produced a case of surgical instruments, a length of hairy twine, and a small white doll fashioned out of torn linen, pierced all over with fish-hooks and screws and tintacks.

"This is a very ancient ritual," he said. "Nobody knows exactly how far back it goes. But throughout the ages, its purpose has always been the same. To open the door to the other world, and coax some of its monstrosities to come through. Interesting, isn't it, how men and women have always wanted to play with fire... to risk their lives and their sanity by calling up their worst nightmares? They could let their demons sleep in peace, but they insist on prodding them into wakefulness, like naughty children taunting a mad dog."

Fiona remained in a trancelike state as he opened up the flat, rectangular case of surgical instruments. It contained two bone-saws, a selection of scalpels, and a shining collection of stainless-steel knives. He took out a long-bladed scalpel, closed the case, and then stood up again.

"I don't know if you want to pray," he said.

Ten

Katie and Liam were early for their three o'clock appointment with Eugene Ó Béara. They pushed their way through the battered red doors of The Crow Bar in Blackpool, across the street from Murphy's Brewery. The bar was crowded and foggy with cigarette-smoke. A hurling match between Cork and Kilkenny was playing on the television at deafening volume, while the pub radio was tuned equally loudly to an easy-listening station.

A few months ago, the pub doors would have been locked between 2 and 4 for "The Holy Hour," even though it would have been just as jampacked inside, but the Irish licensing laws had been relaxed during the summer. Katie and Liam made their way along the darkly-varnished bar to a booth at the very back, partitioned from the rest of the pub by a wooden screen.

Katie got some hard looks as she walked through the pub. Every man there knew who she was, and she recognized Eoin O'hAodhaire and both of the Twohig brothers, whom she had personally arrested for car theft in her first year as detective sergeant. Micky Cremen was there, too, sitting in the far corner glowering at her over his pint. Micky had tried to start up his own protection racket until Eamonn Collins had got to hear of it; and Micky had been lucky to end up in prison instead of the Mercy Hospital.

"What can I fetch you folks?" asked Jimmy the barman.

"We're fine for now, thanks," said Katie. "We're waiting for some friends."

"Friends, is it?" said Jimmy, as if he couldn't believe that gardaí could have any friends, and if they did they certainly wouldn't find a welcome in The Crow Bar. But then the front door opened and Eugene Ó Béara and another older man walked in, with a huge Irish wolfhound on a lead. The pub noticeably hushed, and everybody paid extra attention to the hurling match, or to what they were saying to their friends, or to anything else at all except for Eugene Ó Béara and his white-haired companion, and his giant dog.

Eugene came directly down the length of the bar and slid into the booth next to Katie; while the older man eased himself in beside Liam, facing her. Eugene was about 38 years old, with tight curly chestnut hair that was just beginning to turn gray, and the features of a plump, pugnacious baby. He wore a khaki anorak and a Blackpool GAA necktie, and he laid an expensive Ericsson mobile phone on the table in front of him.

The older man had a hawklike face, and white hair cropped so short that Katie could see every bump and scar on his skull. She thought she recognized him but he didn't introduce himself and neither did Eugene. His fingernails were very long and chalky and he wore three silver rings with Celtic insignia on them. His dog buried itself under the table and lay there with its spine pressed uncomfortably against Katie's legs.

"Eugene tells me you were asking him about some people gone missing," said the older man. His voice sounded like somebody sandpapering a cast-iron railing.

"That's right. But that was before we found out how long they'd been dead. I expect you've seen it on the news. The pathologist estimates that they were probably killed more than seventy-five years ago."

"I saw that, yes. But that's why I called Eugene about it and that's why I'm here today."

Katie leaned forward expectantly but the old man sat back and noisily sniffed and didn't volunteer anything more. Katie looked at Eugene and then she looked at Liam, and Liam made a little wobbling gesture with his hand to indicate that it might be a good idea to buy him a drink.

"A glass of Beamish and a double Paddy's, thanks," the old man told her. He had caught Liam's hand-wobble out of the corner of his eye.

"Eugene? Guinness, isn't it?" Katie asked, and Eugene gave her a barely-perceptible wink, as if he had got a fly in his eye.

Everybody in the pub suddenly roared and cheered as Cork scored a goal, and the old man waited patiently for the noise to die down. Then he said, "I told Eugene that there haven't been any killings like that in recent times, not eleven females, not to my knowledge. But when I saw it on the telly that they were buried there for nearly eighty years, that's what rang a bell."

Jimmy the barman brought the old man's Beamish over and he took a small sip and fastidiously wiped his mouth.

"When he was alive, God bless his soul, my great-uncle Robert told me all kinds of stories about what the boys got up to in the old days. He said that in the summer of 1915 a bomb was planted by the British barracks wall up on Military Hill, and that it went off premature, and killed the wives of two of the British officers, and badly hurt another. Blew her arms off, that's what great-uncle Robert told me.

"A week after that, a young woman went missing from her home in Carrignava, and then two more girls from Whitechurch. By September there were five gone altogether, and of course the boys blamed the English for it, thinking they were taking their revenge for the officers' wives. A sixth woman went on

Christmas Day, and then three more before the end of January.

"The boys hit back in February. They ambushed a British Army truck at Dillon's Cross, and they shot two Tommies. You can read all about it in the history books. There was bad enough blood between the Irish and the English at that time, and all of this made it ten times worse. But girls went on disappearing, right up until the spring of 1916, around the time of the Easter Rising. No more went missing after that, but no trace of none of them was ever found, nowhere."

"How many altogether?" asked Katie.

"Eleven exactly. Eleven, same as it said on the news, which was why I thought you ought to know."

"So what you're suggesting is, the English could have murdered those girls."

"The dates tally, don't they? And there was motive enough."

"You could be right, although it isn't going to be easy to prove anything. I can't see the British Army giving me much assistance, can you?"

"Somebody must know what happened," put in Eugene. "If those girls were taken by official order, that order must be somewhere on file, even after all these years. And even if they were taken unofficially, don't tell me that nobody ever spoke about it or wrote about it."

"Long shot," said Liam. "*Very* long shot. But at least it gives us a better idea of when the women were actually killed."

Katie thought about mentioning the rag dolls, in case they, too, rang a bell; but then she decided against it. The dolls were the only way she had of authenticating any evidence she was given.

"I don't suppose your great-uncle kept a diary of his experiences," she said.

The old man gave another sniff. "Couldn't write. My father

was the very first man in our family who was educated, God bless his memory. Very proud of it he was, too. And that's why he made sure that I was given the gift of language."

"I know who you are now," said Katie. "Jack Devitt. *The Blood of My Fathers*."

The old man smiled, and raised his glass to her. "You're a very fine young lady. 'Tis a fierce pity you're a cop."

They left Eugene Ó Béara and Jack Devitt to their drinks, and elbowed their way out of The Crow Bar into the gray, bright street outside. Steam was rising from the chimneys of Murphy's Brewery and there was a pungent smell of malt and hops in the air, like the fumes from a crematorium.

"What do you think?" asked Liam, as they crossed over to Katie's Mondeo. "Accurate vernacular history or load of old Fenian codswallop?"

"I don't know. But I want you to initiate a search for anything that will tell us more about those eleven disappearances. Have Patrick go through the old police records and the newspaper morgues. Let's see if we can find out what the women's names were, and if any of them still have family that we can trace. If Devitt is correct, we should be able to confirm their identity through DNA tests."

"Okay, boss."

"I also want the deeds and titles of Meagher's Farm, going back as far as you can. I'd like to know who owned that property, back in 1915."

"I'll bet you money it was an Englishman."

Eleven

After she had dropped Liam in the city center, Katie drove to Monkstown to see her father. Monkstown stood on the western bank of Cork Harbor, and if she looked across the half-mile stretch of water to Cobh, she could see the dark elm trees that surrounded her own house on the eastern side. It was drizzling, and the ferry that plied between Monkstown and Cobh was barely visible in the mist.

Her father owned a tall pale-green Victorian house that was perched on a hill with a fine harbor view. He kept a pair of binoculars in the bedroom so that he could watch the ocean liners and the cruise ships coming in and out. Since Katie's mother had died, though, two years ago last July, the house had seemed damper and colder every time she visited it, and it seemed to Katie that her mother's ghost had left it for ever.

Paul had gone along the coast to Youghal "to sort out a bit of business," so Katie had called her father and offered to cook him a lamb stew, which had always been one of his favorites, and one of her mother's specialties. Katie had always loved cooking, especially Irish traditional cooking, and if she hadn't joined the Garda she would have taken a cookery course at Ballymaloe House and opened her own restaurant. But none of her six brothers had wanted to be gardaí, and she alone had seen how deep her father's disappointment was. When she had told him that she was going to carry on the McCarthy family tradition, and sign up for Templemore, his eyes had promptly filled up with tears.

She parked her car in the roadway by the gate, and climbed the steep steps to the front door. The drizzle was coming in soft and heavy now, and the front garden was dripping, with shriveled wisteria and long-dead dahlias. There was grass growing through the shingle path. When her mother was alive, the garden had always been immaculate.

Her father took a long time to answer the door, and when he did it seemed for a moment that he didn't recognize her. He was a small man – bent-backed now, and painfully thin, with wriggling veins on his forehead and his hands. He wore a baggy beige cardigan and worn-out corduroy slippers.

"Well, you came," he said, as if he were surprised.

"I said I was going to come, didn't I?"

"You did. But sometimes you give me the feeling that you're going to come and then you don't."

"Dad, I didn't just give you the feeling this time. I called you."

"So what are you doing on the doorstep?"

"I'm getting rain down the back of my neck and I'm waiting for you to invite me in."

"You don't need an invitation, Katie. This is your house, too."

She stepped into the large, gloomy hallway. The smell of damp was even worse than the last time she had visited, in September. There were two old chaise-longues on either side of the hallway, and a slow, lugubrious long-case clock. A wide, curving staircase led up to the upper floors. There were no flowers anywhere.

She kissed him. His cheek was patchy and prickly, as if he hadn't been shaving properly. "How are you keeping?" she asked him. "Are you eating properly?"

70

"Oh, you know me and my incomparable omelets."

"Dad," she said. She didn't have to say any more. He was standing in the living-room doorway, half-silhouetted by the misty-gray light, sad, tired, still grieving. Nothing could bring her mother back, not even the lamb cutlets and the Kerr's Pink potatoes she was carrying in her Tesco bag.

She took her raincoat off and left her shopping in the hall. Her father went into the living-room and poured out two glasses of sherry. "*Sláinte*," he said, when she appeared. "You're the best daughter a man could ever ask for."

"*Sláinte*."

They sat down side by side on the green velvet Victorian sofa. Over the fireplace hung a large dark oil-painting of people walking through a wood. On either side of the room there were small tables with assorted knick-knacks on them, glass paperweights and Meissen statuettes and a strange bronze figure of a man with a flute and a sack slung over his back. When she was young, Katie had always thought that he was the Pied Piper, whistling children away to the magical land beyond the mountain.

"I saw you on the news," said her father. His eyes had always been green, like hers, but now they were no particular color at all. Does everything fade, when you grow older, even your eyes?

"Those skeletons up at Knocknadeenly," she nodded. "Yes."

"You're not taking your investigation any further, are you? Even if those women *were* murdered, there's not much chance of the perpetrator still being alive today, is there? Or fit to stand trial, even if he is."

"Well, I'll be talking to Dermot O'Driscoll tomorrow morning. He'll probably close it down."

"But?"

"I didn't say 'but'."

"I know you didn't say it but don't forget that I was a detective, too. Maybe I never made the exalted rank of detective superintendent, but I passed out from Templemore with top marks, just like you. And I can always tell when somebody has a 'but' on the tip of their tongue."

"All right. I do have a 'but'. Those eleven women were ritually murdered for some particular purpose and I really want to know what that purpose was. I really, *badly* want to know. If I don't find out – I don't know, I'll feel that I've let them all down – that they died and nobody ever cared."

Her father finished his sherry and put down his glass. "People kill other people for all kinds of unfathomable reasons. I once arrested a farmer in Watergrasshill for cutting a fellow's head off with a scythe. *Whack*! One blow, just like that. He said that the fellow was trying to put the evil eye on him."

"We're talking about eleven women here, dad."

"Well, I don't know. You have to remember that Ireland in 1915 wasn't anything like the Ireland that you know now. Times were very difficult. There was terrible poverty, there was oppression. There was superstition and there was very little education. Who knows why somebody killed eleven women."

"I wish I did."

Her father shook his head. "If I were you, I'd leave this investigation to the archivists and the archeologists."

"There was something else, dad. Something I didn't release to the media. You have to promise me that you'll keep it a secret."

"Oh, yes. I'll ring the *Echo* right away."

"Every thighbone that we dug up had a hole drilled through it, at the thick end, where it connects with the pelvis. And every hole had a string knotted through it, and a little rag dolly on the end."

"A rag dolly? Now that *is* unusual. I never heard of anything like that before. What are they like, these dollies?"

"They're made out of torn strips of old linen, all about four or five inches tall, and pierced through with hooks and screws and rusty nails. More like an African fetish than anything you'd ever see in Ireland."

Her father frowned, and shook his head. "I never came across anything like that before. There used to be all kinds of rituals in Ireland, especially where the roads were bad, and among the Travelers. But if you ask me the only rituals now are television, and the National Lotto. You're probably talking about something that died out years ago, and nobody remembers. My advice to you is leave this case alone. Hand it over to somebody who likes picking through historical stuff. Some retired inspector, I can give you a couple of names. It won't do your career any good if you start looking as if you're obsessed with some peculiar eighty-year-old mystery, believe me."

"I'd better start cooking," said Katie. She got up and went into the large, old-fashioned kitchen with its pine cupboards and its green-and-cream tiles, and her father followed her, and sat on a wooden chair by the window.

"How's things at home?" he asked her.

"You mean me and Paul?" She washed the lamb cutlets and dried them on kitchen-paper. "I'm not sure that I know. We don't seem to be very close these days. Sometimes I think we don't even speak the same language."

Her father looked at her narrowly as she started to chop onions on the thick pine chopping-board. "You're hurting," he said.

"Hurting?"

"You can't fool me, Katie. You were always the quietest of the seven of you, but I could always tell when there was something troubling you."

73

"I'm not hurting, dad. I just wish I knew exactly where I stood."

"You haven't maybe thought about another child?"

"No, dad. I haven't. I can't replace Seamus. Besides, even if I did have another child... well, to be quite frank, I'm not at all sure that I'd want Paul to be his father."

Katie's father pulled a face. "I don't know what to tell you, love. It's always seemed to me that you would make the very best of mothers."

"How can you say that I'm the best of mothers when I practically murdered my own son? I kissed him on the lips before I put him down to sleep. The doctor said that you can kill your child by kissing it on the lips."

Her father stood up, without a word, and put his arms around her, and squeezed her very tight. "Katie," he said. "Katie."

He kept hold of her until the onions started to burn.

Twelve

Fiona was suddenly woken up by the most shattering pain that she had ever felt in her life. She felt as if her right thigh had been forced through the grating of a white-hot furnace. She opened her mouth and tried to scream, but the pain was so horrifying that she couldn't even draw breath, and she could utter only a choked-up, gargling sound.

Oh God, she couldn't bear it, she just couldn't bear it. She tried to move her leg but it wouldn't respond. She wrenched at the cords that fastened her wrists to the bedframe, and thrashed her head from side to side, but she couldn't get free, and nothing helped to lessen the blazing agony that engulfed her hip.

Again she tried to scream, and this time she managed a shrill, distorted whoop, and then another.

The bedroom door opened with a sharp click. He stood in the doorway for a moment, smiling at her, and then he walked up to the side of the bed.

"I told you that I was going to hurt you. Do you believe me now?"

She stared up at him, her chest heaving. She opened and closed her mouth but she was speechless with pain.

"It's amazing, isn't it, how much physical trauma we human beings can endure? You'd think that our brain would shut down once the pain reached a certain level, to prevent us from suffering any more. But it doesn't, does it – as you can testify.

Our minds allow us to experience almost unimaginable agony.

He paused, and licked his lips, as if he could actually taste what she was feeling. "My father died of stomach cancer, you know, and he said that sometimes it hurt so much that the pain was almost beautiful. He said it was like a huge scarlet flower, opening up inside his very soul, one luxuriant petal after another."

Fiona swallowed, and swallowed again. "Please," she panted.

"Please what? Please let you go? Please give you some more aspirin? Please kill you?"

"*Please.*"

"I'm sorry, I can't do anything for you. My hands are tied, so to speak, just as much as yours. I have to perform the ritual according to tradition. If I don't, God alone knows what could happen. It's all very well *summoning* something, you see, but you have to make sure that you can control it, once it appears."

Fiona kept on staring at him, as if she could will him into releasing her, or at least give her something to relieve the pain. But all he did was reach out and lift one sweat-damp lock of hair away from her forehead, and smile.

"You've been wonderful," he said. "It's a good thing you're so physically fit. Physically fit, and beautiful, too. I couldn't have asked for anybody better."

He walked around to the other side of the bed, and peered closely down at her right leg. "Have you looked at it yet? It's amazing. Just like an anatomy lesson."

"What?" she said, in a blurry voice. She felt that she was going to lapse back into unconsciousness at any moment. The pain was now so overwhelming that she couldn't believe that she was the one who was feeling it. There must be another Fiona, who was suffering so much.

"Here," he said. He leaned over her and lifted her head so

76

that she could look down and see her leg. Through all of the pain, she could smell his underarm deodorant, like lavender. "There – what do you think? It's extraordinary, isn't it?"

At first she couldn't understand what she was seeing. Her left leg was normal, suntanned and muscular from jogging and swimming. But where her right leg was supposed to be, there was nothing but a long white thighbone, and a bare kneecap, and then two slender shinbones, and an anklebone, and a skeletal foot. All of these bones were scraped completely clean of flesh, except a few red shreds and thin white sinews which had been left to keep them loosely connected together. The newspapers underneath the bed were thickly splattered with blood.

Fiona stared up at him in panic. "What have you done to me?" she panted. "*What have you done?*"

"I've started to prepare you for the feeding," he told her, easing her head back down onto the bedsprings.

"*What have you done to me, you bastard?*"

"Sssh, quiet," he said, lifting his hand. "You're going to need all of your strength for this ordeal, believe me."

"What, you're not going to – "

"It takes time, and care, and everything has to be performed exactly according to ritual."

"Tell me what you're going to do. *Tell me!*"

"I'm going to prepare you as an offering to the greatest occult power that ever existed – ever."

"You'll never get away with this. My father will find you and when he does I swear to God he'll kill you with his bare hands."

He laughed. "Your father will never know who did this to you, ever. Even on his deathbed he will still be wondering who it was, and why he ever let you come to Ireland on your own. His torture will be far worse than yours."

"Oh God," gasped Fiona. She was suddenly overwhelmed

by another wave of pain, and went into shock. Her head fell back onto the bedsprings, and her face turned as white as wax. He stood watching her for a while, quite impassive, and then he went out to the living-room and pulled the mustard-colored throw off the couch. He came back and draped it over her to keep her warm.

After all, he couldn't have her dying.

Thirteen

Chief Superintendent O'Driscoll looked up from his desk and said, "Ah, Katie." He picked up a green cardboard folder and handed it to her. "I'd like you to take over the Flynn investigation. Sergeant Ahern has been going around in ever-decreasing circles and I'm afraid that he's going to disappear up his own rear end, which is probably what happened to Charlie Flynn."

Charlie Flynn was a well-known Cork businessman who had gone missing in the first week of October. His car had been found by the side of the road near Midleton, about ten miles east of the city, but there had been no sign at all of Charlie Flynn – not a footprint, not a bloodstain, nothing. He was the Lord Mayor's brother-in-law, and so Chief Superintendent O'Driscoll was under persistent pressure from City Hall to find out what had happened to him.

"What about our eleven skeletons?" asked Katie, opening the folder and flicking through the black-and-white photographs at the front. An empty black Mercedes, with its door wide open, from several different angles.

"The Meagher's Farm case? We're going to have to close it down, of course – as an active file, anyway. I was thinking of passing the information over to Professor Gerard O'Brien at the university... he's your man when it comes to folklore."

"But what happened at Meagher's Farm, that wasn't just folklore, sir. Eleven women were murdered."

"Of course they were. But what's the point in pursuing their killer when he's almost certainly deceased? Don't you worry, Katie – even if the murderer never had to answer to an earthly court, he'll have had to stand before God. There's nothing more that you and I can do about it."

"I'd just like two or three more days on it, sir. The way those women were killed – it was so unusual that I think we need to find out what happened."

Dermot O'Driscoll shook his head, so that his jowls wobbled. "Sorry, Katie, it's out of the question. Apart from the Flynn case, I want you to go over to the South Infirmary and have another chat with Mary Leahy. Detective Garda Dockery went to see her last night and he thinks that she may be ready to tell us who shot her Kenny."

Katie pursed her lips but she knew that there was little point in arguing. "All right," she said. "But let me take the Meagher folder over to Professor O'Brien myself. I'd like to talk to him about it."

"You can, of course. But do try to make some progress with this Flynn investigation. It's making us look like a bunch of culchies."

Dermot O'Driscoll had once worked for the Criminal Assets Bureau in Dublin, and he was especially sensitive to any gibes that he was now in charge of a rural police force. His old colleagues at Phoenix Park had even sent him a model of a tractor with a blue light on it.

On the way out, Katie met Sergeant O'Rourke. "I think I have something for you, superintendent. Photocopies of the *Cork Examiner* from the summer of 1915 to the spring of 1916."

"Come through to my office," said Katie. She spread the photocopies out on her desk, and put on her small steel-rimmed reading glasses. Jimmy had circled a dozen stories in red marker. Mysterious Disappearance of Rathcormac Woman. No Trace of Whitechurch Girl After Three Weeks. Mrs Mary O'Donovan Missing for Nine Days.

There was a leader column, too, in which the newspaper's editor spoke of "the local community's grave concern at the spiriting-away of seven young women, all of whom were of spotless reputation and character. We hesitate to point a finger without evidence of any kind, not even a single body having been discovered, but we would remind our readers of the words of Bacon, who wrote that 'a man who studieth revenge keeps his own wounds green'."

"What do you think he's trying to suggest here?" asked Katie. "That the women were taken as an act of retaliation?"

"It seems like it, I'd say. But he doesn't name any names."

"Well, that's what Jack Devitt was telling us, too. Maybe this newspaper editor had a good idea of who was abducting these women, but couldn't say it openly, for fear of a libel action, or worse."

"I don't see how we can ever find out who it was. Not after eighty years."

"Well, maybe Professor O'Brien can come up with something. The chief superintendent's closed the case and we're passing it over to him."

"Oh. You won't want to be talking to Tómas Ó Conaill, then?"

"You've *found* Ó Conaill? Where?"

"I had a tip-off late last night that he and his family have a Winnebago and three mobile homes parked on a derelict farm about a mile outside of Tower, on the Blarney road."

"Well, no... I don't suppose I need to talk to him now. But do me a favor, Jimmy, and keep a sharp eye on him, will you?"

"Oh, yes. I've told the fellows up at Blarney Garda station, too, so that they know where to look for absconding road-drills and runaway tarmac spreaders, and any other property that goes for a walk."

It was so sunny that morning that Professor O'Brien suggested they take a walk through Lee Fields, alongside the river. On the western side of the city the waters of the Lee were much clearer, and they slid over a wide, glassy weir. On the opposite bank, on a high hill, stood the gray Victorian spires of of Our Lady's Hospital, once a lunatic asylum, the building with the longest frontage in Europe.

Children scampered and screamed around the gardens, and a snappy breeze was blowing through the willow trees, so that they glittered in the sunshine. Katie tied a green silk scarf around her head to keep her ears warm.

"Does me good to get out," said Professor O'Brien. "I seem to spend my life in front of a computer screen these days." He was quite young, only about 34 or 35, although he was balding on top and he had combed his hair over to try and hide it. He was small, too, with little pink hands that peeked out from the cuffs of his brown corduroy overcoat like pigs' trotters – what the Cork people call *crubeens*.

Katie said, "Gerard – I want you to think of this as an active murder investigation, rather than just an academic exercise. It may be eighty years since these women were killed, but they were real women and they were murdered for some very specific reason."

"Do you really think that it was anything to do with the British Army, taking their revenge?"

"It's a possibility. After all, the Crown Forces burned most of the city of Cork down to the ground, out of revenge. But it's these little rag dollies that don't make any sense."

"Well, I can't say offhand that I've ever come across anything like them," said Professor O'Brien. "They don't seem to relate to any particular culture or any particular period. Before we were converted to Christianity, we used to have dozens of different gods, and all kinds of extraordinary ceremonies to appease them. But I've never found any mention of human sacrifice, or dismemberment, and I've never seen these particular dolls before.

He held up the plastic evidence bag and peered at the doll more closely, wrinkling up his nose in concentration. "I suppose you could say that there's a passing resemblance to the little cotton figures that some people used to hang on their doorposts when one of their children was sick. They did that so that the Death Queen Badhbh would take away the little figure instead of the person lying inside. But those effigies were invariably sewn out of a remnant of the sick child's clothing, and filled with clippings from its hair and fingernails, so that when Queen Badhbh came sniffing for them in the darkness, she would mistakenly think it was them."

"No hooks or nails or screws?"

Dr O'Brien shook his head. "That does sound more like a voodoo ritual, doesn't it? There were some witches in Denmark, in the seventeenth century, who used to bang magic nails into copies of their victims' heads, to give them splitting headaches, and there's some evidence that Danish sailors could have brought that practice to Cork."

Katie stopped and looked across the river. Three swans were swimming against the current, almost invisible in the diamond-dazzle from the sun. Three white S's.

"I'd appreciate it if you kept me closely in touch with what you're doing" she said. "If you need any help of any kind...

maybe a car to take you out to visit Meagher's Farm, anything at all, just let me know."

"Of course. This is one of the most interesting things I've been asked to do for a long time. Exciting, even."

"Well, then," said Katie, and held out her hand.

The breeze lifted a long strand of Dr Kelly's hair high from the top of his head. "There's one thing," he said.

"Yes?"

"When I've had the chance to go through the file and check up a few preliminary facts... do you think that you and I could talk about this investigation over dinner?"

"Over *dinner*?"

He gave her a sly, schoolboyish grin. "Nothing like mixing business with a little pleasure. Have you ever been to that French restaurant in Phoenix Street?"

She squeezed his little *crubeen* hand. "Let's just see how it goes, shall we?"

"Of course."

She walked back to the parking-lot and he stood by the river and watched her go. She turned back once and he gave her a stiff-armed wave, like a semaphore signal. She didn't know why, but when she unlocked her car she felt quite shocked. Not so much at Gerard O'Brien for asking her out, but at herself, for not having conclusively said no.

"Holy Mother of God," she said to herself, in her rear-view mirror. "You're not *flattered*, are you?"

Fourteen

Fiona was sleeping fitfully when the door banged open and he switched on the overhead light.

She didn't say a word as he approached the bed and peered into her face. She was still in too much pain, even though she had managed during the day to get used to it, the way that anybody can get used to anything, like the roar of traffic, or loud rock music, or the constant rattling of an air-conditioner.

"Are you ready for the next adventure?"

"I don't care what you do. Just do it and get it over with."

"You don't mean that."

"I don't have any choice, do I? You're going to do it anyhow."

"Well, you're right about that."

He opened his case of surgical instruments. "It's been a great day today, hasn't it? I went to Blarney and the sun was shining and it was so warm."

"I didn't notice."

"These are your last few days, Fiona. You ought to make the most of them."

She began to cry, although she didn't feel sorry for herself any more. She had already accepted that she had been abducted entirely by chance, and that if *she* wasn't enduring this agony, it would have been another girl. And who could wish this pain on anybody else? Extreme suffering can bring on a very clear, self-sacrificial state of mind.

He tied a thin nylon cord around the top of her left thigh, and pulled it viciously tight, grunting with the effort.

"Not the other leg," she said, dully.

He nodded. "I'm sorry. It's the way it has to be. Right leg, left leg."

"But why? Why are you doing it? Can't you just kill me?"

"I could, yes. Scalpel, carotid artery, that'd be quick. But a ritual is a ritual. If I don't observe all the niceties, then it wouldn't work, would it, and you wouldn't want to go through all of this for nothing, would you? To die in agony, that's bad enough. But to die in agony for no purpose whatsoever... well, what can I say?"

"What time is it?" she asked him.

"Two-thirty in the morning."

"I need a drink of water."

"That's all right. I'll get you one."

He went out to the kitchen and came back with a thick blue mug filled with warm, peaty-tasting water. She drank all of it, dribbling it down her chin.

"Do you hate me?" she said.

It was incredible, but he actually blushed. "Of course I don't hate you. I think you're very, very special."

"But look what you've done to me."

"I know. I know that. And that's what makes you so special. That's what they don't tell you in the history books, do they, that every human sacrifice was a person, with a mother and a father and ideas of her own? But that's what makes every human sacrifice so valuable. That's why it means so much. You can sacrifice a goat, but what does a goat know? To sacrifice a human life... especially like this... that's what brings the demons out of hiding. That's what really causes a rustle in hell.

He opened his instrument case and selected one of his scalpels. "You know, Fiona Kelly, this is the best time of all for stirring up demons. The third hour of the day, when the angels of death come fluttering down through the darkness to squeeze the struggling hearts of the elderly, and to press their hands over the faces of sleeping babies."

Fiona tried not to listen to him; or even to focus her eyes on what he was doing. She tried instead to think of her mother, sitting at the end of the verandah in her white-painted rocker, sewing and smiling; and she tried to visualize her bedroom, with its pink gingham bedspread, and the crimson bougainvillea that fluttered on either side of the window.

She tried to think of a song that her mother had taught her when she was little. She had never really understood what it meant, but now she sang it over and over, silently, inside her mind, like a mantra. Anything to keep her mind off the pain.

"One girl asked for rosemary
One girl asked for thyme
Another girl asked for locks and keys
And clocks that never chimed

"But all I want is a door that leads
To the road that leads to the sea
And to know when I turn that my shadow
Will still be following me."

She had often asked her mother what it meant, and who had taught it to her, but her mother would never say. When she was older she had looked it up in books of children's poetry and nursery rhymes, but she had never found out. It had always disturbed her, for some reason, especially the line about wanting to know if her shadow was following her. Supposing it wasn't? What then?

She was repeating the rhyme for the third time when he cut into her thigh. He cut deep, right through the skin and the fat and the femoral muscles, until the tip of his scalpel touched her bone. Blood welled out of the wound and pattered onto the newspapers underneath the bed.

The scalpel was so sharp that she hardly felt it. She had once cut her tongue on an envelope that she was licking, and she hadn't realized until blood came pouring down her chin. This incision hurt even less than that, but all the same she let out a long wail of despair.

"Don't cry," he told her. "This is only just the beginning. You wait until tomorrow. Then you'll know what pain is. Then you'll not only feel it, you'll *understand* it."

He sliced through all of the quadriceps, all the way around, right the way through to the femur. All the time he was breathing steadily through his nose, the way that dentists do. When he had cut around her upper thigh, he moved down and made another cut about an inch above her knee. His hands were smothered in blood now, and there were bloody fingerprints all over her leg. She let her head fall back, so that she wouldn't have to look, but then she raised it again, her chin juddering with pain and effort. She found a terrible fascination in watching her own mutilation. He had been right: it was like a journey through an undiscovered country, a country where anything was possible, where no pain was too great and no horror was too excessive.

Having cut one circle around the top of her leg and another circle above her knee, he then took another scalpel from his instrument-case and incised a vertical line down the front of her thigh to join the two together. This time, she felt the point sliding all the way down her bone, and she screamed so long and so loud that he stopped for a moment and watched her with a patient frown until she had finished.

"Are you all right?" he asked her. "This won't take very long, I promise."

"I can't – you can't – I can't bear it, I can't bear it."

"I can stop if you like. Only for a while, though. The bones have to be stripped before the light of day."

"Please, please. I can't bear it any more, please."

"I'm sorry… why don't you try to think of something else?"

"*I can't take any more! I can't take any more!*"

She threw her head back on the bedsprings and hit it again and again, screaming and weeping, as if she wanted to knock herself unconscious. He stood with his scalpel in his hand, the ruby-colored blood congealing on the blade, and frowned at her as if she were nothing more than a toddler who was throwing a tantrum.

At last she stopped screaming and banging her head, and lay back with her eyes rolling wildly from side to side, breathing in high, harsh yelps.

He bent over her again, and continued to cut the rectus femoris muscle all the way down to the knee. Then he laid down his scalpel, and with the thumbs of both hands, spread the incision wide apart, until the bone was visible. The flesh glistened in the bright light of the Anglepoise lamp, as scarlet as freshly-butchered beef.

"There," he said, "the very substance of you, coming to light."

He picked up a small boning-knife, and carefully began to cut the flesh away from the femur. Fiona lay still now, her face gray, her hands gripping the bedhead, her whole body totally rigid and glistening with sweat. Apart from the scrunging of the bedsprings, all she could hear was the sound of wet flesh, like somebody quietly and persistently licking their lips.

She passed beyond agony into a place where she could see nothing but blinding whiteness and feel nothing but utter cold. The North Pole of pain. And still he worried the flesh away from the bone, scraping it meticulously clean.

After quarter of an hour he gave a last scrape, and eased away the muscle of her entire upper leg, in one bloody piece, like a plumber easing the pink foam lagging off a hot-water pipe. He wiped his forehead with the back of his shirtsleeve, and then he carried the flesh into the kitchen and flopped it into the sink. He rinsed his hands and dried them on a ragged tea-towel, and then he leaned his head under the faucet and took a long, noisy drink.

When he returned to the bedroom, Fiona was unconscious. Better that way, he thought to himself. The next part was taking the flesh off the knee, and that was especially agonizing.

He held out both hands, palm upward, and then he turned them over. Not a tremble. He picked up the boning-knife again, and went to work.

Fifteen

Katie was woken up by the sound of the front door slamming and somebody falling heavily against the coatstand in the hall. Then she heard Sergeant barking, and a voice saying, "Shush, shush, you maniac."

"Paul?" she called, sitting up in bed.

"Sawrigh," Paul blurted back. "Everything sawrigh."

She swung her legs out of bed and found her bed-jacket on the back of the chair. "Paul, what the hell's going on down there? Are you drunk?"

"Don't come down," he told her, in a clogged-up voice. "I'll stay down here for tonight. Just don't come down."

She switched on the landing light and went down the stairs. Sergeant was running in and out of the living-room door, panting excitedly. She went into the living-room and switched on the chandeliers. Paul was lying face-down on the sofa, one arm dangling on the floor. His navy-blue coat was split all the way up the back, revealing the torn white lining. One of his loafers was missing and his curly hair was matted with blood.

"Holy Mother of God," said Katie, and knelt down beside him.

He opened one eye and blinked at her. There was a deep semi-circular cut around his eyebrow that was already crusted with dried blood, and his cheekbones were crimson.

"What happened to you, Paul? Let me look at you."

91

"Sawrigh. Everything's grand."

"Paul, for Christ's sake look at the state of you! What's happened?"

He lifted his head and it was only then that she could see how badly he was hurt. Both nostrils were clotted with blood and it looked as if his nose had been broken. His lips were swollen and split, and he was obviously missing some teeth. A long string of bloody saliva connected his mouth to the cushion.

"Who did this to you, Paul? Was it Dave MacSweeny?"

"It doesn't matter, pet. I just need some shleep, that's all. Some *shleep*."

"Paul, I want to know who attacked you."

"Forget it. You'll only make a bother. The only female detective superintendent in Ireland... she can't have anyone beating up her husband, now can she?"

"Sit up, Paul. Let me take a good look at you. You'll be after needing a doctor. Look at that cut. That's going to take stitches."

"Will you stop – *fussing*, for Christ's sake. It's only a couple of knocks. My father used to beat me up much worse than this when I was a kid."

Katie stood up. Paul blinked up at her and his face was so pummeled and swollen that it looked twice its normal size. "Paul... I'm not joking about this. Whoever attacked you, I'm going to have them arrested, and charged."

Paul managed to struggle himself into a sitting position. His left eye was completely bloodshot, like a vampire's. "Ouch, shit," he said, pressing his hand against his side. "Broken my fucking ribs."

"Paul – "

"Katie... forget it. I made a bags of things, that's all. What you might call an error of judgement. If you start making a bother... it's going to be ten times worse. They'll kill me, the

92

next time, I promise you. In fact, they're probably going to kill me anyway."

Katie gently touched his forehead, where his hair was sticky with blood. "God, Paul, you're such a fool sometimes. Don't you realize how much I love you? Weren't we happy once? Wasn't everything perfect?"

He gave her a wry, puffy smile. "That was then, Katie. This is now."

"You can't let them get away with this, Paul. I need to know who did it. It's my duty to uphold the law."

"I'm not telling you, Katie. I can't. They'll kill me. That's if *you* don't kill me first."

She sat back, and lifted her hand away from his knee. "Why should *I* want to kill you?"

"Well, I'm not much of a husband to you, am I?"

Katie said, "It's about that girl, isn't it? That one at the Sarsfield Hotel?"

"God Almighty. Who'd marry a detective?"

"Tell me, Paul. It's about that girl, isn't it?"

"It's partly. But that's not all of it."

"Paul, I'm calling an ambulance."

He snatched at her sleeve. "Leave it, Katie. The last thing they said to me was, 'We bet your old lady's going to come looking for us now.' And what do you think I'd look like, if you did? A man needs his – manhood."

Katie was silent for a long time. She needed time to think, time to get her balance back. Then she said, "How about a drink? You should really go to hospital, but if you won't – "

"It's not so bad as it looks. They punched me around a bit, and kicked me all right. But you don't get anywhere at all unless you take chances, do you?"

Katie went across to the sideboard and poured him a large

93

whiskey. Sergeant followed her protectively, and stood beside her when she sat down, panting. "So what does this girl at the Sarsfield Hotel have to do with business?"

Paul shook his head. "I made a mistake, Katie, that's all."

"Yes, but who was she? And what did you do?"

"I suppose I was looking for something different. Escape, you might call it. The truth is that I still can't look at you without thinking about poor little Seamus."

"You don't think that *I* don't blame myself for what happened to Seamus, every minute of every hour of every day?"

"I don't *blame* you, pet. God wanted Seamus back in Heaven and that was all there was to it. But – I don't know. I suppose I thought you were magic, and that you'd never let us come to any harm. When Seamus was taken, I realized then that you weren't magic after all."

"Paul, I was Seamus' mother but I'm not yours."

He dabbed his nose with his fingertips. "Oh, it was my fault, too. If my business hadn't gone to the wall you wouldn't have had to work."

"What are you saying? That Seamus died because I went to work?"

"Well, I don't know. Maybe you would have paid him more mind."

"Paul – I'm a career Garda officer. I would have carried on with my job whether we had a baby or not. And for you to suggest that he died because I neglected him – Holy Mother of God, what's wrong with you?"

Paul didn't say anything, but lowered his head and sniffed.

"Tell me about this girl," Katie insisted. The central heating didn't come on for another three hours and she was trembling with tiredness and cold and exasperation.

"There's nothing to tell. We went to the Sarsfield and had

a few drinks and it's the old, old story, isn't it?"

"Who is she?"

"That's the whole trouble. She's Dave MacSweeny's girlfriend."

"Geraldine Daley? That tart?"

"I'm sorry, Katie. Losing your only son… that's not exactly an aphrodisiac, is it?"

She slapped him, hard, across the cheek. She didn't mean to, but she had done it before she could think. He shouted out, "*Jesus*!" and lifted one hand to protect himself. "Jesus, Katie. That fucking *hurt*."

"You don't think you deserved it?"

"For what? For trying to get a few minutes' pleasure out of my life, instead of having to tiptoe on – *eggshells* round you and your everlasting grief? You don't have the monopoly on sorrow, Katie, believe me… and you don't have any right to take your misery out on everybody around you. I'm glad I'm not one of your suspects. It's bad enough being your husband."

Katie didn't know what to say. Perhaps Paul was right, and she was dragging her cross around with her wherever she went. Perhaps, on the other hand, he could have put his arms around now and again, in the darkness of the night, and showed her that they could find a way to be happy again.

"Don't you worry," said Paul. "I'll sleep on the couch. At least Sergeant will show me some sympathy."

A long, long pause. Paul picked a bloody scab out of his nostril and stared at it.

"Has it been going on long?" Katie asked him.

"What?"

"You and Geraldine Daley. Was it just the one night, or have you been making a fool of me for longer than that?"

"What does it matter?"

"It matters because the nature of my job requires me to have a private life that's free of any scandal whatsoever. And most of all it matters because we're married, for better or for worse."

"Well, if it's any consolation at all, it was, yes, just the one night. Geraldine was sick to the back teeth with Dave because he never takes her anywhere and she's never allowed to look at other men. He hits her about, too. I guess she wanted to get her own back on him."

"And what about you? Did you want to get your own back on me? What? For killing Seamus?"

Paul flapped his hand dismissively. Katie was about to say something else, something really hurtful, but then she decided against it. Without a word, she turned around and left Paul sitting on the couch, with Sergeant licking his bloody knuckles.

Sixteen

The next morning it was raining again, that fine misty rain that can soak right through your coat before you know it. She walked into her office to find Professor O'Brien waiting for her with a bunch of yellow chrysanthemums, a folded raincoat and a bright, enthusiastic grin.

"Gerard, what a surprise."

He stood up and held out the flowers as if they were a conjuring-trick "I hope you like yellow. It reminds me of sunshine. Just what we need on days like these."

"Thank you," she said. They looked past their best, and one of them was broken, but she took them anyway. "I'll – ah – put them in water."

"You don't mind me coming here to report to you personally? In person, I mean?"

She felt tired and fractured after last night, and the last thing she needed was a flirtatious conversation with Professor O'Brien, but all the same she managed a smile and sat down behind her desk. At the back of the Garda station the crows were still perched along the roof of the parking-lot. Sometimes one or two of them flew off and circled around, but they always came back, the way that blowflies will never leave a decomposing body alone.

"Would you like some coffee?" she asked Professor O'Brien.

"No, thanks all the same. Coffee gives me the jitters. I don't sleep very well as it is. I was up for most of the night, reading through your file on the Meagher's Farm case."

"Oh, yes?" said Katie, prying the plastic lid off her cappuccino. "Did you find out anything interesting?"

He produced a large manila envelope from underneath his folded raincoat, and took out a copy of an ordnance survey map. He spread it out on Katie's desk and smoothed it with the side of his hand. "The first step I always take when I look into any historical event is to look at a contemporary map, if I can. So many things can change over the years – the roads, the place-names, everything. This is the area north of Cork as it was in 1911. This is the road from Cork City to Ballyhooly, and this red outline is Meagher's Farm. You'll notice that there wasn't a farm there, in those days, but there was a small collection of three or four dwellings which was already known as Knocknadeenly. In Gaelic, that's Cnoc na Daoine Liath."

"The Hill of the Gray People?"

"That's right. But 'Beings', perhaps, more than 'people'. It was supposed to be a gateway between the fairy world and the real world – the place where Mor-Rioghain lived whenever she came to Ireland. I think if there was any place in County Cork where anyone would be likely to perform a ritual ceremony, it would be here."

"Excuse me, Gerard," asked Katie. "But who was Mor-Rioghain?"

"Mor-Rioghain? She was an evil sorceress – a malign fairy. She appears in dozens of different legends all over Europe and Scandinavia. In England she was called Morgan Le Fay and she was supposed to be King Arthur's wicked half-sister, who was always plotting to kill him. Here in Ireland she was a cousin of the Death Queen Badhbh, or perhaps another side of Badhbh's personality, and she was supposed to come out of her magic hill, her *sidhe,* in the shape of a wolf-bitch. If you fed her with the flesh of innocent women, she would grant you any wish you wanted."

"So you think these killings could have been part of what? Some folkloric ceremony?"

"Not a ceremony that I've ever come across before, as I told you. But – yes, I believe it's a distinct possibility."

"And that's what you've managed to find out?"

"Yes," he blinked, and sat down. "I mean that's quite an exciting step forward, isn't it?"

"It's a start, I suppose. Do you think there's any way of finding out if there were any pagan sects around Knocknadeenly at the time? Like, devil-worshippers, anything like that?"

"Anybody who wanted to summon up Mor-Rioghain wouldn't have been a devil-worshipper. They would have been ordinary folk looking for wealth, and fame, and power... all of the gifts that the fairies can give you."

"And that was worth murdering eleven women for?"

"I still don't know why that was done; or what the ritual of the little rag dollies was all about, but I promise you I will. We may not bring a murderer to book, but at least we'll find out why he did it. That should give you some satisfaction, shouldn't it?"

Katie frowned at him. "Satisfaction? I suppose so."

"Look," said Professor O'Brien, "perhaps we could discuss this over lunch."

"I'm sorry, not today. I have two other important cases I'm dealing with. Not to mention the disappearance of Charlie Flynn."

"They do a great open sandwich at Morrison's Island Hotel. Tuna, or Cajun chicken. I go there twice a week at least."

"Gerard, I'm sorry. I'm really too busy. But thank you for coming in; and for all of your information."

Professor O'Brien gave her a bashful smile and then he said, "I think you're a very striking-looking woman, superintendent. I hope you don't object to my saying that."

Katie smiled. "No, of course not. It's very flattering. But – "

She nearly said " – *I'm married, Gerard*," but she didn't, because that simply wasn't the reason that she was turning him down. Instead, she said, "I'm sorry. I've got far too much on my plate already."

Professor O'Brien had a noisy wrestling-match with his map. "I understand. But I'll keep on digging. You never know, you see – the Crown Forces may have murdered these women and then hung these dollies on their thighbones to make it look like a ritual sacrifice, even when it wasn't."

"That's another possibility, yes."

Professor O'Brien shook her hand, ducking his head forward as if he was going to try to give her a kiss on the cheek, but then thinking better of it.

"I was engaged once," he volunteered. "Mairie, her name was. She looked very similar to you. Or, rather, you look very similar to her."

"I'm sorry," said Katie, and immediately regretted it, because it sounded so patronizing.

"It was a bit of a surprise. One day she said she loved me and the next day she said she didn't. Women! I don't think I'll ever understand them."

Katie looked at him with his combed-over hair and his folded raincoat and his little hands like *crubeens,* and she thought to herself, why is it that we can never tell people the truth?

Only an hour later, Dr Reidy called her, and he sounded deeply grumpy.

"I sent your dollies in for analysis, and I'm not at all pleased that you've already closed this investigation without having the common courtesy to inform me."

"I'm sorry, Dr Reidy. I was under the impression that Chief Superintendent O'Driscoll was going to get in touch with you."

"O'Driscoll? That fathead! He wouldn't tell his proctologist if he sat on a jamjar. As it is we've spent serious time and budget for no purpose whatsoever."

"Did you find out anything interesting about the dolls?"

"Oh, yes, even though it doesn't matter two hoots now, does it? We've got a very talented young lady here at Phoenix Park who's an expert on fabrics. She dismembered a number of your little effigies and she says they're made out of torn strips of linen, some of which have lace edging. In other words, she thinks they were made out of a woman's petticoats, ripped into pieces. The lace, though, isn't Irish. It's a pattern she's never seen before."

"What about the screws and the hooks?"

"We've made a provisional identification. They were probably handmade in a workshop just off French's Quay in Cork in 1914 or thereabouts. They were in common use in Cork City; in fact, you could probably find quite a few of them now, in some of the older houses."

"So, what do you think, Dr Reidy?"

"I don't think anything, my dear, not unless I'm paid to think and not unless there's some specific purpose."

"I'd like to see your full report as soon as possible."

"My dear, those poor women have already waited eighty years. You don't think that a couple of days more is going to make any difference?"

"Well, I don't know. But I think it might."

Dr Reidy wheezed in and out, saying nothing for a while. Then he said, "You've got a feeling about this, haven't you, detective superintendent?"

"It depends what you mean by a feeling."

"You've got a feeling that this business is going to turn out very black."

"How do you know that?"

"I've been the State Pathologist for twenty-two years, my dear. I saw it in your eyes. I heard it in the way you spoke to me."

Katie didn't know what to say to him. But it was like listening to somebody recount a very old nightmare that you hadn't ever told to anyone.

"Thank you," she said. "I'll see if I can have some of the lace samples analyzed here."

Dr Reidy said, "I'm not a superstitious man, superintendent. I don't believe in signs and wonders. But my knees tell me with great reliability when the weather's going to be wet; and my scalp tingles when there's any kind of evil around; and there is."

That afternoon, Katie took one of the dollies out of its evidence bag, removed all the hooks and the screws, and carefully unfolded it. It had been fashioned out of a long strip of linen, roughly torn, with a lacy hem. She tucked it into an envelope and took it around to Eileen O'Mara, who ran a Victorian-style lace shop in what had once been the old Savoy Cinema, in Patrick Street. Katie opened the door to her little triangular shop, with all of its period nightgowns and its lace pillow-covers and its bowls of pot-pourri, and the bell jingled.

Eileen came out of the back room with an armful of embroidered bathrobes. She was only 24 but she had taken a course in Brussels on lacemaking and needlework and she was an expert on anything sewn or embroidered. She had wavy brown hair and fiery red cheeks and she always reminded Katie of a souvenir doll, too Irish to be true.

"Katie! Haven't seen you for months."

"Oh, well, I've been busy enough. How's business?"

"It's quiet now, but that's what you'd expect in the winter. I saw you on TV, all those old skeletons up at Knocknadeenly. That must have been desperate!"

"That's partly the reason I'm here."

"I didn't kill anybody, honest!"

"No," said Katie, and took the strip of linen out of her purse. "There was some fabric found up there, quite a few pieces of it, that looked like a woman's petticoat. It has a lace edging on it, if you look here, but it's not Irish, that's what they say in Dublin anyway. I was wondering if you knew where it might have come from. Bearing in mind, now, it's probably eighty years old."

Eileen picked up the fabric and held it up to the light. "I don't know. It's very old, I'd say. Not a pattern that I've ever seen before. You'll have to give me a little time on it. But I can tell you straight away that it's handmade and that your man in Dublin has got it right, it certainly isn't Irish."

"My woman in Dublin, actually."

"I might have guessed. But this lace isn't based on any machine-made patterns, like Alençon or Chantilly or Valenciennes. And it certainly bears no resemblance at all to anything I've ever seen in Ireland. My first guess is that it's Belgian, or German."

"Well, I don't know what that tells me," said Katie.

"All it tells you is that whoever it belonged to, she was probably quite wealthy. This is very fine work, and it would have cost a lot of money, even eighty years ago."

"I see." Katie took the lace back and held it up to the light. If it had been really expensive, then the likelihood that it had been taken from any of the women who had died up at Meagher's Farm was extremely remote. She didn't have a complete list of all the women who had gone missing in the North Cork area between the summer of 1915 and the spring of 1916, but those whose names had appeared in the *Examiner* had been farmers' wives and shopgirls and (in the case of Mrs Mary O'Donovan) a postmistress. Not the sort of women who would have been wearing petticoats of handmade Continental lace.

So whose was it? And where had it come from? And if it was such fine lace, why had it had been ripped up?

Katie left the Savoy Center and walked across Patrick Bridge, back to her car. Two crows were sitting precariously on rotten wooden posts in the middle of the river. She was beginning to feel that they were watching her, following her, like a witch's familiars.

Seventeen

John Meagher was standing outside the front door of his farmhouse when Katie drove into the courtyard. It was almost as if he were expecting her. The rain had stopped but the morning was still gray, and the clouds were almost as low as the tops of the elm-trees.

"Hi," he said, opening the car door for her. He was wearing a navy-blue waterproof jacket and tan corduroy pants. He looked more like a model from a men's casualwear catalog than a Cork farmer.

She climbed out. "I just came up to tell you that the case is officially closed and you can carry on with your building work."

"That's it, then? We never get to find out who did it?"

"Well, I hope we do. We're not pursuing it as an active investigation, but we haven't closed it completely. Everybody deserves justice, even if it's eighty years too late."

"Sure, I guess they do."

She looked around the courtyard. "If you do happen to come across anything else... maybe not bones, but anything that strikes you as out-of-the-ordinary..."

"Oh, sure. I won't hesitate. You gave me your number. Listen – I'm being very rude here – how about a cup of tea or a cup of coffee?"

Katie hesitated, but then she smiled and said, "All right. That'd be welcome." John Meagher had an air about him that really attracted her. It wasn't just his looks – even though she had always liked men with dark, curly hair and chocolate-brown eyes. It was his quiet, amused, self-contained manner, and his cultured West Coast accent. She felt that he would always be interesting, and protective, too.

He led her into the house. His mother was sitting at the kitchen table, sewing, with a cigarette dangling between her lips.

"You remember Detective Superintendent Maguire, don't you, ma?"

Mrs Meagher lifted her head and peered through her thick-lensed glasses. "Of course. It seems like time caught your man before you could."

"Yes, I'm afraid it did."

John said, "You should switch the light on, ma. How can you see what you're doing?"

"I can sew on buttons with my eyes closed."

"I can eat hamburgers with my eyes closed, but why would I want to?"

"Get away with you. Ever since you went to America, you've been talking Greek."

"What would you like?" John asked Katie. "Tea? Coffee?"

"Tea would be fine. No milk, thanks."

He switched on the electric kettle. His mother coughed and crushed out her cigarette and went to the larder for shortbread biscuits and fruitcake.

"I didn't realize you were such a celebrity," said John, pulling out a chair so that Katie could sit down.

"Oh, yes. I get wheeled out for TV interviews every time somebody wants to talk about the New Irish Woman."

"Couldn't have been easy, though, getting as far as you have."

"It wasn't. As far most gardaí are concerned, women officers are there to direct traffic, comfort grieving widows and go out for sandwiches – and if they're not too ugly, to have their bottoms pinched at every opportunity."

"Somehow I can't imagine *you* putting up with that."

"I didn't, and I don't. But I was lucky, too. At the time when I applied to become a detective, there was very strong pressure from the Commissioner's office to promote more women to the upper ranks. Not only that, I had a chief superintendent who happened to be a close friend of my father's. Then about two months after I graduated as a detective garda, I solved a double murder in Knockraha, two women drowned in a well, mother and daughter. All I did was overhear a drunken conversation in a pub, but I still got the credit for it."

"You're very modest."

"Well, I try to be efficient, John, as well as modest."

John laughed. "How's your tea? Are you sure it's not too strong?"

"It's fine. It's hot, that's all."

Mrs Meagher shuffled out of the kitchen, leaving them alone. They sat and smiled each other for a while, then John said, "What happens now?"

"About the skeletons, you mean? We've commissioned somebody from the university to see if he can find out how and why they were killed, but there's not much else we can do."

"It was a ritual killing though, wasn't it?"

"Ritualistic, yes."

"My grandfather always used to say that this farm was possessed."

"Possessed? Possessed by what?"

"He never really explained. But he always used to say that if you knew where to look for it, and you knew how to get it, and you were prepared to pay the price, you could have anything your heart desired."

"That's interesting. Professor O'Brien at the university said that this farm was called the Hill of the Gray People because a witch called Mor-Rioghain was supposed to have used it as a way through from the underworld. Mor-Rioghain would give you anything you wanted, so long as you fed her on the bodies of young women."

"That's a pretty gruesome story."

Katie sipped her tea. "I don't take it seriously, not for a single moment."

"Of course not. But, you never know... eighty years ago, *somebody* might have believed it."

"That's one of the possibilities that Professor O'Brien is going to be looking into."

John offered her a shortbread biscuit. "Go on, spoil yourself... they're all home-made. My mother still bakes enough for half the population of Ireland."

Katie accepted, and snapped the biscuit in half. "How about you? How are you coping with the farm?"

"Not as well as I thought I was going to. Everybody back in California said they envied me because I was really getting back to nature. But, I don't know. There's Californian nature, like orange groves and grapes and sunshine, and then there's Knocknadeenly nature. Which is mainly mud."

"You're managing all right, though, aren't you?"

John shook his head. "Not too well, to tell you the truth. The economics don't really work out. Cattle-feed costs almost as much as caviar, but the price of milk is so low that it's cheaper to pour it down the drain than it is to bottle it. The plastic trays I pack my chickens in cost more than the chickens. Apart from that I need a new differential for my tractor and a new diesel generator, and two-thirds of my winter wheat has gone rotten in the rain. I sold my business in the States for a very good profit, but at this rate I calculate that I'm going to be pretty close to bankruptcy by the beginning of July."

"Why don't you cut your losses?"

"Family pressure. I'm the head of the Meagher family now, and what would they think if I sold Meagher's Farm to some developer?"

"That's it? Family pressure?"

"Well, pride, too. I'm not the kind of guy who likes to admit defeat."

Katie smiled. "That's one thing that you and I have in common, then. Blind stubbornness in the face of overwhelming adversity."

John looked at her for a long time, his chin resting on his hand. She looked directly back at him, and for some reason neither of them felt any particular need to talk. Katie hadn't felt so immediately comfortable with anyone for a long time, and it was obvious that he felt comfortable with her, too.

"So what do you do when you're not being a detective superintendent?"

"I don't get much time to do anything. But I like to cook, and take my dog for a walk on the beach."

"You're married."

She twisted her wedding-band. "Yes, well."

"No children?"

She shook her head. She was still smiling but her smile was a little tighter. John must have realized that he had touched a sensitive spot because he raised his hand in a gesture that meant, okay, I won't ask you any more.

After a while, Mrs Meagher came back in, still coughing, and looking for her cigarettes.

"I'd better get back," said Katie, checking her watch.

"Sure... and I've got three hectares of red potatoes to plow up."

They walked outside together and it was raining again. "Thanks for the tea," said Katie. "You won't forget, will you, if you find anything unusual..."

John nodded. He opened her car door for her, and stood watching her while she fastened her seatbelt. As she drove down toward the gates of Meagher's Farm, she glanced in her rear-view mirror and he was still standing there with his hands in his pockets, and she thought that she had never seen any man look so alone.

Eighteen

That afternoon, around half-past three, she had a telephone call from a man with a thick northside accent.

"Are you the one who's after investigating where Charlie Flynn's gone missing?"

"That's right. Why? Do you know where he is?"

"I might."

"Well, either you do or you don't. Which is it?"

"Why don't you meet me and we can talk it over. St Finbarr's Cathedral, in half-an-hour. Make sure you come by yourself."

"I know you, don't I?"

"I should hope so, by now. I'll see you at four."

She drove to St Finbarr's. It was only four o'clock but the afternoon was already gloomy. She parked on a double yellow line outside the cathedral gates and walked in through the graveyard. Beneath the dripping trees, under crosses and obelisks and weeping cherubim, some of Cork's most prominent families lay silently at rest.

A young priest came galloping through the graveyard and called out, "Forgot my umbrella!" as if he needed to explain why he was in such a hurry.

Katie walked in through the main entrance, her heels echoing on the tiled floor, past the sculptures of the wise and foolish virgins gathered on either side of Christ the Bridegroom.

The interior of the cathedral was echoing and dim, with high columns of Bath stone and walls lined with red Cork marble. Hardly any light penetrated the stained-glass windows, and Katie had to pause for a moment to allow her eyes to become accustomed to the gloom.

Slowly, she approached the altar. She genuflected and crossed herself, and then she sat in one of the pews on the right-hand side, and bowed her head. In front of her, a middle-aged woman was praying in an endless, desperate whisper.

After a few minutes, she heard rubbery-soled shoes approaching from behind her. Somebody came and sat in the pew right behind her, and she could smell cigarette-breath and Gucci aftershave.

"Good to see you again, Katie," said the same northside accent she had heard on the phone. "Haven't seen you in a while."

"Dave MacSweeny," she said, without turning around. "I thought I recognized you on the phone. What do you want?"

"I told you... I know where Charlie Flynn is hiding himself. I know *why*, too."

"You've got some nerve coming to me, after what you did to Paul."

"Paul took advantage of me. Just like Charlie Flynn."

"Paul was fooling around with Geraldine, that's all. And don't tell me that Geraldine wasn't just as much to blame as he was."

"That's not the point. She's my woman, at least she was, and he didn't have the right to be messing with her ever. He should have had more respect. Especially since he did me over for half a million euros' worth of building materials, him and that Charlie Flynn."

"What?"

"Charlie Flynn promised Winthrop Developments that he could supply them with breezeblocks and facing bricks and uPVC window-frames and God knows what else, for a very special price. The trouble was, he couldn't. So he came to your husband cap-in-hand asking for help and your husband sold him six hundred and fifty thousand euros' worth of building materials and pocketed twenty thousand euros of commission. Which would have been grand for all concerned... except that those building materials were actually worth more than a million, and they didn't belong to your husband, they belonged to me, and I was left neck-deep in shite trying to explain to Erin Estates why I couldn't meet my contract.

"Me and my friends called on Charlie to ask him what was going on, but he was long gone by then. Florida... look, here's some Polaroids." He passed over four or five photographs of a fat-bellied gingery man in red flowery swimming-trunks. "Charlie by the pool in Kissimmee. Charlie on the beach at St Petersburg. Looks cheerful, doesn't he? Put on weight, hasn't he? That's what happened to Charlie. He cheated me, and now he's afraid to come back."

"And Paul?"

"That's why I wanted to see you today, Katie. That's why I wanted to see you here, on holy ground. Besides, they don't have security cameras. I felt very betrayed when your Paul went off with Geraldine. Well, how did *you* feel? We were both betrayed, weren't we? But, you know, a fuck's nothing more than a fuck, is it, and you can always wash yourself afterward. But now I find out that Paul's made off with my property, almost a million euros' worth, and you can't wash that away."

"So what are you saying?" asked Katie. She felt angry and officious, but at the same time she felt highly alarmed, too. She had seen so many other Garda detectives compromised by men like Dave MacSweeny, their careers ruined for the sake of a housing loan or a new BMW or a holiday in Gran Canaria, and she didn't want the same thing to happen to her. Her father would never forgive her, and more than anything else she had joined An Garda Síochána to win his approval.

Dave MacSweeny was silent for a moment. Then he said, "I'm a very accommodating person, Katie. I don't want any trouble and I know that you don't want any trouble, either. All I'm asking is that Paul brings my building materials back to the yard at Blackpool, all of them, not one brick missing, and we'll forget this ever happened. I'll give him three days, which is fair considering the amount of materials he took."

"And if he doesn't? Or can't?"

"You'd look lovely in black."

Katie turned around; but Dave MacSweeny was already walking back up the aisle, his rubber-soled shoes squeaking on the tiles. Big, wide-shouldered, in a long black raincoat, one silver hoop earring glinting in the dim cathedral light.

She stayed there for a while, and said a novena to St Martha, promising to light a candle every Tuesday, just like her mother used to. Then she stood up, and crossed herself again, and left St Finbarr's with her head bowed, like somebody leaving a funeral.

Nineteen

He came again that night, with his case of instruments. She was delirious now, and no longer knew where she was or what was happening to her. Both her legs were scraped of almost every scrap of flesh, and the bones shone like strange musical instruments carved out of ivory. Her face was a death-mask, gleaming and gray, with two dark hollows for eyes.

"*Mom*," she whispered.

He leaned over her and stroked her forehead. "Don't worry, Fiona. This will soon be over."

"Mom, my legs hurt. They hurt so bad, mom."

"Ssh, you mustn't complain. You ought to be grateful that you're sacrificing your body for such a momentous purpose."

She suddenly opened her eyes and stared at him. "Who are you?" she demanded, in a dry, hoarse voice, almost a squeak.

"Don't say you don't recognize me. I'm your friend. I'm your very best friend."

"No, you're not. What are you doing in my bedroom?"

He touched one finger to his lips and smiled at her indulgently. "Ssh. We don't want to wake up the rest of the house, do we?"

"I don't know who you are. What are you doing here?"

He sat down on the edge of the bed-frame and opened his instrument-case. "I've come here to take you on the next stage of your journey."

"My legs hurt. They really, really hurt."

"Of course they do. But no matter how bad it is, you know, any pain can always be relieved by an even greater pain."

"I have to get up. I have to meet my mother."

"First things first."

He took a length of nylon cord and tied it in a slip-knot around the top of her left arm.

"What are you doing? What's that for? I have to meet my mother."

"You will meet her, one day. I promise."

He pulled the cord tight, grunting with the effort. She let out a high, breathy sound, but it couldn't be called a scream. He pulled the cord tighter still, until it almost disappeared into her arm, and it was then that her eyes rolled upward so that only the whites were staring at him, like a broken doll.

He picked a scalpel, and started to cut a circle around her upper arm. Blood welled out of the incision and poured into her armpit. He started to hum *Bom Dia, Amigo*, but then, as his work grew more difficult, he fell silent, and he frowned in concentration. The only sound now was the quick dripping of blood onto the newspapers under the bed.

Paul didn't come home until 2:35 in the morning but Katie was waiting for him. She was sitting in the living-room in her green-and-white satin dressing-gown with Sergeant lying by her feet, watching Vincent Price in *The Abominable Dr Phibes*.

Paul stood in the doorway, swaying slightly. His bruises had started to turn red and yellow, so that he looked like a small boy who had been playing clowns with his mummy's make-up.

"What?" he said, at last.

Katie used the remote to switch off the sound. "You're asking me 'what?' I'll tell you what. I had a very unpleasant meeting today with a friend of yours."

Paul let out a barking, sardonic laugh. "That can't be right. You know as well as I do, I don't have any friends. Not any more."

"This particular friend was Dave MacSweeny. Apparently, it's not just your messing around with Geraldine Daley that's bothering him. He urgently wants to find out what's happened to one million euros' worth of his building materials."

"Building materials? How should I know?"

"Because you sold them to Charlie Flynn for six hundred and fifty thousand, that's why, and took twenty thousand for yourself."

"Listen, pet. None of that stuff even belonged to Dave MacSweeny. He lifted the whole lot from a housing development up in Kilmallock."

"And you think that excuses you from selling it on to Charlie Flynn?"

"It was already stolen, pet. You can't steal something twice."

"Jesus, Paul, you're certifiable, you are."

Paul came into the living-room and plonked himself down on the couch. "Charlie Flynn needed the stuff and I needed the money. How do you think I paid off this year's prelim tax?"

"Paul – you took property that you knew to be stolen and you sold it illegally. What kind of position do you think that puts me in? By rights I should arrest you. What do you think this is going to do to my career?"

"You don't have to tell anybody."

Katie shook her head in disbelief. "To think I used to boast to my mother that you were the sharpest guy I'd ever met. How can I not tell anybody? I'm supposed to be heading up the search for Charlie Flynn and now I know where he is, and why he's gone there, and that directly involves you. Worse than that, Dave MacSweeny wants his building materials back and if he doesn't get them he's going to kill you."

"Well, arrest *him*, then. He stole the stuff in the first place."

"For God's sake, Paul, if I arrest him I have to arrest him for a reason, and that reason is now in Charlie Flynn's building-yard, thanks to you. There's no way that you can get out of this, and there's no way that I'm going to get through it without having to resign."

Paul stared at her blearily. "Resign? You don't have to resign! Why do you have to resign?"

"Can you imagine the headlines? Top Woman Detective Is Married to Million-Euro Brick Thief. Who's going to believe that you were dealing in stolen property without my knowing anything about it?"

Paul didn't answer. Instead, he got up from the couch and went over to the drinks cabinet, and poured himself an absurdly large whiskey.

"What good do you think that's going to do?" she asked him.

"I don't think it's going to do any good whatsoever, but at least I won't be conscious to know that it isn't."

Katie stood up, came around the couch and put her arms around his waist.

"Paul," she said.

He stroked her hair, but his eyes were focused on nothing at all. "I know, love," he told her. "I know." But he didn't know, not any more, and Katie knew then that he had given up trying.

He had been working for nearly three-and-a-half hours now, and his hands were trembling with effort. He had removed all of the flesh from her upper arm, and now he was using a hooked scalpel to scrape away the muscle between the bones of her forearm. Her fingers would be the most complicated, cutting the last red shreds away from the metacarpals and the phalanges.

She was still alive, but her breathing was very shallow, and he doubted that she would survive until the morning. As soon as she died, he would have to cut open her abdomen and start stripping her skeleton as quickly as he could, so that her flesh was still fresh.

He thought that he would enjoy baring her face most of all, opening the nose, peeling away the fatty tissue underneath the cheeks, and discovering the skull beneath the skin.

Twenty

Katie knew what a risk she was taking, but she had lain awake all night and she hadn't been able to think of any other way out of it, apart from going straight into Chief Superintendent O'Driscoll's office and handing over her gun and her badge and resigning from the Garda on the spot.

She met Eamonn Collins at Dan Lowery's pub at eleven o'clock the next morning, before the lunchtime rush. "Foxy" was dressed as dapper as ever, in a dark green blazer and a camel waistcoat and a Hermes necktie with stirrups on it. His minder Jerry was hunched in the opposite corner, cramming down a bowlful of French fries with so much tomato ketchup that it looked as if his fingers were smothered in blood.

Katie didn't even take off her raincoat. "I need a favor," she said.

"A favor?" said Eamonn. "What kind of a favor could a fellow like me possibly do for a lady like yourself?"

"I have a little problem which I can't deal with in the usual way. There's no evidence, you see, and not much chance of finding any."

"All right. This is nothing to do with those skeletons, is it?"

Katie shook her head. "This is somebody who took something that didn't belong to him."

"I see. A transgression which you know for a fact but which you couldn't prove in court, is that it?"

"Something like that."

Eamonn sat back and systematically cracked his knuckles. "What do you want me to do about it? And dare I ask what I might expect in return?"

"I want you to pay a visit to the party involved and tell him to soften his cough, that's all."

"That doesn't sound too onerous. Who is it?"

"Dave MacSweeny. He helped himself to some building materials up at Mallow, but somebody else helped himself to the very same building materials and sold them on, and Dave MacSweeny's a little unhappy about it."

"Well, he would be. Dave MacSweeny's not exactly a forgiving sort of fellow. Who was the somebody else who relieved him of his ill-gotten gains?"

"That doesn't concern you."

Eamonn stared at her with his dead gray eyes. "It concerns *you*, though, doesn't it?"

"That's beside the point." Katie wished her heart would stop banging so hard.

Eamonn had a long think. At the next table, Jerry was noisily sucking his fingers clean. After a while, Eamonn leaned forward and said, "All right, you're on. I'll have a quiet word in Dave MacSweeny's ear myself. Is there anything specific you want me to say to him?"

"Just tell him to develop amnesia about the building materials and whoever it was that took them. If you like, you can tell him that Charlie Flynn sent you."

"Charlie Flynn? You surprise me. I thought that Charlie Flynn would have been gently floating out to sea by now, or sinking in a bog on Little Island."

"No, Charlie's still with us."

"All right, then. How forceful do you want me to be?"

"Emphatic, that'll do."

"No problem at all. I can be emphatic."

"You'll be wanting something in return. I can have the dealing charges against Billy Phelan reduced to possession."

Eamonn said, "Hm. That's not much of a bargain."

"Okay," said Katie. "I'll see if I can drop the charges altogether."

"That's better. And maybe your people could leave my fellows alone for a while – stopping them and searching them wherever they go. They even stopped Jimmy Twomey when he was coming out of Mass with his grandma."

"I can probably ease off you for a month or so. But any more than that and my chief superintendent's going to start asking awkward questions."

"Well, awkward questions. We can't have those, can we?"

Katie left Dan Lowery's and stepped out into dazzling, colorless sunshine. She felt nervous and sick, and she was almost tempted to go back and tell Eamonn Collins to forget that she had ever talked to him. But it was too late now. She was committed.

She drove back to Garda headquarters and somehow the city looked different – as if scene-shifters had been at work during the night, changing the bridges around, and altering the streets, and re-arranging the quays. And of course it *was* different, because she had changed her life forever, and there was no going back to the day before yesterday.

Twenty-one

The phone rang at 7:05 on Sunday morning. Katie reached across to the nightstand and pulled the receiver back under the covers. "Yes? Who is it?"

"Dermot O'Driscoll here, Katie. Have you seen the Sunday papers yet?"

"I've only just woken up."

"Well, get yourself out of bed and buy yourself a copy of the *Sunday Times*. Page three, you won't miss it. Then call me here at home."

"Yes, sir."

She took Sergeant with her along the road to the newspaper shop. It was a sparkling morning, even though it must have rained heavily during the night, and she could see a large white cruise ship anchored in the harbor.

She bought the *Sunday Times* and the *Irish News of the World*. She opened the *Times* as she walked back home, and immediately she slowed and stopped, while Sergeant bounded around her, wagging his tail and urging her to carry on.

The headline on page 3 read: British Soldiers 'Murdered Eleven Irish Women'. There was a photograph of Katie standing over the excavations at Meagher's Farm, and another photograph of Jack Devitt, the white-haired writer whom Katie had met with Eugene Ó Béara in The Crow Bar.

The story said that "The 86-year-old mystery of eleven young Cork women who disappeared without trace between 1915 and 1916 may have been solved yesterday by the well-known republican author Jack Devitt. He claims to have proof that they were murdered by British soldiers in revenge for a Fenian bomb attack.

"Eleven women's skeletons were uncovered last week during building work at a farm at Knocknadeenly. An examination by State Pathologist Dr Owen Reidy showed that all of their flesh had been scraped from their bones before they were buried, possibly to hamper identification."

Katie read on, the paper flapping in the morning breeze. Sergeant was growing impatient and started to bark at her. But she read the article right to the end, and then she stood where she was, lost in thought.

The *Times* said that Jack Devitt had been given access to private letters and police reports showing that before they went missing, three of the eleven women had been seen by reliable witnesses talking to a young British officer with a moustache, and two of them had been seen climbing into a car with him. "It was never discovered whether the officer was acting on official orders or if he was carrying out a personal vendetta. However, the investigation was pursued no further and no British officers were ever questioned by police or military police. Three months after the last disappearance (Mary Ahern, on the morning of Good Friday, 1916) the case was officially declared to be closed."

Katie could understand that Eugene Ó Béara and Jack Devitt would want to make as much political hay out of the case as they possibly could, but it was obvious that neither they nor the *Times* knew that the skeletons had been ritualistically decorated. If these were the same women, it was entirely possible that they *had* been murdered by a British officer, but why would a British officer drill holes in their thighbones and hang them with rag dolls? Perhaps it had some religious or political meaning. During the Indian Mutiny, British soldiers had sewn condemned Muslims into pig-skins before hanging them, because Muslims considered that pigs were unclean. But if this had been done for a similar reason, to insult and intimidate the Irish, why had all these women been killed in a way that had no significance that anybody knew about, and then buried in secret?

She walked home. Paul was still lying on the couch in the living-room, his head tipped back, snoring in a coarse, steady rasp. She stood watching him and then she went into the kitchen to make herself a cup of coffee.

She called Dermot O'Driscoll. "Sorry," he said, chewing in her ear. "I've got a mouthful of scone."

"I read the *Times*."

"Yes, and what do you think?"

"I still think that there are dozens of questions left unanswered – even if Jack Devitt's evidence turns out to be authentic."

"Well, that's as may be, but the Commissioner called me this morning and said that the Minister of Justice wants us to drop the investigation completely."

"What about Professor O'Brien's research?"

"That too. The minister wants no further action of any kind and absolutely no comments to the media. Things between Dublin and London are touchy enough as they are without taking eighty-year-old skeletons out of the closet."

"But, sir – "

"Drop it, Katie. There's no future in it. How are you getting along with Charlie Flynn?"

"I, ah – I think I may be getting somewhere."

"Good. The sooner you find out what happened to him the better. Perhaps City Hall will give my head some peace."

Twenty-two

John Meagher was driving up toward the farmhouse on Tuesday afternoon when he saw scores of crows flapping over the top field, close to Iollan's Wood. He parked his Land Rover and went to investigate, climbing over the low stone wall and taking a shortcut across the dark, crumbly furrows.

The crows had obviously found something to eat – a dead fox or a rabbit – because they were wheeling and diving and cawing, and squabbling amongst themselves. They were so preoccupied that many of them didn't even notice him as he approached, and continued to flap and quarrel over their feast. A few of them resentfully hopped away, but they didn't go far.

There were so many crows that at first he couldn't understand what he was looking at. But as he came nearer he gradually realized that they were tearing at a radically-dismembered human body.

He felt as if the entire field had suddenly tilted beneath his feet. He stumbled, and stopped. But then he stepped closer, as close as he dared, and stared at the apparition in front of him in total horror.

All of the body's bones had been entirely stripped of flesh, except a few scarlet rags around the joints. Each bone had then been pushed upright into the soil to form a kind of picket fence. On the far side of the fence, the skull was perched on a small cairn of lesser bones, shoulder-bones and toe-bones and finger-bones. On each side of the skull stood the body's thighbones, and the top of each thighbone had been drilled right through and a small linen doll tied onto it with string.

Inside this compound lay a heap of human offal. John recognized the sacklike lungs and the half-deflated stomach – as well as pieces of raw flesh that were still identifiable as calf-muscles and forearms. Even as he stood staring at it, panting in ever-increasing nausea, one of the crows snatched up an ear in its beak and went flying off with it, hotly pursued by three or four other crows, all of them screeching in fury.

He walked back down the field, stiff-legged. Gabriel and the boy Finbar were still digging the foundations of the new boiler-house. Gabriel looked up as he approached, and wiped his nose with the back of his hand.

"What's wrong, John?"

"There's been – some sort of an accident."

"Accident? Where?"

"Up by Iollan's Wood. You see where those crows are. Stay here – don't go up there, whatever you do, and don't let the boy go up there, either. Or anybody else."

Gabriel could see by the expression on his face that something was seriously wrong. "What is it – somebody dead?"

John nodded, and then he abruptly turned around, and leaned against the wall, and gawked up his lunch, potato-and-leek soup and soda bread. Gabriel and the boy stood solemnly watching him, and didn't say anything until he had wiped his mouth, and spat, and spat again.

"You want me to call the guards?" asked Gabriel.

"That's okay. I've got that woman detective's number. You just keep an eye on things."

He called Katie on his cellphone. She took a long time to

128

answer, and when she did the signal was very poor.

"Superintendent?" he shouted, with his finger in his ear. "It's John Meagher, from Meagher's Farm."

"Sorry can't – back in a – "

"It's John Meagher. I've found another body. Another skeleton."

"Another skeleton? Same place? Under the feedstore?"

"No... in the top field. This one's new."

"Sorry, where did you say? I'm just – Jack Lynch Tunnel –"

There was a short crackling pause, and then she came back more clearly. *"Sorry about that, I'm just on my way to the South Infirmary. Where did you say the skeleton was?"*

"It's in the top field, up by the woods. But this isn't the same as the others. The rest of the body... all the flesh... it's all still here. By the looks of it, it hasn't been here longer than a few hours."

"All right. I'm on my way. Don't go near it again, will you? There could be footprints or other evidence."

"I wouldn't go near it again if you paid me."

Liam Fennessy pushed aside the blue PVC sheeting and came inside. He took a long look at the skull and the bones and the glistening viscera and then he shook his head and said, "Jesus."

"Dr Reidy's flying back down this evening," said Katie. She pushed another Ritchie's mint into her mouth. "He wants to see the remains *in situ*."

"It's a woman, yes?"

Katie nodded. "We've found part of her external genitalia and one of her breasts. We've found her scalp, too. Long natural-blonde hair. Apart from that there are large sections of flesh from her back still intact, and her skin looks quite firm. Without second-guessing Dr Reidy, I'd say we're looking at a girl in her early twenties. The skin's quite suntanned, too. Either she's a local girl who's recently been on holiday or else she's a tourist from somewhere warm."

"I'm checking on missing persons inquiries," put in Jimmy O'Rourke, with an unlit cigarette waggling between his lips. "If she was a tourist or a backpacker, though, it could be difficult to find out who she was... a lot of them go away for months before their families start wondering where they are."

"Any identifying marks?" asked Liam. "Any tattoos, studs, or earrings?"

"No tattoos, no studs, and unfortunately the crows made off with the ears. But we have the skull, and we have part of the nose, and most of the facial muscles. It shouldn't be too difficult to build up an identifiable MRI image."

Liam hunkered down in front of one of the thighbones, and flicked the little rag doll.

"Those, of course, are the really baffling part," said Katie. "As far as we're aware nobody knew about those dolls except us."

"And the two fellows who found the skeletons," put in Liam. "And farmer John Meagher himself. And his mother."

"You don't seriously think that John Meagher committed a copycat murder on his own farm?"

"I don't seriously think anything at the moment. But so far we haven't come across any folk legends that mention rag dollies tied to women's thighbones, have we? So it's fair to assume that whoever did this knew about the dollies from the first lot of bones."

He took off his James Joyce spectacles and peered at the thighbone even more closely.

"This hole was drilled with an electric drill, by the look of it. The others were all drilled with a brace-and-bit."

"I've already confiscated three electric drills from the farmhouse toolshed," said Katie. "I've taken all the drill-bits, too. Two complete sets of specialist bits, only two of them missing, plus a tobacco-tin containing eleven assorted bits. Oh – and three balls of twine, too."

"And you don't think that John Meagher had anything to do with this?"

"I'm just being thorough, Liam, that's all."

"How about footprints? This is ideal for footprints, a freshly-plowed field."

"We're taking casts. But considering the way the body was arranged, there seem to be surprisingly few."

"Well, what do you want me to do?"

"Initiate a house-to-house, and pub-to-pub, and knock on the door of every bed-and-breakfast in a ten-mile radius. You're asking about a suntanned girl with long blonde hair."

"And you?"

"I have to talk to Dermot. Then I have to give a statement to the press."

Liam stood up. "The rag dollies are the key to this. If we can find out what they mean, I think we'll know what happened here, and why, and who did it."

Jimmy O'Rourke came over and said, "Take a look at this, superintendent."

He led Katie around the right-hand side of the garden of bones, and pointed to a large section of flesh that had been cut from the victim's hip, buttock and upper thigh. It looked almost like a boned leg of beef from a supermarket display cabinet.

"See there... there's a deep indentation around the upper thigh... really, really deep. The last time I ever saw anything like that was when a fellow caught his arm in a printing-machine in Douglas. His workmates tied a tourniquet around his upper arm to stop him from bleeding to death."

"So what do you deduce from that?" asked Katie.

"I'm not sure. But why would anybody tie a tourniquet around the leg of a dead body?"

"You mean that this woman might have had her leg amputated while she was still alive?"

"Well, not amputated, no. Look at all these bones, they're all intact. They haven't been sawn through, any of them."

Katie looked down at the grisly chaos of the girl's disassembled body. She tried to study the pieces of flesh objectively. She didn't want to think about the cruelty of what had happened to this girl, or the appalling pain she must have endured. "What a mess," she said. "But see how neatly those muscles have been cut. Whoever did this had quite a talent with a knife, didn't he?"

"I'll have a word around the hospitals," said Liam. "You never know. We might be looking for a mad surgeon. Dr Frankenstein in reverse."

"Talk to the local butchers, too," said Katie.

"Good idea. One of my nephews works for O'Reillys in the English Market. That's how I get all my black puddings cheap."

"All right," said Katie. There was a dazzling flicker of flashlights as the photographers got to work, and she had to turn her face away. In spite of her attempts to be detached, she was shaking.

"Here," said Liam. He reached inside his leather jacket and took out a clean white handkerchief.

"What?" she frowned. He unfolded the handkerchief for her but she still didn't understand what he meant until he pointed to his eyes, one after the other, to indicate that there were tears in her eyes.

132

Twenty-three

That evening, Katie held another media conference at Anglesea Street. It was packed with more than sixty reporters and cameramen. She gave the bare facts that the body of an unidentified young woman had been found at Meagher's Farm and that her skeleton had been stripped of its flesh and arranged "in a manner suggesting some kind of ritual or fetishistic behavior."

"Is there any similarity between the way this skeleton was arranged and the way the first eleven skeletons were arranged?" asked Dougal Cleary from RTÉ 1.

"No. The first eleven skeletons seemed to have been buried at random. This skeleton was very systematically laid out in the open, along with the flesh that had been removed from it."

"Removed from it how?"

"Expertly, I'd say. With a scalpel or a knife."

"So you could be looking for somebody with medical skills?"

"Possibly. We're keeping an open mind until we receive the autopsy report from Dr Reidy."

"You keep mentioning this word 'ritualistic' – but what ritual are you referring to, exactly?"

"So far I'm only using it in the sense that this woman wasn't murdered in anger, or haphazardly, but in a carefully considered procedure. We don't know if this procedure has any religious or occult implications. Professor Gerard O'Brien at the university has been helping us in our research but so far he hasn't come up with any complete explanation."

"Does he have an *incomplete* explanation?"

"Nothing that's useful to discuss at this time."

"Does this latest murder cast any doubt on Jack Devitt's theory that a British Army officer was responsible for murdering those eleven women in 1915?"

"Again we're keeping an open mind. Of course the same perpetrator couldn't have committed today's murder. But we're looking into the theory that both murderers could belong to the same cult, or have similar mystical beliefs. In fact, we're looking into every theory that anybody can think of."

"Does this mean that you're re-opening the 1915 murder investigation?"

"We have to... insofar as it could shed valuable light on today's case. We'll be publishing a list of all eleven women in tomorrow's papers, and appealing for anybody who might be related to them to get in touch with us immediately, so that we can perform mitochondrial DNA tests."

"I gather that you, personally, never wanted to close it?"

"Twelve women have been inexplicably killed. No matter when they were killed, no matter who they were, we owe it to all of them to find out who killed them. I want you to know that I am absolutely determined to give them peace."

That evening she left Garda headquarters just after six o'clock and went into Tesco in Paul Street to do some shopping. She walked up and down the aisles with her shopping trolley, trying not to think about the dismembered body in the field. Unless some fresh evidence came up, there was nothing she could usefully do until tomorrow, and she needed time to calm herself down. She had seen the bodies of people who had been shot in the face with shotguns. She had seen the bodies of people who had been drowned, and burned, and crushed. She had even seen the bodies of people who had been systematically tortured with red-hot pokers and pliers. But she had never yet seen a body that had been so completely desecrated, so stripped of its humanity, so totally disassembled. It reminded her more of a burglary than a homicide. It was almost as if her murderer had been tearing her body apart, piece by piece, in a determined search for her soul.

She had been thinking of cooking beef in Guinness this evening, and she bought some carrots and swede and onions. But as she wheeled her trolley toward the meat chiller she found herself breathing more and more deeply, until she was hyperventilating. She clutched the trolley handle tightly and closed her eyes. She could feel cold perspiration sliding down her back.

"Are you all right, love?" an elderly woman asked her.

She opened her eyes and right in front of her, brightly-lit like a traffic accident, she saw glistening dark brown livers and scarlet joints of beef and soft creamy-yellow folds of tripe.

"I'm fine," she said. "I'm just a little faint." She left her trolley where it was and walked quickly out of the store and into the street.

Twenty-four

She was leaving the Paul Street multi-story car-park when her mobile phone warbled.

"Superintendent? It's Liam Fennessy. You'd better get up to the City Gaol, quick as you can."

"The Gaol? What's happened?"

"It's an old friend of ours. It looks like somebody's decided to teach him a lesson he'll never forget."

"At the *Gaol*?"

"Well, you'll see for yourself, superintendent, when you get here."

"All right. I'm down on Lavitt's Quay. I'll be with you in five minutes at the most."

She drove across the river and headed west to Sunday's Well, running three red lights. She turned up the steep incline of Convent Road until she reached the gray sandstone walls of Cork City Gaol. It began to rain, one of those sharp, rattling showers that the Atlantic brings in without warning.

There were two patrol cars already parked in the yard outside the Gaol, as well as Liam's green Vectra. As Katie pulled up beside them, an ambulance arrived, too, with its blue lights flashing. A uniformed garda hurried up to Katie's car and opened the door for her.

"So who is it?" she said.

"Dave MacSweeny, ma'am."

"Dave MacSweeny? Jesus. Is he dead?"

"Not quite, ma'am. But let's just say that he's not feeling too bright."

Katie felt a cold, crawling sensation down her back. Oh my God, she thought. Don't say that this is Eamonn Collins' interpretation of being "emphatic." If it was, then Dave MacSweeny wouldn't be the only one who could expect to be taught a lesson that he wouldn't forget.

She turned up her collar and climbed out of her car. In the dark, and the rain, Cork City Gaol appeared even more forbidding than usual. It had been built high on this hill in 1824 to resemble a medieval castle, with crenellated towers. For years it had been a women's prison, although men had been locked up here, too, during the troubles in 1922. It had closed in 1923, and now it was a tourist attraction, populated with life-size wax figures of warders and inmates to give visitors a feeling of what it had been like to be incarcerated here.

Katie climbed the steps to the front gates, with the garda following close behind her, and walked quickly along the path that led to the Gaol's main buildings. The rain was coming down even harder now, turning her hair into dark red rats' tails.

"One of the cleaners found him, ma'am, after they'd closed. God alone knows how long he'd been here. They've had visitors in and out all day, one hundred and seven according to the ticket sales."

"Is the manager here?"

"We've called her, ma'am, and she's on her way."

They reached the governor's house. The garda opened the front door for her, and then he led her across the chilly, echoing vestibule to the Gaol's West Wing. This was an echoing, high-ceilinged hallway, with three galleries of cells on either side, connected by catwalks and iron staircases. Up on the very top catwalk, the waxwork figure of a prison warder was leaning on the railing and looking down at her. Katie saw Liam Fennessy up on the first floor catwalk, with four or five other gardaí. She climbed the staircase with her shoes clanging on the iron treads.

Liam was standing by an open cell door, with his arms folded. He nodded toward the cell and said, "Dave MacSweeny. I have absolutely no idea how long he's been here. We're waiting on fire and rescue."

Katie looked inside the cell. It was little more than six feet by ten feet, with a wooden bed and a plain wooden chair. The walls and ceiling were painted with scabby whitewash, and there was a strong smell of damp and urine.

Standing up against the right-hand wall was Dave MacSweeny, barefoot, wearing a soiled gray shirt and dark blue trousers, with his left arm lifted as if he were waving to a distant friend. His face was covered with a mask of thick medicine-pink emulsion paint, and his hair had been spiked up with creosote, some of which had slid in dark brown runnels down the back of his neck.

His eyes were closed, although the fine cracks in the emulsion paint around his eyelids showed that he must have opened them at some time after it had dried. There were deep fissures in the paint on either side of his mouth, too, and both of these were filled with congealed blood. His silver hoop earring was missing, torn out of his ear-lobe, leaving a ragged hole.

He remained standing up against the wall, with his arm raised, because he had no choice. His left wrist and his shoulders and both of his knees had been fastened to the whitewashed stone with heavy-duty brads. Whoever had nailed him here, they had turned him into a living parody of all the other waxwork prisoners who occupied the cells around him.

Katie stepped into the cell and tilted her head close to Dave MacSweeny's face. His eyes remained closed but she could hear him breathing. Rapid, shallow gasps, with a harsh rattle at the end of each gasp. He smelled strongly of stale sweat and cigarettes and alcohol and he had wet his trousers.

"Dave?" she said. "Dave, can you hear me?" But he didn't answer.

She turned to Liam and said, "Can't we get him free?"

"That's why we've called for the fire and rescue. They've fixed him to the stone with one of those pneumatic nailers. Ninety millimeter brads at least. We're going to need a pair of bolt-cutters before we can spring our Dave MacSweeny out of the slammer."

"Has he said anything to you?"

"His eyes were open when I first arrived here, and of course I asked him who did it, but he didn't say a word. Or *wouldn't*, more like."

"Any witnesses? Somebody must have seen him being dragged up here. Where was the manager when this was going on?"

"Taking a day off, so I understand."

"What about the rest of the staff? One of the tour guides? A visitor? In the name of Jesus, a sixteen-stone man with his face painted bright pink? And those nailers make enough of a racket, don't they?"

"Nobody saw a thing, superintendent. Nobody heard anything, neither."

Katie thought: that doesn't really surprise me, if Eamonn Collins had anything to do with it.

"All right," she said. "I'll have to make an appeal through the media. Somebody must have seen something – even if it was only a van parked here."

"A van?"

"Had to be. They wouldn't have driven through the city with a fellow painted bright pink sitting in the back of their car, would they? And they would have needed a compressor for the nailer."

Katie turned and looked at Dave MacSweeny again. He had opened his eyes now, and was staring up at the ceiling, as if he were praying to be released. He still said nothing, but bright pink tears began to run down his cheeks and drip onto his shirt.

It took the fire and rescue team over an hour to free Dave MacSweeny from the wall. The nails turned out to be too hard and too deeply-embedded for bolt-cutters so the fire-fighters had to hack away the stone all around them with hammers and chisels and then cut them with a grinding wheel. Katie stood out on the catwalk, covering her ears as metal screeched against metal.

At last they lowered Dave MacSweeny to the floor of the cell and brought in a stretcher. As the paramedics carried him out, Katie bent over him and said, "Dave? Can you hear me, Dave?"

He stared at her but he didn't speak.

"Dave, do you know who did this to you, Dave?"

He gave her an almost imperceptible nod.

"Who was it, Dave? Are you going to tell me?"

One corner of his mouth quivered in the beginnings of a smile.

"I'm sorry, superintendent," put in one of the paramedics, "we really need to get him to the hospital."

"All right." Katie stood up straight, and let them carry Dave MacSweeny away. She turned, and caught Liam looking at her with a slight frown on his face, as if there were something he couldn't quite work out.

"What's the problem?"

"Nothing. I was just trying to work out why anybody would have gone to all the trouble of dolling him up to look like a waxwork and then nailing him to the wall like that. They obviously weren't intent on *killing* him, were they, because somebody was bound to notice him there before too long. So what do you think? Somebody was trying to teach him a lesson?"

"Probably. You know what a cute hoor he is. He could have upset any one of dozens of people."

"But why do this to him – right here in the Gaol? They were taking a hell of a chance, after all. Why didn't they just go round to his house and nail him to his kitchen table? Far less risky, just as much of a punishment."

"I can't guess, Liam. Who knows what goes on in the heads of people who do things like that? Perhaps they were trying to show us that even if *we* couldn't put him in prison, *they* could, whenever they felt like it."

Liam opened her car door for her, and the lights-on alarm began to beep. "I think they didn't do it simply to punish *him* – they did it to show somebody else, too. Maybe as a warning."

"You're absolutely right, of course. All we have to find out who was warning who about what."

"I'll take care of this one. I know you've got your hands full with that body up at Meagher's Farm. I just thought you ought to see it, that's all."

"Thanks," said Katie. "As if I wasn't feeling queasy enough already."

She called Eamonn Collins on her cellphone. A woman answered, with a nasal Dublin accent. In the background, Katie could hear Andy Williams singing *Moon River*.

"Is Eamonn home?"

"Who wants to know?"

"Katie Maguire."

"And who's Katie Maguire may I ask?"

"Detective Superintendent Katie Maguire, that's who."

"All right. There's no need to eat the head off me."

Eamonn came to the phone. "Good evening to you, superintendent. How can I help you?"

"I think you've already helped me more than enough, thanks. What the hell did you think you were playing at? I wanted you to have a quiet word in Dave MacSweeny's ear, not make a public spectacle of him."

"Well, to be truthful, it started off as a quiet word, but then he began to be argumentative. Called my mother a name, you see; and I couldn't have that."

"So you decided to take him to the City Gaol and nail him to the wall? Holy Mother of God, Eamonn, there's going to be a full investigation and the whole thing's going to be plastered all over the papers. And don't tell me that Dave MacSweeny's not going to let everyone know who did it, and why."

"Oh, I don't think he'll be doing that, superintendent. He was given a fair word of warning, as well as his punishment. I'd be very surprised if he gave you any more trouble after this."

"I hope to God you're right, Eamonn, otherwise I'll be going down for this, and I'll make sure that you'll be coming down with me."

"Oh, superintendent! 'Some flow'rets of Eden ye still inherit, but the trail of the serpent is over them all.'"

"I know," said Katie. "Thomas Moore."

Twenty-five

There were crumpled bags under Dr Reidy's eyes, as if he hadn't slept in a week, and he reeked of tobacco. Without a word he held out a large jar of Vick's Vapor Rub and Katie dipped her finger into it and smeared it thickly on her upper lip. It made her eyes water and her nose drip, but that was preferable to the alternative.

Dr Reidy led Katie through to a small side-room, on the other side of the corridor from the main pathology lab, and there, on two stainless-steel autopsy tables, was all that was left of the woman whose remains had been found at Meagher's Farm.

Her skeleton had been reassembled on the left-hand table, and on the right-hand table Dr Reidy had done his best to reshape her skin and flesh and viscera into a semblance of the girl that she had originally been. It was a slack, shapeless parody of a human being, blotchy and bruised and clotted with blood, more like an empty nightdress-case than a woman, but all the same Katie was surprised how successfully Dr Reidy had been able to reconstruct her. She walked up to the table and stood staring at the cadaver for a long, long time. Dr Reidy carried on sorting out his instruments and did nothing to disturb her.

"Cause of death?" she asked, at last.

"Surgical shock, more than likely, caused by diminution of the fluid element in the blood."

"That means that he was cutting the flesh off her while she was still alive?"

Dr Reidy nodded. "I'm sorry to say that it probably does. Judging from the condition of the tissues, it appears that the flesh was removed from both arms and both legs before death supervened. That explains the deep contusions around the biceps and the upper thighs. Your man applied tourniquets to prevent her from bleeding to death for as long as he possibly could."

"No way to tell if she was anesthetized or not?"

"There was some aspirin residue in the stomach, but so far there's no trace of any other painkillers or anesthetics."

"Do you think a surgeon might have done this?"

"No, definitely not. The flesh was removed quite skillfully, I'd say, but this isn't the work of anybody with professional surgical training. We're talking about a talented butcher, most likely."

Katie peered closely at the girl's face. Part of her right cheek was missing, and she had nothing but dark holes for eyes. Dr Reidy said, "We've got most of her internal organs, but her heart's missing. I can't tell if that was deliberate or not."

"Probably the crows took it."

"Nobody's claimed her yet, I gather?"

Katie shook her head.

"Well, not to worry. With what we have here, Dr Lambert should be able to produce a very acceptable likeness. So far I can tell you that she was approximately 5ft 10ins tall, well-nourished and physically fit, and that she probably weighed around 145 pounds, although I haven't got all of her. She was blonde, aged between 21 to 24, and I suspect from the quality of her dentistry that she was American. Her teeth, in fact, are virtually perfect."

"Anything else?"

"There are bruises on her wrists and ankles which indicate that she was handcuffed, and if you can find the handcuffs, I should be able to give you a positive identification. There are also some deep diamond-shaped impressions on her buttocks. It's my guess that she was forced to lie for some considerable time on a bed without a mattress. Again – if and when you find the bed, I can almost certainly give you a positive ID, plus a DNA match. It was an older-style bed, I'd say – and, of course, she would have been bleeding so much that it would have been almost impossible for the perpetrator to remove every tiny fleck of blood.

"Something more – there are no traces of adhesive around her mouth, nor any bruising that might have been consistent with her being tightly gagged – although, as you can see, the skin around the mouth and lips was very severely traumatized when her face was skinned. There are no fragments of latex or tennis-ball flock in between her teeth, either, so she probably didn't have a ball forced into her mouth to keep her quiet."

"She wasn't gagged? And she had the flesh cut off her arms and legs with nothing but a few aspirin to deaden the pain? God, she must have screamed."

"She probably did," said Dr Reidy, unblinking.

"That means that she must have been held somewhere isolated – in a place where nobody could hear her. Either that, or somewhere soundproof, like a cellar."

"That would be my opinion."

"How about the holes in the thighbones?"

"They were both drilled with a number 8 steel masonry bit. Brand-new, by the clean way it drilled through, and there are traces of thin oil, too. We've found some microscopic fragments of metal so we should be able to identify that, too."

145

"All right," said Katie. "You've got all the forensic evidence… all I have to do is find this monster and make an arrest."

Dr Reidy draped two sheets over the autopsy tables. "That's right, superintendent. I'd say you've got your work cut out for you, wouldn't you?"

Jimmy O'Rourke knocked on her office door at 4:45 pm and said, "Boss? The Meagher's Farm victim. We think we know who she is." He held out an e-mailed attachment with a color photograph on it. Katie took it and held it under her desklamp.

It was datelined 6:00 pm the previous day, from the Santa Barbara Sheriff's Department, 1745 Mission Drive, Solvang, California, and it was addressed to Garda headquarters in Phoenix Park. "We have received an urgent inquiry from Mr and Mrs Donald F. Kelly of Paseo Delicias, Solvang, regarding the whereabouts of their daughter Fiona Kelly who is currently undertaking a three-week solo backpacking tour of Co. Limerick, Co. Kerry and Co. Cork, in the Republic of Ireland. Ms Kelly arranged to contact her parents by telephone every two–three days in order to reassure them that she was safe. However – "

Katie looked at the photograph. A young, bright, blonde-haired girl standing on a white-painted verandah, laughing.

"Fiona is 22 years old, 5ft 10ins tall, weighs 147 lbs. She is likely to be wearing blue jeans and a navy-blue windcheater with turquoise panels on the front. She is carrying a navy-blue Nike backpack."

"Oh, shit," said Katie.

At 9:25 pm, Katie spoke on the phone with Chief Deputy Fred Olguin of the Santa Barbara Sheriff's Department.

"I have to warn you that we're investigating a murder here. A young blonde girl who may be American."

146

"I see. I'm real sorry to hear that. Naturally I won't say anything to the Kellys yet awhile. But they're pretty upset. It seems like Fiona always made a point of calling them, almost every afternoon."

"I need a list of every location from which Fiona called her parents since she her arrival. Failing that, the telephone numbers."

"I'll get you all of that information, ma'am. Don't you worry about that."

The list came by e-mail only twenty minutes later, along with a map on which Mr and Mrs Kelly had been carefully tracing their daughter's progress by marking red crosses on a map of the Irish Republic.

Katie asked Liam to call customs officers at Shannon and the Garda stations in Limerick, Killarney and Bandon. Within an hour she had built up a reasonably detailed picture of most of Fiona's movements from the moment she had stepped off the plane from Los Angeles.

At 7:50 Dermot O'Driscoll came in with a blacky ham sandwich in one hand and a mug of tea in the other and asked how she was getting on. She nodded toward the map and the photograph of Fiona pinned up next to it. "I've got a really bad feeling this is our victim."

"American, then? Not Irish."

"Irish by ancestry."

Gardaí called that evening at seven different bed-and-breakfasts where Fiona had stopped for the night, and interviewed every landlady. Almost every one of them said she was "very sweet, very friendly, and very trusting." Mrs Rooney from The Atlantic Hotel in Dingle said, "She was so innocent I have to say that I was feared for her. Hitch-hiking isn't safe like it used to be when I was young."

The last call Fiona had made to her parents was from The Golden Shamrock bed-and-breakfast in Ballyvourney, near Macroom, which was less than an hour's drive west of Cork City.

Just before 8:00 am the following morning, Garda John Buckley from Macroom talked to Denis Hennessy, who ran a newsagent's and confectionery on the main Cork road. He had been tying up the previous days' unsold newspapers when he saw Fiona hitch-hiking just outside his shop. "You wouldn't forget her, you know? She looked like one of those girls in *Bay Watch*." A dirty pale-blue pick-up had stopped for her, with the name *C & J O'Donoghue Builders* painted on the back.

By 11:05 am, Detective Garda Patrick O'Sullivan had tracked down Con and Jimmy O'Donoghue, two young brothers who ran their own building business in Mallow, 20 miles north of Cork. They were restoring a row of old Victorian cottages out near Cecilstown. They remembered stopping for Fiona just outside Macroom and offering to give her a lift as far as The Angler's Rest pub a few miles south of Blarney.

"There's nothing happened to her, is it? She was an angel all right."

"Did she say where she was going?"

"Oh, sure. She was going to kiss the Blarney Stone. She couldn't stop chattering on about it."

Patrick called Katie on his cellphone. "Stay where you are," Katie told him. "Talk to the landlord at The Angler's Rest and any of his customers who might have seen her. I'll come out and join you."

The autumn sun shone brightly in her rear-view mirror as she took the long straight road west out of Cork and headed for The Angler's Rest. Most of the leaves had fallen now, and the landscape was lit in orange and red and yellow, as if she were looking at it through a stained-glass window.

Patrick was waiting for her in the pub car-park, with his windcheater collar turned up against the cold, and his breath smoking.

"You've talked to the landlord?" she said, climbing out of the car.

"He didn't see anything, but there's a fellow here who did."

The fellow was sitting at the bar with a pint of Beamish in front of him and a whiskey chaser. He was small and red in the face, and the top of his head was curiously flat, as if you could have balanced a cup-and-saucer on it. He wore the jacket that had once belonged to a bronze-colored suit and the trousers that had once belonged to a dull blue suit.

"What's your name?" Katie asked him.

"Ricky Looney. Like my father before me. He was Ricky Looney, too."

The fire was crackling in the hearth and all of the drinkers in The Angler's Rest were staring at Katie in shameless, unwavering curiosity. "Well, Ricky, my name's Katie Maguire." She produced the photograph of Fiona Kelly and held it up in front of his face. "Detective Garda O'Sullivan tells me that you saw this girl."

"I did so."

"Can you remember what day that was?"

"Not exactly, but it was the day that Cork lost the junior hurling to Killarney."

"Thursday," put in Patrick.

"That's right. You're right. That would be the day before Friday."

"Were you sitting in here when you saw her?" asked Katie.

"I was, yeah."

149

"So where was she?"

"She was across the road there, like. There was this blue pick-up like and she climbed out of it and crossed the road there, like. And I was watching her thumbing for a lift, you know."

"And did she get a lift?"

"Oh, yes. Only a minute or two, and this big black car pulls up and in she gets, and that's it like, she's gone."

"Do you know what make of car it was?"

"Mercedes, I'd say. With one headlight only."

"You didn't see the registration plate?"

He shook his head. "It was all covered up with mud at the back. Like he'd been driving it through a field."

She put out a call for every black or dark-colored Mercedes to be pulled over and the drivers asked to account for their movements on Thursday last week.

Dermot O'Driscoll rang her back and he wasn't at all happy. "We have a lorry strike blocking the Jack Lynch Tunnel tomorrow. If you stop every dark-colored Mercedes as well, it's going to be chaos."

"I'm on my way to Blarney, sir. I'll talk to you later."

"Katie – I want you back by five. I've arranged another news conference."

"I'm sure you can handle that, sir. You know just as much as I do."

"Katie – "

"Sorry, sir. You're breaking up."

Katie and Patrick O'Sullivan arrived in the village of Blarney and parked outside the castle. Blarney was a tourist-trap, a small village with a supermarket, two big pubs that catered for thousands of foreign visitors in the summer, and souvenir shops selling Guinness T-shirts, leprechaun key-rings, and Waterford crystal goblets at £75 each. This afternoon, however, Blarney was almost deserted, with only one coach in the car-park.

Katie went to the castle ticket-office and produced the photograph of Fiona Kelly. The woman in the pay-booth said, "No, love, I'm sorry... and even if she was here, I wouldn't recognize her. They're all just faces, you know, one face after another."

They walked through the grounds toward the castle itself. A giggling party of Japanese tourists were having their photographs taken on one of the wooden bridges, with the river beneath them sparkling with hundreds of pennies, where visitors had thrown them for luck.

After they had passed the Japanese, however, the lawns and the pathways were peaceful and chilly, with only the cawing of crows and the slowly-sinking sunlight. They climbed the steps that led to the foot of the dark 15th-century tower, but when they reached the entrance, Katie said, "That's it, Patrick. You can go up to the top on your own. You won't catch me climbing four hundred steps, even in the name of duty."

She stayed by the souvenir shop until Patrick reappeared, sweaty and out of breath, in spite of the chill. "You took your time," she chided him.

"I talked to the photographers," he panted. "They don't recall any girl like that kissing the Blarney Stone, not in the past two or three weeks. But they're going to give me copies of every picture they've taken since Wednesday last. Like they said themselves, you can't imagine an American girl coming here on her own and not having her picture taken, so that she could send it to her parents back home."

"All right, Patrick. Good work. Make sure they send you those pictures asap. But my feeling is that she never got here."

"The dark Mercedes?"

"More than likely. It's only six kilometers from The Angler's Rest to the middle of Blarney – don't tell me that any innocent driver wasn't going to bring her all the way."

"So he took her off to Knocknadeenly and tied her up and killed her."

"It looks like it, doesn't it? And he took her somewhere very isolated. A cottage or a barn. A cottage is my guess. He couldn't have tortured her and cut her up all in one night, so he would have needed somewhere to rest, and sleep, and make himself something to eat. A two-bedroom cottage, probably. Get onto the letting agents in Cork and Mallow and Fermoy."

"Anything else?"

"Yes. I want a twenty-four-hour guard on Meagher's Farm. And I want at least half-a-dozen squad cars out tomorrow morning, and have them knock at every door in Ballyhooly and Glanworth and Killavullen and Castletownroche. I want them to drive up and down every single side-road and stop at every single farmhouse and bungalow and outbuilding, no exceptions.

"Whoever did this, I want him found, Patrick, and very quickly."

Patrick scribbled in his notebook with a blunt HB pencil, then clapped it shut and said, "Right. Sorry. What was that first thing you wanted me do?"

There was a message waiting for her when she arrived back at Anglesea Street. A virtual bouquet of red roses on her computer screen, with the message "I'm sorry, Katie. I'm such a gom sometimes. All my love Paul."

She looked at it for a moment, and then she deleted it. She wished he hadn't bothered. It would be so much easier not to love him if he didn't keep giving her glimpses of what he had been like when they first got married.

Twenty-six

Dr Reidy called Katie just after 10:30 on Wednesday morning and said, "Our victim is Fiona Kelly, not an ounce of a doubt."

"You're absolutely sure?"

"Oh, yes. The dental records match exactly."

"All right, then. Anything more?"

"Not at the moment. I'm going to Hayfield Manor to have a belated breakfast. I find it hard to dissect when I'm hungry. By the way, what was the name of that Italian restaurant you recommended? I thought I might go there tonight."

"Florentino's, halfway down Carey's Lane."

Katie put the phone down. Fiona's parents were due to fly to Ireland this afternoon, although Katie had warned Chief Deputy Olguin that even if the body was Fiona, there was no question of them being allowed to see her. She remembered seeing Seamus, in his little white casket. Her darling boy had looked so perfect that she almost expected him to open his eyes and smile at her.

Just before lunch, Jimmy O'Rourke came into Katie's office with full-size photographs of more than twenty complete and partial footprints from the field where Fiona's body had been found. They had been made by a new pair of men's rubber boots, size 10. She sent five detective gardaí to call at every shoe-shop and men's outfitters in Cork, and before 5:00 pm they returned with a pair of Primark boots, which were exclusive to Penney's, a large low-cost department store in Patrick Street. Penney's had sold 27 pairs of this particular boot since they had gone on sale on October 12. Eleven customers could be traced through their credit or debit card records, but the remainder of the boots had been bought for cash. They were only €9.99, after all.

Katie sent her team back out to interview all eleven identifiable customers, but she had very little hope that the killer was among them. Not unless he actually *wanted* to be caught.

By 10:35 pm, the technical officers were back with information about a tire-track they had found in the muddy verge by the entrance to Meagher's Farm. It had been a dry night when Fiona's body had been arranged in the field, so there were no distinctive tracks on the asphalt that led up to the farm buildings. But the perpetrator had probably been driving without lights, and had turned into the farm gates a little too sharply, leaving a triangular impression 66mm long and 37mm wide. The tread had been checked against the database in Dublin, and it had been matched to a ContiTouring Contact CH95 all-season steel-belted radial, size 215/55R16. Among many other vehicles, this was the tire normally fitted to Mercedes-Benz E-series saloons.

The search of cottages and farmhouses in the Knocknadeenly area had so far proved fruitless, although one garda discovered an illegal still and more than 700 bottles of potcheen in a shed in Ballynoe; and another came across a borrowed CAT earth-mover hidden under bales of hay in Templemichael. The potcheen was confiscated and a low-loader was sent out to repossess the earth-mover, but no arrests were made. Katie needed all the public co-operation she could get.

She didn't get home until the early hours of Thursday morning. As she took off her coat she heard screams and shouting from the bedroom. Paul must have fallen asleep in front of the television again. She went into the kitchen and switched on the light. Sergeant looked up from his basket resentfully, and yawned.

She made herself a mug of tea and sat at the kitchen table to drink it. Her mind was too crowded to think of going to bed just yet. It had been a week now since Fiona had been abducted, and her murderer could have left Ireland the day after he laid her body out in Meagher's field. Yet somehow she felt as if he were still very close; as if he had unfinished business. It was only a feeling, nothing more, and it was probably brought on by exhaustion, and because she desperately needed to believe that she was going to find him.

At last, at 2:36 am, she drained the last dregs of her tea into the sink, switched off the light and went upstairs. Sergeant settled down in his basket with a grunt of relief.

Twenty-seven

She didn't reach Garda headquarters until 10:25 the next morning. She had set her alarm for 7:30 am but when it beeped she was deeply involved in a dream about her mother. In her dream it was a warm day in August, with blue skies and rolling Atlantic clouds, and she was sitting in the garden telling her mother that she was expecting a baby. The birds twittered, the leaves gossiped in the breeze. Her mother frowned and said, "Another baby, or the one who died?"

She sat up with a jolt. Her hair was all sweaty. She looked at the clock and she couldn't believe it was 9:07 am. Paul was still buried in the pillow beside her, snoring in a high, sinister cackle.

She dressed hurriedly, in a black coat-suit and a gray sweater, snagging her new black pantyhose with her fingernail. She managed to gulp down half a glass of orange-juice before hopping out of the house with the back of one shoe squashed awkwardly beneath her foot and a folded piece of bread-and-Flora clenched between her teeth. As she neared Cork she found that the main road was jammed with over a mile-and-a-half of traffic. The Jack Lynch Tunnel was closed by striking truck-drivers and there was a checkpoint opposite the Silver Springs Hotel, where four gardaí were flagging down every black and dark-colored Mercedes. When she eventually managed to reach the checkpoint, one of them sardonically saluted her. "Sorry about the delay, superintendent." It began to rain.

In her office, Liam and Jimmy were both waiting for her, staring out of the window.

"I'll bet you ten euros I could pot three of those crows before the rest of them flew away," said Liam.

"With respect, sir," Jimmy replied, "I'll bet you twenty euros you couldn't even hit the fucking car-park."

Katie came in and hung up her raincoat. "Never try to interfere with bad omens," she said, sharply. Jimmy looked at Liam and raised one quizzical eyebrow, but neither of them said anything.

"So, where are we, Jimmy?" she asked him, sitting down at her desk and switching on her computer. "Any more news from Dublin?"

"Nothing so far. But we've had some luck with the missing women from 1915."

He opened his notepad and read out, "A lady from Bishopstown called in to say that Mrs Betty Hickey, who disappeared from Glenville in November, 1915, was her grandmother; and a fellow from Ballyvolane reckons that Mrs Mary O'Donovan was his great-great-aunt. Both of them are quite happy to go to the hospital to have DNA samples taken. That's if we pay for the taxis."

"Well, that's something. Do we know when Fiona Kelly's parents will be arriving?"

Liam said, "They're flying into Dublin at half-past seven tomorrow morning. Don't worry – I've already made arrangements to have them met. Oh – and Professor O'Brien called you. He said that he'd call you back later."

"Oh God."

"He said he had something to tell you. Something fascinating, as it goes, but not desperately urgent."

"Thanks, Liam."

Jimmy said, "We set up all the checkpoints this morning, to stop the drivers of black and dark-colored Mercs. Well, I expect you had to go through one yourself, didn't you? Nothing so far, but we're taking all their names and addresses to check their stories later, and we've taken soil samples from their front nearside tires."

"Good. I hope our lord and master hasn't been grumbling too much about the traffic congestion."

"Of course he has. But that's his job, isn't it, grumbling?"

Katie pressed the button on her phone and asked the switchboard to put her through to Dr Reidy. While she waited, she leafed quickly through her mail, which included two invitations to give careers talks to local schools. At this moment, she had only seven words of advice for young girls: *don't be a guard, be a nun.*

Liam sat on the corner of her desk and said, "By the way, we're making progress with Dave MacSweeny's forced incarceration."

"Oh, yes?" she said, without looking up.

"The nail-gun and the compressor were stolen from that fashion shop they're doing up, opposite the Post Office. They were reported missing first thing yesterday morning, as soon as the fitters found out they were gone."

"Nobody saw or heard anything, of course?"

"We haven't found any eye-witnesses so far. But they must have taken the stuff shortly after four o'clock when the fitters finish work. It's always pretty crowded around there at that time of night, so I'm hopeful."

"Good. But don't waste too much time on it, will you? Whoever did it, and for whatever reason, I'm sure that Dave MacSweeny deserved it."

"Whatever you say. But even the Fenians were given a trial."

The phone warbled. It was Dr Reidy. Katie swiveled around

in her chair so that she could look out at the crows clustered on the car-park roof. There seemed to be even more of them today, twenty or thirty, quarreling and scabrous.

"Ah, superintendent!" Dr Reidy bellowed. He sounded as if he were walking down a long, echoing corridor. "I have only one major finding to report, apart from the bad mussel I discovered in my seafood stew last night. Next time, can you please keep your restaurant recommendations to yourself? That place had the décor of a futuristic public convenience and the food of a nineteenth-century poorhouse."

"I'm sorry about that, Dr Reidy. The last time I ate there it was really very good. You didn't get ill, I hope?"

"Not me, my dear. I can smell putrescence from a quarter of a mile away."

"So what was your other major finding?"

"Aha, well! Fiona Kelly was not sexually assaulted. Obviously the trauma to her body is so extensive that it's practically impossible for me to say if she was otherwise interfered with. But her vaginal and rectal tissues show no signs of forcible penetration, and ultraviolet shows no traces of semen in her body."

"I see. Did the perpetrator leave any other DNA evidence?"

"Not that we've managed to find yet. No foreign hairs, no foreign skin cells, no blood that didn't belong to the deceased, no saliva, no other bodily excretions. I mean, this isn't entirely surprising, considering the condition of her remains, but don't despair prematurely. We're going over her, millimeter by millimeter, and who knows, our diligence may yet be rewarded."

"But it doesn't look as if the killer's motive was sexual?"

"Hmm, very hard to tell with sex. I remember one fellow in Ballybunion who got his jollies by choking women with fresh-caught mackerel. Never penetrated them, though. Never even took his trousers off."

"All right, doctor. Thank you. By the way, it looks as if we might have found direct relatives of two of the eleven women from 1915. Sergeant O'Rourke will be making arrangements with you to have them tested."

"Ah, the wonders of modern forensic medicine! What would you poor coppers do without it? Have you come any closer to finding your monster?"

"We're making good progress, thank you. We have a sighting of Fiona Kelly near Blarney, and a vehicle description. The rest of it is probably going to be routine door-to-door stuff."

"You know something, my dear, you would have made me a wonderful housekeeper. Any time you grow weary of detecting, there's a job waiting for you, I promise."

Katie put the receiver down without saying anything else. Liam said, "Well?"

"She wasn't raped and there are no obvious signs of sexual molestation."

"Isn't that a little difficult to be certain about? Especially when your victim has been reduced to nothing more than T-bone steaks."

"She was a twenty-two-year-old girl, Liam. All her life in front of her."

"I know. I wasn't being flip. I just can't imagine what kind of a maniac could have done that to another human being."

She stood up and walked around her desk. "There may have been some sexual element in what was done to her. But Owen Reidy isn't a fool. I think we have to concentrate most of our attention on finding out what kind of ritual was being performed here."

"Maybe, in that case, you'd better give Gerard O'Brien a call back."

"Yes, maybe I should."

Liam grinned, and patted her on the shoulder. "He's very fond of you, you know, Professor O'Brien. You could do worse."

Gerard's coffee steamed up his glasses. "I think I've made something of a breakthrough," he said. "I looked up Mor-Rioghain on the internet, and I came across a link to a German site about pagan rituals in Westphalia."

"Go on," said Katie. "I don't really have very much time, I'm afraid."

They were sitting in the window of a café on Oliver Plunkett Street. Outside, it continued to rain, and the narrow pavements were jostling with shoppers.

Gerard said, "I'm sorry, yes, I'll – ah – cut to the chase. Around the cathedral town of Münster, apparently, there used to be a witch known as Morgana. She was guilty of all kinds of misdemeanors, like screaming uncontrollably at people's weddings, and boiling live cats, and biting the toes off newly-born babies. But she could be summoned to help you, if you were prepared to give her what she wanted."

"Oh, yes? And what was that?"

"You had to catch thirteen good women, one at a time, and take them to a sacred place, and skin them alive. Then you had to clean their bones of all their flesh, for Morgana to feed on, and arrange their bones around it according to a very specific pattern."

Now Gerard really had her attention. "*Pattern*? What pattern?"

"I don't know exactly. My eighteenth-century German isn't very good. But it had to be very carefully done. *Mit vorsicht.*"

And there's something else. You had to tie a rag doll to each of the victim's leg-bones – a rag doll decorated with fish-hooks and nails. Each of these dolls was supposed to contain half of each victim's soul... the good side attached to the right leg, the bad side attached to the left.

"So long as each soul was separated like that, good in this doll, evil in the other, it couldn't go to Purgatory and it had to do whatever Morgana told it to do. It couldn't use magic to reassemble itself either, because the dolls would prevent its legs being re-attached to its body."

Katie was silent for a long time, twiddling her coffee-spoon around and around between finger and thumb. Gerard O'Brien watched her cautiously, unsure of what she was going to say next.

She was beginning to feel a genuine sense of dread. This wasn't just butchery. This was deeply rooted in the Ireland of legend and mysticism – the Ireland of evil fairies and gray shadows that hurried through the rain, and white-faced mermaids who sat on the rocks and screamed and screamed until a man could go mad. This reminded her of all the terrors that she had felt as a child, when the Atlantic gales had rattled her bedroom window in the small black hours of the morning, as if all kinds of spidery skeletons were trying to get in.

After a while she put down her coffee-spoon. "Then what was supposed to happen? After you'd killed and boned thirteen women and attached these dollies?"

"Then, I suppose, Morgana would give you whatever you wanted. Money, fame, success with women."

"Are there any authenticated cases of people having actually tried to do this?"

"I wouldn't know. But the source of the legend is very respectable. It's mentioned in detail in *Hexenprozesse in*

162

Westfalen by Dr Ignatz Zingerle; and in a seventeenth-century quarto called *Wunderbarliche Geheimnussen der Zauberey*." And a fairy like Morgana is known in some form or another in almost every country in Northern Europe. Morgan, Mor-Rioghain, whatever."

"Gerard, this could be very helpful."

Gerard furiously scratched his head. "It's not a lot to go on, I know. But it's a start, isn't it? At least you know what the dollies were for. And it gives you a clue where your murderer might have come from."

"What do you mean?"

"The lace. You told me that the rag doll was made out of shreds of petticoat, edged with German lace. German legend, German lace. There must be some connection."

Katie nodded. "You could be right, Gerard. The trouble is, we need more than speculation."

"I'll keep at it." Gerard looked at his watch, and blinked. "I don't suppose you could spare the time for lunch?"

Twenty-eight

She was eating a chicken ciabatta sandwich at her desk when Liam knocked at her door. "I'm just on my way to talk to Dave MacSweeny at the Regional. Wondered if you'd care to come along?"

"I'm too busy, Liam," she said, brushing crumbs from the reports she was reading.

"I've been asking around. I think I've already got a fair idea of who nailed him to the wall."

"Oh, yes?"

"Two fellows were drinking in The Ovens Tavern on the afternoon before the nail-gun got stolen. They left the bar at a quarter to five saying that they had a little job to do, but that they'd be coming back later. They had a white Transit van parked just opposite The Ovens, and they climbed into it and drove away. But only about twenty-five yards. They stopped just opposite the Post Office, got out of the van, and opened the back doors. Nobody saw them load the compressor, so I haven't got watertight eye-witness evidence. But I'll bet you a tenner it was them."

"And who were they, these two fellows? Do we know?"

"Oh, yes. Gerry Heelan and Cors O'Leary, and we all know who *they* do little jobs for."

"Eamonn Collins, yes. Them and a score of other scumbags. But why would Eamonn Collins want to do such a thing to

Dave MacSweeny? They don't mix in the same circles; they don't operate the same kind of rackets."

"I know," said Liam. Behind his owlish glasses, his face was very serious.

"Perhaps Heelan and O'Leary did this on their own," Katie suggested.

"Oh, I doubt it. It was far too theatrical. Far too technical, too. Heelan and O'Leary would have caught MacSweeny in a side-street and bashed his head in with a brick."

"Well, I wish you luck," said Katie. She carried on reading and eating but Liam stayed where he was, leaning against the door-jamb.

Eventually, she looked up and said, "Yes? What is it?"

"You can't help hearing stories, you know. And one of those stories was that Dave MacSweeny was looking for some fellow who was messing around with his girlfriend, with intent to do this fellow some grievous bodily harm."

"Oh, yes?"

"In fact, he *did* do this fellow some grievous bodily harm, that's what I heard. Caught him in the car-park in Beasley Street and gave him a good sound bashing. Which makes me wonder if this fellow was looking for revenge, and asked Eamonn Collins to arrange it for him. Or her."

"This all sounds like hearsay and supposition to me."

"You may be right. But it's a possible motive, isn't it?"

"Dave MacSweeny has more enemies than a dog has fleas. Anybody could have taken it into their head to teach him a lesson."

"I don't know. There aren't many 'anybodies' who would dare to. Dave MacSweeny's a very vicious fellow when he's upset. That's what makes me think it was Eamonn Collins. Think about it, superintendent. Not only is Eamonn Collins the only man in Cork who would dream up something like locking him up in a cell in the City Gaol and nailing him to the wall, he's the only man in Cork who would have the nerve to teach him a lesson like that and let him live."

Katie slowly crumpled up her sandwich-wrapper and dropped it into the bin. "Let me know how you get on," she said.

That afternoon she went to see her father. When he answered the door his white hair was sticking up at the back and he looked as if he had been sleeping.

"Katie! This is unexpected. Everything's all right?"

She stepped into the hallway. She could smell mince and onions. "I just needed somebody to talk to, that's all."

"Come on in, then. Can I get you a cup of tea?"

"That's all right. I've just had lunch."

They sat together in the window-seat that overlooked the river. The sun came and went, came and went, so that sometimes they were lit up by dazzling reflected light, like actors, and other times they were plunged into shadow as if they were nothing more than memories of themselves. When the sun shone brightly, Katie's hair gleamed copper, and her skin looked almost luminous white. But it was than that she couldn't help noticing the tomato-soup stains on her father's sweater and how withered his hands were.

"Something very strange is happening," she said. "The trouble is, I don't know whether it's real or imaginary. I mean, I have the strongest feeling that Fiona Kelly's killer is very close, and that there's every chance that he might commit another murder. But I don't know why I feel like that. Maybe it's just me, feeling the strain."

"Do you have any evidence at all that he's still in Cork?"

"None whatsoever. But he must have had a motive for

replicating the murders of 1915. Either he's just a copycat killer, or else he's trying to do what the original murderer was apparently trying to do… to raise up this Mor-Rioghain's spirit out of the underworld so that he can ask her for a favor."

"That would mean that he intends to murder another twelve women, I suppose?"

"I don't know. Maybe the first eleven women still count as part of the sacrifice. They were found in the same location, after all. Maybe he thinks that he only needs to kill one more."

"Even one more would be one too many."

"Of course. But I just can't get a handle on this. We have so much forensic evidence and yet I still don't know who I'm really looking for."

Her father reached out and held her hand. His fingers were so cold that he felt as if he were already dead. "Do you know what you need to do?" he told her. "You need to forget *who* you're looking for and think about *what* you're looking for. You're not a forensic psychologist or a profiler, that's not your job. Nobody can second-guess a psychopath, in any case. Forget about hunches and feelings and bad omens. Concentrate on what you know. The facts, the evidence, the eye-witness reports."

"I only have one eye-witness and I wouldn't call him particularly reliable."

"Eye-witness reports never are. You remember that triple shooting in Togher? One man said that the gunman was short with red hair, another said that he was tall with a heavy moustache, and a third swore blind that he was a woman. But between the three of them I got enough evidence to find out who did it."

Katie said, "Fiona Kelly was last seen climbing into a dark-colored Mercedes outside The Angler's Rest on the way to Blarney. A dark-colored Mercedes with only one headlight. Only one man saw this happen – a drinker in the pub's front bar – and he'd had a fair few pints. It was a very gloomy afternoon and the rear of the vehicle was heavily coated in mud so that he couldn't see the registration plate."

"He didn't see the driver at all?"

Katie shook her head. "The car pulled in about twenty-five metres diagonally opposite the pub window, so the witness could only see a three-quarter rear view of it."

"Draw it for me."

"What?"

"Here… use the telephone pad. Show me where the pub stands, show me where the car stopped, show me where the girl was."

"What good will that do?"

"Trust me, just do it."

Katie drew a square to represent The Angler's Rest, then two lines going off at 45 degrees to the north-east, to represent the road to Blarney. Opposite The Angler's Rest she penciled a small black rectangle, which was the car, and finished off with a small stick figure, Fiona Kelly.

Her father studied it for a while, and then he said, "This is more or less accurate, yes?"

"As near as I can get it."

"So where was your witness sitting?"

"Here, at the left-hand window, with a diagonal view across the road."

"Near enough to be able to identify the make of car?"

"I would say so, yes."

"But how did he know it had only one headlight?"

"What?"

"The car would have driven past the front of the pub without your witness being able to see the front of it. And then it stopped to pick up your victim, just far enough up the road so that he could only see the rear-end of it, and very quickly drove off north-eastward. So how did he know it had only one headlight?"

"I don't know. But why would he say there was only one headlight if there wasn't? He must have been able to see it."

"Remember what they taught you at Templemore. There's no such thing as 'must have been' in any good detective's vocabulary. Either the front of the Mercedes was visible from the pub window or it wasn't, and from what you've just told me, I think it would be worth going to have another word with this eye-witness of yours. You may be wasting your time... but, I don't know. I have a feeling about it."

"And you're telling *me* not to rely on hunches?"

Although it was already growing dark, she drove out to The Angler's Rest again. There were only five people in the bar, four men and a middle-aged woman with crow-black hair and a screaming laugh, but it was warm and welcoming and there was a good strong fire burning in the grate.

Ricky Looney was sitting on his usual stool with a half-finished pint in front of him.

"Buy you a drink, Ricky?" Katie asked him.

"Beamish, if you don't mind. But I can't tell you anything more than what I told you already."

"That's all right. I just wanted to see if you could picture what happened in your mind's eye."

"*Picture it*, like? You mean draw it? I was never any good at the drawing."

"No, you don't have to draw it. All you have to do is close your eyes and try to *see* it, as if you were watching a film."

Ricky Looney looked hesitant, but when she urged him, "Go

on, give it a try," he squeezed his eyes tight shut and clenched his face into a concentrated grimace.

"You can see the girl standing by the side of the road, hitching a lift?"

He nodded vigorously.

"She's got long blonde hair, hasn't she? But what's she wearing? Jeans, perhaps."

"That's right, jeans. And a coat with like green patches on it, you know? And she's carrying a rucksack."

"That's her. Well done, Ricky. Now, can you remember which way the car drove off? Did it go off to the left, or straight on, or did it branch off right toward Blarney?"

"It goes off to the right. No doubt about it. I can see it now, in me head, clear as day."

"That's very good. Is there anything else you can see?"

"It's getting dark. It's starting to rain, like. It's hard to see anything very clear."

"You can't make out the license-plate?"

"The license-plate, no. It's much too muddy. The whole back of the car, it's thick brown with mud."

"Now, tell me about the headlights. Which one isn't working, left or right?"

"Sure I don't know. I can't see it from here."

"I don't understand. Didn't you tell me before that it had only one headlight."

"It does, yeah. But I can't see it this time. I can only see it when it comes back."

"It came *back*?"

Ricky cautiously opened his eyes. "That's right. About twenty minutes later, like."

"You're sure? You're sure it was the same car?"

"It was right outside the window there. I wouldn't have

noticed it but old Joe was pulling out of the car-park rather slow, like, and the Merc was coming down the road here and he blew his horn at him, like he was really in a hurry, you know?"

"And that's when you saw that one of the headlights was out?"

"The offside, that's right."

"You still didn't see the driver?"

"No. I'd be lying to you if I did, and I wouldn't want to lie to you just for the sake of pleasing you."

"But you're absolutely certain that it was the same car?"

"I wouldn't swear my mother's life on it, but it looked like the same car, and in any case my mother died three years ago, God rest her soul."

She drove slowly along the winding road toward Blarney. It was dark now, and the wind had risen, so that blizzards of leaves danced in front of her headlights. She turned down every side-road and entrance, following it as far as it went, looking for a muddy track with an isolated cottage or a barn at the end of it.

If Ricky Looney had been right, and the same car had driven back past The Angler's Rest only twenty minutes after Fiona had been picked up, then she couldn't have been held very far away from here. The driver would have had to reach his destination, overpower her, take her out of the car and restrain her. That wouldn't have left him more than four or five minutes to drive from The Angler's Rest to wherever he had hidden her.

One track about two miles along the road began to look promising. It twisted and turned, up and downhill, and the mud was so thick that she could hear it drumming against her wheel-arches. When she reached the end, however, she found nothing more than a dilapidated shed, heaped in ivy, with its doors and windows missing. She took her flashlight and walked around it, but there was nothing inside it except a kitchen chair, entangled with creeper. She stood still and listened. The evening was almost totally silent, except for the discontented stirring of the fallen leaves, and the surreptitious pattering of rain.

She drove back to the main road and tried the next entrance, but this led only to a large house with heavily-chained gates, which looked as if it had been closed down for the winter. She went further still, and found a narrow metalled road that led her up a steep hill and then down again. She imagined that if she followed it all the way, it would eventually connect up with the main Kanturk road, off to the west. Driving very slowly, she followed it for nearly three-quarters of a mile, while it shrank narrower and narrower, and its edges began to crumble.

Suddenly her headlights caught something tilting and wavering right in front of her. She jammed on her brakes and the Mondeo crunched into the gravel at the side of the road. She heard a hectic clattering sound, and a cry of "*shite*!", followed by silence.

She climbed out. She had almost collided with a skinny old cyclist in a brown tweed coat. He had fallen off his pushbike into the middle of the road, and he was crouched in front of her car on his hands and knees.

"Oh God, I'm so sorry," she said, helping him up. "You're not hurt, are you?"

"What do you think you're doing, *whooshing* around like that?" he asked her, more perplexed than angry. "Look at the condition of me, mud all over. You could have killed me, *whooshing* around like that."

"I'm sorry, but you'd be very much safer if you bought some lights."

"What? What would I be needing lights for? I know the way."

"Well, that's more than I do. I think I'm lost. Does this lead to the Kanturk road?"

"No."

"Where does it lead then?"

"Nowhere at all. It's a dead end. You've missed the turning for Sheehan's Nurseries, but it's been closed down for months now."

"I see. So the place is empty now, is it?"

"Sheehan's not there any more, no."

"Is *anybody* there?"

"I don't know. Maybe. I saw a car up there not five minutes ago."

"Oh, yes? What kind of car?"

"Wouldn't know that, couldn't see it proper through the hedge."

"All right, thanks. You're not hurt, are you?"

"I rolled, like. I'm a bit besmirched but I'll live."

"I'm sorry about that. Here's my card. If there's any damage to your bicycle get in touch. Or, you know, if your coat needs cleaning."

"Oh, it's only an old thing, like me."

Katie returned to her car. She carefully backed up, her transmission whinnying, and it was only then that she saw the narrow, overgrown lane that led off to the left, into total darkness.

She backed up a few feet further, and turned the car so that its headlights shone directly up the lane. She could see several fresh tire-tracks glistening. The lane wasn't used regularly – she could tell that by the way the grass and weeds had overwhelmed the verges. But it had been used quite recently, and several times.

She drove up the lane, trying to keep well to the left so that she wouldn't completely obliterate any of the existing tire-tracks. The lane was rutted and rough and full of potholes, and several times the suspension on her Mondeo gave a loud, brutish bang. At last, however, she saw the silhouette of a large tree on the horizon ahead of her, and next to the tree she could see a cottage roof, and a chimney. As she drove nearer, she could see car sidelights, too, glimmering through a hawthorn hedge.

She steered the Mondeo into the side of the lane, almost up on the bank, and stopped. She sat still for a while, watching the cottage and the car parked outside it. After three or four minutes, she saw a muted light flicker in one of the cottage windows, as if somebody were searching around inside it with a torch. She was tempted to call for back-up, but then she couldn't yet be certain that she had come across anything suspicious, and the last thing she wanted to do was waste police time.

She climbed out of the car and closed the door quietly. The cottage was right on top of the hill, and the chilly wind fluffed and blustered in her ears. She walked across the lane until she reached the entrance to the cottage grounds. The gate was open, and the car outside the cottage had been turned around, so that it was ready to be driven out. She hesitated for a moment, and then she went in, staying close to the laurel bushes on the left-hand side. Now that she was closer, she could see that the car was a Mercedes 320E.

The torchlight flickered in the window again, and then she heard the clatter of somebody knocking a chair over. She edged her way across the yard until she reached the front porch. Then she drew her gun out of its belt-holster and cocked it.

The front door of the cottage was half-open. She approached it cautiously, making sure that she wasn't silhouetted against the sky. She had almost reached it when it suddenly opened wide, and a man stepped out, carrying a torch.

"*Freeze*!" she screamed at him. "Armed Garda!"

The man said, "Jesus! You scared the fucking life out of me!" He shone the torch toward her, but Katie stepped sideways, and shouted, "*Drop the torch*! *Drop it*!"

Immediately, he dropped it, and raised his hands.

"Are you on your own?" Katie demanded.

"What does it look like? Jesus."

Katie said, "Step back." He did as he was told, and she quickly bent down and picked up the fallen torch. She shone it in his face and she recognized him at once. He was very tall, nearly six feet four, with long black dreadlocks like a headful of snakes, and his long, narrow chin was dark with stubble. His eyes were so deep-set that it looked as if he didn't have any eyes at all. He wore a long black overcoat with muddy tails, and muddy black leather riding-boots.

"Tómas Ó Conaill," she said. "I haven't seen *you* in a very long time."

"Who's that?" he asked, in a hoarse, whispery voice. "That looks like Detective Sergeant Katie Maguire."

"Detective superintendent these days. You should read the papers."

"Papers, you say? A fellow like me never has the time to read the papers. You know how hard I have to work to make ends meet."

"This your car?"

He turned his head and frowned at it in mock-surprise. "Never seen it before in my life."

Katie took two steps backward and opened the Mercedes' door. It chimed softly at her to remind her that the sidelights were still on. "The keys are still in it," she said. "You don't expect me to believe that somebody just left it here."

"It's a bit of a mystery to me, too. I was just strolling along the track here when I saw the car stood in the yard with its lights on."

Katie switched the Mercedes' main beams on. She walked around to the front of the car and saw that the offside headlight wasn't working.

"What were you doing inside the house?" she asked.

"I came into the yard and saw that the door was open. There wasn't a sign of anybody so I knocked to see if everything was all right."

"Very public-spirited of you, I'm sure. Do you want to explain where you were going?"

"I was taking a walk, that's all."

"Just taking a walk, were you? In the dark, up a track that doesn't go to anywhere at all?"

"There's no law against a fellow taking a walk, is there?"

"There's a law against stealing cars and there's a law against breaking and entering other people's property."

"I didn't take anything. I've been leading the life of a saint these days, Katie, I can swear to that."

"Detective Superintendent Maguire to you, Tómas," Katie retorted. She switched on her personal radio. "Charlie Six to Charlie Alpha. I need urgent back-up at Sheehan's Nurseries. That's about a mile-and-a-half up the *fifth* turning on the left on the Blarney road, past The Angler's Rest. I have one male suspect to bring in."

"Suspect, is it?" said Tómas Ó Conaill. "Can you kindly tell me what I'm suspected of?"

"I don't know yet, Tómas. Perhaps you can tell me."

"I haven't took nothing and I haven't laid a finger on nobody, God be my witness."

"You won't mind answering a few questions, though, will you?"

"I've got nothing to say, Katie. I'm as innocent as a new-born child."

It was almost twenty minutes before she saw Jimmy O'Rourke's headlights dipping and bouncing along the track, followed by a squad car. All the time that they were waiting, Tómas Ó Conaill talked loquaciously to Katie about where he and his family had been traveling over the past three years, all the way around Roscommon and Longford and Sligo; and how he had been making money from buying and selling horses and second-hand cars, as well as laying tarmac and mending old ladies' leaky roofs. "All good honest work these days, Katie, I can promise you that."

"Detective Superintendent Maguire."

"Oh, come on now, Katie. I'm just trying to be sociable. We've known each other long enough, haven't we?"

"Yes, ever since you cut the baby out of that poor young girl in Mayfield."

"I was acquitted of that, you'll remember."

"Nobody was brave enough to give evidence, you mean. But *I* know you did it and *you* know you did it and that's good enough for me."

"That baby was a child of the devil and if it *was* me that did it, which I can assure you it wasn't, then I would have been doing the world the greatest favor since Jesus Christ."

"Oh, yes. The spawn of Satan. A very colorful defense, I seem to remember."

"If you don't believe in Satan, Katie, then how can you say that you believe in God?"

It was then that Jimmy's car turned into the yard, followed closely by the patrol car. Quietly and quickly, as if he were trying to pass on a last piece of crucial information, Tómas

Ó Conaill said, "Let me tell you something, Katie – there are powers on this earth that most people don't even have an inkling of. There are all kinds of demons and witches just itching to be raised up. You can laugh all you like, but they're there all right, and the only thing that keeps them where they belong is people like me."

"Do you see me laughing?" asked Katie.

Twenty-nine

While Tómas Ó Conaill sat in the back of the squad car under the beefy custodianship of Garda Pat O'Malley, Katie and Jimmy O'Rourke took a look around the cottage. It smelled of damp and decay, but it had obviously been used quite recently. There was a packet of Barry's Tea in the kitchen, and a bottle of rancid orange-juice in the refrigerator, as well as a tub of Calvita processed cheese with green fur on it.

In the living-room, Katie picked up a copy of the *Evening Echo* dated three weeks ago, as well as two screwed-up Mars Bar wrappers. In the smaller bedroom, there was a single bed with pink blankets and a bronze-colored satin quilt on it. It had been neatly made-up, but when Katie lifted the blankets it was clear from the twisted wrinkles in the sheets that somebody had been sleeping in it.

"Beds," she said. "Always a feast for forensics. Hair, skin, dandruff, blood, you name it."

They went into the larger bedroom. Katie reached around the door and switched on the light and it was then that she knew at once that she had found what she was looking for. The room was papered with dull brown roses, most of them diseased with damp. An old-fashioned iron bed stood on the opposite side of the room, without mattress or blankets, so that its diamond-shaped springs were exposed. Underneath it were spread three or four thicknesses of newspaper, copies of the *Irish Examiner*, and they were soaked in dark brown blood. Beside the bed, on a cheap veneered nightstand, stood an Anglepoise reading-lamp.

Apart from the bed and the nightstand, the room was empty. But the feeling of horror it contained was overwhelming, almost deafening, like a scream so loud that the human ear couldn't hear it.

"Holy Mother of God," said Jimmy.

Katie stood and stared into the room for a long time without saying anything. She didn't want to imagine what had happened here, but she couldn't help it. She had seen Fiona's skeleton, reconstructed on Dr Reidy's autopsy table; and she had seen her flesh, and her hair, and her heaped intestines.

One of the gardaí came in and said, "Anything I can do, superintendent?"

"Yes, Kieran. I want the technical team up here right away. Apart from that I need at least ten more guards and I want the track sealed off from both directions. And floodlights. And I don't want the media to know anything. *Nothing*. Not just yet."

"Yes, superintendent."

Katie didn't venture any further into the bedroom. Apart from the fact that there was a pattern of bloody footprints on the linoleum-covered floor, which she didn't want to disturb, the smell of dried blood was like rotten lamb, and there was a chill in the air which made her feel that if she stepped inside, she would never get warm again, ever.

"What was it brought you out here?" asked Jimmy.

"Divine guidance. Apart from that, my father reminded me to think."

Katie went back outside and took a look at the car. Her breath smoked and there were blue lights flashing and radios squawking. She laid a hand on the bonnet and it was still warm, which meant that Tómas Ó Conaill had probably driven it here. Inside, she found a half-empty bag of dessert mints, a folded roadmap, an empty pint bottle of Bulmer's Cider and a box of Kleenex tissues. There were three cigarette stubs in the ashtray, Winfield, an economy brand, only €4.00 for twenty.

The seats were upholstered in camel-colored woven vinyl. The passenger seat had a curved bloodstain on it, as if somebody had been sitting in their own blood, and there were crusty drops of dried blood in the passenger foot-well.

She went to the back of the car and opened the trunk. It was thickly lined with newspapers, like the floor underneath the bed. The newspapers weren't heavily stained with blood, but there were three or four dark brown runnels, and a pattern of seven drops.

Jimmy stood beside her, smoking. He didn't say a word. After a few moments she slammed the trunk shut, and walked across to the patrol car. She climbed into the back seat, right next to Tómas Ó Conaill, and looked him steadily in the eye.

"You have a very grave look on your face, Katie," he told her, but he still had that same sly smile on his face, almost flirting with her.

"I need you to tell me where you were on Thursday afternoon last."

"Thursday? I'd have to think about that. Why?"

"You're going to need a very convincing story, that's why. I'm arresting you on suspicion of murder."

His eyes gradually narrowed. "*Murder*? What murder is this? I didn't have nothing to do with no murder."

"What's all that blood in the bedroom, then? Don't tell me you've been slaughtering a pig."

"I don't know nothing about no blood. I never even went inside the bedroom."

"You're lying to me, Tomás."

"I'm not at all, I'm telling you the God's honest truth. I found the front door open and all I did was take a look around to see if there was anything lying about that nobody had a use for. I never got as far as the bedroom and I swear had nothing to do with any murder."

"Oh, right. Just like you didn't have anything to do with cutting a pregnant girl's stomach open with a chisel? Or hitting a sixty-five-year-old man over the head with a lump hammer because you thought he was cheating you over one of your horses?"

"You should be careful what you say to me," Tómas Ó Conaill warned her. He was still smiling but his mood had turned sour, like milk in a thunderstorm. "I was walking up here totally innocent and all I did was take a look inside. I didn't take nothing and I didn't hurt nobody."

Katie said, "Tómas Ó Conaill, I am arresting you for the murder of Fiona Kelly. You are not obliged to say anything but anything you do say will be taken down in writing and used in evidence against you."

"May the rumbling coach of Dullahan draw up outside your house and may you be drenched in a basinful of blood."

Katie climbed out of the car. "Jimmy, take him back to headquarters. I'll come and talk to him when I've finished up here."

Tómas Ó Conaill leaned across the back seat and said, in the thickest of whispers, "You're a witch, Katie, and you know what we do to witches. I didn't murder nobody and you will never prove that I did."

Jimmy slammed the door on him and turned to Katie with

a shake of his head. "What a header. I just hope that we've got enough forensic to put him away."

"Who else would have killed a girl like that? He's got a smooth tongue on him when he wants to, but my God he's vicious as a mad dog."

"Don't you worry, superintendent. We've got him this time, I'd say."

Katie said, "I'll be applying for a search-warrant right away. As soon as we've got the okay, I want you to go to Ó Conaill's halting site in Tower and go through every caravan and every vehicle with a fine-tooth comb. Take Pat O'Sullivan and Mick Dockery with you, and as many guards as you think you need. Talk to Ó Conaill's family, too. Ask them where he was that Thursday afternoon when Fiona Kelly disappeared, and ask them to account for his movements on the night that her body was taken to Meagher's Farm."

"You're wishing, aren't you? They'll only tell me to go and have carnal associations with my grannie."

"I'm sure they will. But we have to try, don't we? Remember the Maguire motto."

"What's that, then?"

"Don't take shite from anyone."

"All right. But I hope you sign for my overtime."

Thirty

Dermot O'Driscoll came into her office with a sugary jam doughnut and a very satisfied smile.

"You've excelled yourself, Katie. No doubt about it. I'd like to put out a media release in time for the morning papers."

"I'd rather hold off for a while, if you don't mind, sir."

"You don't have any doubts that it's Ó Conaill, surely? You practically caught the bastard in the act."

"All the same, I'd feel happier if we waited for forensics, if that's all right with you. Fingerprints and footprints especially. Ó Conaill swears blind that all he did was sit in the car... he never drove it."

"Oh, stop! If he didn't drive it, how did he get there?"

"Walked, that's what he says."

"*Walked*?" Dermot exploded, with his mouth full of doughnut. "Well, there's nothing like a ritual murderer with a sense of humor."

"You're probably right. But if we can't find any evidence that he *did* drive the car, we're going to have to do a radical rethink, aren't we? I'm not saying for a moment that it would necessarily prove him innocent. After all, he could have had accomplices who picked Fiona Kelly up for him and drove her back to the cottage. But I don't want us to go off half-cocked."

"All right. But see what you can do to hurry those technical fellows up, will you?"

As Dermot left, loudly smacking the sugar from his hands, Detective Garda Patrick O'Sullivan came into her office. "The Merc was registered to O'Mahony's Auto Rentals, of Mallow. They rented it out ten days ago to a man called Francis Justice, who gave his address as Green Road, Mallow."

"How did he pay the deposit?"

"Cash."

"In that case, we'd better go and have talk with Mr Justice, hadn't we? Did the car rental company give you a description?"

"The girl who took the booking is on holiday in Tenerife."

"Then call her up. And talk to Inspector Ahern at Mallow. We're going to need some back-up."

It was nearly eleven o'clock before they were ready to drive to Mallow. Katie called Paul on her cellphone and she could hear laughing and music in the background. A pound to a penny he was in Counihan's, with some of his more unsavory friends.

"I was hoping to see you," he said. He sounded very drunk.

"I'm sorry, Paul. I don't know how long I'm going to be. We've made an arrest in the Meagher's Farm murder."

"You have? That's great news. Great, great. Who is it?"

"Somebody you've heard of, but I can't tell you yet."

"I'm proud of you, pet. Really proud of you. Listen, I can – I can wait up for you if you like."

"Don't bother, really. I probably won't be back until the morning."

"All right, then," he said. He sounded as disappointed as a small boy.

"What is it, Paul? Tell me what's wrong."

"Only everything, that's all. It can wait till tomorrow."

"Tell me now."

"No, love, forget it. It would take the rest of the night."

"Paul – "

"I've made a total mess of everything, that's all. I'm practically bankrupt, I've got Dave MacSweeny threatening to cut my mebs off, I've got two other villains after me for gambling debts. My only kid's dead and now I've lost you, too."

"Paul – "

He was sobbing. "I tried to make everything work out, pet. I did everything I could think of. But all I ended up doing was making everything worse."

Katie didn't know what to say to him. She still didn't trust him, and she knew that she would never love him again, not the way she used to, but she still felt responsible for him, in the same way that she always felt responsible for everybody.

"Go home, love," she told him. "Have a good night's sleep and we'll talk about it tomorrow."

Of course there was no Francis Justice at 134 Green Road, Mallow, and never had been. The street was crowded with squad cars and blue flashing lights but the poor old lady who lived at No. 134 had never heard of anybody called Francis Justice, and neither had the woman next door with the quilted dressing-gown and the curlers and the wrestler's forearms, who insisted in leaning over the fence and giving her opinion about everything.

"You couldn't catch the clap, you lot."

"Is that an invitation, love?"

They drove back to the city. Liam sat in the back of the car with Katie, his head lolling back, staring out of the window and saying nothing at all. As they were driving in past Murphy's Brewery in Blackpool, Katie said, "What do you think?"

"What do I think about what?"

"Do you think that Tómas Ó Conaill could have murdered

Fiona Kelly?"

"I don't know. You'd have to ask yourself *why*, wouldn't you? I know he's got an evil reputation; and he definitely believes in banshees and merrows and all that fanciful shite; but I don't think that he would seriously try to raise up Mor-Rianagh, do you? If he wants something, he steals it. He doesn't have to ask fucking witches for it."

"How do we know what he wants? He may want to be a billionaire, for all we know. He may want to be the next High King of Munster."

"That's true. Or he may be nothing more than an out-and-out sexual psychopath, who gets his rocks off from cutting the flesh off of living women."

"Jesus, Liam."

"I know. It's hard to get your mind round it, isn't it? But there always has to be a 'why?' Sometimes we can't believe why. Sometimes it seems so ridiculous that you have to laugh. I'll bet you don't remember that fellow from Mayfield who crushed his wife's neck in the folding legs of her ironing-board? He seriously believed that she was trying to turn him into a rat."

"I read about it, yes."

"It was ridiculous, it was psychotic, but it was still a reason. What you have to ask Tómas Ó Conaill is, why did you it? Not 'if', not 'how', but '*why*?'"

They drove across the Christy Ring Bridge. The filthy waters of the Lee glittered on either side of them like an oil-slick, and the lights from the Opera House flickered on and off. Katie said, "Listen, Liam, be honest with me. You've never resented my promotion, have you?"

"It wasn't my decision, was it? It was never up to me."

"I know. But it sounds a little like you're questioning my judgement."

"I question everything, detective superintendent. I question the going-down of the sun and the coming-up of the moon. I never believe a word that anybody says and I particularly don't believe a word that anybody in authority tells me."

"You're a good detective, Liam."

"Thank you. The feeling is mutual."

Thirty-one

She questioned Tómas Ó Conaill from 2:30 am until well after five. He remained hunched over the table, his voice rarely rising over the hoarsest of whispers, and he kept his eyes fixed on her unblinkingly, those deep-set eyes that looked as if he had no eyes.

Jimmy O'Rourke stayed with her for an hour, and then Patrick O'Sullivan came to replace him. Ó Conaill had been advised that he could call any solicitor he wanted, but he was content to have the duty solicitor, a young man called Desmond O'Keeffe with thick glasses and a crop of red spots on his forehead.

Ó Conaill smoked incessantly, until the bare, gray-painted interview room was filled with a surrealistic haze.

"Where did you get the car, Tómas?"

"I've told you twenty times, witch. I never saw the fucking car before in my life."

"The engine was still warm when you were arrested. Don't tell me you hadn't been driving it."

"I had not."

"I'll bet you money that your fingerprints are all over the steering-wheel."

"They probably are. I've told you already that I sat in it, like, to see what it felt like. But no more than that."

"You really expect us to believe that?"

"You can believe whatever you wish. I didn't murder any girl."

Katie took out a color photograph of Fiona Kelly and held it in front of his face. He didn't blink, didn't even focus on it.

"I want to know where you were on Thursday afternoon."

"I was over in Dripsey, seeing a man about some horses."

"Which man?"

"Cootie, everybody calls him. I don't know his real name."

"How did you get to Dripsey?"

"I went with my cousin Ger and my second son Tadgh. Ger drove us in his what d'ye-call-it. His Land Cruiser."

"We'll check that, of course. Where were you on Friday?"

"A whole lot of us went to Mallow to see about some felt roofing."

Katie kept the photograph of Fiona Kelly hovering in front of him. "Have you ever heard of Mor-Rioghain?"

For the first time, Tómas blinked. "Of course I have."

"Tell me, then."

"Tell you what?"

"Tell me about Mor-Rioghain. Who she is, what she can do for you."

Desmond O'Keeffe tapped his ballpen on the table. "Sorry... I don't see the relevance of this."

Katie said, "You're here to protect Mr Ó Conaill's rights, Mr O'Keeffe, not to second-guess the lines of our inquiry."

"All the same," Desmond O'Keeffe protested, flushing very red.

"I don't mind answering," said Tómas Ó Conaill. "I didn't do nothing to nobody; as the witch here very well knows. Mor-Rioghain is a *bean-sidhe*, a banshee, which means a woman of the fairy."

"You believe in the fairies?"

"I believe in Mor-Rioghain, and why not? Didn't I hear her myself the night before my poor father died, moaning and keening at the back door?"

"I thought that banshees only cried for five particular families."

"They do," he agreed, and he counted them off on his fingers. "The O'Neills, the O'Briens, the O'Connors, the O'Gradys and the Kavanaghs. But my father was an O'Grady by marriage."

"Do you believe that Mor-Rioghain can be called up out of the fairy world if you offer her a human sacrifice?"

Tómas Ó Conaill shrugged, and flicked ash into the over-crowded ashtray.

"Have you heard about the eleven women's skeletons which were found up at Knocknadeenly?"

"I have, yes. I saw it on the telly."

"One of our experts thinks that somebody may have been trying to make a sacrifice to Mor-Rioghain. If you kill thirteen women and take the flesh off their bones, so that she can feed on it, apparently Mor-Rioghain will reward you by giving you whatever you want."

"I know of that, yes."

"It looks as if our 1915 murderer was interrupted before he could give her all of the sacrifices she demands. It wouldn't have occurred to you, by any chance, that if you killed just two more women, you could call on Mor-Rioghain and ask her to make you rich? Easier than winning the Lotto."

"You shouldn't make mock of the *sidhe*, Detective Super-intendent Witch."

"I'm asking you straight out, Tómas. Did you kill Fiona Kelly?"

"The answer to that is no, I didn't. And if I was minded to

call on Mor-Rioghain, there's only one thing that I'd ask her for, and that's to make you blind and lame."

"You're all heart, Tómas."

A few minutes later, Liam knocked on the door of the interview room and beckoned Katie to come outside. "Interview suspended at 5:09 am," she said, and left Tómas Ó Conaill lighting yet another cigarette.

Liam held up a note from the technical department. "They've made a preliminary check on the car. Ó Conaill's left his dabs all over the doors, the door-handles, the steering-wheel, the gearshift, the handbrake, the radio controls, the keys, the trunk, everywhere. There's a perfect thumbprint on the rear-view mirror where he must have adjusted it to suit his driving-position."

"Anybody else's prints?"

"Fiona Kelly's, on the passenger door-handle, which backs up your witness's story that she willingly accepted a lift."

"Nobody else's?"

"One or two random prints around the filler-cap, which probably came from a garage attendant. But nothing consistent with anybody else having driven the car, apart from Ó Conaill."

"How about the bloodstains?"

"O positive. Same group as Fiona Kelly. They haven't had the DNA back yet."

"Any results from the cottage?"

"Footprints, yes. Size 10 boots the same as we found at Meagher's Farm. But fingerprints, no, and this is the odd part. They found a partial palm-print on the front door-handle, but none of Ó Conaill's fingerprints inside. Plenty of other prints, but not his. Not yet, anyway."

"None at all?"

Liam shook his head.

"Why would he take such trouble not to leave any prints in the cottage if he was going to cover the car with them? Especially since the car still had Fiona Kelly's blood in it."

"You surprised him, didn't you? He was probably intending to drive off and never go back there."

"All the same... it doesn't really add up, does it?"

"There's only one way to find out, and that's to ask him."

"What about his alibis?"

"His family all say that he went to see this Cootie fellow on Thursday and drove to Mallow on Friday. But then they would, wouldn't they? His mother looks as if she eats blocks of pre-stressed concrete for breakfast. And you should see his sister. The words 'red' and 'brick' and 'shitter' came to mind, I can tell you."

"What about their vehicles? Anything?"

"We searched the whole lot of them, seven in all. Two brand-new Jeep Cherokees, a top-of-the-range BMW, one Winnebago Chieftain and three caravans. We took the door-trim out of the cars and we even pulled up the caravan floors. Nothing at all, except twenty-eight bottles of Paddy's and some women's designer clothing that looks as if it was lifted from Brown Thomas."

"All right, thanks, Liam."

She went back into the interview room. Tómas Ó Conaill didn't even raise his eyes to look at her. She sat down and laid the forensic report on the table between them.

"I want you to tell me where you got the car from," she said.

"I've already told you, witch. I found it in the yard in front of the house. I might have touched it but touching isn't a crime, the last I heard."

"Your fingerprints were plastered all over it. Your fingerprints and nobody else's, except for the girl you murdered."

"How many times do I have to tell you that I didn't murder any girl."

"You stole the car, though, didn't you?"

Tómas Ó Conaill was silent for a very long time. Then he took out another cigarette and lit it, and blew smoke out of his nostrils like two long tusks. "I drove it," he admitted. "But I didn't steal it. I found it, and all I did was to lend a borrow of it."

"You *found* it?"

"Yes, found it."

"Do you think that I was born yesterday?"

He stared her dead in the eyes. "No, witch, I don't think you were. You may look young and you may look pretty but you have the hag's face on you."

"So where did you *find* this car, Tómas?"

"It was halfway in a ditch by the side of the road about a mile north of Curraghnalaght crossroads. Not locked, with the keys still in it."

"Parked, in other words?"

"Not parked, dumped. Obviously dumped. There was nobody for miles."

"When exactly was this?"

"Yesterday evening, around nine, I'd say."

"Why didn't you report it to the Garda?"

Tómas said nothing, but gave her an amused shake of his serpentine hair.

"So you found this car abandoned and you decided to steal it?"

"Not steal, I told you, borrow. My own car had gearbox trouble and I needed to get over to Cork for some spares."

"You were simply going to use this dumped car to drive to Coachford and then take it back?"

"That was my first intention, yes."

"All right," said Katie. "Supposing I believe this fantastical story, which I don't for a minute. What were you doing in the cottage up at Sheehan's Nurseries? It's not exactly on the way from Curraghnalaght to Cork, is it? In fact, that track doesn't go anywhere at all."

"I found a piece of paper in the glovebox and it had the name of Sheehan's Nurseries on it, and a bit of a map."

"Oh, really? Do you still have this piece of paper in your possession?"

"I don't know." He poked in his pockets, but all he could find was a packet of Rizla cigarette-papers. "No. I probably dropped it somewhere."

"Very convenient."

"I thought that if I went up to Sheehan's Nurseries, I might be able to find out who the car belonged to, and maybe there might be a reward in it for taking it back."

"Oh, I believe you, Tómas, I really do."

"You don't have any cause not to. I swear to God it's the truth."

"I don't think so. I think the truth is that you used a false name and address to rent that Mercedes, and then you used it to pick up the first innocent girl you could find. You took her up to Sheehan's Nurseries where you tied her up to the bed and you cold-bloodedly mutilated, tortured and killed her. Then you drove her poor butchered remains to Meagher's Farm and arranged them in the field, as a sacrifice to Mor-Rioghain."

Tómas Ó Conaill shook his head and kept on shaking it. "You're a witch, Detective Superintendent Witch. You're nothing better than a *bean-nighe*, you're death's own washerwoman, washing the blood out of dying people's clothing. I'm innocent of any murder and that's my final word."

Katie leaned forward and looked directly into his deep-set eyes. "I will see you locked up for this, Tómas. And long after I'm retired, and I'm sitting at home in the evening, by the fire, I want to have the warm, satisfying feeling of knowing that you're still inside the Bridewell, and that you'll stay inside until the day you breathe your very last breath."

Thirty-two

Siobhan was in such a rush to catch the bus that she forgot to pick up her fashion folder with all her preparatory sketches in it. She was halfway down Wellington Road when she realized that she had left it behind and she had to run back to the house, her big knitted bag swinging from her shoulder. She unlocked the front door and panted up the stairs to her bedsit, snatching her folder from the table, and clattering downstairs again.

By the time she reached St Luke's Cross, the bus was just leaving. She frantically waved at the driver, but he pulled away from the curb in front of the newsagent's without even seeing her, and the bus was off down Summerhill in a big black cloud of diesel smoke, leaving her behind. There was no use running after it. She was going to be late for her design class now, and Mrs Griffin would greet her with her usual sarcasm, and make a show of her in front of the rest of the students, because she was almost always late, and even if she managed to finish her project, she would still feel hot and humiliated.

One arm swinging, she started to walk at a furious pace down the long steep gradient toward Cork, past the gray Victorian spire of St Luke's Church, and the higgledy-piggledy tenement buildings that were stacked up on either side of Summerhill with their damp walled gardens and their rusting cast-iron gates. The low November sun shone into her eyes like a migraine. At this time of the morning, traffic was teeming into the city from the north side and the noise was deafening.

Siobhan had furiously-flaming hair, wavy and almost uncontrollable, which she brushed back every morning and tied with a knotted scarf. She was pretty in a pre-Raphaelite way, like her mother, and like her mother she had deathly white skin and sapphire-blue eyes and whenever she was embarrassed her cheeks caught alight.

Ever since she was a little girl she had wanted to design dresses. In nursery school she had drawn pictures of ladies in glittering ballgowns, and when she was eleven she had won an *Evening Echo* competition for the best party dress design for teenagers. Her father had always been skeptical, and told her to think about training for a "proper job," like working on the checkout at Dunnes Stores, but her mother had encouraged her and protected her and believed in her. She was old enough now to realize that her mother saw her as the girl that *she* had always wanted to be – talented, free, independent, and acknowledged – not pregnant at 17 and exhausted at 23.

She was less than halfway down Summerhill when a large white car drew into the curb beside her and the passenger window came down.

"Hallo, there! You look like you could use a lift."

Siobhan bent down and peered into the darkness of the car's interior. She could see a man's silhouette, a man with tiny dark-lensed sunglasses. There was a strong smell of leather upholstery and expensive aftershave.

"No, you're grand. I don't have far to go."

"You look as if you're in a hurry, that's all."

"It's all right, thanks."

"Suit yourself. I've got a few minutes to spare before my first appointment, that's all. I can take you anywhere you need to go."

She hesitated. She had never accepted a lift from anyone

she didn't know, but it wasn't as if this was two o'clock in the morning, with nobody else around. The pavements were crowded with walkers just like her, making their way down the hill to the city, and the roads were full of buses and cars.

"All right," she said, climbing into the passenger seat and tucking her portfolio down beside her. "I'm going to the Crawford College of Art and Design. Do you know where that is?"

"Oh, yes," said the man, and smoothly pulled out into the traffic. "I thought you might be an art student, from that colorful red coat of yours."

"I designed it myself. I'm studying fashion."

They stopped at the traffic lights at the bottom of Summerhill. The man turned to her and she could see her own white face reflected in his sunglasses. "Such extraordinary hair," he remarked. "The true Celtic fire."

"I used to hate it."

"How could you? It's like a *cohullen druith*."

Siobhan gave him an awkward smile. She didn't have the faintest idea what a *cohullen druith* was.

"It's a scarlet cap, made of feathers," said the man, as if he knew what she was thinking. "It's worn by the Irish mermaids, the merrows, to help them swim through the water. The merrows are strikingly beautiful, like you, and very promiscuous in their relations with mortal men. Not that I'm suggesting, of course – " he paused in what he was saying as he released the parking-brake and drove away from the lights.

They crossed the river and drove along Merchants' Quay. When they reached the next set of traffic lights the man said, "The merrows have to take off their caps when they come on land, and hide them. Any man who happens to find one has complete power over her, because she can't return to the sea without it."

"I think we learned something about that at school," said Siobhan. She was beginning to feel very uneasy. The man had stopped in the right-hand lane, as if he intended to double back across the river, over Patrick's Bridge, instead of straight ahead toward Sharman Crawford Street, where she wanted to go.

"I could walk from here," she told him.

"I wouldn't dream of it."

"It isn't far now, honestly."

The man turned to her and grinned, showing his teeth. "What's your name?" he asked her.

"Siobhan, why?"

"Let me tell you something, Siobhan, every journey is an adventure. When you take that first step out of your house in the morning, you never know where fate is going to take you."

"I think I can walk from here," she told him, in sudden urgency, and tugged at the door-handle. The lights changed to green and the man turned right, over the river, and up to MacCurtain Street, which would take them back eastward.

"Please, stop. I want to get out."

"Impossible, I'm afraid. This is one of those journeys that, once begun, has to continue right to the very end. No dawdling, no diversions. Keep right on to the end of the road, as the song goes."

"Really, stop, please. I want to get out."

The man ignored her. Already flustered, Siobhan began to hyperventilate. They had to stop at the pedestrian crossing just outside the Everyman Theater, and she beat on the window with her fists, trying to attract the attention of the van-driver who had drawn up next to them.

"*Help me!*" she screamed. "*Help me!*"

But the van-driver was talking on his cellphone, and he obviously thought that Siobhan was simply fooling around.

He gave her a wink and a nod of his head, and then the lights changed and they were off again, past Summerhill, past the railway station, and out along the road which ran close beside the wide glassy waters of the River Lee.

The man drove very fast, with only one hand on the wheel. Siobhan wrestled with the door-handle again, but he reached across and snatched her wrist, gripping it painfully tight. "You can't get *out*, Siobhan, so I wouldn't even attempt it. Sit back and enjoy the rollercoaster. This is an adventure, darling... much more exciting than going to college and designing coats! You can design a coat any day. A coat, for Christ's sake! But how often do you come face to face with fate?"

"*Let me out!*" she shrieked. She kicked and struggled and her cheeks were hectic with panic. "*Let me out! Let me out!*"

The man wrenched the steering-wheel first to one side and then the other. The car slewed across the road, narrowly missing an oncoming truck. There was a shrill chorus of protesting tires and a cacophony of car-horns.

"You want to die so soon?" the man demanded, and there was an extraordinary note of triumph in his voice.

"Please stop. Please let me out."

He wrenched the wheel again, and this time the car hit the nearside curb and one of its hubcaps flew off, and bounded into the bushes.

"*What do you want?*" Siobhan screamed at him. "*What do you want?*"

The man steered them deftly across the Skew Bridge – left, then right, tires howling, across the railway. "What do you think? I want everything that you can give me, my darling Siobhan, and a little bit more besides." He lifted her hand up and crushed it triumphantly between his fingers.

She took three or four shuddering breaths, like somebody

stepping waist-deep into cold water. She was trying to stay calm, trying to stay calm. Her mother had always said to her that no matter how threatening men could be, she should never lose control of herself, never get hysterical. They wanted to you to go off the edge. It gave them an excuse for raging back at you, for hitting you. Her father used to hit her mother, every Sunday morning, after Mass, with monotonous regularity, and she never heard her mother even so much as say "Don't, Tom, don't."

The man said, "I could introduce you to all kinds of pleasures… all kinds of sensations… feelings that you never could have imagined. I could give you such ecstasy, Siobhan, you'd be begging me for more. But there's so little time for that, these days. Everything's hurry, hurry, hurry, isn't it, and far too many years have rolled by already."

"I won't let you hurt me," said Siobhan, trying to be defiant.

"Excuse me, you don't have any say in the matter. If I want to hurt you, I will."

"I want you to let me out of the car."

"What? So that you can call the cops and have me collared? I don't think so, my darling. This is much too important. I need only one more life, and then I can have everything I've ever wanted. The day is nearly with us, Siobhan. The greatest day ever in romantic history. And all of the glory will be yours. Well, most of it. Some of it, anyway. A little."

They passed Tivoli Docks, with its tall triangular cranes reflected in the river, and then he turned up the long, steep hill toward Mayfield. Siobhan began to slump down in her seat, lower and lower, as if she were trying to hide.

"You mustn't be scared," the man told her. "The only thing to be scared about is to die a nonentity. And that certainly won't happen to you."

"I'm late," said Siobhan. "I'm late for my fashion class. They'll be wondering where I am."

The man released her wrist and ran his fingers deep into her wiry, coppery hair, tugging at her roots, massaging her scalp. "This is a different path, Siobhan. This is a different way to go. When you woke up this morning you thought that your life was going to be just the same as yesterday, and the day before, and the day before that. But, believe me, it isn't."

He took his fingers out of her hair and sniffed at them. "It's strange, isn't it, that redheads smell so different from the rest of us? Like foxes, I suppose."

After a while, as they approached the crossroads at Ballyvolane, he reached down and groped beneath his seat as if he had dropped something. When he sat up again, he was holding a brand-new claw-hammer, with the price-sticker still on the handle. Siobhan glimpsed something shining, but she didn't understand what he was going to do until he swung his arm back as far as he could and knocked her dead center in the middle of the forehead.

When she woke up she was naked. Her head was thumping from the hammer-blow and her vision was blurred. She didn't have any idea where she was, although it looked like an upstairs apartment, because there was a window opposite, and she could make out the fuzzy tops of fir trees, and a distant skyline, with clouds, and the sun shining behind it.

She tried to stand up, but then she realized that she was tied to the armchair that she was sitting in, her wrists and ankles tightly bound with nylon cord. She was freezing cold. The room was bare, with a green-flecked linoleum floor and an empty cast-iron fireplace, and the cream-colored wallpaper was stained with damp and peeling away from the walls.

There was a damp-rippled picture of Jesus on the opposite wall, surrounded by baby animals. He was smiling at her beatifically, with one hand raised. She licked her lips. Her mouth was dry and she could barely summon the strength to breathe in. "*Help*," she called out, in a pathetic whisper. "Help."

She slept. Several hours must have passed by because when she opened her eyes again the sky had softened to a pale nostalgic blue and the sun had hidden itself behind the right-hand side of the window-frame, so that it illuminated nothing more than the picture of Jesus. She was so stiff that she felt that if somebody were to cut her free, and she tried to stand up, her arms and legs would snap off.

Her skin looked even more white than ever, and she could see the veins in her breasts and her thighs as if they were an arterial roadmap. She had never felt so cold in her entire life.

"Mummy," she said, desperately. Then, much more quietly, "Mummy, I'm here."

Thirty-three

Katie was ready to go home when Conor Cronin from the Traveler's Support Movement knocked at her door.

"I've been expecting you," she said, slamming shut the drawers in her desk and locking them.

Conor was a man of fifty-something, with a walrus moustache and puffy, Guinness-drinker's eyes. He wore an old green raincoat and carried a wide-brimmed hat in his hands. "I'd heard from Tadgh Ó Conaill. It seems like you've arrested Tómas on a charge of murder."

"He's assisting us with our inquiries."

"Voluntarily?"

"When did Tómas Ó Conaill ever help the Garda voluntarily?"

"So he's been formally charged?"

"Yes."

Conor looked around Katie's office as if he had lost something. "Do you mind if I sit down?"

"You can, of course. I'm afraid they borrowed all my chairs for a conference. Here." She took a heap of papers from a small stool and dragged it over toward her desk. Conor sat on it and laid his hat on his knee, as if it were part of a ventriloquist's act, Conor Cronin and his Talking Hat.

"I need to know that you're respecting his rights," said Conor. "Whatever he's supposed to have done, he's not automatically guilty because he's a Traveler. I wouldn't like

205

to think that you've picked on him for racial reasons."

"Conor, you and I know Tómas Ó Conaill of old. He's a totally evil bastard and he gives Travelers a reputation that, for most of the time, they don't deserve."

"He's not a murderer, detective superintendent, until a judge and a jury have decided that he's a murderer. And there's only one power that can decide if he's truly evil, and that's – " Conor pointed to the ceiling.

Katie said, "I'm holding a press conference later today, Conor. I'm going to announce that we've arrested Tómas for the murder of Fiona Kelly, but don't worry. I'm also going to remind them of the media protocols for reporting Travelers."

"All the same, I'm very concerned for Tómas' human rights. You have a very prejudicial attitude, I'd say."

Katie tapped her pencil on the desk. "A young American girl came to Ireland on a touring holiday. Tómas Ó Conaill picked her up, tortured her, cut the flesh off her legs while she was still alive, then dismembered her body and used it make a sacrifical display in the middle of a field. I don't think you can actually blame me for having a prejudicial attitude, can you?"

Conor abruptly stood up. "We'll have to see about that. The Travelers have been persecuted ever since the days of Oliver Cromwell and I'm not having Tómas Ó Conaill made the latest object of your persecution simply because he doesn't have a fixed abode."

"And I'm not going to let him get away with this, just because he calls himself a Traveler."

Conor flared his nostrils. He said, "Good day to you, detective superintendent." Then he jammed his hat onto his head, and pushed his way past Patrick O'Donovan, who was just coming into her office with a sheaf of reports.

"What's got into him?"

"A severe case of sociological self-importance, that's all. What have you got for me there?"

"Two more relatives have come forward to say that their great-grandmothers went missing in 1915. Here you are... Kathleen Harrington and Brigid Lehane. They've both agreed to take DNA tests, too."

"That's good news. Anything else?"

"Mr and Mrs Kelly will be here at four o'clock. Fiona's parents."

"All right, I'll be here."

Katie called Paul on her cellphone as she drove home, but there was no reply. He was probably still in bed, sleeping off whatever he had been drinking last night. She called Liam Fennessy, and his phone rang and rang for nearly half-a-minute before his girlfriend Caitlin answered it. Katie had known Caitlin even longer than Liam: she had dated Katie's brother Mark until Mark had gone off to work in Dublin.

"Caitlin? It's Katie. Is Liam home?"

"He went out about twenty minutes ago. I don't know when he's coming back."

"I need to talk to him urgently but I can't raise him on his cellphone."

"It's broken."

"Oh... I see. Well, as soon as he comes home, can you ask him to contact me?"

Caitlin said nothing, but made a sharp sniffing noise, as if she were crying.

"Caitlin? Is everything all right?"

"I'm fine. Really, I'm fine."

"You don't sound fine."

Suddenly, Caitlin started to sob – a deep, grieving sob that came right from the back of her throat.

"Caitlin, what's wrong? Tell me."

"It's nothing. Time of the month, that's all."

"Listen, I've got a bit of time to spare. I'm coming round to see you."

"Please, don't. It's really nothing."

"I'm still coming."

Liam and Caitlin lived in a two-bedroomed house on a neat new housing estate just outside Douglas, a village and shopping-center off to the south-east of Cork City. Katie parked her Mondeo in the steeply-sloping front drive and walked up to the front door. She pressed the bell and heard it chime inside the house. The sky was the color of slate and the temperature was dropping fast.

She had to press the bell a second time before Caitlin opened the door. She was a thin, pretty girl, with short black hair and a pointed nose. She was wearing a headscarf and a baggy oatmeal sweater and jeans. She was also wearing sunglasses.

"What happened?" said Katie.

Caitlin shrugged in despair. She turned back into the house and Katie followed her, closing the door behind her. In the hallway, a large reproduction of a Jack Yeats painting was propped up against the telephone table, its glass cracked and its gilt frame split. In the kitchen beyond, there was a swept-up heap of broken plates and cups.

"It was all about nothing," said Caitlin, sitting down at the kitchen table. "We were talking about going on holiday, that's all. Liam said that he wanted to go fishing in Galway. I said I'd rather go to Portugal and get some sun."

"That's all right. What's wrong with that?"

Caitlin's fingers traced an invisible butterfly pattern on the varnished pine tabletop, again and again. "He said that I'd probably end up getting my way, whatever, because women always get their way, no matter how irrational they are, because they're women. And – I don't know – I told him not to be stupid and the argument just got worse and worse. He threw his phone across the room. He broke all the breakfast plates. I told him to get out and not to come back until he was calm and that was when he hit me."

She took off her sunglasses. Her left cheekbone was bruised and swollen and her left eye was almost completely closed. There was a cut above her right eyebrow and another on the bridge of her nose.

Katie sat down beside her and took hold of her hand. "I'm so sorry, Caitlin. I'm really so sorry."

Tears streamed down Caitlin's cheeks. "He never used to be like this. He was always so gentle. Like a poet, almost. Now he seems so bitter and so angry."

"Maybe he needs a rest," said Katie. "I've been pushing him very hard in the past six months. I rely on him a great deal – you know – his experience and his expertise. Maybe I've been expecting too much of him."

"You won't make trouble for him, will you?"

"It depends. He's physically assaulted you, Caitlin, and that's a criminal offence. You could press charges against him if you wanted to."

"That would finish him, though, wouldn't it? I mean, it would finish his career?"

"He's a Garda inspector, Caitlin. He's supposed to uphold the law. He has a greater responsibility than most people to behave decently."

Caitlin tugged out a Kleenex and dabbed her eyes. "What will you do?"

"I don't know yet. But I can't just turn a blind eye. I'll have to have a talk with him, when I see him."

"It was partly my fault as well. I shouldn't have told him that he was stupid. I should have realized that he was stressed."

"Come on, Caitlin, shouting is one thing. Battery is quite another."

"He seems to have so much *rage* inside him. So much resentment."

Katie gently squeezed her fingers. "How about I make us a cup of coffee?"

Thirty-four

As she drove home, she met Paul walking Sergeant along the road, about a half-a-mile from the house. It was starting to rain so she stopped and gave them a lift. Sergeant jumped around on the back seat, panting furiously from his walk, and occasionally slobbering her on the back of the neck. Paul looked hungover and distracted. He hadn't combed his hair and he was wearing his old gray jogging bottoms with the white emulsion paint on them.

"So you've caught your ritual murderer, then," he said, not looking at her.

"We're making a media announcement this afternoon at three o'clock."

"Am I allowed to know who he is?"

"As long as you don't tell anybody else."

"I see. Married all these years and you still don't trust me."

"Of course I trust you. Sergeant, for God's sake stop licking me! It's Tómas Ó Conaill."

"Tómas Ó Conaill, that psychopath. That doesn't come as much of a surprise. Has he confessed?"

"He's denying it one hundred percent. Despite the fact that I arrested him next to a Mercedes car with Fiona Kelly's blood in the boot and his own fingerprints all over it."

"Any idea what his motive was? Or did he just do it for the hell of it?"

"I don't know. Gerard O'Brien thinks that he was making a

human sacrifice – trying to raise up the spirit of Mor-Rioghain the *bean-sidhe*. Presumably he was tired of selling used cars and tarmacking driveways and wanted to get rich the easy way. By magic."

"Jesus. I didn't think that even *he* would be as mad as that."

"I don't know. We all like to think that we can get rich by magic, don't we? The Lotto, or the horses, or the football pools."

"Or selling off a million euros' worth of building materials that don't belong to us," Paul put in.

"I didn't say that."

"You would have done, if I hadn't said it first."

They said nothing as they parked outside the house and went inside. It was raining hard now, and the sitting-room was so gloomy that Katie switched on the chandelier. Sergeant went to his bowl in the kitchen and noisily lapped up water. Paul poured himself a whiskey.

"You want one?"

"God, no. It's only ten o'clock. I'm going to take a shower."

"Listen, when you called last night… I didn't mean to sound so down."

"You've got every right to be down. Life hasn't been very good you lately, has it? Even if most of your problems *have* been your own fault."

Paul sat down. "Maybe Tómas Ó Conaill isn't so mad after all."

"What do you mean?"

"Well… think of the things that we could ask this Mor-Rioghain for, if *we* could raise her up."

"Such as?"

He swilled whiskey around in the bottom of his glass, around and around, and then swallowed it. "For a start, we could ask for Seamus back."

"What?"

"That would make things better between us, wouldn't it? I mean if Seamus hadn't – "

He stopped when he saw the look on Katie's face. Without another word she left the sitting-room and went upstairs. She stripped off her jacket, took off her holster and unbuttoned her blouse. She strewed the rest of her clothes across the pink-and-white quilt, and then she went into the en-suite bathroom and turned on the shower. She stared at her face in the mirror over the washbasin and she looked like somebody in shock.

We could ask for Seamus back. Holy Mother of God, how could he have said it?

She took a deep breath and stepped into the shower cabinet. She stood for a long time with her forehead pressed against the tiles and the water coursing down the back of her neck.

We could ask for Seamus back.

She was still in the shower when Paul came rapping on the frosted glass door. "Are you all right, pet?"

"I'm fine. I'll be out in a minute."

"Listen… I didn't mean to upset you. I'm sorry. I've had things on my mind, that's all."

"I can't hear you."

He opened the shower cabinet door. "I've been having some more trouble about these building materials."

"What kind of trouble?"

"A fellow I didn't know from Adam came up to me in the pub yesterday evening and said that I had forty-eight hours and then he was going to come after me."

Katie stepped out of the shower and wrapped a pink towel around her, twisting another pink towel around her head in a turban.

"Did he mention Dave MacSweeny?"

Paul shook his head. "All he said was, 'You've got forty-eight hours, boy, and then I'm coming after you.'"

"But you took him to mean that Dave MacSweeny wants his building materials back?"

"What else do you think he was talking about? Believe me, pet, if I *could* give them back, I'd do it like a shot. But Winthrop Developments won't return them until they're fully reimbursed, and Charlie Flynn's still sunning his fat arse in Florida and how can I get *him* to pay the money back, even if he hasn't spent it, and you know what happened to my commission."

Katie didn't know what to say. Even being nailed to the wall of a cell in Cork City Gaol didn't seem to have deterred Dave MacSweeny from seeking his revenge. If she was going to protect Paul from being badly hurt, it was beginning to look as if she was going to have to admit to Dermot O'Driscoll that she knew where Charlie Flynn was, and why he was hiding, and what Paul's involvement was. In plain language, the shite was going to have to hit the fan.

At least she had arrested Tómas Ó Conaill for killing Fiona Kelly. She may have saved another girl's life, too, if Ó Conaill had been planning to make up the numbers of sacrificed women to thirteen. But that wasn't much of a consolation for losing her career.

The phone rang, and Paul picked it up. "It's for you," he said. "It's Jimmy O'Rourke."

Thirty-five

She was dressed and back at Anglesea Street in less than forty-five minutes, her hair still damp. Detective Sergeant Jimmy O'Rourke was talking to a distraught red-haired woman on the landing outside her office. "Mrs Buckley?" said Katie, holding out her hand. "My name's Detective Superintendent Katie Maguire. Why don't you come in here and sit down? Jimmy – how about a cup of coffee?"

Mrs Buckley sat down on the edge of the chair. She was a very pale, defeated-looking woman. Her wild red hair was untidily arrayed with plastic combs and she wore a cheap gray anorak from Penney's. Katie noticed her nicotine-stained forefinger and offered her a cigarette. Mrs Buckley took it and lit it and blew out clouds of smoke.

"I was going to surprise her by taking her out for her dinner," she said. "I went into the fashion department and she wasn't there. They said she never showed up in the morning and nobody knew where she was, not even her best friend. So I walked up to her flat and she wasn't there, either.

"I was walking back down when I met the fellow who lives downstairs from her. He's had heart trouble or something so he's on the unemployment. He said he saw her walking down the road in front of him at about five past nine, and a car stopped and she got into it."

"Has she ever taken days off before? Just gone off, without

telling anybody?"

"She might have done. She lives on her own now because of our family situation. But today was important. She had to finish the work for her leaving certs. That's why I was going to take her out for her dinner. I thought she might like a bit of a treat."

Jimmy O'Rourke came back, followed by a young woman garda carrying a tray with four cups of coffee. "Frank O'Leary's below, the witness. They just brought him down in a squad car. Do you want me to bring him up?"

"Yes, please." Katie pried the lids off the coffee cups and passed one to Mrs Buckley. "You want sugar? Here. Tell me about your family situation."

"I left my husband about seven months ago, the day after Paddy's Day. He was always spending all his wages on drink and I suppose I just decided that I'd had enough. I went to stay with my sister and unfortunately her husband Kieran was a little too sympathetic, I suppose. We started an affair and this went on for three or four months before my sister found out. Me and Kieran left and for three weeks we had to live in his car because none of the rest of the family would take us in. My mam still won't speak to me even now, and Kieran's family treat him like he's got the foot-and-mouth disease. Siobhan couldn't stay with us, of course, and so my sister helped her to find a little room of her own on Wellington Street."

"You don't think that your family situation could have upset Siobhan enough to want to go away for a while? Girls of that age, you know, they often get very distressed without telling anybody. Bottle up their feelings."

"We were getting along grand. Siobhan liked Kieran all right. She knew that Kieran makes me happy in spite of everything, like. And she would never have missed her college this morning without telling me."

"Do you have a picture of her?"

Mrs Buckley opened her purse and took out a photograph. "This was her nineteenth birthday party."

Katie looked at the laughing redhead holding up a glass of champagne, while Mrs Buckley anxiously bit her lips. "You will find her, won't you?

Frank O'Leary was a proud, portly, slow-spoken man with thick glasses and a bobbly green sweater.

"I saw Siobhan walking down Summerhill about maybe fifty yards in front of me, although the sun was in my eyes. I recognized her red coat and her red hair. She was almost as far as York Hill by the off-license when a big white car pulled up beside her and I could see that she was bending over and talking to the driver."

"You couldn't see the driver?"

"Not from that distance, no."

"How long did Siobhan stand beside the car talking before she got in?"

"Oh, not long at all. I didn't even have the chance to catch up to her. I was going to say hello but she suddenly opened the door and climbed in and then the car was away."

"Do you know what kind of a car it was?"

"It was big, and it was white."

"No idea of the make?"

Frank O'Leary shook his head, but said, "It could have been Japanese, you know. It had a sort of a Japanesey look to it."

"You didn't see the license-plate?"

"It didn't really occur to me to look; and the sun was dead in my eyes; so I was what you might call half-dazzled."

"Did you see which way it went?"

"Down to the bottom of Summerhill, then straight across

the lights into Brian Boru Street, but I couldn't see where it went after that."

"All right, Frank, you've been very helpful. If you can remember anything more – no matter how insignificant you think it is – please don't hesitate to call me, will you?"

Frank O'Leary finished his coffee and stood up. "I remember one more thing. The car had the Cork hurling colors on the aerial – the blood and bandages."

"That could be very useful, thank you."

When he was gone, Katie went to see Dermot O'Driscoll. Dermot was sitting at his desk, going through his in-tray.

"Paperwork," he grumbled, as Katie came in. "They won't need to bury me when I die, I'll already be six foot under in traffic statistics."

Katie closed the door. Dermot looked up. The only time that anybody closed his door was when they needed to talk about something personal, or highly confidential.

Katie said, "I don't know whether you've heard, but a girl of nineteen went missing from St Luke's this morning. A fashion student called Siobhan Buckley."

"Jimmy told me, yes. But she's only been gone for a few hours, hasn't she? It's not exactly unusual for a nineteen-year-old girl to go on the hop from college."

"Well, you're right. But I don't know… I've got an uncomfortable feeling about this one. We have an eye-witness who says that she accepted a lift from somebody in a large white car."

"What are you trying to tell me?"

"It's hard to put into words. I'm just wondering if we might postpone the media conference until we know a little more."

"What are you suggesting? Don't tell me you're having

second thoughts about Tómas Ó Conaill? Most of the press boys already know that we've got him in custody. Conor Cronin shooting his mouth off, as usual."

"All I'm trying to say is that Siobhan Buckley disappeared in very similar circumstances to Fiona Kelly and perhaps we ought to wait for a while before we make any official announcement."

Dermot had a think about that, waggling his fountain-pen between his fingers. At last he said, "You're sure in your own mind that it was Tómas Ó Conaill who murdered Fiona Kelly, aren't you?"

"I wouldn't have arrested him if I wasn't. And all of the forensic evidence we have so far supports it."

"Well, then, what are you worried about?"

"I'm just being cautious, that's all. Especially since Siobhan Buckley's mother doesn't think that she'd have taken a day off college without telling her."

"Is that her?" asked Dermot, nodding toward the photograph that Mrs Buckley had given her. Katie gave it to him and he put on his glasses to peer at it.

"My God. What do girls expect if they dress like this?"

"She wasn't wearing a sequin micro-skirt when she was picked up."

"No, but all the same…"

"Chief, I'd simply like to be sure about what happened to Siobhan Buckley before we tell the world about Tómas Ó Conaill. It could be that Ó Conaill had an accomplice, who's still at large. There could even be a ring of killers."

Dermot handed the photograph back. "I've already told the Commissioner that we've wrapped this up."

"Oh, and you don't want us to look like culchies, is that it?"

"That's nothing at all to do with it," Dermot retorted. "We have overwhelming circumstantial evidence that Tómas Ó

Conaill was involved in the murder of Fiona Kelly and that's good enough for me. Don't tell me that you don't want to see him behind bars as much as I do."

"Of course I do. But I just have this nagging feeling that we're still missing something."

Dermot tossed down his pen. "Listen, girl, I'm retiring in three-and-a-half months from now. I want to go out with the best possible record. Not only that, I want to feel that I've made a difference. Putting a major scumbag like Tómas Ó Conaill behind bars is really going to count for something. Even if he *didn't* kill Fiona Kelly – which I think he probably did – he deserves to be locked up for everything else he's done."

"Not our decision to make, sir – with respect."

"I wish to God it was. But that's enough. The media conference is going to go ahead at fifteen hundred hours, as planned, and we're going to announce to the world that we've caught and charged the man who murdered Fiona Kelly. I'll tell you what you can do, if it makes you feel any better – ask the lads at 96FM to put out a shout for this Buckley girl. She's probably hanging around the Victoria Sporting Club with the rest of the riff-raff."

"Yes, sir."

"By the way, any luck with Charlie Flynn? I've had another call from City Hall."

"I think I may have made a breakthrough, sir. Give me twenty-four hours."

"Do your best, then. I'm supposed to be making a speech at the civic reception on Saturday night… it would be very good for kudos to announce that we've cracked that one, too."

"Yes, sir."

Thirty-six

She went back to talk to Tómas Ó Conaill. When they brought him into the interview room he looked deeply tired, and he sat opposite her with his head resting in his hands, staring at the table.

"Tómas... I want to ask you two questions."

"Go away, Detective Superintendent Witch. Leave me alone."

"Tómas, I want to know if you were working by yourself, or if you had somebody else with you."

"What? What do you mean? When I was selling those trotting-ponies in Limerick, or when I was nailing down that roofing-felt in Glanmire?"

"When you abducted Fiona Kelly."

He raised his head and stared at her wearily. "I told you. I never saw her, I never abducted her, I never killed her. What do you want me to do, make a record, so that you can listen to me saying that a thousand times over?"

"We know you did it, Tómas. Why don't you just admit it? It'll make things much easier if you do."

"And what else do you want me to admit? That I killed those women in 1915, as well? That I'm one of the fairy folk, who never grows old, and never dies, and delights in abducting women and cutting them up into fillets and chops and bodices?"

"Are you?"

221

He sat back, ramming his straight black-jeaned legs underneath the table. "So what if I am? Would you like me to be?"

She picked up a plastic evidence bag and laid it flat on the table in front of him.

"What do you make of this?" she asked him.

His tiny eyes glittered at her. "What do you want me to make of it?"

"I'm simply asking you, what do you think it is?"

"A piece of lace, it looks like."

"That's right, it's a piece of lace. But where do you think it comes from?"

Tómas Ó Conaill slowly shook his head. "I wouldn't like to guess."

"What do you think you could make of it, if you twisted it around, and knotted it?"

He didn't answer for a long time, but then he slowly smiled. "A noose, to twine around your neck?"

She was hurrying downstairs to the media conference when her cellphone warbled. It was Gerard O'Brien, and he sounded excited.

"I've been doing some more research on Mor-Rioghain. A theology professor in Osnabruck has e-mailed me with some fascinating background information. Do you mind if I come round to see you?"

"It'll have to be later, Gerard, or maybe tomorrow. Keep it to yourself for the moment, but we've made an arrest. I'm on my way to announce it to the press."

"Oh, I see," said Gerard, and his disappointment was obvious. "If you've made an arrest, you won't really want to know about any of this."

"I will, of course. But not just now. Call me at five o'clock."

The media conference was packed, and when Katie stepped up to the podium there was an epileptic barrage of flashlights. She hesitated for a moment, waiting for quiet, and then she said, "Yesterday evening we arrested and charged Tómas Ó Conaill, 37, of no fixed abode, for the kidnap and subsequent murder of Fiona Kelly. A file is being prepared for the prosecutor's office. That is all we have to say at the moment, except to thank you, the media, who gave us so much support in this investigation, and the scores of gardaí who put in days of extra work in order to ensure that Fiona Kelly's killer would be brought to justice."

"Has Ó Conaill confessed to the killing?" called out Dermot Murphy.

"No, he denies it."

"What evidence do you have that it was him?"

"At the moment the evidence is still being examined by our technical bureau. But I can assure you that even our preliminary findings are enough to make us feel confident that we have the right man."

"What do you have to say about the allegation that you're using Ó Conaill as a scapegoat, simply because he's a Traveler?"

"I refute it absolutely. And I think the Traveling community themselves would take it as an insult. Ó Conaill is not your typical Traveler in any respect."

"You said before that this might have been a ritual killing. Now that you've made an arrest, do you still hold that view?"

"We're looking into a number of different motives."

"Of which ritual killing is still one?"

"Yes."

"Do you have a clearer idea of what kind of ritual this might have been?"

"I have some idea, yes."

"Would you like to share that with us?"

"Not at this time, no."

"This girl who went missing this morning – what's her name, Siobhan Buckley. Do you think there could be a link with Fiona Kelly's abduction?"

Before Katie could answer, Dermot stepped forward and said, "There's no evidence of any connection whatsoever. We're very optimistic that we'll find Siobhan Buckley safe and well. If she fails to return home within twenty-four hours we will of course be setting up a thorough search. But with Tómas Ó Conaill in custody I can reassure all the young women of Cork that it is very much safer for them to walk the city streets."

When she returned to her office, she found that the light on her telephone was flashing. She picked it up and pressed the button for the operator.

"There's someone downstairs to see you, detective super-intendent."

"I'm sorry, I'm completely tied up right now. Ask him to leave his name and telephone number, and a short note of what he wants to see me about."

"It's a woman, actually. She says it's very important. Something to do with Siobhan Buckley."

At that moment Liam came in, with a stack of technical reports. He put them down on her desk and turned to go. "Liam – " she said, holding out her hand. "Liam, I have to talk to you."

"I've got an appointment in Glanmire," he told her, and he tapped his wristwatch. "I'm running half-an-hour late as it is."

"I'll catch you later, then."

"What do you want me to do about this woman?" asked the operator, impatiently.

"Ask her if she can wait for a couple more minutes. Then I'll come down."

She picked up the technical reports and quickly thumbed through them. Most of them were fingerprint matches from the doors and steering-wheel of the stolen Mercedes, although there was also a preliminary DNA report on several blonde hairs found in the front foot-well. There was almost no doubt at all that they had belonged to Fiona Kelly.

A search of the cottage itself, though, had still failed to produce any fingerprints that matched Tómas Ó Conaill's, although blankets and bedding and cushions had been sent off for analysis, as had cups and glasses and cutlery and a bar of soap.

After she had looked through the folder, Katie went downstairs to the main reception area. Next to the cheese-plant just inside the doorway sat a dowdy middle-aged woman in a brown knitted hat and a brown coat surrounded by plastic shopping-bags. Katie started to walk across to her, but the receptionist called out, "Superintendent!" and when Katie turned around, she pointed with her ballpen toward a tall attenuated figure standing in the far corner, staring at her own reflection in the window.

Katie approached her. Her hair was ash-blonde, cut very short and slashed back with gel. She wore a long black-leather overcoat, calf-length, with its collar turned up; and black leather high-heeled boots, which made her seem even taller than she was. Katie found herself standing up very straight.

Katie said, "I'm Detective Superintendent Katie Maguire. I understand you've got some information about Siobhan Buckley."

The woman turned. She was probably about the same age as Katie, but her make-up gave her skin an extraordinary porcelain smoothness. She had angular, Marlene Dietrich features, with high cheekbones and feline eyes. She wore large rimless spectacles with purple-tinted lenses, above which her eyebrows had been plucked into immaculate arches. She was wearing a perfume that Katie couldn't place, but which had heavy notes of roses and vanilla. She could have been a fashion model, or an actress.

"Lucy Quinn," she said, in a warm American accent, and held out her hand. She was wearing black leather gloves that felt eerily soft. "I'm so glad you could spare me your time."

"I'm very busy, as you can imagine. It would help if you got to the point."

"I read about the Fiona Kelly case in *Time* magazine, and all about those eleven skeletons that were dug up. The article said that they might have been victims of some kind of ritual sacrifice – and of course – well – that aroused my interest immediately."

"I thought you had some information on Siobhan Buckley."

"I'm so sorry, I should introduce myself. I don't want you thinking that I'm one of those weird women who believes in witchcraft and writes love letters to Charlie Manson. I'm a professor in Comparative Mythologies at the University of California at Berkeley. Scandinavian and Celtic legends, those are my specialties. I've done years of research into ancient Celtic rituals, and I really think I could help you."

"Well, Lucy, I appreciate your offer, but we've already charged a man with murdering Fiona Kelly."

"What about Siobhan Buckley?"

"We don't yet have any reason to think that Siobhan Buckley's disappearance is connected to Fiona Kelly."

"Of course they're connected. Siobhan's a redhead, right, and she's a fashion student? That's what they said on the radio."

"Yes," said Katie. "But what does that have to do with it?"

"If anybody wanted to make a ritual sacrifice to Mor-Rioghain, they would have to choose thirteen women; but not just any thirteen women. They would have to be thirteen very special women."

Katie's eyes narrowed. "How do you know about Mor-Rioghain?"

"Eleven women's skeletons with their flesh scraped off? And then another girl murdered in exactly the same way, and her body left in exactly the same place? It has to be a sacrifice to Mor-Rioghain."

"You've say you've studied this?"

"I've done eight years of research on ritual sacrifice alone. The skeletons all had little dolls in the tops of their thighbones, didn't they?"

"Dolls?"

"Little raggy dolls, full of hooks and nails."

"I'm afraid I can't comment about that."

"Of course they all had dolls. You never released that to the media, did you? But I guess you must have had your reasons."

Katie said, "All right, yes, you're quite correct. They did have dolls. We didn't tell the media because we needed a way of checking the credentials of anybody who made a false confession – or anybody who pretended to know who the murderer was, or why he did it."

Lucy Quinn shook her head. "Believe me, detective superintendent, if it's credentials you want, I have a much more extensive knowledge about sacrifices to Mor-Rioghain than almost anybody. I've even published two papers on the subject – *Mystic Ritual in Rural Ireland* and *The Invisible Kingdom*."

"Listen," said Katie, "why don't you come up to my office? Would you like a cup of coffee?"

She led the way upstairs. They passed Jimmy O'Rourke in the corridor and Jimmy raised his eyebrows in appreciation. They went into Katie's office and Lucy took off her coat. Underneath she was wearing tailored black slacks and a tight black polo-neck sweater, which showed off her very full breasts. Patrick O'Donovan passed the office door and then found a reason to pass back again. Lucy sat down and crossed her legs and gave Katie a wide, generous smile.

"Tell me about these thirteen women, then," said Katie.

"Before Mor-Rioghain can take on human form and come out of the world beyond, the person who wants to raise her has to find thirteen women, each of whom has to represent one of thirteen different aspects of womanhood. He has to kill them, dismember them, and lay them out in a very specific pattern for Mor-Rioghain to feed on. He himself has to eat their hearts, to show his devotion. I presume you didn't find Fiona Kelly's heart?"

"We thought that the crows had probably taken it."

"No. Her killer would have sliced it up and eaten it raw."

"Mother of God."

"It's a ritual that goes back to druidic days, maybe even earlier. There was a recorded case in Ardfert, in County Kerry, in the seventeenth century, but until you dug these bones up, and until Fiona Kelly was murdered, the most recent sacrifices we knew about took place around Boston, in the United States, in 1911."

"Somebody tried to raise Mor-Rioghain in America?"

"A man named Jack Callwood. There's no reason why you can't raise Mor-Rioghain anyplace in the world, providing you find the right spot to do it."

"Was he caught, this Jack Callwood?"

"No. The police nearly had him once or twice, but he

disappeared without trace. He sacrificed at least thirty-one women, so he was obviously well into his third attempt to raise Mor-Rioghan."

"What happened?"

"One of his victims escaped, and raised the alarm."

"You'll have to tell me more about this. But what about the man who killed Fiona Kelly? Would he have had to start from scratch, and sacrifice another thirteen women, or would the eleven who were murdered in 1915 and 1916 count toward the total?"

"Oh, those eleven would certainly count – so long as all the sacrifices were made in the same place and according to the same strict ritual. All your killer had to do was murder Fiona Kelly and one more girl, and eat *her* heart, too, and Mor-Rioghain would appear and grant him anything he wanted. Theoretically, of course.

"The killer has to cut all of the flesh off the victim's legs, which is kind of symbolic, you know – so that she can't run away to the nether world. Then he cuts all the flesh off her arms, and the idea of this is so that friendly spirits can't pull her through to the Invisible Kingdom, either. After that, he cuts all the flesh from her face so that nobody in the afterlife will know who she was. Then he cuts her abdomen open so that she can no longer eat or drink, even in the world beyond. He removes her lungs so that she can no longer breathe; and finally her heart is stolen away from her – which represents her soul, her spiritual identity."

"You said that each of these thirteen women had to be special."

"That's right. Here, I've made a list for you." Lucy opened her black leather pocketbook and produced a folded sheet of paper. "The women have to be sacrificed in this order, so you can see that raising Mor-Rioghain isn't exactly a piece of cake."

Katie opened the paper and read the neatly-typed list. 1, A Laughing Virgin; 2, A Sad Mother of Twins; 3, A Singing Cook; 4, A Curly-Headed Prostitute; 5, A Gray-Haired Midwife; 6, A Fortune-Teller With No Children; 7, An Unrepentant Adulteress; 8, A Widow With No Teeth of Her Own; 9, A Youngest Daughter With Eyes as Green as the Sea; 10, An Only Child With Eyes as Blue as the Sky; 11, A Dancer With Hair as Black as the Night; 12, A Traveling Woman With Hair as Bright as the Sun; 13, A Seamstress With Hair as Red as Any Fire.

"One of those women who disappeared between 1915 and 1916 was a midwife; another was a prostitute; a third one worked as a cook for one of the British officers on Military Hill. I don't know about the rest, but three out of eleven…? Fiona Kelly was number 12 and she was a blonde, and she was traveling. When I heard on the radio that Siobhan Buckley was a redhead and a fashion student… well, I don't know. Perhaps I'm making a mistake, but I really don't think so."

Katie said, "I'm keeping an open mind. But all of the evidence that we have so far suggests that the man we have in custody, Tómas Ó Conaill, was the man who killed Fiona Kelly. He left his fingerprints all over the vehicle in which her body was probably driven to the farm where it was found. Not only that, he has a comprehensive knowledge of Irish mythology and he actually believes in the existence of Mor-Rioghain. There's always the possibility that he wasn't working alone, but so far we don't have any evidence that he had an accomplice."

"Do you think it might be worthwhile my talking to him?"

"I couldn't sanction that, I'm afraid. But if you can think of any questions that might give us a clearer idea of how much he knows about Mor-Rioghain… well, obviously we'd appreciate it."

"Okay, sure, I'll give it some thought. How about the place where Fiona Kelly's body was discovered? Do you think I could go take a look at it? It could give you some very valuable insights. When it comes to ritual, you know, location is always extremely meaningful."

"I'm sorry. I'm really going to need some identification if I'm going to allow you to get involved any further."

"Oh, sure." Lucy opened her black alligator purse and took out an identity card. It read University of California Berkeley, Department of Comparative Mythology, 1700 University Avenue, Berkeley, CA 94720, Lucy T. Quinn, PhD, FAIM, and carried a color photograph of Lucy in a black polo-neck sweater.

Katie handed it back. "All right. I'm taking Fiona's parents up to the crime scene tomorrow morning. If they don't object, I can't think of any reason why you shouldn't come along. I definitely want to talk to you some more about this Jack Callwood. Is nine o'clock all right for you? Meanwhile, I'd like to make a copy of this list, if I can. It could help us to verify the identity of some of the women who went missing."

"Please, keep it," said Lucy, standing up and reaching for her coat. "I'll see you tomorrow. I'm just glad that I can help. If you need to get in touch with me I'm staying at Jury's Inn."

When she had gone, Katie sat back in her chair, tapping her ballpen thoughtfully against her teeth. Lucy didn't look at all like an academic. She was so immaculately groomed, and her sexual presence was so strong that even Katie had been aware of it. But she certainly knew all about Mor-Rioghain and the rituals to raise her, and right now Katie needed all the background information she could get. She thought: *Don't be so skeptical, Maguire. Sometimes help can be heaven-sent.*

Patrick O'Donovan knocked on the door. "Who was *that*?"

he wanted to know. "I didn't know that impure thoughts could walk around on legs."

"Stunning, isn't she?" said Katie. "She's an expert in Celtic mythology and she's going to be giving us some background assistance with the Fiona Kelly case."

Jimmy O'Rourke came in, too, and was obviously disappointed that Lucy had already left. He even looked behind the door.

"Don't you start getting ideas, sergeant," said Patrick. "You're married with three children and a tankful of goldfish to look after."

Katie said, "If it's any consolation, you can check on her credentials for me. University of California Berkeley campus, Professor Lucy T. Quinn."

"Can't I just give her a body search?"

Thirty-seven

Fiona Kelly's mother and father arrived half-an-hour late. It had started to rain outside, heavily, and their Burberry raincoats sparkled. Katie crossed the reception area to meet them and Mrs Kelly spontaneously put her arms around her, and held her tight, as if they had both lost a daughter.

Mrs Kelly was blonde, and looked like a tireder and sadder version of the young girl that Katie had seen in Fiona's photograph. Mr Kelly had cropped gray hair and glasses and reminded Katie of George Bush Senior.

"I'm so sorry," said Katie. "The whole Garda station want you to know how much we sympathize." She had dressed in black, too; as had Liam.

Mrs Kelly took out a tissue and wiped her eyes. "Your sergeant told us that we wouldn't be able to see her."

"I'm afraid not. As you probably read in the newspaper reports, her injuries were extremely severe."

"This man you're holding in custody," asked Mr Kelly. "What is he, some kind of gypsy?"

"In Ireland they're officially called Travelers, but a lot of people have other names for them. Tinkers, or knackers. Tómas Ó Conaill has been living the life of a Traveler, and speaks their secret language, their cant, but most of the other Travelers stay well away from him."

Mr Kelly's lips puckered with grief. "I thought she'd be safe,

233

coming to a country like this. I've never been here before, but I've always considered that Ireland was home."

"I know, Mr Kelly, and we deeply regret it. We have very little violent crime here, compared with other countries. But drugs are on the increase, I'm sorry to say, and racketeering, and you can never predict what somebody like Tómas Ó Conaill is going to do. The trouble is he's very glib, very persuasive, like a lot of men who prey on young women. I can't tell you how sad I am that he picked on your Fiona."

"I really need to see her," said Mr Kelly. "You know... just to understand in my own mind that she's actually gone."

"That's impossible, I'm afraid."

"I know she was badly hurt. But I can accept that. My younger brother was killed in a motorcycle accident."

Katie took his right hand between both of hers. "Mr Kelly, what happened to Fiona wasn't like a motorcycle accident. You'd be much better off remembering her the way she was when she last said goodbye to you. Please, trust me on that."

"Patrick..." said his wife, and took hold of his other hand. "Leave it, Patrick. Let her be."

Mr Kelly's shoulders began to shake, and he burst into uncontrollable sobbing. There was nothing that Katie could do but stand beside him while he let all of his agony out.

It was well past midnight when the door opened and the man came back in again. It was almost completely dark, and all that Siobhan could see of him was his silhouette against the curtains. She was shuddering with cold, and about an hour ago she had been unable to stop herself from wetting the foam-rubber seat of her chair.

She said nothing as he walked up to her and stood close beside her. He sniffed twice and took out a handkerchief and blew his nose. "I suppose you're getting hungry," he said, and sniffed again.

"Please let me go," she whispered.

"I can't do that. Not yet. I can't have my merrow swimming back to the sea, now, can I?"

Without warning, he switched on the standard-lamp beside her chair. The light was very bright, 150 watts, and she had to turn her head away. Even so, she was left with a bright green retinal after-image, a ghost of her tormentor which swam in front of her no matter where she looked.

"You've peed yourself," he remarked, without compassion. "Well that, my little merrow, is about as close as you'll ever get back to the briny."

"Please," she begged him. "My mam's going to be so worried about me."

"That's what mothers are for. They're never happy unless they're anxious."

He reached into the inside pocket of his black coat and produced a pair of wallpapering scissors, with blades almost ten inches long. He snipped them a few times, like the long red-legged scissorman in *Struwwelpeter*, and gave her a smile which made her shiver even more, because it was so benign.

"I told you what a man has to do stop his merrow going back to the sea. He has to take her bright red feathery cap, her *cohullen druith*. And that's exactly what I'm going to do to you."

He stepped closer, and gripped her hair. She jerked her head wildly from side to side and tried to wrench herself out of the chair, but he pulled her hair viciously hard by the roots and said, "If you don't keep still, you little bitch, I may change my mind and snip your nipples off instead. It is a matter of total indifference to me."

Siobhan let out a moan of fear, and stopped struggling.

"That's better," he said, and he was so close that she could feel him breathing on her forehead. "There's nothing like a little co-operation, is there? A little co-operation makes the world a very much happier place."

He took hold of the front of her hair, and cut into it with a crunch. She closed her eyes, and hot tears began to pour down her cheeks. She was so terrified now that she was unable to speak – unable even to sob.

The man cut off more and more of her thick red hair, cropping it as close to the scalp as he could. Siobhan could feel it dropping onto her shoulders and onto her breasts. When he came round to cutting the back, she obediently bent her head forward and he cut it so close that the cold scissor-blades were nicking her ears.

When he had finished he gathered up her fallen hair, brushing it off her stomach and her thighs, and he triumphantly lifted it up in front of her. "There... no more swimming away for *you* for a while, my darling merrow. Now you'll have to stay here with me."

He took a rubber band out of his pocket and twisted it around her hair to keep it together. "What a *cohullen druith* this is... what a souvenir of youth and beauty and the strange love between mermaids and men."

Without warning, he tugged down the zipper of his pants and took out his penis, which was already half-erect. He trailed Siobhan's hair across it, from side to side, and gradually it rose harder and harder. Siobhan tried to turn her head away, but there was something so mesmerizing about what he was doing that she kept having to look back at him.

"Do you know what this feels like? It feels like being caressed by animals. It feels like being stroked by a woman who isn't even human."

236

He drew her hair one way, and then the other, and the gaping head of his penis grew a darker and angrier purple. At first he stroked it quite gently, but as he grew increasingly aroused, he began to whip at himself harder and harder. Soon he was lashing at himself in a controlled frenzy, his mouth clenched, his chest heaving, his whole body tense.

Suddenly he cried out, "*Ahh*!" and a thick white jet of sperm jumped out. Siobhan felt it loop against the side of her neck, while one drop of it dangled from her earlobe in a glutinous parody of a pearl earring. The man gave himself two or three luxurious squeezes, his eyes closed, and then he pushed his dwindling penis back into his trousers and zipped them up.

"Do you know much you excite me?" the man breathed, opening his eyes, and giving her that same benign smile. "We're so *close* now... so very, very close. You're going to change my life, Siobhan. You're going to give me pleasure beyond anything that you can think of."

Siobhan looked dully away. It wasn't his abuse that had degraded her, it was the cutting of her hair. She felt as if she wasn't Siobhan any more, as if she were nothing but a scarecrow. A tear ran out of her right eye and dripped onto her forearm. That, and the man's semen, were the only warm things that she had felt all day.

Thirty-eight

That evening, Katie made a point of cooking them a proper meal. She sliced potatoes and mushrooms and onions and interleaved them in a casserole dish with fresh marjoram, before adding pork chops and chicken stock and putting them into the oven.

Paul, watching television and playing with Sergeant's ears, said, "That smells good, pet. I'm starving."

"Sorry. It won't be ready till eight."

She sat down next to him and looked at him for a while without saying anything. His cheekbones were still covered with rainbow-colored bruises, and his split lip had a black crusty scab, but the swellings around his eyes had gone down.

"What are you going to do, Paul?" she asked him.

"What am I going to do about what?"

"Dave MacSweeny and his building materials, of course. I'm really worried that something's going to happen to you."

He poured himself another whiskey. "Can't you give me some Garda protection?" he asked, wryly.

"Seriously, I wish I could. But if I asked for police protection I'd have to explain why."

"You're a guard. Why can't *you* protect me?"

"I've been trying to, believe me. But I can't watch you twenty-four hours of the day, can I? And there's no knowing what Dave MacSweeny will do next."

"What are you suggesting, then? That I do a Charlie Flynn and run off to Florida?"

"You could get out of Cork for a while."

"What good would that do? I couldn't stay away for ever, and what would I do for money? Anyway, I'm a Corkman. I was born here and brought up here and this is my home, and I'm not going to be frightened away by some waste of space like Dave MacSweeny. I'll think of something. Something will turn up."

"Something like what?"

"I was talking to Ricky Deasy today. He wants me to invest in a housing project out near Carrigaline."

"How can you afford to invest in a housing project when you have to raise six hundred and fifty thousand euros to pay back Winthrop Developments?"

"I can't. But the land that Ricky Deasy wants to build on doesn't have planning permission, not at the moment."

"That doesn't sound like much of an investment to me."

"No – but it's going dirt-cheap as agricultural land and there could be a hefty EU subsidy for anyone who takes it on to farm it."

"You've lost me, Paul. You're thinking of taking up *farming*?"

"Of course not. But Ricky's uncle is the deputy chairman of An Bórd Pleanála and once we've bought the land we could see about fixing a change of use. You know, a little sweetener for Jimmy's uncle and a couple of the other board members."

"Paul, you're desperate! You're just digging yourself in deeper and deeper!"

He put down his drink and took hold of her hand. "I have to do something big, Katie. I have to do something dramatic. Otherwise I'm *never* going to get myself out of this mess, ever; and I'm going to have to spend the rest of my life watching my back for Dave MacSweeny."

Katie reached up and stroked his bruised and swollen cheek. "Tell me a joke," she said.

"What?"

"Tell me a joke, the way you used to, when we first went out together."

"I'm fighting for my very life here, Katie. This isn't any time to be telling jokes."

"I know. But just for me."

He looked into her eyes as if he were looking for evidence that she wasn't mocking him. Then he said, "There was this Kerryman who spent an hour staring at a carton of orange-juice because it said 'concentrate'."

Katie gave him the faintest of smiles and kissed him. He still smelled the same as always, too much Boss aftershave. But it was strangely reassuring, as if the past hadn't completely disappeared; as if yesterday were still lying in the chest-of-drawers upstairs, sleeping in the tissue-paper that Seamus' baby-clothes were wrapped in.

Thirty-nine

When she came into her office at 8:35 the next morning, Dermot O'Driscoll was waiting for her, along with a thin, serious-faced man in a dark business suit. Even Dermot looked tidier than usual: he had crammed his shirt-tails into his waistband and even made an attempt to straighten his livid green necktie.

"Katie, this is Patrick Goggin from the Department of Foreign Affairs in Dublin."

Katie held out her hand and Patrick Goggin gave her a soft, recessive handshake.

Dermot said, "Apparently we're having some trouble with your friend Jack Devitt about these disappearances in 1915."

"I never said that Jack Devitt was any friend of mine."

"Figure of speech. Jack Devitt's demanding that the British Ministry of Defence produces documentary evidence to show what happened to those women. Whether they were murdered on official orders, you see, or whether it was a renegade officer who took them, or whether it was just some fellow who was masquerading as a member of the Crown Forces. The trouble is, Devitt's got official backing from Sinn Féin. Here in Cork, and in the Dáil, too. We could have a very embarrassing political situation here, unless we clear this up quick."

Patrick Goggin had a scrawny throat in which his Adam's-apple rose and fell as he spoke, as if he was trying to regurgitate something unpleasant that he had eaten for breakfast. "Do you yet have any idea at all who might have abducted those women? Even an informed guess will do. There's another summit meeting at Stormont next week and the last thing we need is Sinn Féin making an issue out of something that happened more than eighty years ago."

Katie shook her head. "I'm afraid we haven't made much progress. I'm working closely with Dr Reidy, the State Pathologist, and also with an expert in Celtic mythology, Dr Gerard O'Brien. But, you know, these things take time."

"Haven't you even got a theory about it? If the Crown Forces really did order those women to be abducted and murdered, it's going to cause all manner of ructions. The Taoiseach is going to have to ask for an apology from the British government, and some form of compensation for their families, and the whole peace process is going to be knocked back months, or even years. Or even *decades*, for the love of God."

Katie said, "I'm sorry, Mr Goggin, but this is a very complex criminal investigation and I can't cut any corners for the sake of politics. I don't know who murdered those women and the chances are that I never will. As for the latest murder, we have a suspect in custody on the basis of very strong forensic evidence, and that's all I can tell you."

Patrick Goggin rubbed his forehead with his fingertips, as if he had a headache. "I don't think you quite understand the position, detective superintendent. We have to know for certain who murdered those women in 1915; and if it *was* a British soldier, acting on official orders, we have to find a way – well, let me put this the only way I can – we have to find a way of showing that it *wasn't*. A rogue officer, we can deal with that, politically. A psychopath who dressed up in British Army uniform, that would be even better. I'm sure that I can count on you to come up with some kind of evidence that will exonerate the British Army of any direct culpability."

Katie said, coldly, "Evidence is evidence, sir. Facts are facts. If the British Army murdered those women deliberately, then I'm certainly not going to pretend that they didn't."

Dermot lifted his hand and said, "Katie – "

But Katie said, "No, sir. I need to know what happened to those eleven women because it has a direct relevance to the Fiona Kelly murder case. They may have died eighty years ago, but they still deserve our respect, and our conscientious efforts to find out how they really died. They were women, sir. They were living, breathing women."

"Holy Mother of Jesus," said Patrick Goggin. "Now we have feminist solidarity rearing its ugly head. An Garda Síochána is the guardian of the nation's interests, detective superintendent, not the front line of the PC brigade."

"With all respect, sir – " Katie began, but Dermot, behind Patrick Goggin's back, shook his head and mouthed the word "*No.*" She knew what he was telling her. It wasn't worth it. Politicians come and go, but police personnel stay on for years and years – hopefully to collect their pensions, and cook their favorite recipes in peace.

"Yes?" said Patrick Goggin. "You were saying?"

"I was simply saying that we'll do everything we can to find out who abducted those women, sir, and how they died. And when we have... we'll let you know. Of course. And as soon as we possibly can."

Patrick Goggin smiled. "That's what I wanted to hear. That's *exactly* what I wanted to hear." He took out his wallet and produced a card. "There," he said. "That's my private number. If you want to discuss this case any further, or any other Garda business... well – " and here he raised one eyebrow and gave her an extraordinary cherubic smile " – you will let me know, won't you?"

He shook Katie's hand and gave Dermot a mock Garda salute. Then he left Katie's office and walked along the corridor with squeaking rubber shoes.

He hadn't reached the top of the stairs before Dermot burst into an explosion of laughter, and Katie shook her head in amazement.

"He *fancies* you!" said Dermot. "After all that, he only fecking fancies you!"

It was teeming with a fine, chilly rain when they arrived at Meagher's Farm at Knocknadeenly. Mr and Mrs Kelly climbed out of the back of the car and stood looking around at the drab farm buildings and the churned-up mud and the naked poplar trees as if they couldn't believe that anywhere so dreary could exist outside a movie set.

"Jesus," said Mr Kelly. "What a place to die."

"Actually, Fiona didn't die here," said Katie, gently. She opened a large golf umbrella so that she and Mrs Kelly could shelter under it. "She was killed quite a few miles away, and her remains were brought here for a very special reason. We're fairly convinced that it was part of a pagan ritual."

"Jesus," Mr Kelly repeated. He seemed overwhelmed.

Lucy Quinn had been waiting in the front passenger seat for a while, her eyes concealed behind her purple-lensed spectacles, but at last she decided to get out. She was wearing a black raincoat, a black cashmere scarf and long black leather boots. Her bright red lipstick was the only spot of color in the whole gray morning, like the little girl's coat in *Schindler's List*.

"I want to thank you for allowing me to bring Professor Quinn along," Katie told the Kellys.

244

"Not at all," said Mr Kelly. He took out his handkerchief and blew his nose. "Anybody who can help... you know."

At that moment, John Meagher came out of the farmhouse, wearing a tweed cap and a tweed jacket with the collar turned up against the rain. He came up to Mr and Mrs Kelly and shook their hands in silence.

Katie said, "John – this is Professor Lucy Quinn from UC Berkeley. She's something of an expert in ancient rituals."

"You know what happened here?" John asked.

"Yes, " said Lucy. "What can I say? It's a tragedy."

John looked tired and he sounded as if he were going down with a very bad cold. "This is the last thing I need. I've had a hell of a year and now this. I tried to sell three milk-cows yesterday and nobody wanted to touch them. The local farmers seem to think I'm in league with Satan. They practically cross themselves whenever I walk into the pub."

"Do you mind if I see the place where you discovered the first eleven women?" asked Lucy.

Katie turned to Mr and Mrs Kelly. "You can wait here for a while if you want to. Then we'll walk to the place where they found Fiona."

Both Mr and Mrs Kelly were in tears. "That's all right. You do whatever you have to do."

Katie followed John and Lucy to the back of the farmhouse, where the feedstore had already been completely demolished, and brick foundations laid. Lucy circled around the foundations for a while, stepping long-legged over the rubble, and then she stopped, and frowned, and looked left and right, as if she could sense a disturbance in the air. In the distance, a flock of hooded crows rose over the trees, not cawing, but circling, and eventually settling back on the branches.

"This is where the bones were found? All mixed up?"

245

"That's right."

"I doubt if this was where their bodies were originally laid out, after they were killed. I would guess that their bodies were originally spread out in the same place where Fiona Kelly was found. When the birds and the animals had eaten their flesh, their bones were buried here to conceal the evidence."

They trudged up the deeply-furrowed field, with the Kellys close behind them, to look at the place where John had discovered Fiona's remains. The drizzle was so intense that they could barely see the farmhouse, or Iollan's Wood behind them.

"I think we could observe a minute's silence here," Katie suggested; and the four of them stood in the field with the rain sifting down, and remembered Fiona, and all children who die before their parents. Katie crossed herself.

Lucy said, "From a mythological point of view, this spot is very important. Every doorway to the Invisible Kingdom is hidden beneath a copse, or a small wood. This is because the roots of the trees wriggle deep into the ground and the branches reach high into the sky, so that they form a natural connection between the real world and the world of the fairies."

"They call this Iollan's Wood," said Katie.

"Well, yes, that fits in. Iollan was one of the greatest of the Fianna, the ancient warriors who could visit the Invisible Kingdom whenever they wanted to. Iollan even had a fairy mistress, called Fair Breast, and a very jealous mistress she was, too."

"I hate to put a damper on this," Mr Kelly interrupted, "but my daughter died here. I don't think I really want to hear about fairies."

Lucy took off her sunglasses. "When the Irish speak of 'fairies', Mr Kelly, most people think of cheerful little leprechauns out of *Finian's Rainbow*. But Irish fairies are something different altogether. They strangle babies in the middle of the night. They can turn men into dogs. They'll dance in the road in front of you when you're driving, so that you don't see that bridge parapet or that oncoming truck, and when you do, it's far too late."

"My daughter was killed by a psychopath, Professor Quinn, not a fairy."

"Are you a religious man, Mr Kelly?" Lucy asked him.

"Yes, I am."

"Do you believe in God the Father, God the Son and God the Holy Ghost?"

"Yes, I do."

"So you subscribe to the idea that there's another world, beyond this one?"

"Yes, in that sense, I guess I do."

Lucy walked around him, and in an unexpectedly intimate gesture, began to rub his shoulders. "You need to relax more, Mr Kelly. You should open your mind to other realities. If you believe in heaven and hell, why can't you believe in the Invisible Kingdom?"

Mrs Kelly looked anxious, and took hold of her husband's hand.

Lucy said, "The answer to your daughter's death lies right here. She was sacrificed to the witch Mor-Rioghain by somebody who thought that they could summon the witch from the land of the fairies and ask her for anything their heart desired. Somebody who truly believed that it was possible."

"Whoever it was – they must have been out of their mind."

"Do you think you're out of your mind, because you get down on your knees every Sunday and pray to a Divine Being that you've never heard, and never seen, and for whose existence you have absolutely no proof whatsoever?"

Mr Kelly pulled Lucy's hands away from his shoulders. "I

247

came here to mourn my daughter, Professor Quinn. I didn't expect to have a lecture on comparative mythology."

"I'm sorry," said Lucy. "I'm really sorry. I just thought that I could help you to understand why your daughter died. It wasn't a meaningless act of sadism. It was done for a purpose, no matter how cruel and inexplicable that purpose might seem."

"I think you could leave us alone for a while, if you don't mind."

"Of course. I'm really sorry."

Mr Kelly turned away. Katie took Lucy's arm and led her back down the field, leaving Mr and Mrs Kelly standing in the rain on the angled, plowed ridge where Fiona's body had been discovered. As they neared the farmyard, Lucy said, "I hope I didn't upset them too much. I only wanted them to understand that Fiona didn't die for no reason at all."

"I don't think they're very receptive to ancient Celtic rituals at the moment," said Katie.

Inside the farmhouse, John Meagher was waiting for them. "Can I offer you a cup of tea?" he asked them. "My mother's baked some fresh scones if you're hungry."

He took their raincoats and hung them up on pegs in the hallway. In the kitchen, Katie could hear his mother coughing and clattering plates. They went through to the living-room where a turf fire was sullenly smoldering in the grate. "Please, sit down."

Katie sat on the sofa and John sat quite close to her. She could smell peaty soil and aftershave on his sweater. Lucy sat close to the fire, holding her hands out and rubbing them briskly. "I never knew that there was anyplace so *cold*, and so *damp*."

"You came to Ireland specifically to look into these murders?" John asked her.

"Oh, yes. My head of department was really enthusiastic when I told him about it, and the university has given me very generous expenses. You don't very often get the chance to investigate a ritual sacrifice in the flesh, if you know what I mean. Most of the time you're dealing with illegible medieval inscriptions or crumbling old sixteenth-century documents. This is totally different. This is living, breathing mythology."

John turned to Katie and said, "I saw you on television this afternoon. You've made an arrest."

"That's right. The evidence is pretty convincing all right."

"So I'm not a suspect any longer?"

Katie laughed. "Did I ever say you were?"

"It's your job, isn't it, to suspect everybody?"

"I never suspected *you*."

"Why not? It's my farm, isn't it? Who else would have found it easier to lay that poor girl's body out in the field like that?"

She looked at him very hard. He needed a haircut and a shave. His black hair was curling over his collar and the stubble on his chin was like coal-dust. His chocolate-brown eyes seemed to be telling her things, telling her secrets. She willed him to look away but he wouldn't look away and in the end Lucy said, "Well..." as if she had interrupted a deeply intimate moment.

Katie said, "We're still waiting for the results of some of our forensic tests, but I'm ninety-nine percent certain that we've got the right man."

Mr and Mrs Kelly came into the farmhouse and John cleared a heap of newspapers off the sofa for them. His mother came coughing out of the kitchen with a tea-tray and platefuls of scones and slices of rich fruit brack. Mrs Kelly said, "I wish you'd known Fiona. She was such an interesting girl. So romantic, so *adventurous*. She was never afraid of anything."

Mr Kelly said, "This Tómas Ó Conaill character… does he have any kind of record?"

"I'm afraid yes. We've only ever managed to have him convicted for theft and intimidation, but he's extremely violent. He almost killed a girl last year and it wouldn't surprise me at all if he was responsible for a few other murders that we don't even know about. He's a Traveler, you see, and it's extremely difficult to get other Travelers to give evidence against him, even though most of them detest him. There's also the problem of correct identification. We know him as Tómas but his real name might not be. Even the Traveler children call themselves by all kinds of different names. It's a defense system."

"But you seriously think Tómas Ó Conaill killed Fiona because he believes in this – witch?"

Katie nodded. "That's why experts like Professor Quinn can be so useful to us. They can give us an insight into what his motive was. Otherwise, her death looks completely inexplicable."

"How long before he goes on trial?"

"Not for months yet. We still have to finish our investigation and send a file to the prosecutor's office. But I'll keep in touch with you, and let you know when he's going to go to court. In my experience it's a very important part of the grieving process, seeing a murderer convicted for what he did."

Mr Kelly said, "I want to thank you for what you're doing. I'm sorry if I lost my temper back there. You've been very understanding, both of you."

Katie took hold of his hand. "I'm going to make sure that Ó Conaill is punished for what he did to your daughter, Mr Kelly. I'm not just determined, I'm passionate about it."

They talked for a little while longer. They finished their tea, but the scones remained untouched. As they left the farmhouse, John came up to Katie and said, "Do you think we could talk?

I don't mean now, but maybe tomorrow or the day after."

"What is it?" she asked him.

"Nothing special. It's just that – well, I think I need somebody to talk to."

She hesitated for a moment. The rain fell softly between them, as if they were being draped in fine wet veils. "All right," she said at last. "I'll be at home tomorrow lunchtime, in Cobh. Look, here's my address. Call me before you come. It'll only be leek-and-potato soup and soda bread, if you don't mind that."

"Thanks. I don't mean to be a pain the rear end, but – "

"Everybody needs somebody to talk to, once in a while," she told him, and walked back to join Lucy Quinn and the Kellys by the car.

Forty

Katie dropped Mr and Mrs Kelly off at the Country Club Hotel, a sprawling custard-yellow collection of buildings on the high cliffs that overlooked the river.

"I'll send a car for you tomorrow morning," she told them. "You can come into my office and I'll be able to show you exactly how much progress we've been able to make."

"Thank you again for everything," said Mr Kelly. His voice was harsh with grief. Katie was tempted to tell him that she knew how agonizing it was to lose your only child, but she decided that it wouldn't help. The Kellys had enough pain to deal with, without having to feel sorry for *her*, too.

"You want me to run you back to your hotel?" she asked Lucy.

"I was hoping we could maybe have a drink. There's one or two things I wouldn't mind discussing with you."

"All right. But I can't be very long."

She drove up the steep slope of Military Hill until they reached the Ambassador Hotel. It was a fine Victorian building in pale orange brick, with cast-iron pillars and arches, overlooking the higgledy-piggledy nineteenth-century houses that clustered on the hills of north Cork, with all their hundreds and hundreds of chimney-pots.

"Some building," said Lucy, as she climbed out of the car.

"This used to be a British Army hospital," Katie explained.

"And these streets around here – this is where they filmed a lot of *Angela's Ashes*. Apparently they thought that Cork looked more like Limerick than Limerick."

"Sounds like indisputable Irish logic to me."

They went inside the hushed, deeply-carpeted bar. Lucy ordered a vodka-tonic while Katie kept to a sparkling Ballygowan water. They sat together on one of the floral couches. Lucy tried to wipe some of the mud off her boots with a paper coaster. "I should have invested in a pair of rubbers, shouldn't I?"

"You've seen the murder scene, anyway," said Katie. "Are you convinced now that Tómas Ó Conaill was trying to raise Mor-Rioghain?"

"Absolutely. One hundred percent. That locale has everything that the sacrificial ritual requires."

"God, it's such a sad waste of life."

"Not if you believe in Mor-Rioghain it isn't."

"*You* don't believe in her?"

"Who knows? There are so many powers in this world that we don't understand. So many unexplained mysteries."

"I just want to solve this one."

Lucy crossed her long, long legs and leaned closer. Her teeth were almost perfect and there was a small beauty spot on her left cheekbone. "This really means a whole lot to you, this case, doesn't it? Not just Fiona Kelly. The other women, too."

"Yes. They were all killed and forgotten and they never even got a Christian burial. Even when a murderer's dead I don't think that he should be allowed to get away with it."

"I didn't realize – "

"What?"

Lucy's eyes were very bright. "I've never met anybody so passionate about anything before, that's all."

Katie didn't know what to say. She had never met anybody

like Lucy before – a woman who seemed to be so friendly and open, and yet who gave her the feeling that she was hiding the Lucy that she really was, and hiding her very deeply. All the same, she found her easy to be with, and she enjoyed her sexiness. Jimmy the barman had walked past their couch more than half-a-dozen times since they had first sat down, and given them a wink.

Katie's cellphone warbled. "Detective Superintendent Maguire."

"Katie! Thank Christ! It's Paul! I'm glad I caught you, pet! Listen, my car won't start and I'm supposed to be having a lunch meeting at South's in twenty minutes with the fellow from the bank, regarding this building development. I called for a hackney but they can't get here in less than half-an-hour. I was wondering…"

Katie looked at her watch. "You want a lift? All right. I just have to run Professor Quinn back to Jury's Inn."

Lucy said, "Is everything okay?"

"It is, of course. My husband's car won't start so I'll have to drive out to Cobh and pick him up. Perhaps we can have that drink later."

"I could come with you. We can talk on the way."

"If you really don't mind – "

"Of course I don't mind. I'm a stranger in a strange land, and I could use some company, apart from anything else."

They drove eastward on the wide dual carriageway toward Cobh, the windshield wipers intermittently clearing away the misty rain.

Lucy said, "If I'm really excited about this case, I hope you don't think that I'm being ghoulish. This is only the second time I've come across a contemporary ritual sacrifice."

"What was the first?"

"The first?"

"The first ritual sacrifice. Before this one."

"That – oh, *that*. A farmer in Minnesota sacrificed his whole family to the Wendigo. That's a kind of weird creature that's supposed to live in the woods. It's similar to the Irish banshee because it only appears when people are about to die."

"What did the farmer do?"

"You really want to know? He threw his wife and their three children one by one into the grinding machine that he used for pig-food. Alive. The coroner reckoned that they were still conscious even when they were minced right up to their waist. His defense tried to plead insanity but I was brought in as an expert witness, and I showed that everything that he had done was in strict accordance with Native American stories about the Wendigo. You're insane when you kill people for no reason whatsoever. But you're not insane if you're scrupulously observing some specific mythological ritual with the express intention of gaining some advantage out of it. In this case, the farmer was almost bankrupt and he believed that the Wendigo would kill his creditors for him. Wacky? For sure. Disturbed, yes. But not clinically insane. He was convicted on murder two and given life imprisonment."

"So you don't think that Tómas Ó Conaill is insane?"

"Hard to tell for sure, without meeting him. But it took a whole lot of pretty obscure mythological knowledge to do what he did; as well as determination; and physical stamina, too. Think how hard it must have been to scrape the flesh off the legs and arms of a living girl; and then completely dismember her, and drive her out to the middle of a field so that you can spread her out in the special pattern that Mor-Rioghain is supposed to insist on. Your perpetrator is completely rational, if you ask me, Katie. He's calm and methodical and the only thing

255

that makes him different from any other calm and methodical person is that he's an absolute believer in Celtic mythology. He was *totally* convinced that Mor-Rioghain would reappear and give him everything that he deserves."

Katie left the dual carriageway and drove up the ramp toward Cobh, overtaking a tractor. "What do you think about John Meagher?" she wanted to know.

"John Meagher? I'm not entirely sure. He's your typical depressed farmer but have you ever met a farmer who *wasn't* depressed? It kind of goes with the territory, doesn't it? The hours, the weather, the isolation. But there's something else about John Meagher. Another dimension."

Katie said, "He inherited the farm when his father died. He says that he feels responsible for carrying on the family business, but if you ask me he's not cut out for it at all. He's practically bankrupt."

"Was he ever a suspect?"

"Not really. He was working on the farm when Fiona Kelly went missing. His dairy girl testified to that."

"Well… it's quite possible that the man who abducted Fiona Kelly may not have been the same man who murdered her. Quite a few ritual killers work with partners, or in groups. You know, like witches' covens, or pedophile rings."

"I can't see a cultured man like John Meagher working in partnership with a scumbag like Tómas Ó Conaill."

"All the same, if his farm is failing…"

"You mean he might have wanted to ask Mor-Rioghain to save his business?"

"I don't know. I'm only speculating. But I definitely think there's something creepy about him, him and that mother of his. He reminds me of Norman Bates."

"Oh, stop. I think he's charming."

"I know what I'm talking about, Katie. I've interviewed hundreds of people who believe in everything from UFOs to giant monsters. They're always the same – charming, rational, you name it – but after a while you gradually begin to understand that there's a very important screw loose."

They crossed the stone bridge that took them onto Great Island, past a bleak ruined keep with crows flapping around it. It looked like the landscape in an ill-starred Tarot card. Katie said, "I think that John is simply an ordinary decent man who's trying extremely hard to take care of his widowed mother and to keep up his family honor. If he's guilty of anything, it's biting off more than he could chew."

"You're probably right. But Siobhan Buckley's still missing, isn't she? And Tómas Ó Conaill couldn't have taken her."

"We don't have any evidence that she was abducted for a sacrifice. Personally, I have a feeling that she'll show up. Her mother said that she wasn't upset about her parents breaking up, but a lot of the time kids never tell you how they really feel."

"Well, I hope to God you're right."

Paul was standing outside the house waiting for them. His Pajero was parked close to the herbaceous border with its hood raised.

"I don't know what the fuck's wrong with it. It was running perfectly yesterday. I'll have to call the garage when I get back. Meanwhile, I'm going to be late."

He climbed into the back of the car. "Lucy, this is my husband Paul. Paul, this is Professor Lucy Quinn."

"Well, well. I'm overwhelmed to meet you," said Paul, giving her his best cheesy grin. "Katie was telling me all about you last night."

"I hope she was flattering."

"You don't need flattering, professor. You look like the kind of woman who knows *exactly* what effect she has on people."

"God, you smoothie," laughed Katie, as she turned the Mondeo around in the driveway. "Don't take any notice of him, Lucy. Blarney's his middle name."

"Come on, pet, can we get a move on? I can't afford to keep the bank waiting."

They drove back over the stone bridge to the mainland and rejoined the dual carriageway toward Cork City. Traffic was heavy for the time of day, and for the first three kilometers they were stuck behind a slow-moving farm truck, which was trying to overtake an even slower mechanical digger. Paul began to tut with impatience.

"We'll be all right," Katie reassured him. "It won't take us more than another five minutes."

"Can't you use your blue light?"

"To take my husband to a lunch appointment?"

"You used it when you were late for the dentist."

"That was a genuine emergency. I had an abscess."

As they approached the city center, the traffic began to thin out, and as they drove alongside the quays, Katie was able to speed up. Paul said, "That's better... I shouldn't be more than ten minutes late."

At that instant, however, there was a heavy bang at the back of the car, and Katie found herself struggling with a steering-wheel that seemed determined to wrench itself out of her hands. Oh God, blow-out, she thought. The Mondeo's tires screamed on the road-surface, and the car started to slide wildly to the right.

"What the *hell* – ?" shouted Paul.

Katie twisted the wheel into the skid, and the car straightened up. But then there was another bang, and another, and Katie saw the Range Rover looming in the rear-view mirror. "Jesus, they're hitting us on purpose!"

She jammed her foot on the brakes, but the Range Rover slammed into them yet again, and this time it locked its front bumper right up against the Mondeo's trunk, and rammed them onto the sidewalk, so that they burst right through the chainlink fence that seperated the road from the open quays.

"Oh my God," said Lucy.

Katie kept her foot pressed hard on the brake-pedal but the Mondeo was no match for the Range Rover's weight and power. It forced the Mondeo along the quay, nearer and nearer to the edge, its tires shrieking in unholy chorus and black smoke billowing out from under its wheel-arches.

"For Christ's sake!" Paul screamed. "They're pushing us into the water!"

Katie spun the wheel hard and yanked on the parking-brake, so that the Mondeo skidded around in a 180-degree turn. The Range Rover surged forward and hit their offside passenger door with a deafening smash. It ricocheted sideways, stopped, tilted, and then toppled off the edge of the quay and disappeared.

Katie didn't even see it go: she was wrestling to bring the Mondeo under control. It skittered around in another half-circle, and just when she thought she had caught it, one of the rear wheels went over the quay. There was a crunch, as the exhaust-pipe was crushed, and for one long horrible moment they rocked and swayed, right on the very edge. "*Get out!*" Katie shouted. "*Quick as you can, before we go over!*"

Paul opened the rear passenger door, but as he did so the car shuddered and let out a harsh metallic groan, and slid backwards off the quay into the river.

Immediately, the interior was flooded, and Katie was slapped in the face with filthy, freezing-cold water. Paul called out, "*Jesus!*" followed by a sharp gargling noise. Katie tried to turn around and see what was happening to him, but her seatbelt was tightly jammed across her chest. Lucy released her own seatbelt and managed to open her door. The river-water was rushing into the car faster and faster, right over Katie's shoulders, even though – when she looked up – she could still see the gray sky through the windshield, and the edge of the quay, and the faces of people looking over.

Lucy forced her door wider and struggled out. One of her boots kicked against Katie's arm as she swam away. The Mondeo turned slightly, and then sank. Water filled the whole of the passenger compartment, and Katie hardly had time to take a breath before the car dropped slowly down into a peatish-tinted gloom.

She tugged at her seatbelt buckle but it was jammed tight. She cursed herself for not carrying a craft-knife in the car, as she had always promised herself that she would, after seeing a young mother burned alive in an accident out on the North Ring. She jabbed the release button again and again, until she broke her fingernail. She tried twisting and jiggling, but still the seatbelt wouldn't release her.

Oh, Christ, she thought. *I'm going to drown.* Her head throbbed and her lungs ached so much that she was almost tempted to take a deep breath of river-water. Strangely, she wasn't panicky. She felt that she simply wanted to get it over with, without anyone suffering.

Paul must have drowned almost at once. *How ironic*, she thought. *Just when I've decided that I can't live with him, I'm going to die with him.*

It was then that she saw a dark shadow flicker across the windshield. The next thing she knew there was a sharp rapping on her side-window. She turned, and through the brown, particle-filled water, she saw Lucy, her eyes wide, her face colorless.

Lucy opened the Mondeo's door. Katie pointed to the seatbelt buckle and Lucy nodded. Katie saw the glint of a knife, and Lucy cut through her harness in two quick strokes. Then she took hold of Katie's arms and pulled her out of the driving-seat. She kicked up for the surface, supporting Katie all the way, like an angel carrying her up to heaven. As they appeared beside the quay, there were shouts and whoops and applause, and Katie saw to her amazement that the whole quay was already crowded with people and cars. Lucy swam to the side with her, and helped her onto the rusted iron ladder.

"Paul," Katie coughed. "Did you see what happened to Paul?"

"I'll go look," said Lucy. Two men came halfway down the ladder, took hold of Katie under her arms, and lifted her bodily onto the quay, with water pouring from her sodden coat.

"Are you all right, girl?" one of them called to Lucy; but Lucy, without another word, turned and dived under the water again.

"My husband's still down there," said Katie.

"Sacred name of Jesus."

Further along the quay, three men who looked like merchant-seamen had taken a small boat out, and one of them was repeatedly diving where the Range Rover had gone down. Its roof was still visible under the water, like a submerged coffin. A squad car arrived, and then another, closely followed by an ambulance. Detective Garda Patrick O'Sullivan was in the second car, and he came over to Katie immediately.

"My God, are you all right?"

"We were rammed, deliberately rammed. That Range Rover went into us, tried to force us over the quay. Paul's still down there."

"They're sending the divers. Look – hold on – I'll get you a blanket."

Katie stood shivering on the edge of the quay. Over three minutes had gone by and there was still no sign of Lucy or Paul. One of the gardaí dived into the river, but almost at the same moment as he hit the water, Lucy reappeared, supporting Paul. Paul's face was so blue that it looked as if it had been painted for a Hindu festival.

The garda helped to bring Paul over to the ladder, and he was heaved up onto the quay. His eyes were closed and his arms and legs were floppy. The paramedics got to work on him right away, emptying the water out of his lungs and giving him expired-air respiration. Katie stood well back, but in her head she was repeating the mantra, *Please, Holy Mother, don't let him be dead, please don't let him be dead.*

Lucy came up to her, still panting and spitting out river-water. Katie took hold of her hands. "You're freezing! Patrick, will you fetch a blanket for Professor Quinn, too?"

"How's your husband?" coughed Lucy.

"I don't know yet. I don't even know if he's breathing."

One of the gardaí brought a heavy gray blanket and draped it around Lucy's shoulders. Lucy put her arm around Katie's waist and held her close, and they both shivered in unison.

Katie said, "You saved my life, Lucy. You were amazing."

"College swimming champion, two years running."

"Well, thanks be to God."

"How about the people in the other car?"

"They're still trying to bring them up."

"Who were they? Why were they trying to push us into the river?"

Katie ran her fingers through her wet, stringy hair. "I think Paul knows the answer to that."

One of the paramedics came over, a small freckly girl with dark red ringlets. "He's breathing unassisted, superintendent, and his heart-rate's as good as you could expect. He's still unconscious, though. How long was he under the water?"

"Five minutes, not much more."

"We're taking him to the Regional. You ought to you come along with us, both of you. You're going to need a check-up and inoculation against infectious hepatitis."

"I'm fine, thank you," said Lucy. "I just want to get back to my hotel."

"We'd really like to make sure that you haven't suffered any injuries," the paramedic insisted. "And hepatitis can be fatal if you're not inoculated."

"I don't need a doctor and I don't need a jab in the ass, thank you," Lucy retorted. "I need a brandy and a hot shower, that's all."

The paramedic was about to argue, but Katie said, "Professor Quinn doesn't have to have a check-up if she doesn't want to. Lucy – I'll ask Patrick to take you back to Jury's. I'll go with Paul to the hospital and I'll talk to you later."

Lucy gave her an unexpected kiss on the forehead. "You're safe, that's all that matters."

Paul's stretcher was lifted into the back of the ambulance. As Katie climbed in after him, she heard shouting down by the quay. One of the passengers in the Range Rover had been brought up, and lifted into the boat. From where Katie was standing, it looked almost certain that he was dead.

Forty-one

Katie stayed at the Regional until 11:00 pm that night but Paul still didn't recover consciousness. The doctor said, "I have to warn you that there may be some brain damage, due to oxygen deprivation. But it won't be possible to assess him properly until he regains consciousness."

"He *will* regain consciousness?"

"Well, again… that's difficult to tell."

"All right," said Katie. She was suddenly beginning to feel light-headed, and unsteady on her feet. "I'll call in tomorrow, if I can. Meanwhile you've got my cellphone number, haven't you, and you can always get me through Anglesea Street."

"Of course. We'll take v ery good care of him, Katie. Don't you worry."

A young woman garda was waiting outside in a squad car to drive Katie home. She was rosy-cheeked, with fluffy blonde hair drawn back in a pleat.

"Have I seen you before?" Katie asked her.

"No, ma'am. I've just been transferred up from Bandon."

"Ah, so you're getting some experience of the big bad city."

"Oh, it's great here," the garda smiled. "At least you get a bit of excitement."

They drove in silence for a while, but then Katie said, "What made you join the Garda Síochána?"

"I didn't want to work in a shop. All my friends work in

264

shops. I didn't want to do that."

"Is that all?"

"I wanted to do something to help people."

"Ah, yes. Helping people. I remember that."

"Pardon?"

"Oh, you mustn't pay any attention. I've had a difficult night, to say the least. What's your name?"

"Kathleen, ma'am. Kathleen Kiely. Most people call me Katie."

"Do you want some advice, Katie? Some really good advice?"

The garda glanced at Katie apprehensively.

"Never forget that you have limits, Katie. The more you give to people, the more they're going to take."

"Ma'am?"

"I don't expect you to understand what I'm telling you, Katie. But just remember that you're not a saint, or a sister of mercy, or a holy martyr. You don't owe the world everything, because if you think you do, you'll end up with nothing at all."

The garda looked embarrassed, and obviously didn't know what to say.

"One more thing," said Katie, as they crossed the bridge onto Great Island. "Never go swimming in the River Lee with your overcoat on."

Her cellphone rang as she was putting the key into her front door. It was Liam Fennessy. "How's Paul?" he wanted to know.

"It's difficult to say. Very poorly at the moment. He still hasn't regained consciousness."

"I'm sorry about that, Katie. Listen, I'm up at St Patrick's Morgue. We've just had formal identification of the driver and the passenger in the Range Rover."

Sergeant came bounding up to her as she opened the door

and entered the hallway. "Steady, boy! Steady! No – it's all right, Liam. I'm talking to the dog. Was it anybody I know?"

"Oh, yes, it certainly was. Two very good friends of yours, in fact."

"I'm too tired to play guessing-games, Liam."

"What if I told you it was Dave MacSweeny and his muscleman Fergal Fitzgerald."

"You're not serious. Dave MacSweeny?"

"No mistake whatsoever. Earring, tattoos, stigmata and all. That should take a load off your mind now, shouldn't it?"

Katie hung up the raincoat she had borrowed from the Regional. "What are you getting at, Liam?"

"I'm not going to say too much over a cellphone, Katie, but I know that it was Eamonn Collins who had MacSweeny nailed up in that cell in the City Gaol and I know why he did it. There was only one man in Cork who was rash enough to mess with Geraldine Daley, and there was only one man who thought he could get away with lifting nearly a million euros' worth of building supplies from MacSweeny's yard and selling it on to Charlie Flynn.

"Likewise, there was only one woman in Cork who was in a position to ask Eamonn Collins for a very special favor. Come on, Katie, I've known Dave MacSweeny ever since we were in high babies together. Eamonn Collins had no other business with Dave MacSweeny except *your* business."

Katie was silent for a moment, and then she said, "What will you do?"

"Nothing. Why should I? If one scumbag decides to nail another scumbag to a prison wall; and the second scumbag ends up drowned in the river with a third scumbag, who cares?"

"You could report it to Dermot."

"I could, of course, but I'm not going to. I have my loyalties,

Katie; and my first loyalty is to An Garda Síochána. Whatever I think about, it would be a public-relations disaster if our first-ever woman detective superintendent was compromised in any way."

"I could report it myself."

"Yes, you could. But what good would that do us? You'd lose your career, and we'd lose one our best detectives. You should think of your father, too. He'd be heartbroken."

"You can be very creepy at times, Liam."

"Creepy? Hah! I'm perceptive, that's all. Keeping the peace doesn't just mean throwing people in the slammer. Keeping the peace means compromising, doing what's practical, and having infinite patience. Eamonn Collins may have something on you now, but you've got plenty on him, haven't you, and your time will come. Anyway – look on the bright side – Charlie Flynn doesn't have to stay in Florida any longer. None of the rest of Dave MacSweeny's riff-raff is going to have the nerve to threaten old Charlie for money, especially when the goods were nicked in the first place. Dermot can tell the Lord Mayor that his brother-in-law has been discovered safe and well, and you can take all the credit."

"What's this leading to, Liam?"

"I told you, Katie. Nothing at all."

"You know I went round to see Caitlin."

"Yes, I do."

"I was going to talk to you about this yesterday."

"That's right."

A long, tense pause stretched out between them. "Caitlin thinks you've changed. She feels that you're frustrated at work. That's why you can't keep your temper."

"I have my own feelings about things, Katie. But this is my private life you're talking about here, and what happens between me and Caitlin is frankly none of your business."

"You assaulted her, Liam."

"At least I didn't nail her to a prison wall."

Katie didn't answer. It was quite clear, the position she was in. She carried the phone over to the sideboard and opened the vodka-bottle one-handed, and poured herself a large measure in one of her heavy cut-crystal glasses.

"Any news of Siobhan Buckley?" she asked.

"Not much. Three eye-witnesses saw a white Lexus being driven erratically along the Lower Glanmire Road about five past nine in the morning. That was only shortly after Siobhan Buckley is supposed to have accepted a lift in a white Japanese-type saloon. There was a man and a girl in the Lexus, and the woman in the car behind them got the impression that they were struggling. The car was swerving from side to side. It struck the nearside curb and almost drove head-on into the oncoming traffic."

"Any sight of it after that?"

"None."

"I see. I think I need to talk to Tómas Ó Conaill again."

Liam said, "Listen, Katie... however things are between us, you need some rest. I can talk to Ó Conaill tomorrow. I can also co-ordinate the search for Siobhan Buckley. You've just suffered a really traumatic experience, and you've got Paul to think of, too."

"Very compassionate of you, Liam. I just wish you'd show the same compassion to Caitlin. She's my friend, remember."

"Katie – "

"I'll be in tomorrow at nine. I want a report on today's accident on my desk waiting for me. I want an assessment of Dave MacSweeny's family and his remaining gang – who they are, where they live, and whether you think they're still likely to be dangerous."

268

"You're the boss."

Katie switched off her cellphone and put it down on the sideboard. Sergeant roved around her, snuffling and whining. "It's all right, boy. You'll have to do your business in the garden tonight. I don't think I've got the strength for a walk."

She took her drink upstairs to bed. She was too tired even for a shower. She undressed, put on her large blue-and-white striped nightshirt, and climbed under the thick, chilly duvet. She fell asleep almost at once, with all the lights still on.

She had the Gray-Dolly nightmare again. She was walking across a wet, gritty yard toward the door of a factory building. High above the factory roof, black smoke was rolling out of tall brick chimneys, and she could hear the clanking of chains and heavy machinery, and despairing screams.

"*Paul?*" she said, stepping inside the door. "*Paul, where are you?*"

Around the corner, she heard the shriek of bandsaws, cutting through bone. She made her way around a huge heap of bloodied sacking, and then she saw the slaughtermen in their bloodstained aprons and their strange muslin hats, cutting up lumps of dark maroon meat – legs and arms and partially-dismembered torsos.

"*Watch out for the Gray-Dolly Man!*" somebody whispered, close to her ear. But she continued to walk toward the nearest of the slaughtermen, even though she was chilly with fear. "*Watch out for the Gray-Dolly Man!*" The slaughterman was sawing up what looked like a woman's leg – Katie could even see the dimples in her knee – and tossing the bloody pieces into a sack.

Katie came right up behind him. "*Armed Garda,*" she tried to shout out, but her voice came out distorted and unintelligible, like the voice of somebody profoundly deaf. "*Armed Garda, you're under arrest.*"

The slaughterman didn't show any sign that he had heard her, so she cautiously reached out and laid her hand on his shoulder. He stiffened. Then he laid down his butcher's saw and turned around. His face was invisible behind his muslin veil. Her heart stopped, and thumped, and then stopped, and thumped. She felt fear hurrying down her back like woodlice.

Slowly, finger by finger, he tugged off his thick leather glove. He reached up and lifted the veil away from his face. *Oh God*, she tried to say, but she couldn't.

It was Dave MacSweeny, dead, with his eyes as white as a boiled cod's, his face gray, and filthy brown river-water pouring out of the sides of his mouth.

She yelled, "*No! Get away from me*!" Downstairs, Sergeant heard her and let out a sharp bark. She opened her eyes and for a split-second she didn't know where she was. But gradually her bedroom resolved itself, and the bedside lamp was still shining, and the alarm-clock said 3:43; and a photograph of Paul was still smiling at her from the side of her dressing-table. One eye looking in a slightly different direction, as if he could see something over her shoulder.

She went to the bathroom and brushed her teeth. She drank two glasses of water and then she went back to bed, switching off the lights. It took her another twenty minutes to fall asleep, but this time she dreamed only of running along a deserted seashore, running and running, hoping to run so fast that her footprints couldn't keep up with her.

Forty-two

Siobhan was woken by a blinding flashlight shining in her eyes. She whimpered in protest and tried to turn her face away. She was half-covered by a grubby cellular wool blanket but she was still so cold that she could hardly feel her feet.

"What time is it?" she asked. Her mouth was so dry that she could barely speak.

"It's almost time for you to start on your journey, Siobhan," the man told her. "You've managed to get some shut-eye, that's good. You're going to need all the strength that your soft little body can muster."

"Please," she croaked.

He sat down next to her, balancing the flashlight on the arm of his chair. She could only see him as dark outline. "It's strange, that," he said. "How people who are being mistreated are always so *polite*. You'd think they'd get angry, wouldn't you? You think they'd rant and rage. You'd think they'd blaspheme, and rail against God. But they never do. They always say 'please' and 'thank-you'. On the other hand, maybe I'm just lucky. Maybe I only ever abduct the meek and the courteous."

"I just want to go home," sobbed Siobhan.

The man put his hand out and caressed her prickly scalp. "Of course you want to go home. But the sad thing is that you can't. You have another destiny to fulfill. I've arranged a meeting for you – a rendezvous with Auntie Agony. She's going to take you into her arms and give you the most exquisite pain you've ever known."

"Please don't hurt me. I'll do anything."

"I know, I know. But that's not why you're here. You're here to open up the door for me – the door that was sealed so many hundreds of years ago. You're the one, Siobhan. The last of the thirteen, a seamstress with hair as red as any fire. I *am* going to hurt you. I'm afraid. I'm going to hurt you very much. But it's part of the ritual. It's the *point* of the ritual. And it will give you an experience that hardly anybody is privileged to enjoy. It will take you beyond yourself, to a place where you will understand that pain can be an end in itself, even more glorious than death."

"I just want to go home," wept Siobhan. "Please, please, I just want to go home."

"Would you like a painkiller, to begin with?" He sniffed, and stood up. "I think I've got some Disprin in the bathroom."

"I want to go home."

Without warning, the man tilted her chair right back so that she was sitting with her head against the floor, looking upward. She let out a mewl of helplessness and fear. Her wrists were already lashed tightly to the arms of the chair. Now he produced a length of nylon washing-line and tied her ankles, pulling the knots so tight that she felt as if he were cutting her feet off.

"You're cold, that's good. Cold will help to numb the pain a little. But as you warm up again... well, that's when you'll really start to feel it."

"I don't – I can't – I can't bear it! I can't bear it! Please let me go! Please let me go!"

He caressed her bare knees. "You're a fashion student, Siobhan. Did you ever dream of being famous? Well, believe me, *this* is going to make you famous. Your name will forever be associated with one of the most greatest mythic events of the millennium. Whenever people think of the re-emergence of Mor-Rioghain, which they surely will, for centuries to come, they will immediately think of Siobhan Buckley, too."

Siobhan lay on her back, her eyes blurred with tears, her nose clogged up with phlegm. The man was silent for a while, and she wondered if he'd gone away. But then she heard something like a case snapping shut; and a cough. Then – without any warning at all – she felt a terrible cold sliding sensation down the side of her right calf, all the way from her knee to her ankle. It happened again, exactly along the same line, much deeper, actually touching the bone, and this time she felt a flood of warmth and sticky wetness.

She tried to cry out "*Ahh,*" but her throat was flooded with saliva. "*Ahhgghlllghhh.*"

"Very good, Siobhan," he said, making a deep sideways incision directly below her right knee, so that she could feel him cutting through her tendons. In fact, she could actually feel the tendons shrivel, as their tension was released. "Very restrained, under the circumstances."

"AaaAAAAAAAAHHHH!" she screamed, as he continued the incision into her upper calf muscle.

"Do you want me to stop for a while?" he asked her. He coughed again, and said, "Pardon me. It's really much better to get it over with, all at once."

She was shaking with pain. "Don't," was all she could manage to say. "Don't."

"I'll carry on, then. And do feel free to scream if you want to. It's supposed to be cathartic."

Siobhan squeezed her eyes tight and said a prayer to the Sacred Mother to protect her, to take her away from this place, to ease the agonizing pain in her leg. The man sliced through the left side of her calf and she could feel her flesh opening up and the cold draft blowing against her naked muscle. She prayed to Jesus the Savior. She prayed to have her sins forgiven and her soul allowed into heaven.

But when she opened her eyes again she was still in hell. The man was still bent over her, cutting through her Achilles tendon and the extensor muscles around her ankles, and humming.

Forty-three

Katie called the Regional Hospital while her coffee was percolating. Paul's condition was stable and "giving no immediate cause for concern." He was breathing without the aid of a ventilator, but he was still deeply unconscious and so far he had shown no signs of response to any external stimuli. Outside the kitchen window it was raining hard, and water was gushing from the blocked guttering over the garage. The nurse said that Paul would be taken for a CAT scan later in the morning to see if he had suffered any physical brain damage.

As she hung up the phone, Katie said a silent prayer to St Teresa of Ávila, the patron saint of the sick and the afflicted. The same prayer she had said for her mother, before she died. "God makes us suffer, and we worldlings do not understand why, but He chastises us for His own good purpose."

At 8:47 there was a toot outside the house and she looked out to see an unmarked squad car waiting for her. She shut Sergeant in the kitchen, put on her navy-blue squall jacket, and hurried outside.

"Nice soft day," the driver remarked, as they drove away. He was a gray-haired garda called Patrick Logan: friendly, reliable, unambitious, and close to retirement.

"Damn it," said Katie.

"What is it? Forgotten something? Want me to go back?"

"No… I meant to leave the keys of my husband's car under

one of the flowerpots. I was going to call the garage this morning to come and take a look at it."

"That Pajero? What's wrong with it?"

"Won't start, that's all. It was only serviced about a month ago, and it was running all right until yesterday morning."

"My son could take a look at that for you. He runs a mobile breakdown service. He'd charge you a lot less than your garage."

"That would be great, if he could. That's my husband's pride and joy, that thing."

"How is your husband, by the way?"

"Still unconscious. I'm just praying that there isn't any permanent brain damage."

"Please God," said Patrick Logan. Then, after driving in silence for a while, "And how are *you*?"

"Okay," said Katie. "I'm okay, thanks for asking."

"You're not going to take a couple of days' rest?"

"Why should I?"

"Well, if you don't mind me being frank – "

"For God's sake, be frank."

"There's some of your fellow officers who think that perhaps you push yourself a little too hard. Because you're a woman, d'you know, and you seem to think you have to prove yourself."

"I see. Some of my fellow officers think *that*, do they?"

"I'm sorry, ma'am. I didn't want to speak out of turn. But sometimes it's better to know what's going on behind your back before you get stabbed in it."

"As a matter of fact, Patrick, I'm quite aware that most of my colleagues think I push myself too hard. Even more to the point, they think that I push *them* too hard. But I wasn't promoted to detective superintendent because I hung around in the back bar at Counihan's all day, pretending that I was keeping my ear to the ground. I work hard because it's necessary and not because I feel the need to prove myself to my fellow officers or anybody else."

"No, ma'am. Sorry, ma'am."

"That's all right, Patrick, I know it was meant well. Look – I shall be home by half-past one. If your son can come around then, I'd be very grateful indeed."

"Not a problem, ma'am."

There was a message waiting for her from Gerard O'Brien. He had called yesterday evening at 5:00 pm, as she had asked him to, but of course she had been at the Regional Hospital by then. He said, *"Hallo? Katie? Gerard. I know you've made an arrest already, but this new research material I've got from Germany is very, very exciting. I definitely think it could help us to solve this Knocknadeenly business. I could come round to Anglesea Street if you like. Better still, why don't I buy you some lunch?"*

Katie had a moment's thought and then she called Lucy at Jury's Inn. The phone rang for a long time before Lucy answered, and she sounded groggy.

"Lucy? It's Katie Maguire."

"Oh, I'm sorry. I didn't sleep very well last night. Night terrors."

"You weren't the only one. Listen – I just wanted to let you know that Paul's still unconscious but he seems to be reasonably stable. As long as there's no brain damage, the doctor says that he's got a very fair chance."

"That's good news."

"Also, I wanted to ask if you were free for lunch today? There's somebody I'd like you to meet – Professor Gerard O'Brien from Cork University. He's been helping us look into the 1915 killings, and he says he has some exciting new research

277

material from Germany. *His* words, I hasten to add, but he's done well for us so far."

"I don't know, Katie… I don't usually like to tread on another academic's toes."

"You wouldn't be. And who knows, the two of you together might come up with something that really cracks this whole case wide open."

"I'm not sure."

"Lucy, I'd really like to see you – mainly to thank you for yesterday, but I also want to hear more about this Jack Callwood character. Besides, you'd be doing me a personal favor. To put it diplomatically, Gerard O'Brien is a little sweet on me."

"I see. You need a bodyguard."

"I was thinking of 'chaperone', but bodyguard will do. Why don't you meet us at Isaac's in MacCurtain Street at about one o'clock?"

"All right. You've twisted my arm."

Shortly after 10:00 am, Patrick Goggin knocked on the door of her office. She was busy going through the detailed technical reports on the cottage where Fiona Kelly had been killed, and she wasn't particularly happy to see him.

He sniffed, sharply. "That's a very attractive perfume you're wearing, superintendent."

"Thank you. But I'm afraid I'm up to my eyes this morning."

"Of course," he swallowed. "But I just wanted to tell you that I've had a response from the Ministry of Defence in London relating to the disappearance of Irish women around north Cork in 1915–16."

"And?"

"They say that they've made a thorough search of the Public Records Office at Kew and it appears that all the daily dispatches relating to the period in question were destroyed by enemy action during World War Two. Whatever happened to them, they're missing, and nobody can find them."

"How convenient. Do you believe them?"

"I don't have any choice, do I?"

"You don't think they're deliberately being obstructive?"

"They may be. But, I don't know. Jack Devitt has made it his life's work to publicize British atrocities in Ireland. As often as not I think he's justified in what he says, especially when it comes to the Black and Tans and the Irish Volunteers. But personally I find it very difficult to believe that a British commanding officer would officially order the systematic abduction and the murdering of eleven young women, don't you?"

Katie sat back. "I have to say that I'm inclined to agree with you. Especially since the women were sacrificed in an ancient Celtic ritual. The Brits never gave a frig for Celtic rituals – in fact they did their best to stamp them out. And the raising-up of Mor-Rioghain, that's a particularly obscure ritual that very few *Irish* know about, let alone Brits. But… if the Ministry of Defence can't or won't produce the dispatches, it's not going to make things any easier, is it?"

"It isn't, no. That's why I'm relying on you to find out what really happened to those women. If Jack Devitt's right, and they *were* kidnapped and murdered by British soldiers, then I need to know for sure. He may have even more evidence than he's telling us; and we can't do a whitewash until we know exactly what it is we're supposed to be whitewashing."

Katie dropped her ballpen onto the papers in front of her. "I can only tell you, Mr Goggin, that we're doing our best. So far we've located and DNA-tested eleven people who thought they might be related to the victims, and seven of them have proved positive – so I think it's reasonably safe to assume that the skeletons that were found at Knocknadeenly were those of the eleven women who were abducted between 1915 and 1916.

"Some of the relatives have hand-me-down stories of 'the day that Great Auntie Betty disappeared', but unfortunately none of them throw any light on how the women were taken, or who took them. Mary O'Donovan's great-great-grand-niece did mention a scare story that she had told her about a 'demon Tommy', who was supposed to have been preying on young women around St Luke's Cross and Montenotte. But it could have been nothing more than a warning to stop local girls from flirting with British soldiers."

"I could really do without this," said Patrick Goggin, pulling tiredly at his cheeks as if they were Plasticine.

"Well, that makes two of us, Mr Goggin. But I'm having lunch with my two experts in Celtic mythology today and maybe they'll come up with some bright ideas."

"Oh." He looked disappointed. "I was going to ask you if you wanted to come and have a drink with me."

Siobhan's eyes flickered open. Almost at once she was overwhelmed by a tide of pain that swept her away like a broken doll in a heavy sea. She felt the floor rising and falling and tilting beneath her, and the walls rushing towards her and then rushing away again. She vomited, not that she had much left to vomit, only some tinned tomato soup that the man had given her, and a few strings of phlegm.

The pain was so overwhelming that she couldn't think what she was doing here or what had happened to her, or even who she was. All she could think about was pain, and why the room wouldn't stay level.

The man was standing close to her, although she couldn't see anything more than a dark, distorted shadow. "You're awake?" he asked her.

She didn't answer, so he knelt down beside her and peeled back one of her fluttering, wincing eyelids with his thumb. "You're awake? You've done very well, Siobhan. How are you feeling?"

She retched again; and then again; and he stood well away until she had finished. Then he said, "I'm going to leave you to rest now. See if you can get some more sleep. I'll be back in a while to feed you. Would you like something to drink before I go?"

She nodded. She was hurting so much that she couldn't even cry. The man left her for a while and then came back with a large glass of water. He cupped his hand behind her white, red-tufted head, and helped her to take three or four swallows. Almost immediately she retched again, and water splashed over her legs.

She sat with her head hanging down, her eyes clenched shut, while the pain continued to wash her from one side of the room to the other.

"I'll be back later," the man said, gently. "Then we can really discover some pain together."

He closed the door behind him. Siobhan sat limply in her chair while the floor heaved beneath her like a raft. "Mama..." she whispered. "Mama, please help me."

Gradually she opened her eyes. Her legs looked different, and at first she couldn't understand why. Then she realized that she was looking at bones, not skin. Two cream-colored thighbones, and two kneecaps that were still joined to her legs by gristle and fragments of flesh. The seat-cushion beneath her was soaked in blood.

She was in such a state of clinical shock that she didn't fully understand that the thighbones were hers. They reminded her of the skeleton that used to be dangling in the corner of the biology lab at school. She closed her eyes again. The bones frightened her, and she needed to sleep.

Outside the window, the rain began to clear, and the sun came out, so that a wide rainbow gleamed over Lough Mahon and Passage West, where the ships sailed out of Cork on their way to the ocean.

Forty-four

Lucy arrived ten minutes late, wearing a black leather jacket and a thick rollneck sweater of fluffy black angora, and tight black jeans. A large silver cross swung around her neck, studded with dark purple gemstones.

Gerard stood up and knocked his glass of water over. The waitress rushed over to do some frantic mopping with a tea-towel while Katie said, "Gerard, this is Professor Lucy Quinn... Lucy, this is Professor Gerard O'Brien."

"Very pleased to meet you," said Gerard. Lucy was at least four inches taller than he was, and he found himself addressing her bosom. "Katie's been telling me how you saved her from drowning. I'm very impressed."

Lucy sat down. "Anybody would have done the same."

"Anybody who could swim like Flipper," Katie put in. "How about a drink?"

Isaac's was always noisy at lunchtime. It was a modern, starkly-decorated restaurant that was popular with young Cork businessmen and tourists and middle-aged ladies who had finished their shopping. With the same self-protective instincts as Eamonn Collins, Katie had chosen a table in the alcove right at the back, so that she could see everybody who came in.

"Katie tells me that your university funded your trip here specially," Gerard remarked, with his mouth full of soda-bread.

"I wish Cork was so generous. They won't even send me to Wales to look at Celtic stone-circles."

"Oh, those skeletons at Knocknadeenly were a *very* rare discovery," said Lucy. "As I was telling Katie, the only other similar case we know about happened in Boston in 1911. But what really had my head of department all fired up was the fact that somebody was actually trying to complete the ritual – you know, *now*, today."

"Have you got any more out of Tómas Ó Conaill?" Gerard asked Katie.

"I'm planning to interview him again this afternoon, but I'm still waiting for DNA tests and some other technical evidence."

"What do you know about him? It said in the paper that he was a Traveler."

"He calls himself a Traveler, yes. He's the thirteenth son of a very well-known family of Travelers who spend most of their year in Galway and Donegal. But he had a fight with his father when he was fifteen or sixteen. Blinded him in one eye. After that he went off on his own. He likes to think of himself as the King of All the Travelers, but I don't think you'll find many other Travelers who agree with him."

"How does he know so much about Celtic ritual? Presumably he never went to school."

"No... but he told me once that he was taught to read by a schoolmaster who used to live close to the family's halting-site near Claremorris, and that the schoolmaster was also a great supporter of Celtic traditions and the Gaelic language. Tómas Ó Conaill knows everything there is to know about the old superstitions and the old druidic rituals. He seems to believe that he's some kind of chosen descendant of the High Kings of Ireland, and that he possesses supernatural powers.

"Apart from that, he can be very rational at times. He can be charming. He can be amusing. Even – God knows – seductive."

Gerard and Lucy shared a bottle of Chilean white wine. Katie would have given a week's overtime for a double vodka, but she stayed on the mineral water. Their orders arrived: Gerard had chosen a mixed-leaf salad with Clonakilty black pudding, while Lucy had tempura prawns and Katie had grilled monkfish with clapshot – potato and swede mashed together.

"This is very good," said Lucy. "Gerard – Katie said that you had some new research material from Germany. *Exciting* research material, apparently."

Gerard blushed. "Yes, well, *I* think it is, anyway. I managed to get in touch with a famous criminal historian in Osnabrück, Dr Franz Kremer. He's written several books about notorious mass-murders in Germany and Belgium and Poland.

Gerard produced a spring-bound notebook filled with rounded, almost childish writing. "I talked to Dr Kremer on the phone for almost an hour. He said that between the summer of 1913 and the spring of 1914, more than a hundred and twenty women went missing from towns around Münster, in Westphalia. Before their disappearance, several of them were seen talking to a man dressed in a gray Wehrmacht uniform. Nobody knew who he was. No army units in the area reported any of their soldiers unaccounted for. By Christmas, 1913, the local newspapers were calling him *Der Graue Geist*... the Gray Ghost."

"My God," said Lucy. "I can't believe it." But all Katie could think of was the whisper that she had heard in her dreams. *"Beware the Gray-Dolly Man,"* and of what "Knocknadeenly" meant in English. *The Hill of the Gray People.*

Gerard forked too much salad into his mouth, and had to spend a moment getting all the leaves under control. At last he said, "By chance – on June 4, 1914 – a priest in the town of Drensteinfurt happened to see a man in gray army uniform talking to his cook on the opposite side of the town square. The man and the housekeeper left the square together and the priest followed them around the corner where the man had a motor-car parked. The two of them drove off together and of course the priest couldn't follow them, but when his housekeeper failed to return that evening he informed the police.

"Three days later a gamekeeper found the car in a wood. The area was searched with dogs for any sign of the cook, and after only two or three hours the dogs discovered a clearing in the woods where the soil had been disturbed, although it had been cleverly camouflaged with pine-needles and twigs. The police dug up the clearing and discovered the bones of ninety-six women, all fleshless. And here's the cruncher – the thighbones of every one of them had been pierced, and every thighbone hung with a little lace doll full of fish-hooks and nails and other assorted ironmongery."

"So," said Lucy. "The Gray Ghost had been trying to raise up Morgana."

"Without much success, by the sound of it," Katie put in. "Ninety-six skeletons, divided by thirteen – that means he tried seven times, and was halfway through his eighth attempt. Why do you think he persisted, if the ritual obviously didn't work?"

"Who says it didn't work?" said Lucy. "For all we know, Morgana may have given him everything he asked for, only he kept coming back for more."

"Well, yes," said Katie, trying not to sound schoolmistressy. "But that's only if you're prepared to accept that witchcraft actually works."

Lucy gave a little shrug. "When it comes to Celtic mythology, Katie, I try to keep a very open mind. Especially when it comes to fairies."

"All right, then," Katie conceded. "What happened next?"

Gerard finished the last slice of black pudding and earnestly wiped the salad dressing from the bottom of his plate with a piece of bread. "The police waited and two days later the man came back to collect his car. He was arrested and taken to Münster police headquarters. The police chief interrogated him for three days but he refused to say anything except that his name was Jan Rufenwald and that he was an engineer from Hamm. He knew nothing about any missing women and he denied owning the car."

"Sounds familiar," said Katie.

"Anyway," Gerard went on, "Jan Rufenwald was supposed to appear in front of the courts in Münster on July 5, 1914, but by that time Germany was in a state of turmoil because they were already at war with France and they were only days away from going to war with Britain, and for one reason and another his appearance was delayed. On July 7 he managed to escape from his holding cell at the courtroom and he was never seen again.

"A witness said that he saw a woman in a brown dress leaving the court building by way of a staircase at the back. My doctor friend guesses that Jan Rufenwald had a female accomplice who helped him to escape. Either that, or he got away dressed in women's clothing.

"There was a huge manhunt for him, all over Westphalia. The newspapers called him 'The Monster of Münster', and they circulated an artist's impression of him as far away as Hanover in the east and the Dutch border to the west. It was then that the police in Recklinghausen said that a man answering Jan Rufenwald's description had been seen around the town in the late summer and autumn of 1912, at a time when over seventy women vanished; and the police in Paderborn recognized him as a 'Willi Hakenmacher' who had been on their wanted list since the winter of 1911, when literally uncountable numbers of women of all ages disappeared without trace. The investigation was disrupted by the war, and eventually discontinued, but contemporary police records suggest that Jan Rufenwald was probably responsible for the murders of at least four hundred women, maybe even more."

Lucy had been listening to all of this intently, and when Gerard had finished she sat back and said, "Incredible. Absolutely incredible."

"You know something about this?" Katie asked her.

"It's extraordinary. It's exactly like the Callwood murders that I was telling you about. I mean we could be talking about the same guy."

"These were the murders in Boston that you were talking about?"

"That's right. Thirty-one women went missing from all over the Boston area. Before they disappeared, several of them were seen by eye-witnesses talking to a man in army uniform."

Gerard said, "You're right. That *is* extraordinary."

"Think about it – this was well before the days of radio or television or the internet. You didn't get copycat behavior spreading around the world in a matter of hours."

"Was this fellow ever caught?"

"Almost. He got into conversation with a young woman called Annette Songer in a grocery store in Dedham, which is a suburb south-west of the city. Annette Songer was a spinster who had something of a reputation for reading people's horoscopes, so she fitted the pattern of women who have to be sacrificed to Mor-Rioghain – 'a fortune-teller with no children'. Jack Callwood offered to give her a ride home. She had a lot to carry so she accepted. But as soon as she got into the car he drove off in the opposite direction and refused to turn around. She struggled with him and he hit her several times, breaking her jaw. There was a long report about it in *The Boston Evening Transcript*.

"Annette Songer pretended to be unconscious, and when the car stopped and the man got out to open a gate, she climbed out and ran away. She went immediately to the police, but by the time they arrived at the house where the man had been staying, he had gone. The man's landlady said that he had always been quiet and polite and always paid the rent on time, but 'he had a look in his eye which made my heart beat slower.'

"Police searched the house and dug up the garden. They found the bones of at least twenty women, all with little rag dolls in their thighbones.

"They set up one of the biggest dragnets ever seen… just like the manhunt in Germany, by the sound of it. Remember that there were very few cars on the roads in those days, so it wasn't easy for Callwood to get away. He was spotted in New London, Connecticut, heading west; and then again in Westport. A police roadblock was set up and he had to abandon his car.

"Police tracked him as far as New York, and his picture was published on the front page of every Manhattan newspaper. On May 2 a clerk from the Cunard office on Fifth Avenue came forward and said that a man looking like Jack Callwood had bought a ticket from him on the morning of June 29, for a sailing to Liverpool, England, on May 1.

"A wireless message was sent to the ship he was sailing on, and the captain ordered a thorough search, but there was no sign of Callwood anywhere on board. Five days later, when the ship was sailing around the southern coast of Ireland, she was torpedoed by a German submarine and sank with the loss of more than a thousand lives."

"My God," said Katie. "The *Lusitania*."

"Yes," said Lucy.

"So even if he was on board – " Gerard began.

"That's right. Every surviving passenger was accounted for, and Callwood wasn't among them. The New York police even asked the Irish Constabulary in Cork to interview every male survivor, just to make absolutely sure that Callwood hadn't taken on a false identity."

"And he definitely wasn't among them?"

"No. I've seen photographs of every single man who escaped the sinking of the *Lusitania*. Not one of them even remotely fits the description of Callwood that was given to the Dedham police by Annette Songer, his landlady, and about ten other people who knew him."

Katie slowly shook her head. "Yet less than five months later, the first of eleven women was abducted in north Cork and murdered according to exactly the same ritual that Callwood had been carrying out in Boston."

"And the same ritual Rufenwald had been carrying on in Germany," put in Gerard. "And don't forget – the lace that the dolls were made out of, that was German."

"Rufenwald, Callwood, and then our mystery British soldier," said Katie. "It's hard to believe that they weren't the same man, isn't it?"

They talked some more over coffee. Then Katie looked at her watch and saw that it was almost a quarter of two. "Listen, I have to go. But thank you, both of you. This has been very instructive. I'm going to initiate some more checks with the Boston police and the German police. Gerard – maybe your Dr Kremer can help you to find some records of where the German victims were discovered, and who they were. Lucy

– what would you like to do?"

Lucy was busy refreshing her pale coral lipstick. "I think I need to go back to Knocknadeenly and make a thorough examination of the place where Fiona Kelly's body was found. I need to know what its exact magical significance is... whether it lies on a ley-line or not... whether it was once a burial-barrow or a Druid circle... and if there are any local ghost stories about it."

"That's fine. I'll make sure you get an identity badge. It's still officially a crime scene, so they won't let you in there, otherwise."

"Oh... one thing, before we go," said Gerard. "Another of my contacts in Germany e-mailed me a charming picture of Morgana, or Mor-Rioghain, or whatever you want to call her."

He opened his briefcase and took out a large brown envelope. He passed it over to Katie with a smile. Katie opened it and hesitated. "Go on," Gerard coaxed her. "She won't bite."

She slowly drew out a sheet of paper with a dark etching of Mor-Rioghain on it. The witch of witches was standing in a dark wood, holding up a long staff with a human skull on the top. Her face was smooth and pale and unnervingly perfect, and her lips were slightly parted, as if she were just about to speak. But – like Jack Callwood – there was something in her eyes that made Katie's heart beat slow. Something utterly remorseless. She wore an elaborate hat of black crow feathers, beneath which her hair was a mass of tangled curls, crawling with beetles and clustered with freshly-hatched moths. Her decaying robes were pierced with hundreds of hooks and nails and metal pins.

"Sensational, isn't she?" said Lucy.

"You've seen this picture before?"

"Not that particular one, but plenty of others like it. They always say that when the Death Queen arrives at your bedside, you're so mesmerized by her beauty that you forget what she came for."

"Well, then, thank you," said Katie. "Maybe I should have a few hundred copies printed and send them out as Wanted posters."

Forty-five

After lunch she drove round to the Regional to spend twenty minutes sitting at Paul's bedside. He looked peaceful and untroubled, as if he were dreaming, and it was hard for her to believe that she couldn't shake his shoulder and wake him up.

"Oh, Paul, you poor dote," she said, holding his hand. "That was always your problem, wasn't it, getting out of your depth? You always thought you could wangle your way out of trouble, but this time you couldn't. Please open up your eyes, Paul. Please get better. I don't want you to spend the rest of your life like this."

There was a theatrical cough behind her, and a knock on the door. It was Jimmy O'Rourke, carrying a bunch of seedless grapes from Supervalu and a sprawling bouquet of mixed flowers.

"Hi, Katie, how're you doing? How's the patient today?"

"Still unconscious, Jimmy. He's going for a brain-scan in half-an-hour."

"These are from everybody. It's a bit stupid, isn't it, bringing grapes to a fellow who's unconscious, but I suppose his visitors can always nibble on them."

"Thanks, Jimmy."

Jimmy dragged up a plywood chair on the opposite side of the bed. "He *looks* well," he remarked. "I mean, he's got a good colour on him, hasn't he?"

"It's impossible to say yet. It depends if his brain was starved of oxygen while he was under the water."

Jimmy nodded; and then he said, cautiously, "Dermot was asking me about what happened. You know – why Dave MacSweeny should have tried to shove you into the river."

"I really don't know, Jimmy. Paul had been doing a few bits of business with Dave MacSweeny but as far as I can tell they got along well enough. Maybe he was trying to kill *me*."

"This wouldn't have anything to do with Dave MacSweeny being nailed to the wall in the City Gaol, would it?"

Katie shrugged. "It looks as if Eamonn Collins was probably responsible for that, but I doubt if we'll ever be able to prove it."

Jimmy chewed that over for a while, and then he said, "When you think about it, it must have been Paul that Dave MacSweeny was after, not you. He must have been waiting close to your house, ready to follow Paul into the city. He wouldn't have known that Paul's car wasn't going to start and that you were going to come and get him, would he?"

"I suppose not. But if he was really intent on killing Paul, why didn't he simply go to the house and shoot him? Ramming somebody's car into the river isn't exactly a guaranteed way of getting rid of them, is it? Nor discreet, neither."

"Dave MacSweeny was always a lunatic. God knows what was going through that head of his."

Katie gave him a quick, prickly look. The way he said it, it sounded as if he knew very well what Dave MacSweeny had been looking for. Revenge, and punishment. Nobody was allowed to take Dave MacSweeny's property without asking him, and nobody could mess around with Dave MacSweeny's girlfriend, even if he regularly beat her up and broke her ribs and treated her like trash. Dave MacSweeny had lost his temper and paid the price for it; but Paul had been rash enough to provoke him.

"I'm not slow, Jimmy, and I'm a Cork girl, born and bred. I *do* know what's going on here, most of the time."

"All right," said Jimmy. "I'm just looking out for you, you know that."

Katie took hold of his hand with his big thick silver rings and squeezed it tight. She knew that Jimmy wasn't just sympathetic because Paul was in a coma; but because of their marriage; and because everything had fallen apart. You couldn't keep any secrets at Anglesea Street.

"Thanks, Jimmy," she said. Only three feet away from them, Paul continued to breathe, his eyes closed, and he even had a smile on his face, as if he were dreaming about Geraldine Daley, or winning on the horses at the Curragh, or who knew what a man like Paul would be dreaming about, to make him smile?

Siobhan opened her eyes and the man was standing by the window, looking out. There was a melancholy expression on his face, as if he were thinking about things that had happened a long time ago, and far away. The pain in Siobhan's legs had subsided to a dull, regular throb, and the room had stopped tilting up and down, and for the first time she could see the man clearly. He was wearing a tight-fitting black silk shirt and black trousers. He reminded her of a stage magician that her father had once taken her to see, a man who had drawn long strings of scarves from out of his sleeves, and a black rabbit out of a black top hat.

Eventually the man turned away from the window. "Ah, you're awake. Would you like a drink of water? Or maybe a little something to eat?"

"Please... I want to go home now."

"Ah... if only you could. But sometimes destiny has other things in mind for us."

"Please. I don't want to die."

"Don't be in such a hurry. Death has its attractions, you know. Tonight you're going to experience the greatest pain that any human being is capable of suffering; and by tomorrow night you will be begging me to die, *begging*."

Siobhan said nothing, but closed her eyes again, and prayed to be somewhere else, or somebody else, anywhere and anybody, except here, and her. *Please, dearest Virgin, save me, save me, take me away.*

The man said, "I like you very much, Siobhan. Out of all the girls I've known, I think you have the greatest grace. The greatest radiance. They should make you a saint, you know. Saint Siobhan of the Fiery Red Hair. I shall have your hair woven into a locket, and I shall wear it always, for the rest of my life, against my chest, as a tribute to your ineffable composure."

"Why?" asked Siobhan, without opening her eyes.

"Why? Because you, Siobhan, are the chosen one. The thirteenth, and the last. You are the *key*."

"Why?" Siobhan repeated.

"Because you have the hair, Siobhan, and the skills that the ritual calls for. Because you are very, very, *very* beautiful, and you embody everything mystical and magical and mythological that makes Ireland the land it is, where the world of fairies is only a shimmer away from the world of men and women."

"Why?"

He hesitated, confused. "I'm sorry. I don't know what it is you're asking me."

She opened her eyes and stared at him, and there was a wild look on her face that made him involuntarily jerk up his right hand, as if to protect himself. "*Why do you have to hurt me like this?*" she demanded, and her voice was unnervingly coarse, like Regan's in *The Exorcist*.

"Siobhan, Siobhan, you wouldn't understand, even if I tried to explain it to you. It's the only possible way that I can get what I need. Believe me, if there was any alternative at all – "

Tears began to slide down Siobhan's cheeks. "I feel sorry for you," she said. "I feel desperately sorry for you."

"You feel *sorry* for me? Why?"

"Because, when you die, you're going to go to hell, for ever and ever. And you're going to feel like I'm feeling now, worse, and it won't ever end. Never."

The man said nothing for a while, but then he reached out and touched one of her tears with his fingertip. "The true spirit of Catholic sainthood," he said. "I may very well go to hell, Siobhan, but there's no doubt at all where you're going."

Forty-six

John Meagher's Land Rover was already waiting in the driveway when she arrived back home. She climbed out of her borrowed Opel Omega into the lashing rain, and hurried toward the porch. John got out and followed her. He was wearing a long black raincoat and she could see that he had taken the trouble to dress up in a shirt and necktie.

"I'm sorry if I'm late," she said. "I was visiting my husband in the hospital."

"I read about it in the papers. Is he going to be all right?"

She opened the front door and let him in. "They don't know yet. Technically he drowned."

"I'm sorry."

She hung up her coat and then she went through to the kitchen and let Sergeant out. Sergeant rushed out and did his usual over-excited dance and hurled himself up and down, but John laid the flat of his hand on the top of Sergeant's head, between his ears, and said, "Sssh, boy. Sssh. Time enough for prancing about in heaven, believe me."

Sergeant immediately calmed down, and whined in his throat, and slunk off back to the kitchen.

"Well," said Katie. "Who are you? The Mongrel-Whisperer?"

"My father taught me. When I was a kid I was terrified of dogs so he trained me to control them. It's an authority thing. If the dog knows that you won't tolerate any kind of stupid behavior, he'll behave himself."

"Let me take your coat."

Katie approached him and lifted his raincoat from his shoulders. For a moment they were close enough to kiss, if they had wanted to. He looked into her eyes and she looked back into his. "Do you know something?" he said. "The first time I saw you – when we discovered those bones – "

"What? I have to heat the soup up."

"I don't know. Maybe it's stupid. I felt that I'd met you before someplace."

"That's not stupid. Our identification experts will tell you that. There are certain facial characteristics that particular types of people have in common. I reminded you of someone else, that's all. I just hope that it was someone you liked."

"Well… it must have been."

They went through to the sitting-room. "Do you want a drink?" Katie asked him. "I can't join you, I'm afraid. But I have some cans of Murphy's in the fridge. Or some wine, if you'd rather."

"Sure, a Murphy's would be good."

When she came back from the kitchen, John was standing in the far corner of the room, looking through the books on her bookshelf. "I wouldn't have had you down as somebody who liked Maeve Binchy," he said, putting back a well-thumbed copy of *Tara Road*.

"I'm an escapist," she admitted.

"Well, I can't say that I blame you, in your line of work. You must get to see some pretty sickening stuff, I'll bet."

"It's not so much that. It's seeing people at their worst, that's what gets to you, in the end. It's seeing how violent and stupid people can be. Sometimes it isn't easy to keep your faith in humanity."

John raised his beer-glass. "Ah, well. Here's to faith."

Katie sat down on the end of the sofa. "You said you had something you wanted to say to me."

John nodded. "I've tried talking to my mother about it, but you've seen what she's like, bless her. And Gabriel, well… he's not exactly the sharpest tool in the box. The trouble is, I wonder if I'm losing it. I mean, can you *tell* when you're losing it?"

"I don't exactly know what you mean."

"It's that farm. It's really grinding me down. Day after day, week after week, month after month. It's milking and plowing and digging and fence-mending and getting soaked to the skin and all I can hear in the middle of the night is the rain beating against the windows and my mother snoring like a walrus. You don't know what I'd give to go out in the evening and meet my friends at Salvatore's and fill my face with *linguine pescatora*."

Katie couldn't help smiling; but John said, "I'm sorry, I shouldn't whinge. I chose to come here and do it, but I genuinely think that I'm losing my marbles."

"Sit down," said Katie. "Have some more Murphy's, it's good for what you're suffering from."

John sat on the far end of the sofa, next to the pink-dyed pampas grass. Sergeant came back from the kitchen and stared at him balefully for a while, but then he made a squeaky sound in this throat and trotted to his bed.

John said, "I saw something."

He hesitated for so long that Katie said, "Go on. What was it?"

"I'm not entirely sure. I was putting the tractor back in the shed when I thought I saw somebody standing in the field up by the woods, in the place where I found that young girl's body."

"Did you call the garda on duty?"

John shook his head. "He was right down by the front gate.

300

It just seemed easier to go up the field myself. I thought it was probably somebody taking a short cut. Some of the young kids on the estate do that sometimes, to get to the main road."

"And?"

"I climbed over the fence and walked up the field. The sun was just going down behind the trees and it was shining right in my eyes. But when I got nearer I could see that it was a woman, wearing a long gray coat, with a gray shawl around her shoulders, or a pashmina, something like that."

He paused again, and then he said, "I called out to her. Like, 'Excuse me, but nobody's allowed in this field at the moment.' And it was then that she disappeared."

"You mean she walked away?"

"No. She literally disappeared. She faded. Very gradually, so that I could still see the faint outline of her when I was only twenty or thirty yards away. But by the time I reached the place where she had been standing, she had completely vanished. No trace of her. No footprints, nothing."

"What did you do?"

"What could I do? There was nobody there."

"You didn't tell the garda on duty?"

"What was the point? He would have thought that I was off my head. That's what I'm saying. Maybe I *am* off my head."

"So why did you decide to tell me?"

"Because I couldn't keep it to myself and I couldn't think of anybody else to tell. My mother thinks there's something strange about me because I don't eat mashed potatoes with my knife."

Katie looked at John for a long time without saying anything. The way she saw it, there were several possible explanations. One, he was simply trying to attract her attention, because he liked her, and this was the only way he could think of doing it. Or two, he had seen nothing more ghostly than the setting sun, shining on the early-evening mist. Or three, he was suffering from delusions, brought on by isolation and depression and stress.

"What do *you* think it was?" she asked him.

"I don't have any idea. I guess it could have been a mirage or an optical illusion."

"But you don't think it was?"

"No. I was looking at it for far too long and it was far too – I don't know, *substantial*. It wasn't just a trick of the light or a puff of smoke."

"Nobody could have simply laid down in one of the furrows so that you couldn't see them?"

"I told you. She didn't fall over, or drop down, or anything like that. She *faded*."

Katie had another long think. Then she said, "Can I show you something?"

"Sure, if it explains what I saw."

She went to the front door, but as she did so the doorbell chimed. She opened it up and there was a young man in oil-stained blue coveralls with a Maxol badge on his pocket. He had curly fair hair and a smudge of oil on his upturned nose and there was no mistaking that he was Patrick Logan's son.

"Superintendent Maguire? Declan Logan. My father called me to look at your car so."

"That's great. Thanks for coming. I don't have any idea what's wrong with it, but my husband couldn't get it started."

"My dad said that your husband was in the hospital. I'm sorry to hear about that."

"Thanks. Look – here are the keys."

Katie went outside, and Sergeant followed her, intently sniffing at Declan's trainers. His bright yellow Transit van was parked by the front gate, with Declan Logan Auto Doctor emblazoned in red on the side. Katie went to her car and took out the picture of Mor-Rioghain that Gerard had given her.

"Come on, Sergeant," she called. "You're being a pest."

"Oh, he's grand," said Declan, slapping Sergeant's flanks. "I like dogs."

Katie went back into the sitting-room. "Would you like another beer?" she asked John.

"I'm okay, thanks. You have to keep your wits about you when you're operating farm machinery. Especially when you're going nuts, like me."

"Here," said Katie, sliding the drawing of Mor-Rioghain out of the envelope. "Does this look anything like the woman you saw?"

John studied the picture intently. Then he nodded. "It could have been. Obviously she wasn't so distinct. But, yes."

He handed the picture back. Outside, they could hear Paul's Pajero whinnying as Declan tried to start it up. Katie opened her mouth to say something, but suddenly the air in the sitting-room became strangely *compressed*, like an airplane at high altitude. There was a deep creaking sound, and Katie immediately knew what was happening. She threw herself across the sofa and dragged John onto the carpet, just as the windows exploded with an ear-splitting bang, and the curtains flew up in a blizzard of glittering glass.

Clouds of thick black smoke rolled in through the window, so that Katie could barely see from one side of the room to the other. Thousands of cushion-feathers drifted down on top of them, as well as shreds of burning Dralon and fragments of sponge-rubber.

John struggled to sit up. He said, "What the hell was that?" but then he realized that he was deafened, and he couldn't even hear what he was saying.

"Bomb," Katie shouted at him. "Don't get up. Stay where you are. There might be another."

"*Bomb*? I didn't think that happened in the South."

"Just stay where you are."

She stood up. The smoke was clearing, and through the frameless window she could see Paul's Pajero blazing in the middle of the driveway. Declan's van was parked right next to it, connected by jump-leads. The Pajero's roof had been blown upward into an extraordinary question-mark shape. The driver's door was lying in the herbaceous border by the front gates, and Declan was lying next to it, with his hand still clutching the handle. Katie could see blood.

She heaved aside a tipped-over armchair and ran out into the rain. John followed her. The air was pungent with the smell of wet laurels and exploded Semtex.

"Told you to stay where you were," snapped Katie.

"Look at him – this guy needs medical attention, and he needs it right now."

Katie rang Anglesea Street and called for an ambulance, a fire pump and the bomb-disposal unit, as well as Liam Fennessy and Jimmy O'Rourke and eight other gardaí, no matter where they were or what they were doing.

"Stay well away from the car," she warned John, but he was already skirting around it. He crossed the lawn, which was scorched with streaks of black, and knelt down next to Declan in the flower-bed.

Declan was quaking like a man suffering from an epileptic fit. His hair was cinder-black and sticking up on end. His face was blackened, too, and when John gently lifted his head, his right eye slid glutinously out of its socket and dangled on his cheek. But the worst blast damage was on his left side. His left arm was missing, so that his shoulder-bone was gleaming through the bloody shreds of his sleeve, and his left leg had been blown off just above the knee. Katie saw his leg, right in the middle of the road, with his neatly-tied Adidas trainer still on it.

Blood was jetting out of Declan's femoral artery and darkening the soil beneath his leg. Without any hesitation, John pulled off his belt, tore back the tatters of Declan's overalls, and lashed the belt around his thigh, pulling it so tight that the blood stopped spurting almost at once. "Get me a towel," he told Katie. "We've got to stop his arm from bleeding, too. And blankets, to keep him warm. He's in serious shock."

Katie ran into the house and stripped blankets off her bed. When she came back out John had stripped off his coat and was using his bundled-up shirt as a pad to press against Declan's shoulder. Rain dripped from his hair and ran down his bare, muscular back.

"Here," she said, and gave him two bath-towels. Then she covered Declan with blankets, and knelt over him to keep the rain off his mutilated face. The Pajero's tires were burning now, with a malevolent hissing noise, and there was a stench of rubber that made her eyes water and went right down her throat.

"How long before the ambulance gets here?" John asked her.

"They're very quick, mostly. But it depends where they're coming from."

"He won't make it unless we can treat him for shock."

"He'd be dead already if it wasn't for you."

"I did two years' training at San Francisco General Hospital. I was going to be a doctor."

They waited in the herbaceous border for another ten minutes, and then they heard the ambulance siren coming from Fota Island. Even before the ambulance appeared, they heard squad car sirens as well, five or six of them, and a fire pump.

Katie looked at John through the rain. Declan was still

shuddering, and occasionally he let out a quick, surprised gasp. Then the ambulance pulled into the driveway, and the doors were opened up. A young paramedic laid a hand on her shoulder and said, "You're grand, superintendent. We'll take it from here."

A garda gave her a hand and helped her up, and it was only then that she realized that she was shuddering, too, and that the tarmac drive, when she tried to walk across it, had turned to water.

Forty-seven

After an hour Jimmy O'Rourke came into the sitting-room, brushing the rain from his shoulders. "We've checked everywhere. Garages, shed. All through the house. There's no more booby-traps that we can find."

"Does it look like the kind of device that Dave MacSweeny might have planted?"

"Well, let's put it this way, it doesn't look as if it was very professional. The bomb boys think they wired about half a pound of Semtex to the self-starter, but the connection may have been faulty. It was only when Declan put the jump-leads on it that there was enough current to bridge the gap."

"God, I don't know how I'm going to break the news to Patrick."

Jimmy laid a hand on her shoulder. "I'll do it if you like. Patrick and I go back a very long way."

"No, you're all right. It's my job. And besides, I was the one who asked Declan to take a look at Paul's car, and it should have occurred to me that there was some good reason why it wouldn't start. That was what Dave MacSweeny was doing here yesterday. He wasn't waiting to follow us. He couldn't even have known that I was going to give Paul a lift. He was hanging around, the bastard, waiting to hear his bomb go off."

"And when it didn't, he lost his temper, and rammed you into the river?"

307

"It's the most likely scenario, isn't it? Pity Dave MacSweeny isn't around to tell us whether it's true."

Jimmy turned to John, who was wearing one of Paul's shirts, and a thick brown Aran sweater. "John... the paramedics asked me to tell you that you probably saved Declan's life. He's critical, but they think he's going to pull through."

"John was a medical student in San Francisco," Katie explained.

"Well, that was God looking out for Declan, I'd say."

John said, "It wasn't any big deal. In any case, I quit after two years. I guess I wasn't really cut out for it. It gets to you, after a while, all that blood and guts. I was more interested in alternative healing, you know. Aromatherapy, reflexology, herbal medicines, that kind of thing."

"Witchcraft?" asked Jimmy, making a potion-stirring gesture. "Eye of toad and bollock of bat?"

John gave him a wry smile, but didn't reply.

Liam came in. "Superintendent? Can I see you for a moment?"

"Of course."

"Outside, if that's all right. There's something I have to show you."

Katie followed him into the front garden. The burned-out wreckage of Paul's Pajero was still smouldering, but the fire was out. Officers from the technical bureau were examining the ignition mechanism, and others were taking photographs of the blast-pattern. Three bomb-disposal experts from Collins Barracks were standing around smoking and shuffling their feet. Liam led Katie to the side of the garden, toward the laurel bushes.

"We didn't see him at first. I hope this isn't going to upset you too much."

"What is it?" asked Katie, and there was something in

308

Liam's expression that gave her a sudden surge of chilly dread.

Liam pulled one of the bushes aside, and said, "I'm sorry. I really am."

At first Katie couldn't understand what she was looking at. Halfway up one of the silver-birch trees that stood behind the laurels was a tangle of red-and-yellow ropes, with thinner strings hanging from it, and large lumps of glistening maroon with bubbles of white all around them. It was only when she saw Sergeant's head on top of the tangle, and one of his legs dangling down between the thinner strings, that she realized she was looking at the blown-apart body of her dog.

"Oh my God," she said. She turned away and walked stiff-legged across the driveway, while Liam let the bushes rustle back. He came after her and stood beside her, ignoring the rain that speckled his glasses.

"I'm sorry," he told her, and held out his hand.

"It's not your fault." She thought that she sounded like somebody else altogether – somebody on the edge of cracking up. "I should have followed the proper security procedure."

"This is nothing to do with procedure. You've had Sergeant for how many years?"

"Eight," she said, and then cleared her throat. "He was eight."

She felt like walking out of the front gate and walking and walking and never coming back, but she knew that she couldn't. She had to follow this through to the end, if only to redeem herself for what had happened here today. Liam said, "Why don't you take the rest of the afternoon off? I can cover for you."

"I'll be fine. And besides, I've got too much to do. I have to interview Tómas Ó Conaill again."

"You'd tell *me* to take the rest of the afternoon off, if something like this happened to me."

"I'm too busy, Liam. I'll take some time off when Tómas Ó Conaill is convicted."

"Will you look at yourself? You're white. Even your lips are white."

"In that case I'd better put some lipstick on."

She went back into the house. Liam followed her. She sat on the sofa with her hands pressed against her ears and her eyes tight shut. She felt as if she wanted to block out the whole world. If only she could be deaf and blind for long enough, she could open her eyes and find that Paul was out of his coma and Sergeant was still alive and that nobody had been murdered or mutilated or drowned.

John frowned at Liam and mouthed, "What's happened?"

Liam said, "Her dog got caught in the blast. We've just found it." To Katie he said, "Would you like a drink? Brandy maybe?"

Katie shook her head.

"Listen," said Liam, "I'll have them take Sergeant away as soon as I can, and I'll make sure that they treat him with respect."

She opened her eyes. It was no good trying to deny what had happened. "Thank you," she sniffed. John passed her a box of Kleenex.

"He wouldn't have known what hit him, believe me. He wouldn't have suffered."

"I know that, yes. But he was such a mad, friendly dog, you know? He didn't deserve to die like that."

"You're sure you don't want that drink?"

"If I take a drink I won't be able to go back on duty."

"You've had a bad shock," said John. "Maybe you should give yourself the rest of the day to get over it. I had a neighbor in San Francisco whose dog got hit by a truck and she was depressed for *months*."

Katie took a deep breath. "I'm fine. I'll survive. Did we get the rest of those technical reports yet, from the cottage?"

"They came in about half-an-hour before. I haven't had time to look at them in detail, but it seems that there are very few fingerprints, and none of them match Ó Conaill's. Some of the footprints in the blood are his, so he was obviously lying when he said that he had never been into the bedroom. But the lab says that he only trod on the blood after it was congealed. The other prints were made when it was still fresh."

Katie said, "I still believe Tómas Ó Conaill did it, or had a hand in it, at least. But it's certainly beginning to look as if he wasn't alone. That makes me even more worried about Siobhan Buckley."

"No news on her, I'm afraid."

John's cellphone rang and he went out to the hall to answer it. When he came back he said, "Is it all right if I go now? I've just heard from Gabe that one of my cows has gone into labor. I'll come down to the Garda station if you want to talk to me again."

"That's all right. I'll want you for a witness statement about what happened here today, but it's not desperate."

"Listen," said John, "I'm so sorry about your dog. I really am."

Katie accompanied him out to his Land Rover. The force of the bomb had cracked the driver's side window and two triangular pieces of shrapnel had penetrated the bodywork, narrowly missing the fuel tank. "So much for my no-claims bonus," he remarked.

Katie said, "About that other thing... the figure you saw up by Iollan's Wood."

"Maybe I was hallucinating."

"Tell me something... do you *believe* in things like that?

Ghosts, or fairies, or spirits from the other side?"

"I don't know. I can only tell you what I saw. I mean, plenty of other people in Ireland claim that they've seen apparitions, don't they? Did you see that TV program about leprechauns? Somebody's keeping a twenty-four video watch on a magic tree in County Laois, hoping to see real live little people."

"If you could conjure up Mor-Rioghain, what would you wish for?"

"Me? A couple of million dollars I guess, like most people would. And a long vacation someplace warm and sunny. And a beautiful, intelligent woman to take with me. How about you?"

"I don't know. It's no good trying to put the clock back, is it?"

Forty-eight

Tómas Ó Conaill was supremely calm, so self-possessed that Katie found him as threatening as dark afternoon, before a thunderstorm. He was wearing a faded black denim shirt which was open to reveal the Celtic chain that was tattooed around his throat and the herringbone pattern of black hair on his death-white chest. In his left hand he held a packet of Player's untipped cigarettes, which he constantly rotated, over and over, until Katie felt like snatching it away from him. But she knew that was what he was challenging her to do; and so she kept her temper, and didn't.

He smelled strongly of male sweat, and Ritchie's clove sweeties. He had a new lawyer this afternoon, a smooth gray-haired fellow in a shiny gray suit from Coughlan Fitzgerald & O'Regan, one of the grander firms of solicitors in South Mall. Before Katie could even open her mouth he announced himself as Michael Kidney and didn't stop interrupting Katie's interrogation all the way through.

Katie said, "Tómas, there were several footprints in the blood on the bedroom floor and they were identified by our technical people as yours."

"Then I must have wandered into the bedroom, mustn't I?"

"*Wandered*? You didn't just wander. You had Fiona Kelly imprisoned in that bedroom and you murdered her there, didn't you?"

Michael Kidney lifted his expensive ballpen. "I'll have to interrupt here, detective superintendent. My client has admitted that he may have strayed into the bedroom; but that was only *after* the event, long after the murderer had left; and he was quite unaware what had happened there."

"The bedroom was plastered with blood. Only a gowl couldn't have been aware what had happened there."

"Being a gowl, as far as I know, is not a criminal offence. If it was, then half of the male population of Ireland would be languishing behind bars."

"Tómas," said Katie, leaning forward across the table. "Tómas, listen to me. I think you know what happened to Fiona, but I'm also prepared to believe that you didn't do it entirely on your own. There was somebody else involved with you, wasn't there? You may have known all about the ritual for raising Mor-Rioghain, but there was somebody else with you who did the killing, wasn't there? I know you have a reputation, Tómas. But this wasn't your doing, was it? Not the actual murdering."

"I swear on the Holy Bible that I never murdered nobody and I swear on the Holy Bible that I never helped nobody to murder nobody, neither."

"You swore that you never went into the bedroom, but you did."

"I might have done, yes. But there was nobody there and as I say I never murdered nobody. I swear."

"What's your friend's name?"

"What?"

Michael Kidney immediately raised his hand. "Superintendent, my client is innocent, and he doesn't have to implicate anybody else to prove it. It's your job to discover who committed this murder, not his."

"I simply asked him the name of his friend. The one who actually murdered Fiona."

Tómas shook his dreadlocks like a filthy floormop. "I've done nothing but tell you the truth, Katie. I never murdered nobody and I don't have no murdering friend."

Michael Kidney sat back, took off his glasses, and started to polish them with the end of his necktie. "Seems like an impasse, detective superintendent. And I have to say that your evidence is very insubstantial."

"Insubstantial? We can prove that Tómas drove the car in which the dead girl's body was taken to Knocknadeenly, and we can prove that he was present in the room where she was killed."

"*Where* she was killed, yes, but not *when*. You can't inconclusively establish that he committed murder, and you don't even have a credible motive. All this talk of fairies and witches. You're not seriously going to accuse my client of black magic?"

"We have sufficient evidence to prepare a file for the Director of Public Prosecutions, no matter what his motive was. I'm just giving him the opportunity to make things easier for himself, by giving us a little co-operation."

There was a moment's silence. Then Michael Kidney said, "I heard that you lost your dog today. I want you to know how sorry we all are. Everybody at Coughlan Fitzgerald."

Katie took in a sharp, involuntary breath. "Thank you," she said. Then she turned to Tómas Ó Conaill again and she knew instantly from the look in his eyes that Tómas had sensed her distress.

"I love dogs myself, Katie," he told her, in the softest of voices. "I had a grand black Labrador once, who died. He was mostly Labrador, anyway. It was almost as bad as losing a friend."

315

Katie said, "A young art student called Siobhan Buckley was abducted from Summerhill two-and-a-half days ago and we still haven't been able to find her. A witness saw her accepting a lift in a car, just like Fiona Kelly. If you know anything about this – if you had an accomplice when you took Fiona Kelly – I need to know who he is, Tómas, and I need to know where to locate him, and very fast. Because if you know where she is, and something bad happens to her, I swear to God that I'll have you in prison for the rest of your life."

Tómas took out a cigarette, and lit it, and blew out voluminous quantities of smoke. "I've told you, Katie. I had no accomplice, and I don't know nothing. But if it helps, let me tell you this."

"Tómas – " Michael Kidney warned him.

"No, Michael," said Tómas. "I've done nothing particularly wrong and if it helps Katie with her investigation, then why not? I'll confess it now. Bless me, dearest Katie, for I have sinned. I didn't find the Mercedes where I said I found it. I saw it in the driveway of the old garden center and there was nobody around and the keys were still in it and I admit to you freely that I was thinking of robbing it. I didn't actually rob it because you turned up, didn't you, like the baddest of bad pennies. But I did look around the cottage and I did see that something fiercely horrible must have happened there, and I was ready to go away when you shouted 'Armed Garda' at me and I was caught.

"But if this is something to do with the raising-up of Mor-Rioghain, let me advise you of this, if you didn't know it already. Mor-Rioghain can only be summoned by a witch, and only a witch can speak the final words which will set Mor-Rioghain free. So if it's a man who took Fiona Kelly and murdered her for the purpose of bringing Mor-Rioghain through from the other side, then he wasn't working alone, as you rightly guess. He must have been working along with a woman."

"My client didn't say that," put in Michael Kidney, crossly. "You can't accept any of that as part of his interview."

"Shut your gob, Mr Kidney," said Tómas Ó Conaill, placidly. "What I'm doing now is helping Katie to find the fellow that she's really looking for, because when she finds the fellow that she's really looking for, she'll know that it wasn't me who laid a finger on Fiona Kelly or nobody else."

"So you think that I should be looking for a man and a woman, together?" asked Katie.

Tómas Ó Conaill lifted his cigarette as if to say it, that's it, you've got it.

Katie stood up. "Mr Kidney... I think we'll need to talk to Mr Ó Conaill again in the morning."

"I'm not sure that's going to be convenient."

"Then make it convenient, if you don't mind; or send somebody else."

"All right, superintendent. No need to get upset."

Gerard O'Brien called her just as she was driving out of Anglesea Street.

"Katie, I think we need to have a talk."

"Gerard, can't it wait until tomorrow? I'm on my way to the Regional to see Paul."

"I've been on the internet all afternoon. I've come up with something. I don't know exactly what it means, but I think you ought know about it."

"All right," she said, steering one-handed towards Sullivan's Quay, with the gray afternoon light reflected in the river. "Why don't you tell me what it is?"

"It's difficult to tell you everything on the phone. Perhaps you could meet me for a coffee later on; or even dinner."

"Gerard, I really appreciate it, but this investigation is taking up all of my time, and a number of things have been getting on top of me, and I'd really – "

Somebody blew their car-horn at her, and she suddenly realized that the lights at the junction of George's Quay had changed to green.

"Gerard," she said, "I can't talk now. Give me an hour and I'll call you right back."

"*I called the university*," he said, and then his voice broke up into a crackle.

She dropped her cellphone onto the seat beside her, and waved her hand in acknowledgement to the car behind her. She drove to the Regional Hospital past St Finbarr's Cathedral. A few spots of rain spattered onto her windshield, and already it was beginning to grow dark.

She couldn't stop thinking about her interview with Tómas Ó Conaill. All of the circumstantial evidence indicated that he had at least been a party to Fiona Kelly's murder; even if he hadn't actually dissected her himself. But what if he were right, and the legend of Mor-Rioghain *did* demand a female witch to summon her up from the Invisible Kingdom? Who was the most likely candidate for that?

The only person she could picture was John Meagher's mother, coughing her way from room to room. It was hard to imagine that John alone was capable of killing anybody, even though he was depressed and lonely and financially strapped. But if his mother was acquainted with the ritual, and if his mother had always been aware of the skeletons that were buried under the feedstore, she would have known how to finish the sacrifice, how to add two more victims to the toll of eleven, and bring Mor-Rioghain out of the darkness.

John thought that he had seen an apparition by Iollan's Wood; a ghostly wraith that could have been Mor-Rioghain.

In the mental state that he was in, his mother could have led him to believe that he had actually seen her, even though it had probably been nothing more than a twist of evening mist, or smoke, or the last of the sunlight falling between the trees.

Katie decided that she would go up to Meagher's Farm again tomorrow morning and talk to John and his mother, separately, and see if she couldn't push this line of thinking a little further. There might be a *Psycho* factor behind these sacrifices: a mother exerting her influence over her favorite son, in order to give him the strength and the confidence that he hadn't been born with.

Dr O'Keeney came into the waiting-room. He was a tall, rangy man with bulging eyes like Buster Keaton and hands that flapped around at the bottom of his sleeves as if they didn't belong to him. He smelled of antiseptic and smoke.

"We've had the results of Paul's tests, Katie, and I have to be honest and tell you here and now that they're not very encouraging."

Katie felt cold. She had been right on the point of standing up, but now she remained seated, although she kept her back rigidly straight. Dr O'Keeney had a large wart close to the side of his nose. She had always wondered why people didn't have warts removed, especially doctors.

"Paul's brain was deprived of oxygen for long enough to cause a considerable amount of damage. His disability isn't life-threatening, I have to tell you, but it is very unlikely that he will recover consciousness, and he is likely to remain in a vegetative state for the remainder of his life."

"He won't wake up? *Ever*?"

Dr O'Keeney shook his head. "I don't know what's happening inside of his head, Katie, what thoughts he might be having, what dreams. But I don't think they could possibly be worse than the sort of existence that he would have to suffer if he were to come out of his coma, and try to live in the waking world. He would be unable to speak, unable to feed himself, doubly incontinent, but always conscious of his predicament."

"So what can I do?"

"Nothing, I'm afraid. I do have several other coma cases here, where parents and children sit with their afflicted loved ones, and talk to them every day, and play them their favorite music. It's always very well publicized when somebody recovers, but in my experience this very rarely happens. You'll have to face up to something very grim, Katie. To all intents and purposes, Katie, the Paul you knew died in the back of that car."

"What if he's aware?"

"He's not, I assure you."

"How can you be certain? You just said yourself that you didn't know what thoughts he was having."

"Katie, barring a miracle from God, he's lost to you for ever. I'm very sorry."

She went alone into Paul's room and stood beside him. He looked deeply peaceful, as if he were simply sleeping after a long day's betting on the horses at Fairyhouse and too much Guinness. She knew now that her life had changed for ever; and that the dreams she had harbored when she was young were never to be. She felt as if her dreams had been a curse on everybody who came into contact with her, even her dog.

She didn't kiss him, couldn't. What was the point? Instead, she walked out through the swing doors and into the parking-lot where it was raining in torrents and ran to her car. She started the engine, then she turned it off again. Then she picked up her cellphone and dialed Jury's Inn.

"Lucy? Lucy, it's Katie Maguire. Do you mind if we meet?"

Forty-nine

As she pulled away from the Y-junction at Victoria Cross, a pick-up truck came right through the lights opposite The Crow's Nest pub and collided with her nearside passenger door. The truck wasn't going fast, but the noise was tremendous, and Katie's car was pushed sideways across the road so that her rear offside bumper was hit by a hackney coming in the opposite direction.

She climbed out into the pouring rain. The pick-up's wheel-arch had become entangled with hers, and when the driver tried to reverse there was a crackling, groaning sound of metal and plastic.

Turning up her collar, she walked around to the driver's door and held up her badge.

"Oh feck," said the driver. He was a young man with a shaven head and earrings and a donkey-jacket with orange fluorescent patches on it.

"You went right through a red light without stopping," Katie told him. "I want your name and address and the name of your insurance company."

"I'm sorry, my girlfriend's having a baby and I was trying to get home quick."

"I don't care if the hounds of hell are after you, you could have killed somebody, driving like that."

She called the traffic department at Anglesea Street and then ordered the pick-up driver to pull in by the side of the road. Her car was still drivable, even though the tire chafed against the twisted wheel-arch with a chuffing sound like maracas. By the time a squad car had arrived and she had redirected two miles of congested traffic, she was soaked through, and trembling with cold.

"Not your week, superintendent," said Garda Nial O'Gorman, climbing out of the squad car and putting on his cap.

Lucy was waiting for her in the bar, at a table by the window, working on her laptop. She was wearing a fluffy white rollneck sweater and black leather trousers. "My God," she said, when Katie walked in. "What happened to you?"

"Minor car accident, that's all. Nobody hurt, nothing to worry about."

"You're drenched. Do you want a drink?"

"I'm still on duty, but I'll have a coffee maybe."

She sat down. Through the window she could see the lights of Western Road and the glossy black river, sliding by. "What are you working on?" she asked, nodding at the laptop. "Are you making any progress with this Mor-Rioghain thing?"

"A little," said Lucy. "I went up to Knocknadeenly again this morning and had a look at the site by the wood. There's no doubt that it's the sort of place that would have had great magical significance in druidic times. There are Celtic stone markers at Ballynahina to the south, at Tullig to the west, at Rathfilode cave to the east, and at the megalithic tomb at Kilgallan to the north. If you draw lines from each of these locations, they converge precisely on Knocknadeenly, practically down to the meter. Then, of course, we have Iollan's Wood, which is a natural gateway through to the Invisible Kingdom."

Katie was trying to listen, but Lucy's voice was beginning to echo, and she felt as if she was not really there, and was looking at Lucy through the eye-holes in a mask.

Lucy said, "I've already found two early poems by a local filí which mention Mor-Rioghain in the context of Knocknadeenly. One of them talks about 'the frantic death-dancing of thirteen women on the hill of the gray people', and it also mentions 'the woman with living hair who comes from the land beyond the land'."

She hesitated, and said, "Katie – are you all right? You're looking very white."

"I'm grand. Cold, I think, that's all. And tired. I had some bad news about Paul this afternoon."

Lucy took hold of her hand. "Tell me," she said.

"It seems as if he's never going to – " She stopped, and puckered her lips. She couldn't make her throat work.

"Take your time. It seems as if he's never going to what?"

"The doctor said that – " She waved her hand, trying to pull herself together, trying to explain herself. But then she couldn't stop the tears from running down her cheeks and she couldn't stop herself from sobbing.

The waiter came up with her coffee, but Lucy said, "That's all right, forget it, this lady's kind of upset. Come on, Katie, you come up to my room with me and have a lie-down for a while. You're shaking like a leaf."

Lucy helped her up from her chair and led her across the bar and she didn't resist. Just at the moment, after everything that had happened, she had no more resistance left. Even her pride and her natural determination and her strict Templemore training couldn't protect her from grief.

They walked upstairs to Lucy's first-floor room and Lucy held her hand all the way. Room 223 was plain, but it was warm and comfortable, with beige walls and a double bed with

323

a rusty-colored bedspread. Lucy drew the curtains and then she pulled down the covers.

"Here," she said, and helped Katie out of her sodden coat. "God, even your blouse is wet. Listen – why don't you let me run you a bath, that'll warm you up."

"You don't have to go to any trouble."

"What are friends for? You'd do the same for me, wouldn't you?"

"All right, a bath would be very welcome, thanks."

Lucy brought Katie a white toweling robe from the bathroom and then started running the water. Katie sat on the side of the bed and undressed very slowly. She felt aching, exhausted and disoriented as if she had tumbled down six flights of stairs and knocked her head at the bottom.

"I hope you like Chanel No. 5 bath foam," Lucy called out. "It does wonders for the skin."

"I usually use whatever's on special offer at Dunnes Stores."

"There," said Lucy, coming out of the bathroom. "You have a good long relaxing soak and I'll hang your blouse on the air-conditioner."

Katie climbed into the bath and sat there for a long time staring at nothing at all. She wanted to empty her mind of everything. Of struggling to escape from her car, as it sank backward into the river. Of Declan, shuddering in the flowerbed with half of his leg missing. Of Sergeant, a Daliesque nightmare hanging in the trees. Of Paul, on his long dark journey to the end of his life. Of little Seamus, cold as ice.

"Everything okay?" said Lucy.

"Fine, thank you, yes. This bath smells gorgeous."

"You know what my mother used to say to me? She said, sometimes you just have to admit to yourself that you've had enough, you know? Sometimes you just have to say, I can't cope, I can't fight this any more. I have to give in."

Katie nodded, even though Lucy couldn't see her. She picked up the facecloth from the side of the tub and it was then that she really started to cry. It hit her so unexpectedly that she couldn't believe she was doing it, and she was actually cross with herself for sobbing. But the crosser she got, the more she cried, until she was leaning forward with her nose almost touching the bubbles, her mouth dragged down, her throat aching with self-pity.

Lucy tapped gently at the door. "Katie? Are you all right?"

Again, Katie nodded, but she couldn't speak.

"Katie? You're not crying, are you?"

Lucy hesitated for a moment and then she opened the door. "Oh, Katie," she said. She knelt down beside the bath, rolled up the sleeves of her sweater and put her arms around Katie's shoulders. "Katie, you poor darling. Everybody expects you to be so strong, don't they? They forget that you're human, like all the rest of us."

She kissed Katie on the cheek, twice, in the way that a mother would kiss a weeping child. Then she said, "You relax. I'm going to wash your hair for you and massage your back and you'll feel ten times better, I promise you."

Katie sat without saying a word as Lucy unhooked the shower attachment and wet her hair. She worked shampoo into her scalp with a strong circular movement and the feeling was so soothing that Katie found herself closing her eyes.

"I always wash my hair whenever I'm feeling tired or depressed or hung-over," said Lucy. "I wash my hair and then I sit down and eat a whole bar of chocolate. Like, if nobody else is going to pamper me, then why not pamper myself?"

She rinsed Katie's hair and then she took a handful of body shampoo and started to massage her neck muscles and her back.

"That's wonderful," said Katie. "Where did you learn to do that?"

"My boyfriend used to work for Gold's Gym. He taught me massage and reflexology and all kinds of tricks that you can do to relax yourself."

With her thumbs, she located all of the knots of tension down Katie's spine, and loosened them. "I could do with more of this," said Katie.

"You really are *incredibly* tense," Lucy told her. "It's like your whole body is wound up tight, like a clock-spring."

"Do you still see him?"

"Who?"

"The boyfriend who taught you how to massage people."

Lucy shook her head. "I'm afraid I've never been very lucky with men. Either I frighten them, or else they see me as some kind of challenge. I guess it's the penalty you pay for being tall and well-educated."

"Better than being small and bossy, like me."

"It's your job to be bossy, isn't it?"

"It's not my job to be obnoxious."

Lucy massaged her neck and her upper back. Katie kept her eyes closed and she could almost feel her stress dissolving into the bathwater. Then, without any hesitation, Lucy squirted more body shampoo into her hand and started to massage her breasts.

Katie thought, *Holy Mary, what's she doing?* She opened her eyes and stared at Lucy, but Lucy looked completely calm, as if this was a natural part of the massage. She gave Katie a friendly little smile and Katie thought that if she tried to pull her hands away she would look like a prude. This was a woman, massaging her, that's all, and even if she hadn't been expecting her to touch her breasts, it didn't seem to be intended as a sexual advance.

Lucy squeezed and caressed her shampoo-slippery breasts and Katie dared herself to close her eyes again, and relax, and simply enjoy what Lucy was doing. Lucy came from California, after all, and she knew that American women were much more at ease with nudity than most convent-educated Irish women. God, if only Sister Brigid could see me now.

"You should do this yourself, at least once a week," said Lucy. "It helps to firm your breasts and stimulate your breast-tissue, and of course it's important to check for lumps."

Katie said nothing. The sensation of having her breasts massaged was beginning to arouse her, especially when Lucy pulled gently at her nipples and rolled them between her fingers. It had been a long time since anybody had touched her as lovingly as this, as if they really cared about her. She began to think that if she allowed Lucy to carry on, she might even be able to reach an orgasm, simply from having her breasts caressed.

But then Lucy said, "Come on, now, you don't want to get cold," and kissed her on the forehead. She pulled the plug and helped Katie to climb out of the bath and wrap a towel around herself.

When Katie was dry, Lucy poured them both a whiskey from the mini-bar and they lay side by side on the bed, talking. Katie felt as if she could lie there for ever.

"You know, I don't think I've ever had a really close woman friend," said Lucy. "I guess it's because I get so-o-o bored by women's conversation. All they want to talk about is their repulsive children, or their husbands' careers in accountancy or how to make a tantalizing pie out of left-over turkey."

Katie smiled. She felt warm now, and much more peaceful, and she realized that while Lucy's massage had been disturbingly intimate, it must have been the kind of hands-on sisterly gesture

327

that Californian women considered to be perfectly natural. Just because Sister Boniface at Our Lady of Lourdes would have been scandalized…

She said, "I used to have some wonderful friends at school, but most of them are married now, with seven kids. One of them's a teacher at a special school in Kilkenny, and one went to Dublin to sing in a choir, but the rest of them fell pregnant as soon as they'd finished their leaving certs, or even before."

She turned to Lucy. "Did you ever think about getting married?"

Lucy shook her head.

"Children?"

"One day, maybe, if things work out the way I want them to."

"Do you know, I'm not sure what I'm going to do now, with Paul in a coma. I'm still going to be married, aren't I? But how can you be married to somebody who's never going to wake up?"

Lucy touched her bare shoulder. "He's gone, Katie. You're going to have to get used to the idea."

"I suppose so. But it's hard."

They lay in silence for a long time. Katie closed her eyes and felt that she could easily drift off to sleep. But after a while Lucy said, "This guy, Tómas Ó Conaill. Do you really think that you're going to get a conviction?"

Katie opened her eyes and blinked at her.

"You have a whole lot of evidence, don't you? The fingerprints, the footprints."

Katie said, "Well, you're right. The circumstantial evidence is very strong, and Ó Conaill's got a bad reputation, but still – I don't know – something doesn't quite fit. He said that Mor-Rioghain could only be raised by a witch, a woman. Yet our eye-witness report suggests that Fiona Kelly was almost certainly abducted by a man, and Dr Reidy says that the physical strength required to kill her and cut her up would have been way beyond a woman's capabilities. Not only that, I've been reading through the FBI profiles, and it's extremely rare for a lone woman to be a serial killer, and almost unheard-of for a woman to be a serial killer with any kind of mythical or fantasy motive."

"So you think it *could* have been a partnership?"

"It's a possibility. Especially since we still haven't been able to find Siobhan Buckley, and Mor-Rioghain needs one more sacrifice before she can make her appearance."

"You're beginning to sound as if *you* believe in Mor-Rioghain."

"I'm simply trying to think like our killer, that's all. Or killers. *They* believe she exists, and because of that, I have to believe in her, too."

"And do you have any suspicions about who they might be?"

"John Meagher told me that he actually saw Mor-Rioghain. Or a figure of some kind, anyway, standing in the field where he found Fiona's body."

"You're kidding me."

"He swore it. He said he saw it as plain as the nose on his face."

"He's probably hallucinating. It must have been a hell of a shock, finding Fiona's body like that."

"All right. But when you think about it, John Meagher has a very compelling motive for wanting to raise up a spirit like Mor-Rioghain – a spirit who can help people to solve all of their problems. He hates farming, he's gradually going bankrupt. And his mother... well, she may not be a real witch but she certainly looks like one. And she might very well have known about the bones buried under the feedstore. After all, she's been living at Meagher's Farm ever since she was nineteen years old."

"Do you have any material evidence that the Meaghers could have been involved?"

"None. We searched the fields, the outbuildings, the farmhouse. We even dug up the floor of the piggery."

"In that case, maybe you can get them to confess? Always presuming they did it, of course."

"Easier said than done. If they did it together, mother and son, it's going to be very difficult to break that kind of a relationship. I had to deal with a father-and-daughter situation a couple of years ago, in Carrigaline, the father got together with the daughter and crushed his wife's head under his tractor, with the daughter actually holding her mother down. I knew they'd done it, and they knew that I knew that they'd done it, but I could never get either of them to admit it, and they're still free today. Jesus, I saw them shopping in Roches Stores."

"Maybe I can help you," said Lucy, propping herself up on one elbow. "After all, I know just about everything there is to know about Mor-Rioghain, and how she's summoned up, and the rituals that have to be performed to persuade her to help you. If you and I can talk to the Meaghers together... well, there's a possibility that we could get them to slip up, isn't there?"

Katie shook her head. "I think you've been watching too many American cop shows."

"Unh-hunh. I hardly ever watch TV. I did a two-year postgraduate course in business psychology at UC Santa Cruz. I was trained to ask people the kind of questions that show them up for what they really are. Ambitious, boastful, deceitful, whatever. Whoever killed Fiona Kelly must have been supremely confident that he or she was going to get away with it, and when somebody's as confident as that they're *very* prone to making mistakes. They think that everybody else is stupid, that's why, so they don't bother to work on their stories."

Katie thought about that for a moment and then said, "All

right. Why don't you and I take a trip up to Knocknadeenly tomorrow morning – say around ten?"

Lucy laid her hand on Katie's shoulder. "The main thing is – are you feeling better?"

"Thanks to you, yes."

"So what are you going to do now?"

Katie looked into her rain-gray eyes and she could almost have loved her. "I'm going home now, I suppose."

"I don't know why you don't close your eyes for an hour. It's only seven."

"No, I have to get back."

Lucy leaned over her, and stroked her hair, and traced a pattern around her eyebrows with her fingertips, and touched her lips. "Close your eyes. It'll do you good, I promise you. In the gym, they always make you take a short sleep, after a massage. Otherwise you walk out feeling like your brains have turned into scrambled eggs."

"It's only seven?"

"Six fifty-five, as a matter of fact."

There was no question that Katie felt overwhelmingly drowsy. She felt almost like Dorothy, wandering through the field of poppies in *The Wizard of Oz*. The hotel-room was warm and her toweling bathrobe was warm and there was Lucy lying next to her, shushing her and stroking her and touching her ears. She had never even allowed Paul to touch her ears, because they were sensitive, but Lucy tenderly ran her fingers around them as if they were winter roses, and she was coaxing the scent from their petals.

"I should go," she said, trying to raise her head.

Lucy gently pushed her back down onto the pillow. "An hour won't do you any harm. And you'll feel much better afterward, I promise you."

"You'll wake me up, though, at eight?"

Lucy kissed her on the lips. It was totally chaste, but somehow it made Katie feel as if she had discovered a whole new dimension; a mirror-world, where everything was still familiar, but everything was back-to-front. It was alarming, in a way, but it was also strangely alluring.

"I'll wake you up, I promise you."

Katie lay still for two or three minutes with her eyes still open, but then it seemed as if it was impossible not to close them for a while – only for a minute. When she was a detective sergeant, sitting in a squad car watching a house all night, she had developed the capability of sleeping for three or four minutes at a time, and she knew that she could still do that now.

"You're warm enough?" asked Lucy, drawing the bedcover over her.

"Myumh."

"You're comfortable?"

"Mmh."

"You're fast asleep?"

Silence.

Lucy sat in a chair beside the bed and watched Katie sleep for nearly an hour. She was just about to get up and take another whiskey from the mini-bar when Katie's cellphone rang. She picked it up from the coffee-table and said, "What?"

"*This is a message from Eircell. You have one new message in your mailbox. To listen to your message, press one.*"

She pressed 1. It was Gerard O'Brien, and he sounded worried.

"Katie? It's Gerard again. Listen, Katie, I really need to talk to you very urgently. I don't want to tell you too much over the phone, but I think I've found out who Callwood was, and what happened to him; and I've also found out some very worrying information that might affect the way you decide to pursue this investigation, which is about the discreetest way I can think of to put it."

He paused, and then he said, "Call me back as soon as you can. I'll try leaving a message with Liam Fennessy, too."

Lucy kept the cellphone pressed against her ear. After a while, the Eircell voice said, *"To erase your message, press 7."*

She looked down at Katie, who was now sleeping deeply with her mouth open and one hand intermittently jittering on the pillow next to her as if she were trying to catch the smallest of dusty-gray moths.

Fifty

Liam was about to leave his office when his telephone rang.

"Inspector Fennessy? It's the switchboard here. Is Super-intendent Maguire there with you?"

"I haven't seen her all afternoon. Have you tried her mobile?"

"I have, but she isn't answering. It's Professor O'Brien, he says he has something important to tell her but he can't seem to find her."

"Is he on the phone now? Put him on."

There was a sharp crackle, and then Gerard said, "Is that Inspector Fennessy? I've been trying to locate Superintendent Maguire."

"Anything I can help you with?"

"It's to do with these murders. I really have to talk to her urgently. I've tried her cellphone, I've tried calling her up at Meagher's Farm – "

"Professor, I'm assigned to this case, too. If you've found out anything critical – "

"Critical? It's absolutely *cataclysmic*. I'm waiting on some final bits and pieces of information from America, but when I get it, I think we may be able to solve the 1915 murders *and* the Fiona Kelly murder, too. And change the face of modern history, besides."

"Listen, professor, I don't actually know where Katie is, right at this moment, but I expect that I'll be hearing from her sometime this evening. Why don't you tell me what it is that you've found out, and then I can pass it on to Katie when she calls me?"

"Well, ah – I think I'd better try to talk to Katie first. I'm not sure she'd be – "

"We're talking about a murder inquiry, Professor O'Brien. If you have material evidence that could help to bring somebody to justice, then you ought to tell me about it, and you ought to tell me as soon as possible."

There was a long pause, and then Gerard said, "All right, then. But this is not a thing that I can explain to you over the phone."

"I'll come to see you, then. Where are you now?"

"I'm at home. Number 45 Perrott Street, up at the back of the university."

"Give me twenty minutes. There's one or two things I have to sort out first."

"All right, then. But if you do hear from Katie in the meantime, you'll let her know?"

"I will of course."

He met Jimmy O'Rourke in the lobby. "Fancy an old beer, sir, before you go?" Jimmy asked him, blowing out cigarette-smoke.

"Just a quick one. Have you seen Katie anywhere?"

"She went home I think. Did you hear about her accident?"

"I did, yes. Christ. That must have been the end to a perfect day."

"She needs to take a week off, if you ask me."

Outside it was clattering with rain. Liam pulled on his overcoat and buttoned it up to the neck. "I always thought this job was too much for a woman. If Katie's not careful she'll be cracking up."

"I'd be careful, if I were you," said Jimmy. "She's a whole lot tougher than she looks."

"We'll see," said Liam. "Where do you want to go? O'Flaherty's?"

Katie was dreaming that she was walking through a slaughterhouse. Cattle-carcasses were heaped on every side, and the whole building reeked of blood. Above her she could see a filthy skylight, clotted with fallen leaves, onto which the rain was ceaselessly pattering. Somewhere, music was playing, echoing and indistinct, as if a radio had fallen down the bottom of a well. *The Fields of Athenry.*

What are you doing here? somebody whispered, close to her ear. *This is a place of death. This is where the Gray-Dolly Man lives, and cuts up people for his own purposes. Women and children, innocent and guilty. He cuts off their arms and legs and saws their screaming heads in half.*

She turned a corner and found herself in another part of the slaughterhouse. The floor was glistening with rainwater and strewn with indescribable pieces of flesh and fragments of bone. Not far away a tall man in a strange five-cornered hat was standing at a metal table, feeding carcasses into a bandsaw. The saw let out a fierce, intermittent scream, and blood and bone was flying everywhere.

Cautiously, she approached him. She lifted her hand to touch him on the shoulder, but as she did so he slowly turned around. She was so shocked that she almost lost her balance. His face was not a face at all, but a mass of crawling beetles.

"*Your turn next,*" he whispered, between lips that literally dripped with insects. "*Your turn next, and you'd better believe it.*"

It was almost ten o'clock now and Gerard was growing irritable. He drew back the sitting-room curtains and peered down the street. It was raining like the Great Flood tonight and he was beginning to suspect that Inspector Fennessy might have decided that he would rather sit at home in front of the TV than visit a professor of Celtic mythology in a large, damp-smelling Victorian apartment that was crowded with books and *National Geographic*s and empty Bulmer's cider bottles. That was all right by him. He preferred to talk to Katie in any case. He just wished Inspector Fennessy could have had the common courtesy to call him and say so.

Gerard was wearing a partially-unraveled sweater of thick green wool that he had bought on a walking holiday in Kerry, and a pair of baggy beige corduroy trousers. In his tiny study, the only light came from his computer, which he had switched on so that he could show Liam Fennessy what he had discovered.

He tried ringing Katie again. But her cellphone rang and rang, and then he was answered by the Eircell answering service. "*If you want to re-record your message…*"

That was the limit. Katie couldn't be found and Liam Fennessy couldn't be bothered to turn up. Gerard believed that he had discovered one of the most dramatic secrets of the twentieth century and when it came down to it, nobody cared. He went back to his study to switch off his computer. He would take his golf umbrella, walk down to Reidy's Vault Bar in the Western Road and console himself with a few pints of cider.

Just as he had clicked the computer off, however, his doorbell shrilled. He gave an old-womanly cluck of exasperation and went over to the intercom by the front door. "Inspector Fennessy?"

"*It is, yes.*" Liam's voice was distorted and barely audible, as if he were standing too far away from the intercom. "*It's raining buckets out here. Are you going to be after letting me in?*"

"You're very late. You said twenty minutes. I was just about to go out."

"I'm sorry, but I'm here now."

Pressing the entry buzzer, Gerard went back to the study and switched on his computer again. While it booted itself up, he blew his nose on a tiny fragment of crumpled Kleenex. He had really wanted to tell Katie what he had discovered, and Katie alone. He had even rehearsed what he was going to say to her, and he knew how impressed she would have been. Perhaps then she would have looked beyond his plumpness and his combed-over hair and seen what he was really like inside: a man who had all the romance of a mythological hero from the days of Tara and Aileach and Cruachan. All the same, he supposed that it would still be fairly dramatic to tell Inspector Fennessy. "What I am about to reveal to you, inspector, will change the way that historians think about the twentieth century for ever."

There was a sharp knock at the door of his apartment, and then another. He called out, "All right – I'm coming!" and drew back the chain.

Before he could open it properly, the door was kicked with such force that it hit him on the side of the face and he fell back against the door of his coat-cupboard. He said, "What – ?" but before he could say anything else a man in a black coat and black balaclava stormed in through the door, seized his sweater, and threw him across the floor, knocking over his coffee-table and all his empty Bulmer's bottles.

Gerard tried to stumble to his feet but the man grabbed his sweater yet again, lifting him almost off his feet, and slamming him against the door-frame that led to his kitchenette. He felt his shoulder crack, and an indescribable pain in the small of his back.

"What are you doing?" Gerard shrilled at him. "For God's sake you're hurting me!"

The man said nothing, but twisted one of his arms behind his back and pressed him against the wall beside his study door.

"The gardaí are coming!" gasped Gerard. "I just called them and they'll be here at any minute."

"Shut up," the man ordered him, calmly.

"I'm telling you the truth, I've got an appointment with Inspector Liam Fennessy. That's why I let you in. I thought you were him."

"And what were you going to tell him?"

"Nothing. Just some research I've been doing, that's all."

"Oh, yes? And what have you managed to find out?"

"Nothing – nothing important. For God's sake, you're hurting me."

"Something about those bones up at Knocknadeenly, was it? Something about Fiona Kelly?"

"I'm not telling you. You can do whatever you like, I – "

The man gripped Gerard between the legs and twisted. Gerard let out a cry of agony that sounded more like a tortured dog than a man. The man twisted him again, even more fiercely, and this time Gerard babbled out, "*I found out who killed all those women! That's all!*"

"And what about Fiona Kelly? Did you find out who killed Fiona Kelly?"

Gerard shook his head. Tears were streaming down his cheeks and if the man hadn't been holding him up he would have collapsed on the carpet.

"I'm asking you again. Did you find out who killed Fiona Kelly?"

"I don't know, I swear to God. The gardaí still think it was Tómas Ó Conaill, but if it wasn't Tómas Ó Conaill then I don't know who it was."

"You'd better be telling me the truth."

The man released his grip, and Gerard crouched his way over to the sofa and lay down with his knees drawn up under him, coughing.

The man went into his study. All around Gerard's computer, his desk was heaped with books and magazines and spring-bound notebooks. The man picked up a notebook on top of the heap and said, "What's this? Does this have anything to do with it?"

"Gaelic legends," Gerard coughed, miserably. "Preparation for a lecture on Friday. Nothing to do with – Knocknadeenly."

The man tossed the notebook aside and swept the papers onto the floor. Then he lifted up Gerard's computer and threw it against the wall. The monitor imploded with a dull bang and a shower of glass. The man stamped on the drive unit, denting the case and breaking the plastic inlets. Then he came back into the sitting-room.

"Up, come on."

"What?"

"You heard me. Up!"

One-handed, he heaved Gerard off the sofa. He jostled him out of his front door, along the landing, and down the high Victorian stairs. Gerard did everything he could to resist, flapping his arms and trying to make his legs turn to jelly, but the man was frighteningly powerful, and when his legs collapsed beneath him the man simply picked him up by the scruff of his Kerry sweater and made him dance along like a puppet.

"Where are we going?" Gerard panted, as the man forced him along the corridor that led to the back door.

"Shut up."

He opened the back door and pushed Gerard out into the narrow courtyard at the back of the house. It used to be part of a larger garden but now it was all tarmacked over and Gerard used it to park his old red Nissan. Through the teeming rain, Gerard saw a large white car parked only inches away from his.

"Where are you taking me? You can't do this... this is abduction!"

"No it isn't," the man assured him.

"You can't take me away against my will!"

"I don't intend to. Now, shut up."

The man pulled Gerard to the back of the car. He unlocked the trunk and took out a length of nylon washing-line. Then he kicked the back of Gerard's calves, so that Gerard dropped to the ground like a knackered cow.

"What do you want? Who are you? I haven't done anything to anyone."

The man said nothing. He bent over Gerard and deftly tied his wrists together. He cut the washing-line with a craft-knife, and then he looped Gerard's wrists over the car's towing-hook.

"What the hell are you doing to me?" Gerard shrilled at him. "If you think you're going to drag me along the road – "

"I'm not," said the man. "So shut up."

"Look, I don't know what this is all about, but if there's something else that you're after..."

"Shut up," the man repeated. He took the rest of the washing-line and tied it to Gerard's ankles. Then he knotted it tightly around a sign saying *Residents Parking Only*.

Gerard lay on the ground and looked up at him, so terrified that he could hardly breathe.

"What are you going to do to me? Are you going to *leave* me here?"

"Some of you, I expect."

"*What are you going to do to me?*"

The man stood over him for a while, and Gerard could see the raindrops sparkling all around his head, caught in the streetlights so that they looked like an endless shower of tiny meteorites.

"Help!" Gerard called, but he was so frightened that his throat closed up and he could only manage a hoarse whisper. "Somebody help me!"

The man went back around the car and climbed into the driver's seat. There was a moment's pause and then he started the engine.

"*Help*!" Gerard screamed. "*Holy Mary, Mother of God, somebody help me*!"

The engine revved. Gerard twisted and grunted and struggled, trying to lift his wrists over the towing-hook at the back of the car. If only he could stretch himself another inch, he was sure that he could get himself free. This man was trying to scare him, that was all, trying to warn him off. Somebody must have alerted him that he was asking questions about Jack Callwood, and that he was getting very close to the truth. It hadn't occurred to him before that the British government might have intelligence officers in the Irish Republic to make sure that nobody tried to look under any stones that they didn't want looked under, particularly from their colonial days, and the days of the Black and Tans and the Irish Volunteers.

"All right!" Gerard shrieked out. "I promise you I won't say anything to anybody! Not a word! Ever!"

The engine-revving died down. Gerard lay back in relief, with the rain falling directly in his face and almost blinding him. "Just let me up, will you? Untie me and let me up. I won't say anything, I swear to God. I swear on my mother's grave."

Without warning, the car was revved up again. The man threw it into gear and drove off, tearing every muscle in Gerard's body with a sound like ripping linen and pulling both of his arms off.

Gerard instantly stopped shouting. He realized that something appalling had happened to him but he didn't want to know what. He lay on the wet tarmac with blood pumping with horrible regularity from his each of his arm-sockets. He felt no pain at all. In fact, he felt oddly relieved, glad that the worst was over. He heard the car stop, and the driver's door slam, but he didn't see the man walk back and stand over him, because his eyes were closed.

The man said, "Some things aren't meant to be found out, professor. It wasn't your fault, but there you are."

For some reason, Gerard couldn't think of a prayer. All he could remember was W.H. Auden's poem about the iceberg knocking in the cupboard, and the desert sighing in the bed, and the "crack in the teacup that opens... a lane to the land of the dead."

Fifty-one

It took Katie almost five minutes to wake up properly. When she finally managed to lift her head, she felt as if her dead mother had stuffed her knitting in her mouth. Lucy was sitting in the armchair, watching a documentary on the *Lusitania* on the Discovery channel with the volume turned down.

"What time is it?" she asked, thickly.

"Half-past nine."

Katie sat up and dry-washed her face with her hands. "Jesus! I thought I asked you to wake me at eight."

"I tried, believe me, but you were dead to the world. Do you want me to make you a cup of coffee?"

"No – no thanks. Is there anything fizzy in that mini-bar?"

"Sure. Here."

Katie popped open the miniature can of Diet Coke and drank it in four quick swallows. Lucy stood up and said, "How do you feel?"

"Terrible."

"That's because you haven't relaxed in ages. Not really relaxed."

"I can't relax. I've got too much to do."

Lucy sat down on the bed beside her, and stroked her hair. "I used to be just like you sometimes, all nerves, all stressed out, never allowing myself to rest. But that's because I was never focused. I couldn't decide what to do with my life. It was only when I narrowed my vision down to one single objective that I began to understand myself. You have to say, 'This is what I want and I'll do anything to achieve it.' And I mean *anything*. If you can do that, you'll find this tremendous inner calm, I promise you."

"I have to check in with Anglesea Street."

"Katie – you don't actually have to do anything but relax."

Katie turned her head and looked into her eyes. "I can't. Not yet. But I promise you that I will, as soon as this case is complete. We could go down to West Cork together if you like, and I can show you Baltimore and Cape Clear. It's beautiful down there."

Lucy leaned forward and kissed her lightly on the forehead. "That sounds wonderful."

"Well, it'll be a way of paying you back, for everything you've done for me. You saved my life when I was drowning in the river, and now you've saved me from going to pieces."

"You don't have to pay me back."

Katie went to the dressing-table, where she brushed out her hair. She hadn't dried it properly after her bath, and it stuck out wildly. "Look at me," she said. "I look madder than Tómas Ó Conaill."

"Wet it again and I'll blow-dry it for you."

"You should have been a therapist, instead of a professor of mythology."

"Mythology *is* a kind of therapy, in a way. It's the way we understand our place in the world. There are no merrows and *bean-sidhe*s, Katie. Not really. There's only us."

Liam didn't reach Perrott Street until 10:47. He climbed out of his car and hurried to Gerard's front door, his collar turned up against the pelting rain. He pressed the doorbell and waited.

Then he pressed it again. Fuck it. The stupid bastard hadn't even had the patience to wait an extra twenty minutes. Well, whatever Gerard had wanted to tell him, it couldn't have been *that* critical. It was Liam's guess that he had probably been exaggerating its urgency so that he could persuade Katie to come round to see him. He didn't entirely blame him. When Katie had first been stationed at Anglesea Street, Liam had been attracted to her, too.

He ran back to his car and splashed straight into a pothole full of water, soaking his sock.

It was still raining when Katie arrived home, and the house was in darkness. Paul's burned-out Pajero had been towed away and the sitting-room window had been boarded up with plywood. She let herself in and switched on the lights. The house was cold and it even *smelled* empty.

She went into the sitting-room and poured herself a large vodka. Then she tried her message-recorder. Jimmy O'Rourke said, "*I've been trying your mobile but it seems to be switched off. We might have a lead on the Siobhan Buckley case. A woman remembers seeing a man and a girl answering Siobhan's description in a large white car up by the traffic lights by Mayfield shopping center. She said it looked as if they were arguing, and the girl was crying. I'm going to set up a new search tomorrow morning, concentrating on Mayfield and Glanmire and maybe up as far as Knockraha. I'll talk to you later.*"

Then Liam, sounding as if he had taken drink. "*Katie... I couldn't get you on your cellphone so I just wanted you to know that lover-boy Gerard O'Brien was trying to get in touch with you. He said he had some very important new information so I went round to meet him at his house. I was only a few minutes late but the silly bastard had gone out.*

346

I reckon it's you he wants to meet, if you want to know the truth."

She rang the Regional and talked to the sister on Paul's ward. "*There's no change at all, I'm afraid.*"

No change at all? she thought, sitting on the chilly sofa by the empty black hearth. She could still picture Paul pacing up and down with his glass of Power's in his hand as he blethered to all of his dodgy builder friends, and Sergeant resting his head on her knee so that she could fondle his floppy ears.

After a while she went into the kitchen and made herself two slices of toasted cheese, with Mitchelstown cheddar and lots of cayenne pepper. She ate them standing up, and sucked her fingers when she had finished, because that's what you can do, when you're alone.

Fifty-two

The next morning it was still raining and the sky was a grim greenish-gray, like corroded zinc. It was so dark that Katie had to switch on the overhead lights in her office. On the roof of the car park opposite, the crows sat bedraggled and even more sinister-looking than ever, and she was sure that there were more of them. She hung up her raincoat and then she sat down with a cup of cappuccino to read through her mail and her paperwork.

Dermot O'Driscoll came in, with his bright red necktie askew. "There you are, thank God. I've had Patrick Goggin panicking since eight o'clock this morning like a washerwoman with her knickers on fire. He says there's a meeting at Stormont at three o'clock tomorrow afternoon and he needs to be able to report some positive progress."

Katie didn't look up. "Sir – this is a very difficult and complicated investigation. There are very few written records; there are no living witnesses; and even if I can prove beyond a shadow of a doubt that Tómas Ó Conaill murdered Fiona Kelly, it won't throw any more light on what the British did in 1915."

"Politics are bad for my digestion," Dermot grumbled. "I couldn't even face a second sausage this morning."

Katie said, "Gerard O'Brien may have some more information. He called me yesterday afternoon to say that he had some new research for me to look at."

"Have you got in touch with him yet?"

"I'm going up to Knocknadeenly first, to talk to the Meaghers again."

"Look, call him. The sooner I get Patrick Goggin off my back, the sooner I can get back to a normal diet."

"All right." Katie punched out Gerard's number while Dermot waited in the doorway, slowly rubbing his stomach as if to calm it down. Gerard's number rang and rang, but Gerard didn't pick up. Katie called Jimmy O'Rourke instead.

"Jimmy? Where are you now?"

"Dennehy's Cross, stuck in traffic."

"Listen, on your way in, can you call at 45 Perrott Street and see if Professor Gerard O'Brien is at home? If he's not there, try his office at the university."

"I'm very pushed for time, superintendent."

"I realize that, Jimmy. But this is important."

Katie switched the phone off. "Sorry," she told Dermot. "Just for the moment, that's the best I can do."

"Well, try to get me something by the end of the day. I don't want my dinner ruined as well. By the way, how's your Paul getting along?"

"No better. No worse."

Dermot nodded and said, "We're all thinking of you, Katie. You know that."

She left Anglesea Street at 10:22. She tried to call Lucy to tell her that she was running late, but all she could hear on Lucy's cellphone was a thick crackling noise. With her coat-collar turned up against the rain, she hurried to the bronze Vectra that she had been allocated in place of the damaged Omega. She climbed in, brushed the rain from her shoulders and checked herself in the sun-vizor mirror. She looked almost as bedraggled as one of the crows.

Cork Corporation had started new main drainage works at the corner of Patrick's Bridge so she had to wait for almost five minutes with pneumatic drills clattering in her ears and Father Mathew the hero of temperance staring at her balefully from his plinth in the middle of the road. As she drove up Summerhill the rain started to hammer down so hard that she had to switch her windshield wipers to full speed. Buses passed through the spray like ghostly illuminated boats.

She reached Knocknadeenly at 10:57. The garda on duty at the gate was sitting in his squad car with the windows steamed up, having a cigarette, but when she drew up beside him he climbed out and came across, still breathing smoke.

"Nice soft day, superintendent," he remarked.

"Everything okay? Has Professor Quinn arrived here yet?"

"About twenty minutes ago. Nobody else."

"All right, then, Padraig. What time do you go off duty?"

"Not for another two hours yet. If it doesn't stop raining soon I'll have to go home by canoe."

Katie drove slowly up the driveway, with her windshield wipers still flapping hysterically in front of her. She turned her car around in the muddy forecourt in front of Meagher's Farm and climbed out. A blue Ford tractor was parked next to John Meagher's Land Rover with its engine running, but there was no sign of anybody around. She walked across to the farmhouse and into the porch. The front door was open and the house was filled with the strong crusty aroma of baking bread. She knocked and called out, "John? Mrs Meagher? Anyone at home?"

Nobody answered, and the rain continued to pour down out of the sky as if it was determined to drown her.

Katie opened the farmhouse door a little wider, and stepped into the hallway. There were old coats hanging on pegs, and muddy boots tangled together. "John?" she said. "Lucy?" But still there was no reply. Only the giggling of Teletubbies, in the sitting-room.

She looked into the kitchen. It was gloomy but reasonably tidy, apart from a mixing bowl with a tea-towel over it, and a floury bread-board, and a rolling-pin. Katie hesitated for a moment, and then she went through to the sitting-room.

The Teletubbies were rolling on their backs and kicking their legs in the air. Mrs Meagher was sitting in the tall armchair facing the television, her gray wiry hair barely visible over the back of it. Katie could see one arm dangling down the side of the chair, in a hand-knitted olive-green sweater, with orange flecks in it. A burned-out cigarette had fallen onto the carpet.

"Mrs Meagher?" she said. "Mrs Meagher? It's Detective Superintendent Katie Maguire. Do you know where John is?"

Mrs Meagher didn't answer. The Teletubbies called out, "*Eh-oh*!" and went scampering off behind their improbably green hill. Cautiously, Katie walked around the side of her chair. Mrs Meagher was staring at her with milky eyes, her mouth hanging open to reveal her tobacco-stained teeth. Her throat was cut from side to side and the front of her sweater and her pleated skirt were drenched in blood. Drops of blood were still creeping down her shins and into her slippers.

"Oh, Jesus," said Katie. She stood staring at Mrs Meagher for a moment and then she had to turn away.

Her hands shaking, she took out her cellphone to call for back-up. As she started to punch out the number, however, John Meagher stepped into the sitting-room and barked, "*Don't*!"

Fifty-three

Jimmy O'Rourke parked his car outside 45 Perrott Street and heaved himself out of his car. Personally, he thought that this part of their investigation was a total waste of time. He didn't give a monkey's who had killed those eleven women in 1915, and if it had been up to him, he would have dropped the case into the "pending for all eternity" file, even if Sinn Féin were acting the maggot about it. All that mattered was who had killed Fiona Kelly, and Jimmy believed, like Katie, that Tómas Ó Conaill had at least been a party to it.

He went to Gerard's front door and rang the bell. No answer. He rang again. Still no answer. He walked round to the side of the house and peered up at Gerard's window, his hand held up to shield his face from the rain. Gerard was out, no doubt about it, and that meant that he would have to go looking for him at the university. He said, "Shit," under his breath. He had plenty of other things to do this morning, like interviewing seven Romanian so-called asylum-seekers who had broken into a mini-cab office in MacCurtain Street and made off with €132.75 from the petty-cash box.

Jimmy was just about to leave when a bedraggled black Labrador came around the corner of the house, carrying something in its mouth.

"Here boy," said Jimmy.

The Labrador looked guilty, and dropped its trophy onto the pavement. At first glance Jimmy thought it was somebody's lost gardening glove, but when he took a closer look he realized that it was a man's hand.

"Here boy, where did you find that, boy?"

The dog loped off. Jimmy walked over to the hand and hunkered down next to it. He took out his ballpen and poked it but he didn't try to pick it up. There was a cheap gold ring on the hand's third finger, with a black onyx in it.

Jimmy walked around the back of the house, into the driveway. There were twenty or thirty crows flapping and hopping around, and when Jimmy appeared they flustered off into the sky. It was then that he saw Gerard O'Brien's body lying on the ground, with wet strands of black hair sticking to his face like a veil. His arms were lying amidst a heap of litter over seven feet away, still tied together by the wrists.

"Holy Mary," said Jimmy. He leaned over Gerard to make absolutely sure that he was dead, and then he stepped away. "Who the feck did *this* to you?"

He took out his cellphone and tried to call Katie, but he couldn't get through, so he called Liam Fennessy instead. "Inspector? I'm at 45 Perrott Street. I've found Professor O'Brien, or what's left of him. That's right, somebody's done for him, practically torn the poor bastard apart. Yes, 45 Perrott Street."

Liam sounded out of breath. *"I'm away from the station at the moment, Jimmy, but I'll send Patrick O'Sullivan and Brian Dockery, and the technical team. When you say they've torn him apart – ?"*

"Somebody's ripped his arms off. Looks like they must have tied him to the back of a car."

"You're codding me."

"I'm not. I'm serious. Professor O'Brien on one side of the car park, arms on the other."

"I'll have to get back to you, hold on."

Jimmy wiped the rain from his face. The crows kept circling back, but they came no further than the wall between 45 Perrott Street and the house next door, where they shuffled together like the scruffy punters in a Blackpool betting shop. Jimmy tried the back door and found that it was still unlocked. He unholstered his Smith & Wesson revolver and shouldered his way inside. The stairway was dark and smelled of frying mince. Jimmy paused at every turn in the stairs, keeping his gun held high, and listening. By the time he reached Gerard's flat, however, it was obvious that his killer must have been long gone. Somebody downstairs was playing *Days Like This* by Van Morrison and from upstairs came the clatter of somebody running a bath.

Jimmy nudged open the broken door of Gerard's flat and went inside. He checked the sitting-room and the kitchen and the bathroom but there was nobody there. He went into the study and found papers strewn all over the floor and the smashed computer, and the chair tipped over.

He tried calling Katie again, but he still couldn't get through. There was nothing much he could do now, until the technical team got here. He poked around the study, picking up one or two papers, but most of them were lecture-notes on Celtic mythology. He decided to go outside for a smoke.

Before he left, he bent down and picked up the notebook that was lying on the study floor. The first few pages were packed with hand-scribbled notes, mostly in Gaelic. He was about to toss it down again when his eye was caught by the word "*iobairt*," underlined five times. It was the Gaelic word for "sacrifice."

Jimmy picked up Gerard's leather armchair and sat down. He skimmed through the first few pages and realized that they were comments about Badhbh the Death Queen and Macha and Mor-Rioghain and how thirteen ritual killings could be used to call Mor-Rioghain out of the Invisible Kingdom. Jimmy's Gaelic wasn't as good as it should have been, considering that every garda was required to be reasonably fluent, and that 11-year-old Jimmy O'Rourke had come second in Gaelic studies at Scoil Oilibhéir at Ballyvolane. All the same, he was able to understand most of it.

Gerard had written: "Several authoritative sources suggest that *once Mor-Rioghain appears, it is necessary for the summoner to offer her a living woman as a final sacrifice to seal the bargain between them. This living sacrifice would have to be the wife of a chieftain, or the most influential woman in her community.*" The reason for this apparently being that once she materialized in the mortal world, Mor-Rioghain did not want to have her influence challenged by any mortal woman.

"*The living sacrifice has to be tied and blindfolded. Her stomach has to be cut open ready for Mor-Rioghain to step through from the Invisible Kingdom, so that when the witch conducting the sacrifice has recited the sacred texts, and Mor-Rioghain has made her appearance, she can drag out the victim's intestines and drape them around her shoulders as a cloak of her absolute authority.*"

"Yuck," said Jimmy, out loud. He flicked through the next few pages, recognizing words like "*mort*" for murder and "*cloigionn*" for skull, but there didn't appear to be anything particularly new in Gerard's notes. He had already taken out his cigarette-packet when he reached a page that was written in English.

"I have talked to two different heads of department but the

355

British Public Records Office in Kew *insist* that they have no information about the disappearances of the 11 Irishwomen between 1915–1916!! But I contacted my old friend John Roberts at the Imperial War Museum and he was able to put me on to the relatives of the late Colonel Herbert Corcoran in Nantwich. Major Corcoran (as he then was) was attached to the Crown Forces in Cork between 1914 and 1922, and was considered something of a spy-hero in the style of William Stephenson ('A Man Called Intrepid').

"Major Corcoran had a Cork accent which assisted him in infiltrating the republican movement with considerable success. It was his information that led to the ambush of the 1st Cork Brigade at Dripsey in 1921 and the killing of nine IRA men. In the late 1920s he wrote two books of memoirs, *War of Whispers* and *Undercover in Ireland*, although these were *drastically* censored by the British War Office, and amounted to little more than *Boy's Own*-type adventures. In fact he also wrote three fictitious stories for *Magnet* and *Boy's Own*, based on his adventures in Ireland.

"His family sent me these pages with the caveat that, in later years, Colonel Corcoran had become obsessive about his time in Ireland and was constantly writing rambling letters to the newspapers about it. In his last job at the War Office before he retired he was affectionately known as 'Crackers' Corcoran."

Jimmy turned the page, and there they were: curled-up fax-paper copies of Colonel Corcoran's diaries, stapled in a thick bunch to the back cover of Gerard's notebook.

Colonel Corcoran had written: "I pen these pages knowing that they will probably never be seen for a hundred years to come. However, I feel that this story should be recorded in the interests of military history and of humanity.

"While I was operating as a senior intelligence officer

in County Cork in the summer of 1916, I was contacted by Brigadier Sir Ronald French at the War Office. He informed me that the local commanding officer in Cork, Lieutenant-Colonel Gordon Wilson, had been instructed to find and arrest a man who had been masquerading as a British officer in order to abduct Irishwomen.

"It appeared that this man had been offering women rides in his motor-car, after which they had never been seen again.

"After seven Irishwomen had disappeared, I was told to assist Lieutenant-Colonel Wilson to apprehend the perpetrator at whatever cost, not for the sake of justice alone, but to ward off a very dangerous political situation, since the Irish republicans were accusing the British of taking and murdering their womenfolk in retaliation for several bomb attacks on military garrisons in Cork City.

"After the tenth abduction, I set up an ambush at Dillon's Cross, with Mrs Margaret Morrissey, the wife of Sergeant Kevin Morrissey of the Signal Corps, bravely volunteering to act as a 'Judas goat'. The abductor approached her but as soon as he realized that she had an English accent he took to his heels. We almost succeeded in catching him, but our vehicle became bogged down in thick mud at Ballyvolane and we lost him over the fields. Two months later, however, after an eleventh abduction, I set up another ambush with an Irishwoman who worked in the garrison laundry, Kathleen Murphy. When we challenged him, the fellow escaped over a wall in York Hill but we had three Army bloodhounds with us which followed his scent to a second-floor room in a boarding-house in Wellington Road, where we arrested him.

"To begin with, he claimed that his name was Jan Vermeeling, and that he was a Dutch merchant-seaman. However, we discovered papers and letters under the floorboards of his

357

room in the names of John or Jack Callwood, Jan Rufenwald and a birth certificate in the name of Dieter Hartmann, from Münster, in Westphalia. To my astonishment we also found a ticket that showed that he had arrived in Ireland from New York on the ill-fated *Lusitania*, and so must have been one of her 765 survivors. Yet when I checked the manifest of all the *Lusitania* survivors, and their photographs, Dieter Hartmann (or whatever his real name happened to be) did not appear to be among them.

"The answer to this conundrum, however, was in Dieter Hartmann's wardrobe. Apart from a British Army uniform and a tweed jacket and several men's shirts, we found three women's dresses, as well as bodices and lace petticoats. At first we assumed that he was co-habiting with a woman companion, but then it occurred to me to look again at the photographs of those who had been rescued when the *Lusitania* was torpedoed. My intuition proved to be correct: among the survivors was a woman called Miss Mary Chaplain, described in the original list of survivors as a retired teacher from White Plains, New York. The face in the photograph, however, was of a much younger person than any retired teacher would have been, and on closer examination I realized that 'Miss Mary Chaplain' was in fact Dieter Hartmann in women's clothing and a wig.

"Under intensive interrogation, Hartmann eventually admitted that he had taken on the identity of 'Miss Mary Chaplain' to avoid detection on board the *Lusitania*. He confessed that he was wanted for questioning by the Massachusetts police and he was afraid that a wireless message might be sent to the *Lusitania*'s captain to detain him. His fear was well-founded because there had been a thorough search of the vessel in mid-Atlantic, although as 'Miss Mary Chaplain' he evaded discovery. He claimed that there had been some 'misunderstandings' between him and the Massachusetts police concerning the disappearance of several women.

"I contacted my superiors at the War Office and informed them that we had successfully arrested the man we believed to be responsible for abducting the eleven Irishwomen. I told them that I believed him to be Dieter Hartmann, although I also gave them his several aliases – Jan Rufenwald, John Callwood and Mary Chaplain. I was satisfied that I would be able to send him for trial to the Cork County courts.

"Almost by return, however, I received a coded wireless message ordering me to execute Dieter Hartmann summarily and to 'eliminate' all evidence of his existence. I was to tell Colonel Wilson and all of the other officers and men who had assisted me that my investigation was now concluded and that they were not to speak of it again, in the interests of national security.

"With three NCOs I took Dieter Hartmann that same evening to a bog close to Glanmire, where he was made to kneel and shot once in the back of the head with a service revolver. He was buried very deep in the bog and we left no marker.

"I wondered for many years afterward why I should have been ordered to execute Dieter Hartmann so expeditiously and so secretly. After all, he was a German, and in my estimation at the time it would have been matchless propaganda for the Crown Forces if we were credited with catching the man who had abducted and presumably murdered so many Irishwomen – not that we ever found their remains."

Jimmy lit up his cigarette and blew smoke out of his nostrils. Katie would love this stuff, and it would mean that they could wind up their own investigation, too, thank God.

Colonel Corcoran had written: "I thought no more about Dieter Hartmann until 1923, when I received a copy in the post of a rather sensational American magazine called *True Crime Monthly*. It had been sent to me without any attached comment whatsoever by Lieutenant-Colonel Wilson, who was now working for a merchant bank in New York. The magazine carried an article about the notorious ritual murders of scores of women in Massachusetts. The man suspected to be responsible was 'Jack Callwood' – believed to be one of Germany's worst mass-murderers, 'Jan Rufenwald'. The article said that Jack Callwood had booked passage on the *Lusitania* to escape from the United States and had almost certainly drowned with the other 1,195 victims – 'so even if he escaped the electric chair, natural justice caught up with him.' But of course Colonel Wilson and I knew full well that Callwood had survived, and that it wasn't natural justice that had caught up with him – but us.

"My curiosity about the affair was once again aroused, and through old friends in Naval Intelligence I managed to obtain the records of the wireless signals that were sent to the *Lusitania* prior to her sinking. At the subsequent board of inquiry, the *Lusitania*'s captain, William Turner, was blamed for ignoring the Admiralty's directives for evading German submarines. He said that he had slowed down because of patchy fog off the southern coast of Ireland, and that he had not understood that he was supposed to steer a zig-zag course unless a U-boat was actually sighted.

"But here in the top-secret Admiralty files was the handwritten record of a wireless message which had *ordered* him to slow down, and that he take a particular heading close to the Old Head of Kinsale. It was here that U-boats habitually lurked, waiting for British merchant-ships, and he was intercepted by the German submarine U-20, under the command of Kapitanleutnant Walther Schwieger.

"On further investigation, which took me many months, and in which I naturally had to be extremely circumspect, I discovered from records at the War Office that a telephone call was made to the German Embassy in Dublin on the night of May 4, 1915, to the effect that Jan Rufenwald, alias Jack Callwood, was traveling on board the *Lusitania* to Liverpool. When the liner passed the southern coast of Ireland, they would have an opportunity to exact their revenge on the worst mass-murderer that Germany had ever known.

"Of course, I have no absolute proof. But even at the time, rumor was rife that the British intelligence services colluded in the sinking of the *Lusitania* as a way of provoking outrage against Germany in the United States (which had previously shown little interest in the war in Europe and had even been protesting against the British blockade of German ports.)

"My personal belief is that it was British intelligence who advised the Germans of the presence on board the *Lusitania* of Dieter Hartmann, and that the *Lusitania* was specifically instructed to slow down to a speed at which she would present herself as an easy target to U-20. In a war which had already cost hundreds of thousands of lives, a further 1,195 were of very little consequence compared with the benefits of bringing the United States into the conflict on the Allied side.

"*That* is why I was ordered to dispose of him so secretly. If it ever emerged that the War Office had used him as a bait to encourage the Germans to sink the *Lusitania*, the damage to Anglo-American relations would have never have recovered."

There was a cautious knock at the door, and Detective Garda Patrick O'Sullivan appeared, red-faced, looking as if he had just eaten a rather large Irish breakfast.

"Jesus, the state of that fellow downstairs. No fecking arms. Jesus."

"All right, Patrick," said Jimmy. "Liam's called out the technical team. Any idea where superintendent Maguire has got herself to?"

"Not a clue. I wouldn't blame her if she was drowning her sorrows."

Fifty-four

Katie followed John up the angled field, her shoes clogged with mud. The rain was lashing down slantwise now, and she was completely soaked and shuddering with cold. John turned back and looked at her, but there was nothing she could do to help him, not yet. What was most important now was their survival.

"Move it, will you?" Lucy snapped at them.

"For God's sake," Katie protested.

"There is no God, Katie. You should have realized that by now."

"You're crazy. You really think this is going to happen? You really think that Mor-Rioghain is going to appear?"

"Shut up. Everything's ready. Thirteen sacrifices, it's all been done, everything."

"You're crazy."

"And *you're* not crazy? Going to Mass every Sunday, and eating a biscuit, and thinking that it's Jesus you're eating?"

"Mor-Rioghain is a *myth*. Nothing but a fairy-story."

"And Jesus isn't?"

Lucy looked wilder than Katie had ever seen her before. Her blonde hair was brushed up in spikes, and she was wearing her long black leather coat, which was rolling with raindrops, and her knee-length black leather boots. She was walking beside them, with Katie's nickel-plated gun in her right hand and a four-inch butchers' boning-knife in the other, and Katie was in no doubt at all that she was prepared to use both of them. She had forced Katie to hand over her weapon by sticking the point of the knife into John Meagher's ear, lancing his eardrum. Blood was still dripping from his earlobe and into his shirt-collar.

They reached the crest of the field by Iollan's Wood, where John had found the remains of Fiona Kelly. Katie dreaded to think what they would see there, and her stomach started to spasm. She gagged up a mouthful of half-chewed breakfast, and had to stop.

"Come *on*, will you?" Lucy shouted at her, hoarsely. "We can't waste any more time! Mor-Rioghain has waited too long already."

They trod over the last thick furrows, their feet almost disappearing into the saturated soil, and there spread out in the mud in front of them in reds and grays and fatty yellows was a disassembled human body. Katie had seen Fiona Kelly's remains, but this was still difficult to take in, especially since she was badly scared now, and had no control over what was going to happen to her.

"Siobhan Buckley," said Lucy, stalking around the remains in satisfaction. "Pretty girl, sensitive, artistic. Just what Mor-Rioghain was looking for."

In the same way that Fiona Kelly's remains had been arranged, Siobhan Buckley's ribs were stuck into the ground in a circle and her fleshless skull was perched on top of her pelvis. Her intestines were heaped into the middle like a knot of large pale snakes. Her liver lay shining in a puddle next to her deflated lungs. The rain was pelting down so hard that even the crows were discouraged from coming down to peck at them.

There, too, were her thighbones, with holes drilled through them, and little gray dollies dangling from them.

"She made me help her," said John, with almost overwhelming self-disgust. "She said she'd kill my mother if I didn't, but then she did anyway."

"I never thought that I would see this day," said Lucy, pacing from side to side and making a curious ducking movement with her head every time she turned. "I never thought I would ever see this happen. Mor-Rioghain, the great and terrible Morgana, summoned through from the other side!"

Katie and John stayed where they were. John's fists were clenched tight and his face was very white.

"My colleagues will be wondering where I am," Katie called out. "I was supposed to interview Tómas Ó Conaill again at twelve. If I don't show up, and they can't get in touch with me by telephone, they're going to come looking for me."

"Let them come looking for you," said Lucy, still pacing from side to side. "By the time they find you, there won't be very much left of you."

"What are you talking about?"

"You don't know, do you? When Mor-Rioghain comes through from the other side, she needs a fourteenth sacrifice, a living woman, the strongest woman in the tribe. You were perfect, right from the very beginning. It was always going to be you."

Katie said, "What do you mean, 'right from the very beginning'?"

"Right from the moment I saw you on the television nightly news, when you first discovered all of those women's bones. I heard you talking about ritual murder, and I knew at once what kind of ritual it was, because I could see one of the thigh-bones in the background, with a dolly hanging from it."

"You told me your university sent you."

"University? I've never been to any university. I was living in Boston when I first saw you, working as a window-dresser. Haltmann's Stores, at Downtown Crossing."

"So how did you know so much about Mor-Rioghain?"

"She's my reason for living, Katie. She has been for years. I studied Jack Callwood's sacrifices in endless detail, trying to locate the exact spot where he laid the bodies out, and how many women he had managed to kill. I went out almost every weekend, but I was beginning to think that I would never find what I was looking for. His house in Boston had long since been demolished and there was no way of finding the magical place where he had buried the bones. But there you were, like an angel from heaven, if there were angels, and if there was a heaven. There you were, talking to me on my television, showing me the very place where Mor-Rioghain could be summoned, and telling me how many more women I would have to sacrifice to summon her."

"You're sick. You're totally deranged."

"Well, hah, I'd agree with you, if Mor-Rioghain didn't exist. But when Jack Callwood was Jan Rufenwald, in Germany, he managed to summon Morgana three times, so he said, and each time she gave him wealth, and property, and the company of some of Germany's most desirable women. I first found out about him when I was seventeen years old, and ever since then I've *known* that I would summon Mor-Rioghain myself one day, and today's the day."

"So what do *you* want from Mor-Rioghain? Don't tell me you cut up those poor girls just for money, or houses, or men."

Lucy stopped pacing and stared at Katie and Katie had never seen an expression like that on anybody's face, man or woman, ever. She was alight with triumph.

"Mor-Rioghain will give me *myself*. That's something that I've never had. Mor-Rioghain will give me *me*."

Katie smeared the rain away from her eyes with the back of her hand. She didn't understand this at all, but she knew that she had to think of a way of getting them away from here. Even though it was raining so hard, the smell around Siobhan Buckley's body was sickening, a metallic mixture of blood and peat and feces, and the proximity of actual grisly death made Katie feel even more afraid.

"Take off your clothes," Lucy ordered her. "You have to be ready for the sacrifice."

"No, I won't," said Katie.

Lucy came back around bloody remains and held the boning-knife up to Katie's face. "Take off your clothes or so help me I'll stick this in your eyes."

Katie unbuttoned her sodden green blouse, and peeled it off. Lucy stayed where she was, very close to her, the gun held high, the knife pointing directly at Katie's face. It suddenly occurred to Katie that Lucy must have always carried this knife. How else had she managed to cut so deftly through Katie's seatbelt when her car was sinking in the Lee?

She took off her skirt and stepped out of it. "Underwear now," Lucy insisted. Katie hesitated but Lucy prodded the knife at her. She unfastened her bra and then pulled down her Marks & Spencer panties. The rain ran down her naked back and gave her goosebumps all over.

"Kneel," said Lucy.

"If you so much as lay one finger on me – " Katie began, but Lucy screamed, "*Kneel*!" and so she knelt, her knees sinking into the mud.

Lucy took a black scarf out of her coat pocket and handed it to John. "What do you want me to do with this?" he asked her, his voice sounding tight and terrified.

"Blindfold her, tightly, so that she can't see anything at all.

Even Mor-Rioghain's living sacrifice is not allowed to set eyes on the great one when she appears."

John did as he was told. Then Lucy gave him a length of nylon cord and said, "Tie her hands behind her back."

"I'm not too good with knots."

"Just tie her, will you?"

It took John a few fumbling minutes before he was able to fasten Katie's wrists. All the time he kept mumbling under his breath, "I'm sorry, Katie, I'm sorry. I'm so damned sorry."

When he had finished, Lucy said, "Step away. This is the time for the summoning to begin."

It had grown even darker than ever, and the rain was drifting across the field from Iollan's Wood like the winding-sheets that the *bean-nighe* washes. John took one step back, and then another. "Turn around," Lucy told him, and so he did. With three quick paces she approached him from behind, put her right arm around him and sliced the boning-knife across his Adam's apple.

Fifty-five

Jimmy O'Rourke turned to the last few pages of Gerard's notebook. Outside he and Patrick O'Sullivan could hear police and ambulance sirens approaching from the Western Road. Patrick took out a cigarette, too, and lit it, and took a look around. "Wasn't too tidy, was he? Look at the state of this place. Dirty dinner-plate under the couch."

"He was an academic, Patrick. Very learned fellow. Academics aren't interested in dirty dinner-plates."

Patrick picked up a heap of *Examiner*s and found a dog-eared copy of *Playboy*. "Interested in dirty books, though, I'd say."

"Can't fault the chap's research, though. This is going to cause one hell of a bloody great political row, I can tell you. Wouldn't be surprised if it starts a war."

"I thought you weren't bothered with all of this guff."

"Well, I am now, boy. There could be some promotion in this."

He finished reading the final few paragraphs of Colonel Corcoran's diary, and then he came to some slanted, hastily scribbled notes which Gerard had written at the very end. "Had reply to my email to UC Berkeley re Prof Quinn's research papers!! She published her first study *Celtic Legends* in 1962!! Odd!!"

Jimmy put down the notebook and frowned. "He says here that Professor Quinn published her first paper in 1962. Nineteen sixty-two? That would make her at least sixty-five years old, wouldn't it?"

"I thought you checked her out yourself."

"Yes, but I only checked that she *existed*. I didn't ask if she was a pensioner."

"Have you heard from Katie yet?"

"No, but she's due back at lunch to talk to that Tómas Ó Conaill again."

"Due back from where?"

"She went out to Knocknadeenly with Professor Quinn. She wanted to talk to the Meaghers again."

"Katie's taken Lucy Quinn with her to Knocknadeenly?"

"That's right. She mentioned it this morning."

"Have you tried her cellphone?"

"I can't get through. The mountains screw up the signal, especially in this weather. She said she wouldn't be later than twelve or so."

Jimmy picked up Gerard's notebook again. Why had Gerard needed to talk to Katie so urgently, and why had somebody come to Gerard's flat, smashed up his computer and pulled him apart? Maybe that somebody hadn't wanted him to tell Katie what he had discovered. But if that were the case, why hadn't he taken his notebook, with all his research in it? Unless that somebody could read no Gaelic, and hadn't realized from the first few pages what it was all about.

He tried Katie's cellphone number again. Now the signal said that the phone was out of service. He tried Liam Fennessy instead.

"Inspector? Jimmy O'Rourke here. Are you anywhere near Knocknadeenly?"

"*Not far. I'm just on my way back from Rathcormac. Assault with a deadly leg of pale ham. Fellow knocked his poor old father's teeth out.*"

"I've been trying to contact Katie Maguire. She's up at the Meagher farm with that Professor Lucy Quinn, supposed to be talking to John Meagher and his mother. Trouble is I can't get a signal, and, well – "

"*What?*"

"I've been looking through Gerard O'Brien's research papers here, and there's kind of a cryptic note about Lucy Quinn, like she may not be exactly who she says she is."

"*So who exactly is she?*"

"I don't know, but it might be an idea to call up at the Meaghers' and make sure that everything's okay."

"All right, then. I'll be down with you in Perrott Street in twenty minutes or so. You've got everything under control, then?"

Oh, yes, thought Jimmy. I've got a dead university professor with no arms and a notebook containing the most explosive political secret of the twentieth century. Everything's well under control, boy.

Liam arrived at the entrance to Meagher's Farm and tooted his horn. The garda on duty came hurrying through the rain and Liam wound his window down. "Is Detective Superintendent Maguire still here?"

The garda nodded. "She's been here about forty-five minutes, sir."

"Okay, thanks."

He drove up to the farm buildings. Katie's car was parked outside, as well as the tractor with its engine idling. He climbed out of his car and puddle-hopped over to the front door. The door was half-ajar, and so he knocked at it and called out, "Superintendent? Anybody home?"

371

Katie knelt in the mud with the rain dripping from her nose and her nipples and sliding down her spine. She could hear Lucy on the far side of Siobhan Buckley's remains, chanting and humming. "Come to me, Mor-Rioghain. Come to me, you queen of death and darkness. Come and see what I have to offer you. Come and feast off flesh and pain."

Katie didn't know what had happened to John, even though he lay only a few feet away from her, his shirt dark with blood. All she could think of was: supposing I got up and tried to run, how far would I get, tied-up and blindfolded? But what else can I do? I can't just kneel here and wait for her to cut my stomach open.

"Come to me, Mor-Rioghain, mistress of misery. Come to me, enchantress. I will give you freedom again. I will give you substance and shape. I will set you back where you belong, on a mortal throne, in a mortal kingdom."

Katie was sure that she heard a kind of cackling hiss, like a tortured cat. It was difficult to tell, because of the splattering sound of the rain falling on the field, and the sighing and creaking of the trees in Iollan's Wood, but it went on and on, and if anything it was growing louder.

"Come to me, Mor-Rioghain. I can feel your presence close by. Come to me, sister of disaster, bringer of woe, you who walk by night through cemeteries and sepulchers."

Katie thought: this is madness. There is no Mor-Rioghain. There is no Invisible Kingdom. How she can sacrifice me to somebody who doesn't exist? Yet she continued to strain her ears to hear the cat-hiss, and she thought she could detect another sound, too – a very low-frequency throbbing, like a large unlit tanker making its way up the River Lee in the middle of the night.

"Mor-Rioghain, listen to me! Mor-Rioghain, bring me your magic! I will serve you, Mor-Rioghain, for ever and ever!"

Lucy's voice grew higher and harsher, and behind her blindfold Katie suddenly thought: *This doesn't sound like the Lucy I know. This doesn't even sound like a woman. More like a beast.*

"Mor-Rioghain! Queen of the night! Empress of every decay! Come to me, Mor-Rioghain, I have given you everything you ever demanded! *Come to me, damn and curse you, Mor-Rioghain! Come to me! Come to me!*"

Katie heard a deafening bang, and an echo that came from the woods, and a further echo. She threw herself sideways into the mud because she recognized it instantly. Not a witch, or a *bean-sidhe*, but a gunshot.

"Armed Garda!" shouted Liam. "Drop the gun and put up your hands!"

Lying on the ground, she closed her eyes behind her blindfold and whispered, "Mary, Mother of God, thank you. Mary, Mother of God, thank you, thank you."

She heard Liam squelching toward her. He bent over her and eased the blindfold away from her eyes, one-handed. With his other hand he was keeping his gun leveled at Lucy.

"Are you all right, Katie?"

She blinked against the lashing rain. "I'm grand, Liam. Thank you. I'm grand." She was too relieved to be embarrassed by her nakedness.

"You can't stop Mor-Rioghain now!" Lucy screamed. "This has taken years, and years, and so much blood! You can't stop Mor-Rioghain now!"

Liam yanked at the cord that bound Katie's wrists, and after three sharp tugs she was free. Muddy all over, she climbed to her feet and picked up her clothes. It was only when she went to retrieve her blouse that she saw John lying in a deep furrow with his throat cut.

"You can't stop this now!" Lucy was croaking, and she was staggering around and around in hysterical fury. "*You-cannot-stop-this-now-not-after-everything*! Don't you understand? *Don't you fucking understand*? I have to be me! I have to be me! *I have to know what I am*!"

Katie knelt down beside John and felt his pulse. The boning-knife had cut his larynx but it had missed his carotid artery, and although his breathing was very shallow he was still alive. She took out her handkerchief, folded it into a pad, and pressed it against his throat. Then she said, "Liam, quick, give me your phone. We have to get the paramedics up here."

Lucy kept on spinning around, her arms flailing. Liam threw his phone to Katie and then he approached Lucy with his gun held in both hands. "Keep still! Don't move! Stop going round and round, for feck's sake! Put your hands on top of your head and kneel on the floor!"

Lucy abruptly stopped spinning, and lifted her head, and gave Katie that mad wide-eyed stare that she had given her before.

"Do you hear something, Katie?" she said. "Do you hear something, coming through the woods? The door's open, Katie. The door's open! Mor-Rioghain is rushing our way!"

"Will you ever put your fecking hands on top of your head!" Liam roared at her.

Katie slowly lowered Liam's cellphone. She could hear something, she swore it. That cackling hiss, that ground-quivering rumbling sound. And there was a *feeling*, too, an indescribable feeling that something huge and terrible was coming closer and closer.

"She has to have a living sacrifice, Katie, and if it can't be you then it'll have to be another strong woman, won't it? And who can you think of who's stronger than me?"

374

"Lucy! Calm down! Calm down! Do what Liam tells you! Put your hands on your head and kneel on the ground!"

"Too late, Katie darling! Mor-Rioghain's coming!"

With that, Lucy wrestled herself out of her black leather coat and threw it aside. Then she pulled off her black polo-neck sweater, and her black lacy bra. Her breasts were big, and dark-nippled, and veined with blue.

"*Kneel down!*" Liam yelled at her.

"*You don't understand anything!*" Lucy screamed back at him. "*You don't understand anything at all!*"

Then, suddenly, she stiffened, and stood still, as if she had heard what she was waiting for, and she smiled a waxy-looking smile.

"Mor-Rioghain," she breathed. Behind her, the branches of Iollan's Wood were thrashing from side to side like the arms of drowning bathers. Katie swore that the temperature was dropping, and that the rain was even colder, and when she looked up the sky was crowded with silent, wheeling crows.

Raising her voice against the rain, Lucy said, "All my life I never knew what I was, or understood myself. And then I found out about Mor-Rioghain – that she could give you everything you ever wanted. Other people get everything they want, other people understand themselves. Why not me?"

The wind was rising. The wet leaves of autumn were being lifted from the floor of the woods, and there was a death-rattle of bracken-stalks, like a thousand old people with bronchitis. Soil began to fly from the furrows in a black blizzard.

"You can't have *anything* at the price of somebody else's life!" Katie shouted. "You can't!"

Lucy unbuckled the belt of her tight black leather trousers. "*Who are you to judge me?*" she shrieked. "*Who are you to judge? If I can't have you as a sacrifice, then I'll sacrifice myself, and ask for Mor-Rioghain to give me my life back!*"

She forced her trousers down to her knees. She wasn't wearing any underwear, and when Katie saw her she slowly raised her hand to her mouth, and stared at her, and simply couldn't believe what she was looking at.

Lucy had a fully-developed penis, and testicles, and curly black pubic hair.

"Christ," said Liam.

Something happened then, but Katie didn't mention it in her report, and neither did Liam, and they never spoke about it again, even to each other. But they both felt as if the world had gone blind, as if the atmospheric pressure had dropped so much that nobody could breathe. Lucy picked up her boning-knife and what was Liam going to do? Shoot her?

Katie felt as if a huge dark presence swept over them, or perhaps it was only a katabatic gust of wind. But Lucy threw her head back and stuck the boning-knife into her chest, right up to the handle, and drew it downward, not hurrying, as if she were relishing the way she was opening herself up. For a long, calm moment she stood in the rain with her intestines sliding out of her, all down her thighs, and her face was as strange and pale as beautiful as the face of Mor-Rioghain herself.

"Now, Mor-Rioghain, you have your sacrifice!" she cried, even though her voice was juddering with pain. "Come through, O Pitiless One, and take my offerings! Come through, maker of widows and orphans, carrier of grief and shadows! *I call you once, I call you twice –* "

Katie thought, *God, this is the final summoning. Mor-Rioghain's coming – she's actually coming through!*

She stumbled toward Lucy through the muddy furrows. She fell to her knees once, but she managed to pick herself up again. Liam shouted, "*Katie! No! For Christ's sake!*"

But Katie picked her shining revolver out of the mud, raised it double-handed, and fired it almost point-blank at Lucy's face. Lucy pitched backward in a spray of blood, and a slap of an echo came back from the trees.

Almost at once there was a loud sucking noise, like closing a car window at high speed, and a sudden increase in pressure that made Katie's ears pop. The soil beneath her feet physically *rippled*, a shock-wave of earth that ran all the way back to Iollan's Wood. The trees dipped and thrashed as if something wild were tearing at their roots, and then they were suddenly still.

Katie stood where she was, panting. A small ghost of gunsmoke hurried off into the woods. Liam cautiously came up to her, still pointing his revolver at Lucy's bloody white body.

"It's all right, Liam. She's completely dead."

Liam looked around him. The wind had died down already, although the rain continued to fall across the fields.

"You only fecking topped her," he said, in disbelief.

"I didn't have any choice."

"Jesus, Mary and Joseph, she was past saving already." He peered at the body. "*It* was past saving already."

"You don't know that. She was going to ask Mor-Rioghain to bring her back to life."

"Katie, there *is* no Mor-Rioghain. Did you see any Mor-Rioghain? There was wind all right, but it was only a squall."

"You're probably right. But I wasn't prepared to chance it. And I wasn't going to let down any of those thirteen women, not now, not after everything they suffered. Lucy's dead, Mor-Rioghain's back where she belongs, in the Invisible Kingdom, even if you don't believe in her. Those women have got their justice now... those women and everybody who drowned when the *Lusitania* went down. That's all that matters."

Liam holstered his gun. Katie looked away. The duty garda was running up toward them, up the field, like the back marker in a marathon, plodding on, plodding on, even though he's never going to win.

Fifty-six

"Herm*aph*rodite?" said Dermot Driscoll, putting down his half-eaten cheese-and-pickle sandwich onto his blotter.

"Yes, sir. It appears so. We've sent to America for any medical records."

It had stopped raining and the sun was glittering on the drops of water that clung to Dermot's office window.

"So... what do you think we tell the media?"

"I don't think it's going to pay to complicate things, sir. Let's say that a disturbed individual tried to copy the ritual murders from 1915 and 1916, and killed himself to escape being arrested and charged."

"Killed *him*self? Or *her*self?"

"We don't know yet, sir. We know that she wasn't Professor Lucy Quinn. She's a seventy-six-year-old living in retirement in Mill Valley, just outside San Francisco. But quite *who* she was we're still not sure. Not everybody in this world has an identity, do they? I think that was Lucy's problem. She was neither a man nor a woman, and from the way she talked, she had never had anybody to help her come to terms with it. Not even God. That's why she went looking for somebody magical like Mor-Rioghain."

"And poor old Gerard O'Brien found out about her, and suffered the consequences?"

"Yes, sir."

"How's John Meagher?"

"He'll live, but he won't be singing opera for a while. And I don't think he'll ever be farming again, I shouldn't wonder."

"Horrible case, Katie. Gives me the shudders. Do you think you can play it down, when you talk to the press? You know, forget about the witch bit?"

"Yes, sir."

"As for Tómas Ó Conaill… well, I think we can forget about any charges against him. Never pays to upset the Travelers' support people."

"No, sir."

Katie left Dermot's office and walked along the corridor. Jimmy O'Rourke was waiting for her, with his hands behind his back, looking serious.

"You saved my life, Jimmy. You don't have to look quite so miserable."

"I've given up smoking. It's playing havoc with my equilibrium."

She went into her office and sat down. "Was there anything special?" she asked. "I've got a hell of a lot to do."

From behind his back, Jimmy produced Gerard's notebook. "I should have put this in as evidence, but I had a bit of a think about it and I decided not to. Not right away, like. There's things in here that could possibly cause some very bad blood, and in my opinion there's enough bad blood in the world already. If you think I'm wrong, then I'm ready to be reprimanded. I know gardaí aren't supposed to think. Well, not to philosophize, anyway. But I thought you ought to have the chance to read it first. Seeing as I respect your opinion, like."

Katie looked at him, not smiling, but feeling that she might at last have made some kind of breakthrough.

"Thank you, Jimmy," she said, and took the notebook, and put it down in front of her.

"Well, then," he said, obviously embarrassed. "I just wanted to say that I'm glad I saved your life. Otherwise, you know, you'd be dead, like."

She put a hold on her calls and took twenty minutes to read Gerard's notebook and then read it a second time. After the second reading she sat at her desk in silence. Then she put the notebook into her handbag, and closed it. Jimmy was right. Even if "Crackers" Corcoran had been nothing but a wild theorist, there was enough bad blood in the world already.

At eleven-thirty the following morning she met Eugene Ó Béara and Jack Devitt in The Red Setter, a cramped triangular pub up at Dillon's Cross. During the whole of her time there, the rest of the clientele stared at her balefully, as if she were a nun who had walked in with dogshit on her shoe.

They sat in a small booth in the corner. The smoke was so thick it was surprising that nobody called the fire brigade. Even Jack Devitt's wolfhound was snuffling and coughing.

Katie said, "We've found intelligence records in London that conclusively show that the man who abducted those fifteen women in 1915 and 1916 wasn't a British soldier at all. He was almost certainly a German from Münster in Westphalia known as Dieter Hartmann, and he wore a British uniform as a disguise. We're still searching for more information from the German government, and we'll let you know if we find out any more. I just want you to know that we also have evidence that the Crown Forces in Cork went to extraordinary lengths to find him and arrest him. Once they almost had him, but he managed to escape and after that he was never heard from again."

"We can examine this evidence?" asked Jack Devitt, solemnly.

"Of course, once we've finished with it. But you have my word that it's genuine."

"Very well, then, Superintendent Maguire. I knew your father well, and if you give me your word that it's genuine, then I accept it. Although I have to admit to a certain sense of anti-climax."

Katie gave him a tight smile. "Keeping the peace is a never-ending anticlimax."

Eugene Ó Béara suddenly let out a loud, staccato laugh, and then – just as abruptly – stopped. "You're a good woman, Katie Maguire, for a cop."

Just before one o'clock, she met Eamonn Collins in his usual seat at Dan Lowery's. His minder Jerry was having a séance at the opposite table with a bowl of fish chowder.

"Hallo, Eamonn."

"Hallo yourself, Detective Superintendent Maguire. You look very fetching today. I always say that black always becomes a woman, nuns and widows especially."

Katie said, "I thought I'd let you know that I've decided not to press any charges against you relating to the abduction of Dave MacSweeny. Lack of evidence, as well as the fact that my principal witness is lying on a slab in St Patrick's Morgue."

Eamonn took out a very white handkerchief and blew his nose. "Not to mention the minor embarrassment that it might have caused yourself, of course?"

"Let's just say that Dave MacSweeny deserved everything that ever happened to him, and more besides."

"So we're friends again, are we, Katie? Just remember, if you ever need another favor, at any time, you know who to call on."

"Actually, I would rather sell my soul to the Devil."

"Oh, come now! You know how much you need decent upstanding criminals like me. God knows what state this city would be in, otherwise."

Katie stood up. "I'll have you one day, Eamonn, I swear it, you jumped-up Knocknaheeny gobdaw."

Eamonn raised his whiskey-glass, and sang to Katie in a low, husky voice. "'Believe me, if all those endearing young charms, which I gaze on so fondly today... were to change by tomorrow, and fleet in my arms, like fairy gifts fading away!'"

She left Dan Lowery's and was crossing MacCurtain Street when her cellphone rang. It was Sister O'Flynn from the Regional.

"Mrs Maguire?" It was the first time that anybody had called her "Mrs Maguire" in a very long time. She knew then that it was bad news.

She pushed open the door of Isaac's restaurant. John Meagher was waiting in the back, self-consciously holding a large bouquet of lilies. He stood up when he saw her, and pulled out a chair.

"I'm afraid I won't be able to stay for lunch. I've just heard from the Regional that Paul died about fifteen minutes ago."

"I'm sorry, Katie. I really am."

She took a deep breath to steady herself. "Well... I suppose it's for the best. He wouldn't have wanted to spend the rest of his life like a cabbage."

"Why don't I give you a lift to the hospital?"

"Would you? I'd like that. I can't say I really feel like driving."

The waitress came up with their menus. "Do you want to know what the specials are?"

Katie stood up and managed a lopsided smile. "Not today. Some other time."

They walked back along MacCurtain Street to John's Land

Rover. The sun was shining but it was raining again, so that the wet pavements were almost blinding.

"Oh," said John. "I have something to show you. I was going to wait until after lunch, but – "

He opened the Land Rover's tailgate. In the back there were coils of rope and shovels and blankets. There was also a circular wicker basket, in which, fast asleep with its tongue lolling out, lay a glossy young Irish setter.

"He's yours. His name's Barney."

Katie stood in the rain and the sunshine, her fingers tightly pressed against her lips because she was trying not to cry. Behind her, over the tall gray spire of the Evangelical Church, a rainbow appeared, and brightened, and faded, and brightened again.

AUTHOR'S NOTE

On May 1, 1915, in the second summer of the First World War, the luxury Cunard liner *Lusitania* set sail from New York bound for Liverpool, England. By this stage of the war, a considerable number of British merchant ships had already been sunk by German submarines, and the German authorities had published warnings in US newspapers on the very morning of the *Lusitania*'s departure. However, it was thought that her superior speed would enable her to outrun any U-boat attack.

Six days later, as she approached the coast of south-west Ireland, Captain William Turner was warned that there was U-boat activity in the area and that three British ships had already been sunk in the waters through which he intended to sail. However, he maintained his course and even – inexplicably – slowed down.

As the *Lusitania* approached Queenstown harbor (now called Cobh) she was sighted by the submarine U-20 under the command of Kapitanleutnant Walther Schwieger. He fired a single torpedo which penetrated the *Lusitania* just below the waterline. The first explosion set off a devastating second blast, and the huge liner sank in 18 minutes, with the loss of 1,195 of her passengers – men, women and children – including 123 Americans.

President Wilson and the American public were outraged, but

in a note to her embassy in Washington on May 10, Germany gave no satisfactory explanation for the sinking, and eventually even struck a medal to commemorate U-20's successful action. More than any other single event, the loss of the *Lusitania* turned public opinion and led to the United States entering the First World War.

Many unanswered questions still surround the disaster. At the time, there were claims that the huge secondary explosion was set off by contraband American munitions hidden in the liner's hold. But recent dives on the wreck revealed lumps of coal scattered widely over the seabed – suggesting that the most likely cause was a detonation of coal-dust and oxygen in her almost-empty bunkers.

Captain William Turner was washed from the bridge when the ship went down, and survived. But he was never able to give a satisfactory explanation as to why he was sailing so close to the shore, and why he was taking no evasive action. He claimed that he had slowed down because of patchy fog, yet the danger to the *Lusitania* from U-boats was obviously far greater than the risk of collision.

A memorial to all those who died on the *Lusitania* stands today in the center of Cobh, the figure of a sorrowing angel.

A SELECTED GUIDE TO CORK SLANG

Corkonians have a very distinctive accent of their own, which sounds very different from the Dublin brogue which is usually presented as "Irish" in movies and television. They also have their own local slang vocabulary, although many of their expressions are used throughout the Republic.

Men and women of any age commonly address each other as "boy" and "girl." Even a temporary departure will elicit the remark, "Are ye going away?" followed by the reassurance that "I'll see ye after."

Acting the maggot: behaving foolishly or annoyingly.

Bags: making a mess of a job – "he made a bags of it."

Banjaxed: broken.

Bazzer: a haircut.

Bodice: spare ribs.

Bold: naughty – "you're a very bold boy."

Claim: fight – "I claim ya."

Codding: teasing or fooling – "I'm only codding."

Craic: good fun and stimulating conversation.

Craw sick: hung over.

Culchies: hayseeds or country people.

Cute hoor: sly, untrustworthy man.

Desperate: in a bad state.

Eat the head off: snap at, attack verbally.

Fair play: approval of somebody's actions – "fair play to him, mind."

Feck: slightly less offensive version of the other word.

Fierce: extreme – "there was a fierce crowd in there."

Fine half: nice-looking girl.

Flah: to have sex with.

Flah'd out: exhausted.

Full shilling (not): mentally challenged.

Funt: kick.

Ganky: unpleasant (of a person's looks).

Gawk: stare at, or vomit.

Gob: mouth.

Gobdaw: fool.

Gowl: idiot.

Grand: good, fine, okay.

Header: mentally unstable person.

Holliers: holidays.

Holy show: spectacle – "you made a holy show of yourself."

Hop (on the): playing hooky.

Hump off: go away.

Jag: a date.

Langered/langers: drunk.

Letting on: pretending.

Massive: lovely – "your dress is only massive."

Me Daza: very nice.

Mebs: testicles.

Messages: shopping – "I have to get the messages."

Mooching: sponging for money.

One: woman – "some oul one."

Rubber dollies: plimsolls.

Sconce: look – "have a sconce at that."

Scratcher: bed.

Septic: vain (of a girl).
Shades: the police.
Show: movie.
Shelityhorn: snail.
Slagging: making good-natured fun, teasing.
Soften his cough: teach him a lesson.
Soot: satisfaction – "I wouldn't give you the soot."
Twisted: drunk.

GRAHAM MASTERTON

BROKEN ANGELS

"One of the most original and frightening storytellers of our time"
Peter James

One

At first he thought it was a black plastic garbage bag that some Traveller had tossed into the river, full of dirty nappies or strangled puppies. '*Shite*,' he said, under his breath.

He reeled in his line and then he started to wade through the shallows towards it, his rod tilted over his shoulder. As far as he was concerned, the Blackwater was sacred. His father had first brought him here to fish for spring salmon when he was eight years old, and he had been fishing here every year since. It was Ireland's finest river and you didn't throw your old rubbish into it.

'Denis!' called Kieran. 'Where are you off to, boy? You won't catch a cold over there, let alone a kelt!' His voice echoed across the glassy surface of the water, so that it sounded as if he were shouting in a huge concert hall. The wind blew through the trees on the opposite bank and softly applauded him.

Denis didn't answer. As he approached the black plastic garbage bag it was becoming increasingly apparent that it wasn't a black plastic garbage bag at all. When he reached it, he realized that it was a man's body, dressed head to foot in black. A priest's soutane, by the look of it.

'Jesus,' he breathed, and carefully rested his rod on the river-bank.

The man was lying on his side on a narrow spit of shingle, with his legs half immersed in the water. His hands appeared to be fastened behind his back and his knees and his ankles were tied together. His face was turned away, but Denis could see by his thinning silver hair that he was probably in his late fifties or early sixties. He looked bulky, but Denis remembered

1

that when his father had died, his body had sat in his basement flat in Togher for almost a week before anybody had found him, and how immensely bloated he had become, a pale green Michelin Man.

'Kieran!' he shouted. 'Come and take a sconce at this! There's a dead fella here!'

Kieran reeled in his line and came splashing through the shallows. He was red-faced, with fiery curls and freckles and close-together eyes so intensely blue that he looked almost mad. He was Denis's brother-in-law, eight years younger than Denis, and they had nothing at all in common except their devotion to salmon fishing, but as far as Denis was concerned that was perfect. Salmon fishing required intense concentration, and silence.

Salmon fishing brought a man closer to God than any prayer.

'Holy Mother of God,' said Kieran, joining Denis beside the body and crossing himself. 'He's a priest, I'd say.' He paused and then he said, 'He *is* dead, isn't he?'

'Oh no, he's just having forty winks in the river. Of course he's dead, you eejit.'

'We'd best call the guards,' said Kieran, taking out his mobile phone. He was about to punch out 112 when he hesitated, his finger poised over the keypad. 'Hey . . . they won't think that *we* killed him, will they?'

'Just call them,' Denis told him. 'If *we*'d have done it, we wouldn't be hanging around here like a couple of tools, would we?'

'No, you're right. We'd have hopped off long since.'

While Kieran called the Garda, Denis circled cautiously around the body, his waders crunching on the shingle. The man's eyes were open, and he was staring at the water as if he couldn't understand what he was doing there, but there was absolutely

2

no doubt that he was dead. Denis hunkered down beside him and stared at him intently. He looked familiar, although Denis couldn't immediately think why. It was those tangled white eyebrows and those broken maroon veins in his cheeks, and most of all that distinctive cleft in the tip of his bulbous nose. His lower lip was split open as if somebody had punched him, very hard.

'The cops are on their way,' said Kieran, holding up his mobile phone. 'They said not to mess with anything.'

'Oh, I will, yeah! You should come round this side. He's starting to hum already.'

'I just had my sandwiches, thanks. Tuna and tomato.'

The two of them stood beside the body, not really knowing what they ought to do next. It seemed disrespectful to go back to their fishing, even though now and again, out of the corner of his eye, Denis caught the quick flashing of silver in the water. He had hoped to catch his first springer today, and the conditions were perfect.

'Who killed him then, do you think?' said Kieran. 'Whoever it was, they gave him a good old lash in the kisser before they did.'

Denis tilted his head sideways so that he could take another look at the man's face. 'Do you know something? I'm sure I reck him. He's a lot older than when I last saw him, if it's him, but then he would be, because it was fifteen years ago, at least.'

'So who do you think it is?'

'I think it's Father Heaney. In fact, I'm almost sure of it. His eyebrows used to be black in those days. I always thought they looked like two of them big black hairy spiders. You know, them tarantulas. He's not wearing his glasses, but I'd know that gonker anywhere.'

'Where did you know him from?'

3

'School. He used to teach music. He was a right whacker, and no mistake. There wasn't a single lesson went by that he wouldn't give you a smack around the earhole for something and nothing at all. He said I sang like a creaky door.'

Kieran sniffed and wiped his nose with the back of his sleeve. 'Looks like somebody smacked *him*, for a change.'

Denis didn't answer, but standing in the river next to Father Heaney's dead body with the wind whispering in the trees all around him made him feel as if he had been taken back in time. He could almost hear the school choir singing the '*Kyrie eleison*' in their sweet, piercing voices, and the sound of stampeding feet along the corridor, and Father Heaney's voice barking out, '*Walk*, O'Connor! You won't get to heaven any quicker by running!'

Two

Katie opened her eyes to see John standing by the bedroom window, one hand dividing the rose-patterned curtains, staring at the fields outside.

The early morning sunlight illuminated his naked body so that he looked like a painting of a medieval saint, especially since he had grown his dark curly hair longer after he and Katie had first met, and he had a dark crucifix of hair on his chest. He was thinner, too, and much more muscular, from a year and a half of working on the farm.

'You're looking very pensive there,' said Katie, propping herself up on one elbow.

John turned his head and gave her the faintest of smiles. The sunlight turned his brown eyes into shining agates. 'I was looking at the spring barley, that's all.'

'And thinking what, exactly?'

He let the curtain fall back and came towards the bed. He stood beside her as if he wanted to tell her something important, but when she looked up at him he said nothing at all, but kept on smiling down at her.

She reached her up and cupped him in her left hand, gently stroking his penis with the tip of her right index finger. '*This* fruit's beginning to look ripe already,' she teased him. 'Why don't you let me have a taste of it?'

He grunted in amusement. But then he leaned forward and kissed the top of her head, and sat down next to her. She kept on stroking him for a while, but he gently took hold of her wrist and stopped her.

5

'There's something I have to tell you, Katie,' he said. 'I was going to tell you last night, but we were having such a great time.'

Katie frowned at him. 'What is it? Come on, John, you've got me worried now. It's not your mother, is it?'

'No, no. Mam's fine for now. The doctors even said that she might be able to come home in a week or two.'

'Then what?'

He was just about to answer her when her mobile phone played the first three bars of 'The Fields of Athenry'. 'Hold on a second,' she said, and reached across to the bedside table to pick it up. 'Superintendent Maguire here. Who is this?'

'Detective O'Sullivan, ma'am. Sorry to be disturbing you, like. But we were called out to Ballyhooly because these two fisher fellas found a body in the river.'

'What does it look like? Accident or suicide or homicide?'

'Homicide, not a doubt about it. He was all trussed up like a turkey and strangulated.'

'Who's in charge up there?'

'Sergeant O'Rourke for the moment, ma'am. But he thinks you need to come and see this for yourself.'

'Oh, for God's sake, can't *he* handle it? This is my day off. In fact this is the first day off I've had in weeks.'

'Sergeant O'Rourke really thinks you need to see this, ma'am. And we need somebody to talk to the media about it, too. We've got RTÉ News up here already, and Dan Keane from the *Examiner*, and even some girl from the *Catholic Recorder*.'

Katie picked up her wristwatch and peered at it. 'All right, Paddy. Give me fifteen minutes.'

She snapped her mobile phone shut and swung her legs out of bed.

'What is it?' asked John.

'The call of duty, what do you think? Somebody's found

6

a body in the Blackwater. For some reason, Jimmy O'Rourke wants me to come and take a look at it first-hand.'

She stepped into the white satin panties that she had left on the wheelback chair beside the bed, and then fastened her bra. John said, 'You want me to drive you?'

She pulled on her dark green polo-neck sweater so that her short coppery hair stuck out like a cockerel's comb. 'No, thanks. I could be there for hours. But I'll call you as soon as I can. By the way, what was it you were going to tell me?'

John shook his head. 'Don't worry. It can wait until later.'

She buttoned the flies of her tight black jeans and zipped up her high-heeled boots. Then she went through to the bathroom and stared at her reflection in the mirror over the washbasin. 'Jesus, look at these bags under my eyes! Anybody would think I spent all night at an orgy.'

'You did,' said John. He watched her as she put on her eye make-up and pale pink lip gloss. He always thought that she looked as if she were distantly related to the elves, with her green eyes and her high cheekbones and her slightly pouting mouth. She was only five feet five, but she had such personality. He didn't find it difficult to understand how she had managed to become Cork's first-ever female detective superintendent. He also knew why he had fallen so inextricably in love with her.

She came out of the bathroom and gave him a kiss. 'How about Luigi Malone's this evening, if I don't finish too late? I'm dying for some of their mussels.'

'I don't know. Maybe.' But then he thought: *Over dinner, that could be the right time to tell her.*

He wrapped himself in his dark blue towelling bathrobe and followed her barefooted to the front door. She turned and kissed him one more time. 'You take extra good care,' he told her, like he always did. Then he watched her walk across the steeply angled farmyard, with his tan and white collie Aoife trotting after her. She climbed into her Honda and blew him a quick final kiss before she drove off.

Three

On the way to Ballyhooly she played Guillaume de Machaut's 'Gloria' by St Joseph's Orphanage Choir, from their *Elements* CD. The singing was so piercing and so clear and so intense that it always made her feel uplifted, and she sang along, just as high as the boys in the choir but badly off key. Despite the crime she had to deal with every day – the violence and the drug peddling and the prostitution and the drunkenness – 'Gloria' reminded her that there really must be a heaven, after all.

She drove along Lower Main Street until she reached the turning for Carrignavar. The road was narrow and bordered on each side by grey stone walls covered in ivy, but it was deserted, and she saw no other sign of life until she reached a farmhouse about three miles down the road. Seven or eight cars and vans were lined up along the grass verge outside the farmhouse gates, and inside the farmyard three squad cars were parked, with flashing blue lights, as well as two police vans and an ambulance.

A garda directed her in through the gates and opened her car door for her. As she climbed out, Sergeant O'Rourke came across the farmyard to greet her, holding up a large pair of green rubber wellingtons. He was a short, sandy-haired man, with a rough-cut block of a head that looked much too big for his body.

'You'll be needing these, ma'am,' he told her.

'What size are they?'

'Tens. But you wouldn't want to be wading in the river in stiletto heels, would you?'

She sat down in the driver's seat, unzipped her black leather boots, and put on the wellingtons. They were enormous, and when she started to walk in them, they made a loud wobbling sound.

'So, what's the story, Jimmy?' she asked, as she followed him around the side of the farmhouse. The farmer and his wife and two teenage sons were standing together in their front porch, glowering at them. Katie waved at them and called out, 'All right, there? Sorry about all the disturbance!' but they didn't reply. They looked like a family of ill-assorted gargoyles.

'What a bunch of mogs,' said Sergeant O'Rourke.

'Now then, Jimmy. Respect for your ordinary citizen, please.'

They walked together across the pasture that led down to the edge of the Blackwater, and the breeze whispered softly in the long shiny grass. As they came nearer, the black-clad body came into view, lying on its side in the shallows. Two gardaí from the technical bureau were crouching in the water next to it in pale green Tyvek suits, taking photographs. Three more uniformed guards and two paramedics were talking to a TV crew and two reporters on the bank. A little further away stood two men with fishing rods, smoking, and three small boys.

Sergeant O'Rourke pointed to the anglers. 'Those two fellas over there – they were the ones who were after finding the body. One of them says that he knows who he is – or he's reasonably certain, anyhow.'

'Really?'

'He's pretty sure that he's a parish priest from Mayfield, Father Heaney. Apparently he taught music at St Anthony's Primary School back in the eighties.'

'Good memory your man's got.'

'Not surprising, if it *is* him. Father Heaney was one of the twelve priests in the Cork and Ross diocese who were investigated seven years ago for sexual abuse. Taught the boys music?

10

Taught them to play the fiddle, I shouldn't wonder.'

'Was he ever charged with anything?'

'I had O'Sullivan check for me. There were eleven complaints against Father Heaney in all. Inappropriate behaviour in the showers, that kind of thing. In the end, though, the Director of Public Prosecutions wouldn't take the matter any further because it had all happened too long ago.'

'But that's why the press are here? Because of the sexual abuse angle?'

'Partly, like.'

'What aren't you telling me, Jimmy?'

'Like I said, ma'am, this is something you need to see for yourself.'

He stepped down into the river and held out his hand to help Katie follow him. The water felt icy cold, even through her rubber wellingtons. Sergeant O'Rourke waded ahead and Katie came behind him, trying to keep the wellingtons from falling off. As they approached, the two gardaí from the technical bureau stood up and took a few paces back. One was grey-haired, in his mid-forties. The other could have just left school.

'Well, he *looks* like a priest,' said Katie, bending over the body. 'Any identification on him?'

'Nothing, ma'am,' said the younger technician. He had a wispy blonde moustache and such fiery red acne that he looked as if he had been hit in the face point-blank by a shotgun. 'All we found in his pockets was a rosary and a packet of extra-strong mints.'

'He took care of what mattered, anyhow,' remarked Sergeant O'Rourke. 'His soul, and his breath.'

'Any ideas about the cause of death?' asked Katie. 'Not to prejudge Dr Reidy's autopsy, of course.'

11

The older technician cleared his throat. 'One of two or three things, I'd say; or a combination of all of them. He was garrotted with very thin wire, which was twisted tight at the back of his neck with the handle of a soup spoon. The same type of wire was used to tie his wrists and his knees and ankles. But he could just as well have bled to death, or died of shock.'

With that, he bent over the priest's body and turned him on to his back. The priest's left arm flopped into the water with a splash. The technicians had cut the wires that had fastened his knees and his ankles together, and then they had unbuttoned his black soutane all the way up to his waist.

He was wearing no underpants. His flaccid penis lay sideways on his fat white thigh, but underneath it, where his testicles should have been, there was nothing but a dark gaping hole.

'My God,' said Katie. She leaned forward and peered at the wound more closely.

'Whoever did it, it looks like they used something like a pair of garden shears,' said the older technician. 'You can tell by the slight V-shaped nick in his perineum where the blades crossed over each other.'

'Christ on crutches,' said Sergeant O'Rourke. 'Makes my eyes water even to think about it.'

'This didn't happen to him here,' the technician continued. 'He's no longer in full rigor, so he's probably been dead for at least three days. My guess is that he was strangled and castrated somewhere else and dumped here sometime last night.'

'What do you think, ma'am?' Sergeant O'Rourke asked her. 'Revenge killing, by somebody he messed with when he was teaching his music? There's been wagons of publicity about child abuse lately, hasn't there? The pope saying sorry and all. Maybe somebody's been holding a grudge against him all these years, and decided it was time to do something about it.'

12

'Well . . . you might be right,' said Katie, standing up straight. 'But let's not jump to any hasty conclusions. Maybe his killer simply didn't like him, for some obscure reason or another. You remember that case a couple of years ago in Holyhill? That young woman whose husband died of cancer, and she stabbed the parish priest with a pair of scissors because she said that his prayers hadn't worked?'

'There's a few priests *I* wouldn't mind having a good old stab at, I can tell you,' said Sergeant O'Rourke.

Katie turned to the older technician and said, 'You can send him off to the path lab when you're finished. I think I've seen everything that I need to see.'

'Before you go – there's one quite interesting detail,' he told her. He held up the two lengths of brass wire that had been used to bind the dead priest's legs. The ends of both of them had been twisted into neat double loops, like butterfly wings.

Katie said, 'That's very distinctive, isn't it? Is there any particular profession that finishes off its wiring like that?'

'Not that I know of. But I'll be making some inquiries.'

'Okay, good.'

Katie waded out of the river and Detective O'Sullivan gave her a hand to climb up the bank. Immediately, the TV crew from RTÉ came over – Fionnuala Sweeney, a pretty gingery girl in a bright green windcheater, accompanied by an unshaven cameraman – as well as Dan Keane from the *Examiner*, red-nosed, in his usual raglan-sleeved overcoat, and a pale, round-faced young woman with very black curls and a prominent beauty spot on her upper lip, whom Katie presumed was the reporter from the *Catholic Recorder*. She had very big breasts and she wore a grey tent-like poncho to cover them.

Fionnuala Sweeney held out her microphone and said, 'Superintendent Maguire! All right with you if we ask you some questions?'

'Let me ask *you* a question first,' said Katie, sharply. 'Who tipped you off about this body being found?'

Fionnuala Sweeny blinked rapidly, as if Katie had mortally offended her. 'I couldn't possibly tell you that, superintendent. You know that. I have to protect my professional sources.'

'Oh, stop being so sanctimonious, Nuala,' said Dan Keane, lighting a cigarette. 'I had the same tip-off myself but the caller didn't leave his name, and I certainly didn't recognize his voice. In fact, I couldn't even tell you for sure if it was a man or a woman. Sounded more like a fecking *frog*, to tell you the truth.'

'All right, then,' said Katie. 'Ask me whatever you like. But I can't tell you very much at all, not at this early stage.'

Fionnuala Sweeney said, 'Your witness here identified the deceased as Father Dermot Heaney, from Mayfield.'

'No comment on that. Whatever the witness said to you, we don't yet know for certain who he is.'

'In 2005, Father Heaney was one of the priests who were investigated on suspicion of child abuse.'

'So I'm told. But as far as I know, the DPP took no action against him, and this may not be him. What's your question?'

'I just want to know if you'll be considering the possibility that one of Father Heaney's victims was looking to punish him for what he did. Or what he was alleged to have done.'

Katie held up her hand. 'Listen, Fionnuala, how many times? We haven't yet established the deceased's identity, not for certain. He might not even be a priest, for all we know. And even if it *is* Father Heaney, we have no evidence at all who might have wanted to kill him, or what their motives might have been. All I can say at this stage is that we'll be searching this area with a fine-tooth comb, and interviewing anybody who might have witnessed anything unusual. If any of your viewers think that they can help us to identify the victim, and whoever wished him harm, then as usual we'll be very grateful.'

'Do you know what the cause of death was?' asked Fionnuala Sweeney.

'Again, we're not sure yet. Either Dr Reidy, the state pathologist, or one of his two deputies will be carrying out an autopsy as soon as we can arrange it.'

The girl with the beauty spot spoke with a lisp. 'Ciara Clare, superintendent, from the *Catholic Recorder*. If your dead man does prove to be a priest, you *will* be consulting the diocese, won't you, about the most discreet way to handle it?'

Katie frowned at her. 'I'm not sure I understand your question.'

'Well, this has been a very difficult time for the church, hasn't it?' said Ciara Clare. 'The bishop has asked the public for forgiveness for past errors, as you know. I'm only suggesting that this is a time for healing, rather than more scandal.'

'Excuse me, Ciara? Are you saying what I think you're saying?'

'I'm only concerned about this murder being sensationalized. I mean, it does seem likely that your man was killed by a victim of child abuse, doesn't it, in revenge for molesting him, and that could very well incite other victims to take the law into their own hands. We don't want more priests to be attacked, whatever they might have done in the past.'

'That's about three too many *if*s,' Katie told her. 'Like I said, we need to take this one step at a time. Just because the deceased is wearing a cassock, that doesn't prove anything at all. He may have been on his way to a fancy-dress party.'

Dan Keane took his cigarette out of his mouth and let out a cough like a dog barking. 'He was castrated, though, wasn't

15

he? That would indicate some kind of sexual motivation.'

'I'm sorry, Dan. We'll have to wait for the pathologist's report to find out exactly what injuries he suffered.'

'You don't need a pathologist to tell you when a man's had his mebs cut off. Your anglers saw it with their own eyes. Gelded, that's what they said.'

'Well, I'd rather you kept that to yourself for the time being. You too, please, Fionnuala. And you, Ms—'

'I'm not sure I can do that, superintendent,' said Dan Keane. 'It's the best part of the whole story, don't you think? "Father loses fatherhood."'

'Dan!' Katie retorted. 'Do you want me to give you any further co-operation on this case, or not?'

Dan blew smoke and coughed again and said, 'Very well, superintendent. I'll hold off for now, until you get the pathologist's report at least. But if it comes out from any other source, I'm going to have to run with it.'

Katie walked back to her car and kicked off the huge green wellingtons so that they spun away across the grass. As she was tugging on her black leather boots again, Sergeant O'Rourke came up to her and leaned against the car door. 'I'm having the whole area searched for tyre tracks and footprints and any other evidence. The fields, the pathways, the river bed. Everywhere. We've already started a door to door in Ballyhooly and all the surrounding communities. Somebody must have seen something.'

'Thanks, Jimmy. Keep me in touch. For some reason, I have a very uneasy feeling about this one. I always do when the church is involved. You never get an outright lie, do you? But then you never get an outright truth, either. It's all incense smoke and mirrors.'